Praise for Sarah Mlynowski

"Mlynowski is out for a rollicking good time
from the start."
—*Arizona Republic* on *Fishbowl*

"Undemandingly perfect...wonderfully bitchy."
—*Jewish Chronicle* on *Fishbowl*

"A fresh and witty take on real-life exams in love,
lust, trust and friendship."
—Bestselling author Jessica Adams on *Fishbowl*

"This entertaining debut [offers]
both humor and substance....
[Anyone] who's ever been bored by an unfulfilling job...
jealous of a roommate who has it all together...
or thoroughly perplexed by boy-speak will
find something to enjoy here. Mlynowski
may not be able to provide all the solutions,
but she certainly makes the problems fun."
—*Publishers Weekly*

"A likable heroine."
—*Booklist*

"*Milkrun* by Sarah Mlynowski is funny,
touching, sassy, and bright. It's as spicy as
cinnamon-flecked foam on cappuccino
and as honest as strong black coffee."
—*Anthology* magazine

For Bonnie, Ronit, Lisa, Jaime, Mel and Todd:
my roommates, past and present.

SARAH MLYNOWSKI

fishbowl

ISBN-13: 978-0-7783-2710-3
ISBN-10: 0-7783-2710-8

FISHBOWL

www.MIRABooks.com

Printed in U.S.A.

ACKNOWLEDGMENTS

Thank you, thank you, thank you to the people who read and reread drafts of this book: Sam Bell, my devoted editor; Elissa Harris Ambrose, my grammar-queen mom; Jess Braun, my long-standing coconspirator; Bonnie Altro, my favorite storyteller; Todd Swidler, my exceptionally patient boyfriend; and Kathrin Menge and Ana Movileanu, my perceptive, speed-reading ex-coworkers.

Special thanks to the Oakville firefighters who—extremely sweetly—explained the technicalities of burning down one's kitchen. Oh, and let me try on the funky gear.

Cheers for the RDI team: Laura Morris, Margaret Marbury, Margie Miller, Tara Kelly, Tania Charzewski, Pam Spengler-Jaffee... and I mustn't forget Craig Swinwood.

Finally, thanks to the endless support of family and friends (Dad, Louisa, Bubbe, Grandma, Squirt, Rob, Lynda, Sohmer, Merjane and the Wednesday Night Dinner Girls).

Prologue
A TINY BIT OF FORESHADOWING

Allison, Jodine and Emma are going to set their apartment on fire. No, they're not going to do it *on purpose*. What kind of lunatics do you think they are?

Now, don't go worrying. No one will get hurt. There will be no heart-stopping da-da-da *E.R.* music in the background, no one in white yelling *Stat!*, no George Clooney look-a-like climbing aboard a gurney to thump life back into someone's heart, and no artificial respiration of any kind, including the mouth-to-mouth variety.

And we're all thankful for that, of course. Although when Janet, the substitute teacher who lives in the apartment upstairs, tells the story, she'll kind of wish something slightly more significant will have happened, like maybe the girls get trapped in the bathroom while the flames lick the closed door, and they stand sweating and shivering under the running shower, and they see smoke creeping in from the hallway, and just as they're about to pass out... No, wait! Maybe one of them *will* pass out. She'll faint away just as the cute fireman throws open the door and tosses all three girls over his muscle-rippled shoulders. He'll look as if he stepped right off a Chippendales calendar (except his fireman's getup is done up) to carry them into the midnight air to safety. And then he'll give the passed-out girl resuscitation (yes! yes! the mouth-to-mouth variety) and she's breathing! She's going to make it! Isn't it wonderful to be alive!

But this isn't going to happen. This is Janet's fantasy, and Janet is not an important player in this story.

Sorry, Janet.

Anyway, the girls will have to go to the E.R., but it'll be more of a formality than because of any real concern. Something about sucking in too much carbon monoxide and needing oxygen. They'll also need to shower. When they get out of that burning apartment, they won't exactly be making a fashion statement, although they'd make excellent "before" or "fashion don't" pictures, if any glossy magazine decides to snap their pictures. Which, of course, isn't going to happen, either, because why would a fashion photographer be sitting in the waiting room of the E.R.? Be serious. The girls' faces are going to look as if they've been rubbed with black chalk, if black chalk even exists, as there are no white blackboards. And their hair...if their mothers were to see their hair in that rat's-nest sooty condition, they'd probably cover their eyes and scream, "Cut it off! Just cut it all off!" while flashing back to incidents of pink chewing gum. Mothers can sometimes get a wee bit overdramatic.

These girls ain't going to be a pretty sight.

But do you know what they're going to need? Even more than a shower?

Insurance. Sounds kind of superfluous next to oxygen and water, but when you don't have protection, things tend to get a little messy.

Anyway, you don't have to worry about all this fire mumbo

jumbo right at this moment. The girls haven't even met yet. So relax. Have a cup of coffee. Never mind, there's no need to stimulate any heart-stopping da-da-da *E.R.*-beat hyperactivity. Have a cup of herbal tea instead. And pay attention to the first name in each chapter title or you're not going to have a clue who's talking. Oh, and forget you ever heard about the "burning down" of any "apartment."

So did you hear about the fire at 56B Blake?

(Fire? What fire? Insert your blank stare here.)

Well done!

1
ALLIE'S MISTAKE

ALLIE

Eeeeeeeeeeeep.

Shut. Up.

Eeeeeeeeeeeep.

Shut. Up. Pause.

Eeeeeeeeeeeep.

Shut! Up! I'm trying to mind my own business while I stir my instant coffee (my brewer has gone back to Vancouver with its owner, one of my former roommates. My other college roommate, most furniture, all forms of cutlery and the living-room TV have also deserted me for the rainy city of Vancouver), but this teeth-scratching *eeeeeeeeeeeeep* keeps interrupting me. It's like when you bite your lip by accident and it gets all puffy, and because it's puffy, you keep biting it—you know?

Eeeeeeeeeeeeeeep.

Please, please, please stop.

Three minutes and ten seconds later: *eeeeeeeeeeeeeeeep.*

Time to detonate the smoke detector. I've lived in this apart-ment for over two years and in all that time, not once have the batteries run out. But isn't that always the case? They had to wait for Rebecca and Melissa to move out before they decided to kick the bucket. My ex-roommates are each at least half a foot taller than my five-foot frame (I prefer to be called petite, not short, and none of that vertically challenged crap, thank you very much) and could have reached it by standing on a stool without the aid of a phone book. Both could have easily, without breaking a glow, popped out the offending batteries, making the *eeeeeeeeeeeeep* go away. Go figure.

The beeping offends my ears yet again, and I examine my right thumb for a piece of stray nail to chew on. Gross? Yes. A bad habit I picked up from my mom.

Maybe this *eeeeeeeeeeeeeeping* is a sign. A sign for me to get dressed, walk to the nearest Starbucks and order a cappuccino before going to work. Maybe while I'm there I will meet someone capable of stopping this *eeeeeeeeeeeeeeping*. Maybe I will make new friends. I need new friends. Now that my former roomies have left town, I have only one friend left in Toronto, Clint, but secretly, I'm a little in love with Clint, so I don't think he counts. I've tried not to be in love with him, because he's not in love with me. I realized this last year (me loving him *and* him not loving me). I had a little too much Mike's Hard Lemonade (Canadian girl beer) and said, "I love you, Clint." And he got as pale as loose-leaf paper and said, "Thank you."

Thank you? What is thank you? Thank you for making me a turkey sandwich, Allie, maybe. Thank you for taping *TWIB* (that's *This Week in Baseball* for all those not in love with Blue Jays–obsessed men) while I was out sleeping with the slut from my economics class. Worst-case scenario, obviously, but still applicable. But thank you for the "I love you"? What does that mean? He started stammering all boylike that he had to go, he had an early class (as if he ever went to class), and I realized what a mistake, what a *huge* mistake I had just made, and I said, "As a friend, I mean. I love you as a friend. You're my best friend."

So technically I don't know for sure he *doesn't* love me. It's certainly possible that he believed me about me not loving him *that* way. And if he doesn't think I'm in love with him, he probably doesn't want to risk potential embarrassment and disappointment by admitting his true feelings for me. He's probably afraid of making the first move, because of his fear of rejection. Not that he's ever been afraid of being rejected by other girls.

But I'm different from other girls. I am. Clint says no one appreciates him the way I do.

So you see, I'm having a bit of a current living-in-Toronto friend drought. Obviously, I'll have two built-in friends when my two new roomies arrive in a couple weeks, but who should I talk to until then? I wish I had a dog. I've always wanted a dog. A dog that will sleep on my pillow. A dog that I can take for walks and feed snacks and teach to roll over and walk on two legs and do other fun tricks, and maybe one day I can present him on David Letterman's Stupid Pet Tricks. But shouldn't I ask my new roomies if I want to get a dog? In case they're allergic? Is it the ethical thing to do? Could I hide the dog? It could sleep in my room. I have the biggest one.

But if I can call them to ask them this, that means I have someone to talk to. And if I have someone to talk to, then I really don't need a dog, now do I?

Eeeeeeeeeeeeeep.

Maybe by the time I get back from coffee and work the *eeeeeeeeeeeeeping* will have stopped. Sometimes you wish for something and it actually does happen. Really. Like in fourth grade. I went to sleep crying because in the morning I had to take the

Monday multiplication test and I was stuck on table nine. For five weeks, Mrs. Tupper (who probably never used Bounce, because her skirt always stuck to the inside of her thighs) had been making me stand up in front of the class and answer, "Allison, what is nine times two?" And when I answered eighteen, she'd ask, "What is nine times five?" She'd ask me six questions in all, assuring me that if I passed the test, I could move on to the tenth table, but if I answered even one wrong, I'd have to repeat table nine again the next Monday.

Anyway, for five weeks I went to bed crying because even though nine times ten and nine times eleven were no-brainers ("Multiplication isn't your foe, times it by ten and add an O. Don't let math give you trouble, times it by eleven and you're seeing double!"— Mom made those up for me), I would either forget nine times eight (seventy-two!) or nine times nine (eighty-one!), and for some inexplicable reason answered sixty-five to both. Anyway, I had been on the ninth table for five weeks now, and the test was in the morning. I knew that one (maybe two) more days of practice would really be helpful, and then poof, the next morning there was a flood. There's never been a flood in my part of the city in its entire history. How weird was that? Needless to say, the schools were closed, since no one could get to them unless they had a boat or Jet Ski. Totally bizarre. And when I took the test (on Tuesday) I passed.

See? It happens.

Eeeeeeeeeeeeep.

I brush my teeth, throw on jean shorts, a tank top and sandals. I grab my purse and head out the door.

Mission not accomplished. Work—good. Well, not *good* as in fulfilling *good*. How can telemarketing be fulfilling? Although, I raise money for the Ontario University Alumni Fund so it's actually telefundraising, which isn't as immoral or annoying as tele-marketing. And I did raise over five hundred bucks today, which is pretty good. Anyway. Cappuccino—also good. Meeting taller friends so they can fix the *eeeeeeeeeeeep*—bad.

But what's this? Silence? I look up at the offender on the wall in the living room next to the kitchen's entranceway. Has the sour-milk-sipping noise come to an end?

No sound except passing traffic. I leave the windows open because it is a breath-hampering, fluid-draining ninety-seven degrees outside. And I can't afford an air conditioner. I once had a fan, but like everything else that gave me joy, it is now in Van-couver.

Quiet. See? I told you it could happen. Sometimes when you wish for something hard enough—

Eeeeeeeeeeeep.

Damn.

Hmm. There's a pharmacy next door to Starbucks. Why didn't I think to buy batteries? Wouldn't that have made more sense than to assume that the obviously dying batteries would self-heal while I was getting caffeinated?

I roll the computer chair from my bedroom into the living room and place it beneath the smoke detector. This is a bad plan. A very bad plan. My computer chair is one of those $15.99 You-Put-It-Together! chairs whose wheels are about as sturdy as legs in high heels after three glasses of zinfandel. Unfortunately, my other chairs, which are metal, sturdier, more appropriate for this situation (and which used to be arranged around a glass kitchen table which had to be placed beside the kitchen instead of inside it due to space limitations) are gone. With the glass table. In Van-couver.

I pump the computer chair as high as it can go. And now, the moment of suspense. It's just me, an *eeeeeeeeeeeeeeping* smoke alarm, and a rolling computer chair in a couchless, coffeemaker-free apartment.

Steady. Stea-dy. Lift right arm to smoke detector. Lift left hand to mouth. Insert pinky nail between lips. Excellent nail overgrowth. Mmm. Missions accomplished. Superfluous nail piece is freely rolling around my tongue. And both hands are placed squarely on the smoke detector.

Now what?

Press button?

EEEEEEEEEEEEEEEEEEEEEEEEEEEEEEEEEEPPPPPPP. Whoops. Remove batteries? Why can't I remove batteries? Chair! Swerving! Seconds from head injury! Need both hands to balance! Steady! Stea-dy!

Eeeeeeeeeeeeeep.

Stop. That. Now. Remove smoke detector? Crunch. Smoke detector removed. Three-minute wait. Beeping stopped.

Tee-hee.

I think I broke it. I guess I should put it back on the wall. I can't just leave it on the table. What table? (Do milk crates covered in a tablecloth count as a table?) Okay, smoke detector is now back on ceiling.

I carefully crouch into a sitting position and insert another finger into my mouth. I wait three minutes.

No *eeeeeeeeeeeeeep.* Not even one tiny *eee.*

Now, isn't that better?

2
JODINE DOESN'T WANT TO TALK

JODINE

August 27—Agenda:

1. Call car to bring me to airport.√
2. Call mother to remind her to pick me up at airport.√
3. Purge fridge of remaining food.√
4. Sweep.√
5. Throw out garbage.√
6. Close windows.√
7. Return apartment key to superintendent.√
8. Save car receipt to airport (firm has agreed to reimburse).√
9. Verify frequent-flyer points credited to account.√
10. Bring suits to dry cleaner.
11. Call Happy Movers to confirm truck rental for move to new apartment.

"Hello," the annoying businessman sitting in the window seat beside me says as he removes his suit jacket. "How are you doing on this fine day?"

Terrific. Shouldn't the fact that I'm in the middle of reviewing something be a sign that I'm not interested in pursuing a conversation? "Fine, thanks."

He squashes his arm on the seat rest. "I'm doing well, too."

I pull out the *New York Times*. People are usually less likely to intrude on one's personal time when one appears to be engaged, especially if the engagement happens to be reading the *Times*. It's not a comic book, or worse, a fashion magazine. It spells *serious* all over it.

"What are you reading, little lady?"

It takes me another moment to get over the traumatizing shock of being called a little lady. Is he blind? "The paper," I answer in yet another dismissive attempt. Maybe now he will set sail the notion of small talk? Float away, annoying man! Float away!

"So what do you do?"

"I'm a student." Now vanish. Enough.

"Oh, that's nice," he says in a pat-me-on-the-head voice. Notice he does not think to ask the obvious question, What are you studying? Not that I care. I do not wish to engage in a conversation with this man. I'm not sure why people believe being seated next to someone implies an ensuing conversation.

He puffs himself up like a blown-up life jacket. "I run an international appliance sales force. It's one of the largest in the world."

I don't remember asking, but now that you've opened the field up for discussion, let me ask, is that why you're sitting in 23D in the economy section, next to me? Because you're so rich and powerful? "That's nice," I say instead. It's not that I'm a coward; why should I be rude?

I slip my Discman headphones out of my carry-on and over my ears. Unfortunately, my CD player is broken. I realized this while waiting to board. But the important thing is, he doesn't realize this.

Maybe if I nod my head and shake it side to side as if I'm in the swing, I'll be able to pull it off.

Forty-five minutes until landing.

My mother had better be on time to pick me up. In her last attempt to pick me up at the Toronto airport, when I flew back from a law conference in Calgary, she was fifty-five minutes late. Apparently she was under the false impression that my arrival time was at five, despite the photocopied version of my itinerary taped prominently to the refrigerator, which clearly stated that my flight was landing at four. When she drove up at four-fifty-five, she was congratulating herself for arriving five minutes early. My primary question, ignoring the more obvious why-didn't-she-pay-attention-to-the-time-on-the-fridge query, was why didn't she call the airport to verify the arrival time? Why, why, why, would one drive to the airport, a forty-five-minute trek in Toronto, without first confirming the accurate arrival time? The possibility of my flight being delayed was more than likely. It was December; a snowstorm was practically guaranteed. It made no sense.

This time, I specifically instructed her to call the airport. I even gave her the number. I should have insisted, however, on taking a cab. Sigh. Her inability to make it here for the assigned time is now beyond my control.

Dear, sweet Mom. In the last year, at least four times that I can remember, she's left her keys in the car while it was running and had to call my father to bring her the spare. Not that my dad is much better. Once when my mom—"But it slammed shut so fast! Before I could catch it!"—locked herself out, smack in the middle of downtown Queen Street, my dad trekked all the way to meet her, only to realize he'd left the spare keys back at the house, on the—"But I could have sworn I'd put them in my pocket"—kitchen table. They called me to rescue them. And when I got there, after two hours of subway-hell, they were having a giggly submarine picnic lunch on the hood of the car. How frustrating is that? Fine, I admit they can be a tiny bit adorable. They thought it was the funniest thing that had ever happened to them.

One week of living with my parents. Seven days. One hundred and sixty-eight hours. That's all I have left. Seven days of explaining to my mother how to work that "intercourse machine" so that she can go "to the line" ("Internet, Mom. Online, Mom"). Seven days of picking up my father's seemingly strategically discarded socks on the kitchen floor. Why would one take off his socks in the kitchen? There is no carpet, just cold tiles.

They will be fine without me around to take care of them, won't they?

I should get a cell phone to make sure I can be reached at all times.

Besides enabling me to live in New York for the summer, my summer job allowed me to save up enough money to afford my own place here in Toronto. If I had to make the one-hour subway trek to school from my parents' house in nosebleed land for one more year, I think I might have dropped out of school and taken a job at the corner coffee shop. Yeah, right.

Last year, I had to walk fifteen minutes just to get to the bus stop that would take me to the subway that would take me to school. My new apartment is a five-minute walk from school. Five minutes!

My brother, Adam, forwarded me an e-mail about this apartment. The younger sister of one of his friends was looking for renters. It's a three-bedroom, bottom floor apartment of a duplex, and her two roommates were moving back to British Columbia. But the best part is that she's lived in the apartment since before rent control—it's therefore only $500 a month per renter. My ridiculously high-paying $2,000-a-week summer law job has provided me with the funds to cover at least one year. Then, in May, I'm off to New York again, for a full-time job. The requisite being, of course, that I keep my grade point average above a B, which I can do without batting an un-mascaraed eye.

Not that I'm a regular eye-batter. I'm actually more of an eye-rubber. This annoying eye-massaging fetish I somehow picked up usually follows fits of exhaustion in the library. And then I leave the building looking as if I've been elbowed in the bridge of my nose. There is an abundance of library time in my schedule. I'm there every morning from nine to ten, in school from ten to three, and then back in the library until ten at night, with only quarter-hour breaks for a fat-free cheese sandwich lunch and a low-carb dinner.

But the best part about living five minutes away from school is the close proximity of Ontario University's gym. My day's newfound one hour and fifty minutes of saved travel time will facilitate my additional working-out time. For the past two years, I've had to work out at the Y near my house after putting in time at the school library, which on a regular, day-to-day basis, resulted in a complete emotional and physical breakdown.

My lack of spare time may also have been partly responsible for the demise of my relationship with Manny. Or, unless apathy is considered an emotion, the demise might have been caused by my lack of any feeling toward him. I won't deny that he's a good guy—he is. He ranks number one in our class, and has sat with me for hours whenever I had a case I couldn't wrap my brain around.

But here's the thing: he has to pee all the time.

This might sound insignificant and possibly irrelevant or even discriminatory, but isn't the woman normally the one with the smaller bladder? I find it extremely irritating to constantly have to wait for him by the bathroom. For example, we're on our way from class to the library, and he says, "Hold on one second, Jodine, I have to pee." Or "Tell me what I miss of the movie, I just have to run to the bathroom, excuse me, excuse me..."

It makes no sense. Can't he hold it in?

Annoying-Lying-Businessman in the seat next to me appears to be asleep. His eyes are closed and a thin river of drool is leaking out of the corner of his opened mouth. It's only two o'clock. Who falls asleep at two o'clock? The person sitting next to him refuses to entertain him for a lousy one-hour flight and he can't muster enough stimuli for staying conscious? At least he's leaning toward the window, not toward his seat divider, the supposedly adequate buffer between us.

Little lady. Hah.

I hate being patronized. My mother's favorite story of me is when she took me, a scared-but-trying-not-to-show-it six-year-old, to the pediatrician for my annual TB test. It's the one where they insert three little dots into your arm, and you hope these dots won't blow up into explosive pimples, because then they have to amputate or something. Anyway, when I asked the doctor if I was going to get a needle, he shook his head dramatically, insisting on drawing a happy face with a red marker on my arm while emphatically declaring, "No, needle, only a nose!" Then he stuck a three-pronged needle between the haphazardly drawn eyes and leering grin. I remember thinking, Why, oh why, is this silly, patronizing man speaking to me as if I were a child?

My mother thinks the story is hysterical. She tells it at family gatherings. She's been calling me a thirty-year-old stuck in a little girl's body for as long as I can remember. So what does that make me now? Fifty?

I remove my headphones and close my eyes. I always request the row behind the emergency exit. I like to be as close as possible to an escape while still having the ability to lean back. Annoying-Lying-Drooling-Businessman is now snoring. How can any one person make so much noise? His emissions are even drowning out the screeching baby in the row behind me. Yet another peeve of mine. Parents should be required by law to drive any offspring under the age of three to long-distance destinations. Young children, babies in particular, obviously don't like to fly, so why must we all suffer?

Apparently I must suffer because I forgot to ensure that my Discman was intact. A moronic oversight for which I must (sigh) accept responsibility. If one doesn't think and carefully plan ahead, one loses the right to complain about unpleasant outcomes.

Case Study Number One, regarding planning ahead: if one does not order a vegetarian meal beforehand, even though one is not, in fact, a vegetarian, then one has no choice except to eat the heap of brown plasticine offered at mealtime. One must not try to dwell on that lovely mushroom omelette and fruit salad the woman across the aisle is eating, or else one might go crazy.

Case Study Number Two, regarding planning ahead: Benjamin, an I-bank associate in New York. At first he seemed relatively normal. Always called after a date to say thank you. Never did anything annoying like send flowers to the office or send embarrassing e-mails. Great smile, great date, great kisser. An A minus in bed. All a perfectly gloss-coated experience until last week when he started blubbering about how much he loved me, couldn't handle me leaving, wanted to transfer to Toronto and move in with me. Transfer to Toronto? We were only dating five weeks! Does that make sense? How could he move in with me? First of all, I already signed a lease. Second, I wasn't sure he was the person I wanted to spend my life with, never mind an entire semester. Allowing him to pick up and move to a foreign country was somewhat implying that I was considering him as a potential life mate, right?

I reach into the small space that Annoying-Lying-Drooling-Snoring-Businessman has left at my feet and pull out my "List of Benjamin's Flaws" from my carry-on.

1.   He has a feminine laugh.

I don't think I need to elaborate on this. What woman wants a man with a feminine laugh?

2.   He constantly wants to go dancing.

I hate dancing, mostly because I can't dance. I wish I could, but I can't. So I don't. To most men, this is not a big concern, since most normal men do not start squirming in their chairs when "Sexual Healing" comes on.

3.   He is too impulsive.

If he's supposed to be so much in love, why can't he wait nine more months for me—in New York? I could visit him. My Christmas vacation plans aren't finalized yet. The New Year's reservations are booked but not *confirmed*. Kidding. I'm not that anal. Really.

4.   He is too sentimental.

He said he loved me. I started laughing.

5.   He called me cold.

Now that's insulting. I am not cold. He said I am just like that Simon and Garfunkel song. A rock that does not feel. I am realistic, but I repeat, not cold. So I am not like most women. I don't appreciate when men who have only known me for five weeks tell me they love me. I don't sit around with my other girlfriends, wondering what shades I should use to highlight my hair so that men will send me flowers. I can buy my own flowers, thank you very much. I am not afraid of never having a man fall in love with me. I have already had men fall in love with me. This summer, Benjamin. Last year, Manny. In college, Jonah. High school, Will. All three told me they loved me—and meant it. They called it making love when we slept together. They all wanted me to meet their mothers.

Dilemma Number One: I did not want to meet their mothers. I already have one of my own, thank you very much.

Dilemma Number Two: I call it "having sex."

Dilemma Number Three: I said, "You love me? That's sweet."

I put down the list and reflect on something my mother once told me: "There's a lid for every pot." No. I dismiss her attempts at motherly wisdom. People are not household appliances. Everyone is born alone and dies alone. You are not created to fit with anything else. Of course I would like to find the person who is most likely to make me happy in life. The person who fits me *best*. But I refuse to adjust so that I can fit to someone else's jagged shape.

"You're a real piece of work," Benjamin said, his voice cracking, before slamming my apartment door.

I pull my hair out of its usual low ponytail, shake it out and then tie it back again.

Fine, I admit it. Hurting him made me feel a little shitty. A lot shitty. I'm not out to crush men's feelings. It's a nonpremeditated causal effect.

Is there something chemically wrong with me? Everyone else seems to fall in love all over the place. When will I feel like belting out, "And I…I…I…will always love you-ou-ou-ou…?" and cherishing those other sweet Whitney memories? And how will I lose that loving feeling if I've never even found it? What if there is some sort of gross abnormality in my DNA? What if I *am* a rock? AN EMOTIONLESS, DEAD-INSIDE ROCK?

Or maybe unlike most people, I'm not willing to brainwash myself into believing I'm in love.

Meaning behind Case Study Number Two, otherwise known as the Benjamin Experience: One mustn't allow someone else to derail her carefully laid out plans. If one isn't cautious, a carefree fling might snowball into a messy relationship.

Thirty minutes until landing.

A perfect opportunity for leg lifts.

Lift left knee. Hold to ten. Release left knee.

Lift right knee. Hold to ten. Release right knee.

Lift left knee. Hold to fifteen. Release left knee.

Lift right knee. Hold to fifteen. Release right knee.

Too bad there is not enough room for sit-ups. Would Annoying-Lying-Drooling-Snoring-Businessman notice if I lifted the seat divider and used his lap as a headrest?

Not worth his potential consciousness. Then I might have to talk to him.

3
EMMA GETS PISSED

EMMA

"You're not wearing that. Go back inside and change."

Why is Nick so full of shit? Was he a toilet in his last life? "I most certainly am wearing this. I bought it today. It's gorgeous." *It* is a soft, luscious, red silk tank top with a plunging neckline. *It* cost a fortune. *It* could be the most stunning tank top ever designed. *It* feels like lotion against my skin. Like my favorite thirty-dollar lip gloss against my lips. I love *it*. If he makes me choose between the tank top and him, he's not going to get off on my decision.

He pounds his fists against the steering wheel. "Why do you want to wear something that makes you look like a slut?"

I don't understand the question. Because I like looking like a slut? "Funny that you hate when I look like a whore, but love when I act like one."

He scrunches his face as though he just swallowed a shot of tequila. "Fuck off," he swears.

"You fuck off."

Another lovely night out with Nick. Best thing about Nick: he's amazing in bed. And I mean *fucking incredible*. It's always all about me. He won't settle for anything less than two orgasms every time. Even if I tell him it's okay, tonight can be a blow job night, he still insists on making me come. Worst thing about Nick: he's more stubborn than a TV remote control without batteries.

"Go change," he says, crossing his arms in front of his chest.

Big baby. He didn't mind my cleavage-revealing tops when we started dating last year. Lately, he's like a pig-in-shit whenever I wear a sweatshirt and sweatpants. In his ideal world I'd be wearing a full-piece snowsuit twenty-four hours a day. Or fourteen hours a day. The other ten hours he's happy to have me parading in front of him in the cheesy-ass lingerie he buys me. Red, lace, crotch-less panties. Feather garters. Snakeskin teddies. Could he want me to look any more like a porn star? He even likes when I design my pubic hair so that I look like a twelve-year-old. I think he's been watching too much Playboy TV. For his eyes only there's no such thing as too tarted up, but when he takes me out in public, it's like we live in Iraq. Other men aren't entitled to catch a glimpse of my ankles or neck or whatever else they're not allowed to see in foreign countries. Talk about your Madonna-whore complex.

"I am not changing." Why should I change? I have a great body. I'm not one of those fake-modest do-I-look-fat? does-my-ass-look-big? girls. I do not look fat. My ass does not look big. My bras are 34Ds. I look forward to bikini shopping come spring. That may sound conceited, but aren't magazines always telling women to be proud of what they have? Judging from my mother's chronology of old pictures, I have about eight years, tops, to flaunt my looks before everything starts to go. At thirty-three my mother's size-five pants were a little too snug. At thirty-six, her husband was sleeping with someone my age. My age now, not my age then— I'll give him credit for that, at least. The window of opportunity to have men salivate at my scantily clothed perfect breasts exists for just a limited while; it is therefore my sacred duty to use them at full capacity.

"Then we're not going anywhere," Nick says, his lips pouting. Ironic, really. He was first attracted to my breasts, and I was first attracted to his stubbornness. We were at a club on Richmond and he kept staring at my black negligee with no back and barely any front. He repeatedly sent me vodka martinis and I repeatedly sent them back to him. We ended up in his bed—where I've been pretty much ever since, except for the four times I've broken up with him. And then got back together once he proved his undivided love and desire.

By now he should be trained not to pull this bullshit with me. Who does he think he is, dictating what I get to wear? I will wear whatever I want. I am in charge of my own body. I am in charge of what parts of my body will be flaunted and what parts will be kept under snowsuits. Not that I even have a snowsuit. I have a ski suit, which is too trendy and too tight and too lacking in protective layers to be appropriate for anything but the chalet. I haven't worn it since I moved to Toronto, because the skiing is shit in this city. Compared to Montreal, anyway. Not to mention lacking in the nightlife, restaurants and men department.

"Fine!" I yell, throwing the door open and swinging my feet out of the car, feet dressed in gorgeous new patent leather red sandals purchased last week. "If you're going to behave like a fresh piece of shit, I'm going home."

Why must I play this game? He's in love with me. He can't live without me. It's now his turn to proclaim that I'm being silly, I can wear whatever I want, I look beautiful, et cetera, et cetera, et cetera...

"Em..." He leans toward the open window.

"Yes?"

"Don't wait up," he says, and drives off.

"Go to hell!" I scream and give the finger to the tail of his Mustang as it tears down my street. "If you don't stop that car, don't ever bother calling me again!"

His car slows down…and then turns the corner.

Bastard. Pervert-bastard. This time it's over-over.

"I thought you were going out?" my father asks as I slam the front door, post breakup cigarette. He and the stepbitch are sitting at the kitchen table, probably involved in one of their many discussions about how fucked up I am. I'm their favorite topic of conversation. If it weren't for all my supposed screwups, I bet they'd be divorced for lack of a common interest.

"You sound disappointed. Don't stop discussing me just because I'm here."

"Of course we're not disappointed, dear," AJ says, patting my father on the arm and speaking extremely slowly. "Don't be silly. Stephen and I just thought you were going out, that's all."

Blah, blah, blah. I ask you, is AJ an appropriate name for a stepmother? What happened to Marge? Or Stella? AJ sounds like a boy I pinned down at recess in the fifth grade during an episode of kissing tag. I'm pretty sure AJ stands for Annoying Jerk-off. First of all, she's only thirty-six. That's ten years older than I am and eighteen years younger than my cradle-snatching father. AJ has the annoying habit of speaking for my father, and my father has the annoying habit of letting AJ speak for him. She also tends to speak to me in the identical voice she uses while speaking to her six-year-old daughter.

"Spare me the bullshit, please," I say. "You're counting the seconds until I'm out of the house."

AJ, aka Stepbitch, rolls her eyes at my father.

I am moving out in eight days. AJ found me a room in an apartment with two complete strangers. She works with one of the girls, Allison, but unlike Allison, she's a volunteer. They do something for Ontario University a few times a week. AJ acts like I should be grateful, as if she's doing me a favor, but she only set it up to get me out of the house, away from her precious daughter, Barbie. I'm not kidding. Her name is Barbie. Not that she's ever going to look like a Barbie. She's a chunky, short kid. And let's not forget her big nose and glasses. I guess conniving ol' AJ (actually, *young* AJ) will manipulate my father into spending my inheritance on a nose job and laser eye surgery.

Apparently I have a bad attitude and I'm negatively influencing Barbie's development.

Fuck that.

Barbie is not really a bad kid. When I baby-sit, I let her watch music videos and I teach her how to do the moves. She might be a pretty good dancer one day, that is, if her legs ever get long enough to reach the floor from a sitting position.

I even let her play with my hair. I'm amazed at how long it took that kid to learn how to make a braid. Of course, she uses only two strands, which is kind of like juggling with two balls instead of three.

I brought back some of my old clothes, after visiting my mother in Montreal. Too bad AJ feeds her so much, because poor Barbie couldn't even get one of her bloated thighs into one of my dresses.

I'm trying to get her to dance the weight off.

I try to pretend to like AJ in front of the kid so I don't add to her list of things she's going to need to talk about in therapy one day.

"I'm not going to listen to this abuse," AJ whines, and leaves the kitchen.

Silence.

I pour myself a glass of juice and sit down in her deserted seat. It's hot. She probably farted in it.

"Why do you insist on upsetting her?"

I'm upsetting *her?* Let's tally up, shall we? She had an affair with my father. She convinced him to desert my mother and me, move to Toronto and marry her. As far as I'm concerned, I'm entitled to blame her for every messed-up thing I do. I have problems maintaining relationships? AJ's fault. I don't trust people? AJ's to blame. I killed someone? AJ. I haven't actually killed anyone, but if I did she would have driven me to it. How can anything I do possibly equal her actions? She drove a clearing truck right through the soft patch of snow that was my life.

"Fighting with your boyfriend does not give you the right to take out your anger on us," my father says.

"Nick and I aren't fighting." I hate when he blames Nick for everything. It's like when Nick says I'm being a bitch because I'm on my period, which is a dumb expression because how can someone be on her period? Are they straddling it? And just because I'm being a bitch doesn't mean I have my period. It may mean that I have PMS, mind you, but that Nick doesn't need to know.

"Does AJ ever ask you for a thank-you? For letting you live here for the past two years? No. For getting you a job at *Stiletto?* For finding you an apartment? No. For lending you her basement furniture for your apartment? No. All she asks is that you treat her decently. And can you even do that? No."

First of all, why was she "letting" me live here? Isn't part of a father's responsibility to take care of his kid? I wanted to do the two-year design program at the Toronto School of Art. I would have been happy to live on my own and let them foot the bill, but my father thought all of us living together would be a good opportunity for us to get to know one an- other. Apparently AJ has now changed her mind.

Second, she didn't get me the job at *Stiletto* to help me. She used employment as an excuse for exiling me from her Rosedale palace. Is it my fault that she happens to know someone in the industry of my dreams? What does she expect from me? It's not even a high-paying job. If my salary were a shirt, it would barely be enough material to cover my nipples.

"Thank you, Daddy," I say in a Popsicle-sweet voice. "I truly appreciate everything AJ has done to make my life more successful. If she hadn't fucked you while you were married to my mother, I might not have ended up right here at this kitchen table, drinking juice."

So I'm a big baby. Shoot me.

My father gets up and leaves the kitchen. He's always taking off. Maybe he was an airplane in his last life.

The moonlight spills into the kitchen and my body glitter dances.

Maybe I'll play dress-up with Barbie.

Maybe I'll take her shopping tomorrow.

Things could be worse. Daddy dear hasn't taken back his credit card.

Another breakup equals another shopping spree.

4
ALLIE GETS EXCITED

ALLIE

One hour till Clint comes. Well, not *comes* exactly, but comes over. Maybe comes.

So that's it, then. I'll organize for potential coming. I'll take the vodka out of the cupboard and put it into the freezer. Hea-vy. Why did I buy the supersize bottle? Was I planning on bathing in it? How much vodka can two people drink?

Ditto for the cranberry juice. Supersize? Puh-lease. But it will make a perfect vodka diluter later and a fab dry-mouth remedy immediately. Mmm, good. Back into the fridge. Whoops...cranberry juice leakage. Why can't I ever remember to screw the top back on properly?

Will cranberry juice make me have to pee? It's supposed to cure bladder infections, but I don't want to be running to the bathroom every five seconds, do I? Talk about ruining the mood. Although I read you have a better orgasm when you have to pee. I think that's just for women. I don't think guys can have to pee and be hard at the same time. I also read that if you're about to have a G-spot orgasm you feel like you have to pee.

I've never had a G-spot orgasm. I've never had an orgasm during sex. I've never had sex.

I'm a twenty-two-year-old virgin.

Is that crazy? It's not like I have a third eye or a missing front tooth or anything. There *are* other virgins. Thousands of them, probably. It's just that the others are either waiting for marriage, religious or ugly.

Or thirteen years old.

I'm pathetic.

But I'm waiting to meet a man I'm utterly in love with! Or a little in love with. Or, at least, a man I like.

Or, at least, a man who likes me.

Okay, fine. I'm waiting for a man, any man, as long as I like him and want to sleep with him, and as long as he likes me and wants to sleep with me. I don't think that's too much to ask for, is it?

Open mouth. Insert nail of left ring finger. Mmm.

I almost did *it* in high school. With Gordon. God knows he wanted to. He asked me pretty much every day: "When are you going to be ready? Are you ready yet? How come everyone else is doing it? How come everyone else is ready?" I wanted to, but for some mind-numbing, inexplicable reason, I felt it was my duty to say no. *We're too young. We're not ready.* Why is that exactly? Some-one remind me, please. Teenage girls want to do it as much as guys do. We daydream about doing it, we imagine ourselves doing it, but we believe it is our duty not to do it. Except for the girls who actually do it. They're the ones we call sluts when their backs are turned. They're the ones we pretended to be when our eyes were closed.

Is it possible I waited too long and now it won't even work? Does that happen? Can a hymen ferment?

Gordon dumped me and slept with Stephanie Miller. "Thank

God I didn't sleep with him," I said, crying into the purple bed-spread of my then best friend, Jennifer (while wishing I had slept with him and that he still loved me).

You'd think I would have done it at least once over the next four years, but I haven't had a boyfriend since Gordon. I've dated, of course, and I've fooled around a lot (everything but), but I feel gross about losing my virginity on a one-night stand. I don't have to marry the guy, but I should be dating him for at least three months. Is an entire season too prudish? Maybe six weeks. Reality TV shows take place in under six weeks and look how complex those relationships become.

Okay, how about four weeks? I can accept that. I don't think it's crazy to plan on being with someone for four measly weeks. A lot can happen in four weeks. For example, you get your period at least once. Most people, anyway. For some inexplicable reason, I'm on the "Surprise! It'll come whenever you're wearing white pants!" cycle, which is sometimes every four months, sometimes every two weeks. But at least it comes. (Not that I've ever had to agonize about it *not* coming. Nope, I've never been in that particular pre-dicament.) By the time I got it for the first time, I was already geri-atric enough for my parents, my brother, my friends, my teachers and even the grocery deliveryman to be repeatedly harassing me with "So? Are you a woman yet? What's taking so long?" type comments.

Apparently I'm a late bloomer.

In college, I would have slept with Ronald. Yes, I admit it. I dated a guy named Ronald, although I always tried to call him Ron. ("I prefer Ronald, thanks." Why, why, why? Why would anyone except for the nerd-turned-cool-guy in *Can't Buy Me Love* prefer Ronald?) We dated for two weeks in junior year, and one night, when we were fooling around, I told him "the truth." Big mistake.

Huge. (That's a line from *Pretty Woman*—you know, when she walks into the snobby store that wouldn't let her shop there before, to show them how much she spent in the other store? I love that movie. I've seen it forty-six times. Maybe I shouldn't be admitting that, either.)

Somehow I had always been under the impression that when I finally did offer my virginity to a guy (Would you like some tea with this virginity, sir? Or would you prefer it to go?), it would be something he'd want. Apparently this is not the case. It FREAKS guys out. His you-know-what turned as soft as a decaying banana. And then Ronald left, saying he had an eight o'clock class in the morning. (Funny, his eight o'clock class was the last thing on his mind five minutes ago, when his banana wasn't overripe.) He ignored me for the next week in the cafeteria, and when I saw him at a dorm party that weekend, he drunkenly admitted that he felt there would be too much commitment involved if we were to get intimate.

Who wants to have sex with a guy whose name is Ronald, anyway?

Who wants to have sex with a guy who uses the word *intimate?*

Is it possible I haven't had sex with anyone because I've been subconsciously saving myself for Clint? No…maybe…but what if it never happens? Will I stay a virgin forever?

The clock on the VCR, which even when it was connected to a TV refused to play videos, says 6:10, which actually means that it's 7:10, because it's still on eastern standard time. In a few months it will be right again.

Fifty minutes till Clint-time. It has to happen.

Time to prepare the body and make it sexable.

Tonight's shower requires many props. Got the loofah. Got the razor. Got the pear body wash. Got the citrus face wash. Got the

watermelon-fortified shampoo. Got the avocado leave-in conditioner that was stuck through the mailbox and because it's just me
picking up the mail, it's mine, all mine! (The girls and I used to
rock-paper-scissors for these mini treasures.)

I place my glasses on the sink. I know I should put them into
their case, because if I don't, I'll never remember where they are
and spend a minimum of twenty-five minutes frantically searching for them tomorrow morning. But I don't know where the case
is.

Fab! So much hot water! No one flushing the toilet while I'm
trying to cleanse myself! The apartment has two bathrooms. One
has a shower and toilet, and the other one has just a toilet. I'm in
the one with the shower and toilet, obviously. The other bathroom
is off the smallest bedroom, soon to be Emma's room, once
Rebecca's room. Isn't that weird? Why build an apartment like
that, where the master bedroom, mine, has no bathroom, and the
smallest one does? It must be built for students—to make it fair.
If a family moved in here, the kid would have its own bathroom
and the parents would have to share!

I'd need my own bathroom if I lived with a boy. When I'm with
Clint, I leave the water running when I pee so he doesn't realize
what I'm doing in there.

Melissa let me use her bathroom if someone was using the
shower in the main bathroom. I hope that Emma won't mind the
same rule.

That felt great. Why don't I ever remember to keep my towel
next to the shower? Thirty minutes until he's here. The skin
around my thumbnail is bleeding. I reach over to the toilet paper
roll and rip off a few squares, and bandage my injured finger and
apply pressure. Why do I do that? And when did I do that? Why
don't I even notice when I'm biting anymore?

Post-shower is really prime biting time. The skin gets all pruned. There are so many little pieces and layers for teeth to grab on to. That sounded disgusting. That's it. It's over. I'm stopping. No more biting. How can I make ecstatic nail marks on Clint's back if I have no nails?

"What are you doing?" he asked me earlier today. When I realized it was him on the phone, I got into my Phone Concentration position. This is basically lying down on my unmade bed in a right-angle position, my feet up against the wall above my pillow. I love my bed. I have a yellow daisy-covered duvet cover and six soft throw pillows in varying shades of yellow. I love my bed most when it's made. Which only happens on sheet-changing day or when a guy comes over, the latter not being too often. The former being less often than I should admit. What can I say? I hate doing laundry.

"Not much," I answered. "You?"

"Maybe I'll come by later to watch *Korpics*." *Korpics* is that new let's-hang-out-at-the-water-cooler-to-talk-about-lives-that-aren't-ours detective show. The fact that it's only available on the Extra channel—Canada's version of HBO—only increases its water-cooler coolness factor since only select people are capable of chiming into the conversation.

Luckily, I'm part of the select few.

I know he doesn't get *Korpics* at his place, but he could have gone to see it at a bar if what he was really interested in doing was "watching." It's an excuse. It has to be. He's never asked to watch TV here before.

Hemorrhage averted. I throw the soiled toilet paper into the slightly overflowing garbage, leave the towels discarded on the tiled floor (I will remember to pick those up before he gets here. I will, I will, I will…) and wander naked to my closet, something I would never do if anyone else were home. What to wear… It can't be something that looks like I want action. I need a hangout outfit. Not too Victoria's Secret, because why would I be wearing anything sexy if I'm just sitting around the apartment? I have to look like I don't care what I look like, right? That's the rule with guys. They want what they can't have. So if I look like I'm not interested in the slightest, he'll be interested. The grosser I look the more he'll want me.

Decision made. I'll wear my old camp overalls, the ones with the tear on the left knee from when I tripped on the bench in the rec hall. Which killed.

A cattle rancher stares back at me from my reflection in the mirror. What if being this extreme on the gross-a-meter repulses him? Maybe I should go casual. Gap modelesque. And makeup that doesn't look like makeup. Natural makeup with no lipstick. No lipstick looks more natural.

The truth is I hate wearing lipstick because I'm perpetually afraid of getting it on my teeth. I have a tiny overbite and I'm always convinced that I'll spend half the day walking around with red-stained front teeth.

Jeans and a little T-shirt?

Modrobes (look like doctor scrub pants but in funky orange) and a tank?

A wrap skirt?

Why would I be wearing a skirt to sit around in my apartment? The buzzer sounds.

Oh, God. He's here! I'm going for the true natural look, then. Jeans and a tank top it is. Why is he so early? He couldn't wait to see me? He couldn't wait to see me!

The buckle digs into my stomach. I hope it's because I put my jeans in the dryer by mistake, and has nothing to do with that cheesecake I polished off last night.

Mmm. Cheesecake.

They'll stretch, right?

Note to self—hold in stomach. And butt.

Can you hold in your butt?

"Coming!" I holler. I certainly hope I'll get the chance to say that again later.

My reflection catches me off guard in the mirror next to the door. Yuck. I got deodorant on the sides of my tank top. Why does that happen? The bottle says "Clear!" So why are there white tire tracks on all my shirts?

"Hold on!" I scream (I hope I won't have to say that later tonight) while running to my room. I throw my tank into my laundry basket and squeeze into a white T-shirt.

"Who is it?" I ask. You never know. I don't want to let an ax murderer into my house.

"It's Em," replies a voice that does not belong to a yummy-smelling hard body. Em? Who's Em? Oh, Emma.

"Hi!" I say, opening the door.

"Hey. I just came by to drop some shit off. Hope that's all right." She's holding a fancy-looking metallic-green box.

"Sure, no problem. Come in."

She leans toward me and air-kisses me near the right cheek. I pull my head back just as she heads in for a double, and I end up smashing her in the face.

"Sorry. Didn't mean to kill you there," I say.

"It's the Montreal double-kiss. You'll get used to it. It's addictive."

I don't think I'm a double-kiss type of girl, but you never know. "Aren't the movers bringing over your stuff?"

"Yeah, but I don't want them touching my perfume collection. They'll help themselves to a present for their girlfriends or mothers or whomever. I thought I'd drop them off myself on my way out. Is that cool?"

"Of course. Cool. Do you need any help?"

"No, I got it. Thanks."

As she walks toward her new room, her gold hair swishes below her shoulders. Why can't I have gold hair? What are you if you have gold hair? A golde? I don't think I could pull it off. I couldn't pull off the Uma Thurman *Pulp Fiction* bangs that frame her face, either. Or the perfectly arched eyebrows. They look like they stepped right off a McDonald's sign.

"So how are you?" she asks, flashing her head back at me.

"Fine. Thanks. How are you?" The chunky silver belt around her hips scratches her size-zero silver jeans as she walks. How do I get pants that make my butt look like that? And a top that makes my boobs look like that? She's wearing a black cotton V-neck, the perfect sexy hangout shirt.

I follow her into her recently painted red room. Her father sent a man named Harry over to paint the walls, install new silver blinds and disinfect the bathroom. Emma pulls the blinds open, exposing the black sky and our reflections in the window. Emma glitters.

"I like your belt," I say. Ooh, I hope she lets me borrow her clothes. I wonder how long it'll take me to get down to a size zero? I must stop staring. She'll think I'm a creep.

Must not look. Pretend she's an eclipse.

Where does she buy belts like that?

"Thanks."

"Nick didn't want to come with you?" I met Nick when Emma came to see the apartment last month.

"That fuckhead? It's over. What an idiot."

But he was so hot! "What happened?"

She closes her eyes as if the scene is unfolding in her head. "He called me a slut." Her eyes flutter open.

"No!"

She scrunches her lips as if she's just swallowed a French fry soaked in vinegar. "He's absurdly controlling. I shouldn't have to put up with that."

"Of course not!"

Her eyelids slam shut. "He wanted me to *change* my clothes. Do you believe?"

I shake my head to show that no, I do not believe (despite the fact in the past twenty minutes I've tried on about a gazillion outfits, but those were without Clint ever knowing, so it doesn't count). But she can't see my reaction because her eyes are still closed. Hello?

"And then he *drove* off. Do you believe that?"

I pointlessly shake my head again.

"Then he went out with his friends and didn't call me until *the next day*. Do you believe *that*?"

I shake my head again, this time adding a little sigh for emphasis and audio concurrence.

"Of course I told him to go jerk himself off when he finally had the decency to apologize. Obviously."

Yes. Obviously. Now I'm picturing a masturbating Nick. I wonder if that's what she's seeing behind her eyelids, too.

"I'm exorcising my life of shit-suckers."

I don't know exactly what a shit-sucker is, but I'm pretty sure it's not something I want to be.

"No more dickheads telling me what to do." She opens her eyes and places the green box in the corner of the room.

Why didn't I ever paint my walls red? Now I can never do it because I'll look like a copycat. Why didn't I think of that first?

Why why why? She's officially moving in the day after tomorrow. Maybe I can have my room painted purple by then. No can do. Jodine is moving in tomorrow.

"New apartment, new frame of mind," she says. "So what's Jodine like?"

Oh my God. She practically read my mind! Is that a sign we're going to make good roommates or what?

"I haven't met her. We spoke on the phone a couple of times, though," I say.

"I hope she's normal."

"I'm sure she's normal. I met her brother and he seemed nice. And we've been e-mailing back and forth for about a month."

"If she's freakish we'll keep her locked in her room," she says, revealing a perfectly white tooth-bleach commercial smile. She's wearing a brownish lipstick and of course none of it has smeared onto her teeth. "I wonder what she looks like."

"She's tall with long brown hair."

"How do you know? She sent you a picture?"

"What? Oh, no." Hmm. I have absolutely no reason to think she's tall with long brown hair. That's how I pictured her looking, because she sounded exactly like Christine Torrins on the phone, a girl I went to college with, and I had brilliantly deduced that they must look exactly alike as well. "I don't know, actually."

"She hasn't seen the place? What kind of a person rents an apartment without seeing it first? I bet she's a flake."

I suddenly feel defensive for Jodine. "Her brother took some digital pictures for her."

"Don't judge an apartment by its pictures. That's how you know her? You know her brother?"

"Yeah. My brother is a friend of her brother."

"Is he hot?"

"Her brother or my brother?"

"Either," she answers, and laughs.

"I don't know." How do I answer that? First of all, I can't tell if my brother's cute. He's my brother. He looks like me. Second, no I don't think Jodine's brother is cute—he has a unibrow and a big head, but I'm not going to start making fun of my new roomie's family, am I? Besides, maybe Emma will like him, I don't know. How cool would it be if Emma started dating Jodine's brother?

"Are they single?"

"My brother isn't. I don't know about Jodine's. We can ask her tomorrow."

"Shit. I gotta go. I'm meeting some friends in Yorkville. What are you up to tonight? Wanna join us?"

I almost regret having made plans. Almost. "A friend is coming over to watch *Korpics*. I get Extra and he doesn't."

"We get Extra?"

"Yeah. We get movies and most of the HBO shows, and it's only a few extra dollars a month."

Emma's lips scrunch back into their just-ate-vinegar position. Uh-oh. "Unless you guys want to—to cancel it," I stammer. Please don't want to cancel it. I really, really like it and I keep forgetting to fix the VCR.

"No, we shouldn't cancel it. Do you think we can splice the cable into my room? I'm bringing a TV."

"Oh, definitely. I splice it into my room."

"Who do you have plans with? You don't have a boyfriend, do you?"

"Not a boyfriend exactly…"

She smiles knowingly. "I get it. A 'special' friend."

"You could say that." Very, very special. "Do you think this looks okay?" I twirl.

She eyes me up and down. "Your hair is so long."

I'm not sure if that's good or bad. "But what about the outfit?"

"It's cute."

Cute? Is that good? It doesn't sound good. A younger cousin with spaghetti sauce on his chin is cute. "I wish I had a shirt like yours. Where did you get it?"

"Some store on Queen Street. I'll take you. Do you want to wear mine?"

"The one you have on?" Is it possible? Is she so awesome that she'll not only help me shop for a new wardrobe but she'll lend me the shirt off her back (literally) in the interim? It's a good thing the material is stretchy—not that she's lacking anything up front. There's just more to me on the sides. "But what are you going to wear?"

"I'll borrow a sweatshirt. Don't worry—I know where you live."

She follows me into my oh-so-boring white-walled but maybe soon-to-be-purple room. Unfortunately I haven't yet cleaned it for Clint's visit. I was supposed to be doing that now, instead of chatting. She was inevitably going to find out I was messy, but it didn't have to be before she even moved in, did it?

I pull a semiwrinkled blue Champions sweatshirt out of a pile and hand it to her. What should I do now? Should I leave my room and let her change? Apparently not. My new roomie is not as conscious of public nudity as I am. She whips off her shirt in a fluid stripperlike motion and sits on my bed, wearing a see-through beige bra. She has huge nipples. I shouldn't stare at her nipples. What is wrong with me? I don't mean to be staring at her nipples. Did she see me staring at her nipples? It's just that women hardly ever see each other naked. Really. Men see each other's private parts every time they use a urinal. Women see breasts on TV, of course, but these aren't real breasts, they're Hollywood-perfect breasts, which are far from the real thing. Far from my real thing, anyway.

How does she manage to look like a Victoria's Secret model even in my five-year-old safe-to-paint-a-garage sweatshirt?

She hands me her cleavage-revealing shirt.

She doesn't expect me to try this on in front of her, does she?

Apparently she does. I'd like to turn around while I take off my shirt. Will she think I'm weird if I turn around while I take off my shirt? It's not that I think she really cares what my boobs look like or anything. Can I turn around when she didn't turn around? Is that bad-mannered? Is she entitled to see my bra now that I've seen hers? I'll show you mine if you show me yours? At least I'm wearing a good bra for Chrissake (or Clint's sake).

I try the trick we used to use in camp when you had to change in front of the whole cabin. I put on the cleavage shirt before taking off the old shirt. It doesn't work. Now both shirts are tangled around my neck and I feel like a five-year-old struggling to take off her snowsuit.

I remove my top from my neck and slip on her shirt. The armpit material has an already-been-worn aroma, but nothing that a little extra spritzes of perfume won't fix. (Maybe a few extra spritzes of *her* perfume? Am I becoming *Single, White Female?*) Hmm. Maybe she doesn't wear deodorant and that's why there are no white marks on her shirt.

"What do you think?" I ask, catching a glimpse of my new sexy-yet-casual self in the mirror over my bureau.

"Very hot."

Hot? Hot is good. Much better than cute. Yes, I think I like my new roomie.

* * *

After Emma leaves, I run around my room and bathroom, trying to make it look Clint-presentable. And then I stumble upon an additional dilemma. Do I move the TV in my room into the living room, or keep it in the bedroom? The only place to sit in my room is on the bed. Unless he wants to sit on my lone computer chair. Into the living room the TV must go. Hea-vy. Arms hurt. How can something so small be so heavy?

Hmm. Do I just plug it in and turn it on? Where's the cable? Do I use the red cable or the yellow cable? Red or yellow? Five minutes until he's here…I feel like I'm in a *Lethal Weapon* and I'm about to cut the yellow wire and there are only three seconds left, and what should I do? Yellow, red, yellow red yellowredyellow…red. Definitely red. I plug in the red.

Nope.

Yellow?

Nope.

Okay. TV goes back to my bedroom. He'd have to sit on the floor in the living room, anyway. Thank God Emma will be here soon with couches.

Heavy heavy heavy.

Korpics starts in three minutes. Where is he?

I sit on my bed.

It smells good in here, right?

Maybe I should open the window.

Should I spray perfume on the bedspread?

It's starting!

I should fluff up the pillows so they look more inviting.

Fluff-fluff.

Fluff.

One minute into *Korpics*.

Where is he?

Two minutes into *Korpics*. People are already dying and he's not even here. He's going to come in the middle and I'm going to have to miss some of the show and I hate missing parts of shows.

Hah! The fact that he's late proves that he doesn't care about watching the show, because if he cared he wouldn't be even a minute late for it, right? If he were coming all the way here to watch it, then he would certainly be on time for it, right?

Unless he changed his mind and found somewhere else to watch it. And he's not coming. And I'll be staring at the television not absorbing anything that goes on, sitting here wallflower-like as the minutes turn into hours, the hours into days.

The doorbell buzzes.

Finally! I speed through the hallway and throw open the door.

"Hey," he says. And smiles. He has a big smile. A big, beautiful smile exposing big, beautiful teeth. (All the better to eat you with, my dear, I think. Now that's sick. Why do I always start having perverted thoughts when he's around?) His smile finally looks proportioned. His face has filled out since he put on about twenty pounds last summer, but the good kind of twenty pounds. The muscle kind. He used to be a bit too skinny and his smile looked kind of out of place. Now he's completely gorgeous. Of course, I thought he was completely gorgeous before, even when he wasn't really, you know?

Did his eyes just sneak a peek at my cleavage? I think they did! Hah! It's working! He's falling in love! Or in lust. I'll take lust. He already loves me as a friend, so all I need really is to provoke a little lust. If he feels lust, then there's nothing missing. I might as well start ordering the wedding invitations immediately. Kidding!

Kind of.

"You're missing it!" I tell him, impossibly trying to pout but too happy to see him to be angry with him. "It started five minutes ago."

"I'm sorry, I'm sorry." He kisses me on the cheek. "You smell like a fruit salad."

Who doesn't like fruit salad? He's slightly more casual than I am. Not that I expected him to dress up. He's not one of those dress-up guys at all. Not that he dresses badly or anything. He's more of a sporty dresser. He wears a lot of baseball caps and those bubble shirts. You know, the kind of shirt that has tiny indented squares patterned all over it—but in one color. He's wearing a white one now, a white bubble shirt with tiny white bubbles. And snap pants—the blue nylon pants that have snaps all down the sides. They'd be so easy to just rip right off.

"I had the craziest day. Troy Cobrint wants to do the Cobras."

I try not to stare blankly. Apparently I should be aware of who Troy Cobrint and the Cobras are. "What are the Cobras again?" I figure pleading ignorance to a probable brand name is better than pleading ignorance to a probable Toronto athlete.

"Our new basketball shoes." Aha! Troy Cobrint must be a basketball player! Brilliant deductive reasoning, Nancy Drew!

"He walked into the office at around ten-thirty. He was supposed to be there for nine, but I guess when you're that crazy rich and famous you can come and go whenever the hell you want. Anyway, he agreed to endorse the shoes. He said he tried them and liked them. My VP is loving my ass for coming up with the idea to create a shoe for him called Cobra. Get it? Cobrint—Cobra?"

"Got it."

"I bet I get a crazy raise." Clint's favorite adjective is *crazy*. He sprinkles it in every sentence he can.

"Didn't you just get a raise?"

He started his marketing job right after we graduated and is already some kind of office hotshot. "Yeah. But since I come up with the craziest ideas, I should be compensated, huh?"

"I'm shocked you're not VP by now. Maybe next week they'll make you CEO."

This whole "attitude" thing is pretty new for Clint. He struggled to keep a B average at school, and was always better at criticizing other people's athletic abilities than showcasing any of his own. He dated a bit, but not the girls he talked about. And then out of nowhere he got a prime marketing job (possibly through one of his dad's connections, but that doesn't mean he's not qualified), and he now has this whole "big man on campus" attitude going on.

"C'mon." I grab the piece of his shirt near his wrist (there's not too much spare material around the chest area anymore) and pull him into my room. How many girls dream about walking into their bedrooms with a guy who looks like this? Hah! And he's here!

He picks up the freshly arranged yellow pillows one by one and drops them onto the floor. Then he kicks off his shoes and sprawls across my bed. Reaching over, he picks up one of the pillows and squashes it against the wall to prop up his head.

Hmm. Where should I sit? On the corner of the bed? By his feet? Should I lie down? Sprawl next to him? It *is* my bed. There's nothing obvious about me sitting on my own bed, is there? Will he think, Wow, it's so obvious she invited me over because she's so desperate and no one else wants her? Will he think, I definitely don't want her and that's why she's lying so pathetically on her bed, to make me want her? Will he also think (God forbid), She even moved the living room television into her room so I have no choice but to fool around with her?

I sit on the computer chair.

Swivel.

"Your hair got so blond from the sun!" I say.

He smiles sheepishly. "I highlighted it last week. Do you like it?"

Are men supposed to highlight? "It looks great. Very California. Do you want to know what you missed so far?"

"I can figure it out."

Oh. Okay.

Twenty minutes later, I'm starting to wish the show were on regular cable, not Extra, so it had commercials through which we could talk. Although if it were on regular TV, he wouldn't be here, now would he?

Why did I choose the swivel chair? Why why why? Should I make him something to eat? Is he hungry? He's probably hungry. "Do you want some popcorn?"

"Sure. Thanks. You're such a sweetheart."

My heart fully stops. A sweetheart. I am a sweetheart. Men marry women they think are sweethearts. Reason Number One why he should fall in love with me: I am a sweetheart.

Reason Number Two is that I make great popcorn. I do. In the kitchen, I pull out my fancy popcorn maker that goes on the stove, and the real butter.

As soon as I set up the popcorn I peek my head into my room so that I can follow what's going on. I hate missing my shows. Which is a problem because I have a lot of favorite shows and no VCR to speak of. Now that I'm out of school, I can watch TV all day, which is fab, but I miss the prime times because during the week my shift is at night. This isn't as annoying as in the summer when it's repeat season, but soon all the new shows will be on and I'm going to miss them.

Making popcorn is definitely a good call. I'll be expected to share some of it, which means I'll have to be on the bed, too. We'll be lying right next to each other, our hands delicately grazing each other's in the salad bowl, since Rebecca took the popcorn bowl with her when she left.

What's taking so long? Standing here by the door is starting to hurt my legs. But I know that as soon as I sit down, it will start to pop, and I'll have to get up again. C'mon, popcorn, please hurry. The show will be over by the time it's ready. Although that might not be such a terrible thing. It will force him to stay longer.

Pop. Pop pop pop. It's almost ready. Pop. FINALLY. Ready.

"Thanks, hon," he says without lifting his eyes from the television. I love when he calls me hon. You don't call someone you have no feelings for, hon, right? I oh-so-casually slide onto the bed.

He reaches for the popcorn. Our hands touch in the bowl. His fingers linger. Is he thinking about sneaking his hands under my sexy shirt? And then gently kissing me, and then passionately kissing me and then taking off all my clothes, lying on top of me and pressing his hard broad-shouldered musky-yummy-smelling body into mine? Is the fan on?

He stuffs a fistful of kernels into his mouth.

"What did I miss?" I ask.

He rambles about some sort of murder and "crazy fight scene." Can't really concentrate. Clint is in my room. Clint is on my bed.

Why are we wasting time watching TV?

I spend the next thirty minutes trying to casually drop my hand into the popcorn bowl whenever his hand is there, without looking obvious about it.

Is he going to make a move? Maybe when the show is over?

When the credits roll he leans toward me. This is it! This is it! My heart is hammering about a thousand beats a minute. I'm not sure how many beats are normal, but this seems excessive. Can he hear it? I'll bet he can hear it. I'll bet he's wondering if someone is at the door, because the sound of the pounding is echoing throughout the apartment.

And then…he kisses me.

On the cheek.

On the cheek? "Thanks, hon. You're the best." He jumps off the bed.

Come back, I telepathically scream. Where are you going? Return to my bed. Return to my bed!

"I'll see you later this week, okay? We'll grab dinner."

"Oh. Okay, sure." What are you doing? Where are you going? "No problem."

"You have plans tonight?" He is looking at himself in the mirror, running his fingers through his recently processed hair.

"Um…I'm meeting some friends. My new roommate. Later. You?"

"I'm hooking up with the boys on College. First I have to stop by my place to change." Apparently his snap pants are of the hangout not make-out variety. "Call me on my cell if you girls end up on College."

"Definitely." Definitely not. What a wasted opportunity. If I had gone with Emma then I could have plotted bumping into him. I push myself off the bed with my hands, and my buttered-covered fingers leave a trace on one of the daisies. Ew.

"You're such a mess," Clint laughs as I try to scratch the stain off with—oops—the sleeve of Em's shirt.

Mess? I just cleaned my room for him. What mess? A little butter? Ew. This sleeve procedure isn't helping the matter. Apparently butter stains must be some sort of contagious virus—the circle has now spread to twice its original size. Since letting him watch this cannot be a good strategy for the Get-Clint-to-Want-to-Have-Sex-with-Me objective, I walk him to the door.

"Have fun tonight. Maybe we'll see you later," I say.

See, wasn't that sneaky of me? When I don't show up later, he'll think I'm far too busy to make time for him, thereby increasing my level of desirability. "Sure," he says, and pats me on the head. "It'll be fun to hook up."

Hook up—hook up? Uh-oh, he's really going. He's walking away. Wait! I forgot about the vodka! Before next time I'd better forget about my popcorn abilities and focus on my bartending skills.

5
JODINE ARRIVES

JODINE

"You're here! You're here!" Through the open passenger's seat window of the Happy Movers truck, I hear a girl squeal. She's short, has an incredibly long brown braid, and is wearing gray jaggedly uneven cutoff sweat shorts and a red cotton T-shirt. Is it possible? Can someone look more like Pippi Longstocking?

She was waiting for me on the porch of 56 Blake, my new abode, and is now jumping up and down, trampoline-style. "You're really here!" she says. Jump. Jump, jump. Each jump is punctuated with a clap of her hands. "It's you!"

I hope she doesn't lose her footing and topple down the stairs. "It is I," I answer, and she runs, no, *skips* toward me. "You must be Allie."

"That's me!" Her wide, overjoyed smile overtakes at least fifty percent of her face. "And you're gorgeous!"

I am? "Thank you." Terrific. A suck-up.

"And your eyes are so green! They're like the color of grass!"

"Um…thanks?"

"Mine are blue. And Emma's are brown. Isn't that cool? We're like a rainbow!"

I raise an eyebrow. What in the world is this person rambling about?

"And you have a fish! I've always wanted a fish."

She is referring to the glass bowl I am carrying, which contains one medium-size, mouth-agape goldfish. "You can have mine," I tell her.

Adam snorts as he walks to the back of the U-Haul. "Don't take it. She already tried to pawn it off to both me and our parents."

"Why? What's wrong with it?" she asks.

"Nothing is wrong with it. My brother makes it sound as if it's nuclear."

"She got it as a Valentine's Day present and has been trying to pawn it off on someone else," he explains.

"But it's so cute!"

I watch as Allie pokes the bowl with her—what is that revolting thing? Her finger! It's her finger! What is wrong with her finger? Why is it bleeding? Is she diseased? "What happened to your hand?"

She hides her hands behind her back. "Nothing. I bite."

Nail-biting makes no sense. Why would someone mutilate her own body parts? "You did that to yourself? Let me see."

"No." She keeps her hands behind her back. "I'm stopping."

I didn't mean to offend her, but really, no one should be causing herself that kind of pain. "Good. It's disgusting."

"So no one else in your family wants your fish?" she asks, changing the subject.

"I'd take it," Adam says, "if I didn't think it was infinitely more amusing to force Jo here to take care of it." He laughs.

I hate when he calls me Jo. "If it has an unfortunate accident down the toilet, it will be your fault."

"Poor fish," Allie says, looking at it as though it was Little Orphan Annie.

"Oh, he doesn't take it personally," I say. "He knows I'm not discriminatory—I hate all animals."

"But I'm sure you'll like Whiskers."

Whiskers. What's a whiskers? My body begins to feel clammy. Any chance her boyfriend is named Whiskers?

"My cat," she says, smiling. "Adam told you about my cat, didn't he? You'll love him. He's adorable. All black with gold whiskers."

I swallow. Cat? Allie has a cat? I can't have a cat. I can't live in the same vicinity as a cat. I hate cats. They scratch and bite and meow and do nasty things in the moonlight. Terrific. "Um. No one mentioned a cat."

She giggles.

Dread has manifested itself into a vacuum cleaner, sucking the moisture out of my mouth. Why is she giggling? This is the most horrendous news I have ever heard. I can't live here. The move is off. Turn the truck around. Back to the parents.

"I'm kidding, Jodine!" she says, and giggles again.

Huh? What? What kind of a sick joke is that? "You're kidding?"

"I don't have a cat. Don't have a heart attack. You just turned white. Are you okay? I'm sorry. I was kidding."

Kidding? Is this funny? This isn't funny. Certainly not ha-ha funny. Maybe this is some kind of new Olympic sport, the how-fast-can-she-make-me-dislike-her event. Or maybe all new roommates have to undergo this kind of inane ritual, as though initiating for a sorority. What a way to begin my next life stage. With a heart attack. I hate being teased.

"I'll take care of the fish," she says, attempting a peace offering. "I like animals. We'll keep it in the kitchen. Maybe even think about getting him some playmates. You know, some roomies of his own." Again, she giggles.

"Okay." Amity reinstalled. Can I still accidentally drop the fish down the drain?

"What's up?" she asks my brother as he opens the back of the U-Haul, fish story concluded. "It was nice of you to come help."

It's hot. I rub my arm against my hairline and feel beads of sweat. I hate sweat. I have a minor sweating problem. There are certain shirts I cannot wear because I get stains under my arms. It's because I work out so often. Despite what comedy sketches and character impersonations seem to imply, when your body is accustomed to working out, you break a sweat much faster than if you're out of shape.

"Not much, Al," Adam says with a wave. "What's up with you?"

Allie turns pinkish, possibly at the comfortable way he throws around the name Al, as if they're best friends. Does she go by Al? When she called, she used the name Allie. But Adam talks to everyone as though they've been best beer buds since tenth grade.

"Nothing's up," Allie answers, smiling. "I'm just excited that your sister is moving in."

Is that smile for him or for me? Are they flirting? Oh, God, listening to my brother get it on with my new roommate would be about as pleasurable as having a tooth pulled.

"Don't say I didn't try to warn you," he says. "Jo is a pain in the ass."

"Don't call me Jo," I say. I hate when he calls me Jo.

"Oh, come on, Jo. Al is practically family."

I hate when he gets like this. But at present, I am unable to publicly be angry with him, as he was decent enough to help me move. "That doesn't mean that shortening our names should become a tradition."

"What's wrong with Jo?" Allie asks.

"I prefer Jodine."

"If my name were Jodine, I'd prefer Jo," Adam comments. "What kind of a name is Jodine? What is a Jodine?"

I ignore him as he unloads the boxes off the truck. If I'm going to make him angry, it's wise to do so after he has unpacked.

"What took you guys so long?" Allie asks, picking up one of my two wicker baskets. "I was getting worried. Did you fly in today?"

"No. I flew in last week. The flight was surprisingly on time. And Mom even remembered to pick me up on time from the airport," I say to Adam. "But loading the truck took longer than I anticipated."

Adam shakes his head. "Your new roommate insisted on checking off every item on her list as it entered the truck. And then she double-checked it all. Three times."

"I had to make sure I didn't forget anything. And by the way, double-checking three times would imply that I checked it six times, which I most certainly did not."

"No, it would imply that you're neurotic, which you most certainly are. So what if you'd forgotten something? You're not in Siberia. Mom would have brought you it eventually."

"You are always mocking my list system. Yet you're the one who is constantly forgetting things, whereas I am on top of things."

This time, he ignores me. "How's Marc?" he asks Allie. I deduce that Marc is Allie's brother. Adam and Allie's brother were friends in university.

"He's great. He and Jen just bought their own place. It's in Belleville, about five blocks from where I live."

Interesting the way she says where I "live," not "lived" or where "her parents live." She obviously considers her Belleville house her home. My parents' house is just that—my parents' house. And I've been on my own for less than ten minutes.

"His umbilical cord was always sewn on too tight," Adam says.

"At school he drove home every week to see his parents and Jen."
Incredulity is written all over his face, as though he has just realized
that Marc's preferred mode of transportation was his unicycle, or
that he ate only food that was beige. My brother, unlike his family-
oriented friend, came back maybe at Christmas, if we were lucky
enough to be blessed with his company. As soon as he graduated,
he moved back to Toronto and rented a place downtown.

I suppose I could have rented my own place, too, rather than
have to put up with roommates. Except for one small factor: I can't
afford it. My parents can't afford to subsidize me, either, not that
I would have asked them. As for Adam, he can't really afford his
own two-bedroom apartment downtown, but he took out loans,
which is something I would never do. Presently, he owes his life
to the bank.

Still, even though I have roommates, at least I have a place I can
call *almost* my own. And I can afford it. And unlike Allie, I consider
this to be my main residence. My parents, however, don't agree
with me on this. For example, they refused to let me take my bed,
dresser and night table with me, claiming they want me to have a
place to sleep and unpack when I come "home." They tried to
placate me by surprising me with a new double futon and a box
filled with pieces of a put-together-yourself dresser. Yes, of course
I was thankful for their thoughtfulness and monetary help, but
letting other people pick out my furniture is about as pleasant as
rubbing bug repellant into a skin irritation. Why not surprise me
with money and allow me to do my own choosing? Your bed is
where you spend—in an ideal world eight hours but in reality
you're lucky if you get six—a large portion of your time. Having
one's bed chosen by someone else is too personal. And by your
parents, unthinkable. What could be worse than having someone
else pick out your bed?

"I can't believe you haven't even seen the place yet!" Allie gushes as she hoists a duffel bag of my clothes over her shoulder, and unknowingly sparks a far greater concern in my mind and stomach: *an apartment.* An apartment is far more personal than a bed. It's where one spends all of one's pre-school/post-gym waking and nonwaking hours. Someone else picking your apartment is far more invasive than having someone else picking one's bed.

Terrific. What have I done? Why did I let my brother convince me to take this apartment sight unseen? I would not even purchase a dictionary sight unseen! What if it contains hyphenated words that have since become closed compound nouns? Unthinkable.

How did I let this happen? I suppose, like the evolution of language, some things are unavoidable. I think back to the e-mail my brother forwarded me in New York. Dappled with exclamation marks, it was accompanied with pictures of this supposedly huge, too-good-a-deal-to-pass-up apartment at only five hundred a month. I wasn't planning on moving out of my parents' place in Toronto, but the more I tossed the idea around in my head, the more agreeable it became. I e-mailed Adam, asking him to take a look at it, knowing I was making his day—he'd been harassing me for years to move out on my own. His e-mail reply said that the apartment was solid, and that although Allie was a sweetheart, she needed to know right away. Suddenly I got cryogenic feet. I told him I'd think about it. I needed to see it for myself, which was not feasible, considering that I was in New York.

Adam e-mailed that some other girl was interested, and it had to be a yea or nay immediately. He also said I'd be an idiot to go with the latter. "Are you actually going to give up one of the nicest and cheapest apartments I've ever seen in this city, in one of the coolest areas for a twenty-something to be living in, right off Little

Italy, to spend at least a year on the subway and having to listen to dinner stories about our father's hangnails?"

It's true. My father repeatedly refers to his hangnails.

"Be spontaneous," Adam said. "It's good for you."

I'm not the spontaneous type. For instance, at coffee shops I always order regular black coffee with one Sweet'n Low. But in spite of this character flaw—or strength, depending how you view it—I found myself answering, "Okay. I'll take it"—and then immediately questioning my rash decision. What did I do? Sight unseen, I fully put the fate of my happiness into the hands of my big brother.

From inside the truck, he hands me a box and then lets out an elongated burp.

Terrific. Why did I listen to him? He has no concept of refinement. I've seen his apartment. He has beer cans overflowing in the garbage. My apartment is going to look like a smelly, rat-infested frat house.

"Let's go inside! I can't wait for you to see!" Allie says. I am afraid that at any minute she will break out into a chorus of "Follow the Yellow Brick Road." The street is pretty, I admit, although there are no yellow bricks. Impressive maple trees line the one-way road, dwarfing the small homes that look like white-and-red Lego houses.

Allie turns the handle of the unlocked front door, and Adam and I enter the foyer to face two additional doors.

"Is it 56A or 56B?" Adam asks. For some inexplicable reason, I find myself rooting for 56A.

Allie takes her key chain from her pocket and opens 56B. I deem this as a bad omen.

Welcome to hell. Here it comes.

The first thing I notice is the brightness. The door leads into a small entranceway off a sun-drenched den. The white blinds are pulled up and the windows are open. Soft air wafts through the room.

"We're lucky there's a breeze outside right now. It gets hot here in the summer," she says.

Terrific. I'm going to have permanent sweat marks. Mercifully I'll be moving out before next summer.

"My last roomie sponge-painted the walls yellow. We can repaint if you don't like it."

If she starts referring to me as her "roomie," I may have to throttle her. The word itself makes me think of "goomie"—the colored rubber bracelets I was obsessed with in grade school. I used to have over a hundred of them, and I would choose my colors meticulously every morning to match my outfits. We're not sharing a room, anyway. It's more of a flat. *Flatmate* sounds too British. "Housemate"? What about "floormate"? No, it sounds too much like "floor mat."

"I like the yellow," I say, surprising myself. "The room looks sort of sun-kissed." Amazingly, my brother was right about this place. It *is* solid. It's fabulous. The ceilings are high, the floors polished wood. The kitchen, which is self-contained and to the left of the living room/dining room area, is white-walled and filled with silver appliances. "I'm impressed."

"See? You should always listen to me," Adam says, heading back out the door. "I'm getting more boxes."

I follow Allie down the corridor. "That's Em's room," she says, pointing to the room on the right. She's already Em? When did Emma become Em? "And here's yours," she says, pointing to a bedroom that's only slightly larger than Em's. It's not as large as my room at my parents, but it's big enough. I think everything will fit.

This is it. My new home.

I exhale the breath I hadn't realized I was holding.

After we finish unloading the boxes, we escort Adam back to the truck. "You sure you didn't forget anything?" he asks as he climbs into the driver's seat. "Should we consult your seven hundred lists?"

Allie giggles.

Wonderful. My new roommate, who hasn't even known me an hour, is already aware of my neuroses.

"She's slightly sensitive," Adam tells Allie. "Especially about the lists. Eh, Jo?"

"I like my lists. Get over it. And stop calling me Jo."

Allie giggles again. Quite the giggler, this girl. Although I'm not quite sure what it is that's so giggle-worthy. And I wish Adam would wipe that patronizing smile off his face.

"Okay, Jo," he says. "If you say so."

"Why do you call her Jo if she hates it?" Allie asks him.

"Excellent question," I add.

"My sister was supposed to be a boy."

I can tell by her wrinkled nose that Allie needs further explanation. "He wanted to name me after Joe Namath," I offer, sighing.

"Who's Joe Namath?"

"He was a quarterback for the New York Jets," Adam says.

"My parents attempted to appease him by naming me Jodine. He decided to ignore the Y-chromosome factor in my DNA and refer to me as Jo."

Allie giggles again. "That's cute."

"No, not really. He told his friends he had a brother. They used to make fun of me for looking like a girl. I'd appreciate it if you stick with Jodine."

Allie's eyes widen as if her shower just ran out of hot water. "I'm sorry."

Am I a bitch? "I'm sorry if I sometimes come across too abruptly, but on this particular issue regarding my identity, I'm a little sensitive."

Adam smirks and starts the engine. "Enjoy her, Al," he says. "Jo, remember, if you make her cry she's going to ask you to go back to our parents." He drives off.

"Sorry," I say, forcing a big smile to reassure her that, no, I am not Psycho Bitch. "I just hate when he teases me."

"Hey, I have an older brother too, remember?" Her eyes return to their previously un-Frisbee-like proportions and squint in a smile. Her lips smile correspondingly. "He used to call me Hyena. For no reason at all." She puts her arm through mine. "Hungry?"

After finishing a cheese-and-salsa omelette—apparently Allie likes to cook—I'm anxious to start organizing. I'm glad I managed to convince my parents not to come along. My mother begged to help me unpack, but I am truly looking forward to attacking it on my own.

"It's going to take me hours to unpack everything," I announce, hoping Allie will insist on doing the dishes and send me on my way. Technically it's my responsibility to do them, since she cooked and it was all her food, but I assume these are special circumstances. And the kitchen is a mess, which I did not partake in the making. She can cook, fine, but the ingredients seem to have exploded all over the countertop. For instance, how, specifically, did salsa get on top of the refrigerator?

"Don't worry, it won't take us that long. We'll do one box at a time. We should start with your bed stuff. Then, if we don't finish everything today you'll be all ready for tonight. Of course, if you want to paint the walls or something, you can always sleep with me in my room. Whatever you want."

What was all this "we" talk? What "we"? This stranger is not going to rummage through my stuff. "Oh, don't worry about it. I can take care of it. I'm sure you have better things to do than be stuck in my room all day unpacking crusty boxes."

"Umm…not really." She giggles again. I will have to throttle her if she doesn't lose that giggle. Or start calling her Hyena. "I guess I shouldn't say that, eh? You'll think I'm a big loser and you just met me."

"Why don't you do the dishes and I'll start unpacking?"

Her eyes widen the way they did when I chastised her for calling me Jo, only this time it's because I've brought about a concept utterly alien to her, the concept of cleaning the kitchen. "Don't worry about the dishes," she says. "I'll do them later. First, I want to set you up. That's what roomies are for, right?"

My definition of *roommate* is someone who shares a kitchen and a bathroom—although from the present chaotic state of this kitchen I probably should have negotiated my own bathroom.

In order to avoid crushing her obviously frail feelings, I allow her to help me unpack my bed ("What nice green-colored sheets! They match your eyes! I love them! They're gorge!"), my shampoo and conditioner ("You use Thermasilk? Does it work? Can I smell it? Wow! It smells awes!"), and my clothes ("Too bad you're so much taller than me! These pants are fab!"), until I can no longer handle any more abbreviated acclamations and need to take a pizza break. Anyway, all that remains is building a dresser, putting away clothes and hanging a few posters.

I realize that I am a complete freeloader—I have nothing to contribute to the rest of the apartment. Wait! Not true. I have a salad spinner. My parents had two for some inexplicable reason, so I took one.

I'm hoping to finish organizing when Allie is asleep. I'm going to try and fake her out. You know, pretend I'm going to sleep but then continue working? She's sweet, really, just as Adam said. It's just that she has so many questions and comments and I'm tired because I was up all night packing and I don't feel like revealing my life story at this particular moment.

At ten she invites me to watch TV in her room, but I decline. "I think I'll just read a magazine in bed."

"Okay. We don't have to watch TV. Let's read. I'll get my book and we'll read together."

Haven't we spent enough time together? Is she ever going to leave me alone? Will we have to get bunk beds? "You know what? I'm exhausted. I don't think I can even keep my eyes open. I'm going to go to sleep." I can leave my light on for a bit to read without getting caught, can't I?

"Okay. Tell me when you're ready for bed and I'll tuck you in."

She has got to be kidding.

"Nightie-night," she says ten minutes later as I climb under the covers. She pulls the sheets up to my chin and turns off the lights. "What do you want for breakfast?" she asks, popping her head back in the doorway.

Breakfast? She's already thinking about breakfast? "Whatever."

I hear her muffled voice speaking on the phone, and although I want to tell her to keep it down, I decide to turn on my recently unpacked stereo and try to drown her out.

A knock on my door awakens me. The sun pours into the room because of my lack of curtains, the glare blinding me from seeing the numbers on my alarm clock.

"Jodine? Are you awake?"

"Mmm."

"Can I come in?"

"Mmm."

Allie opens the door with her right hand while balancing a tray with her left. "You're up?"

A little late for that question, isn't she? "I am now."

She strides into my room. "I made you breakfast in bed!"

I am somewhat surprised, as no one has ever made me breakfast in bed. Even lovesick Manny never made me breakfast in bed.

Using my elbows, I prop myself up into a half-stomach-crunch position. Allie gently places the silver tray onto my lap and then sits cross-legged on my bed.

This disturbs me for four reasons:

1.   She will now proceed to watch me eat. It is always odd when a person is eating and another one isn't.

2.   No one is allowed to eat in my room, for fear of lingering odors, unsightly crumbs and potential spillage. Perhaps this rule would be expunged during emergency circumstances such as...I can't think of one at this moment, but I will concede that possible situations could arise.

3.   More significant, no one is ever allowed to eat in/on my bed. Ever. No emergency could ever require food to be eaten in/on my bed, including but not exclusive to whipped cream and/or edible food paint. I'll admit that I've indulged in these sumptuous delicacies from time to time, but we were on Manny's bed, thereby leaving no sticky lactose residue on *my* sheets.

4.   Allie is sitting on my bed without socks. And she did *not* wipe her feet prior to sitting on my bed. She walked, walked, walked along the floor, accumulating the germs and dust bunnies and whatever other bacteria ferment amid the crevices, and has now contributed these germs to my chosen area of rest. Instead, she should have worn slippers, removing them prior to sitting on the bed, or at the very least, used some sort of excess material to

wipe clean her polluted body parts. (I really, really want to ask her to wipe, but I don't want to embarrass her for her barnyard behavior.)

She uses her left big toe to scratch her right ankle. Scratch, scratch. I can taste the food I haven't even eaten yet regurgitate in my throat. She is spreading germs all over my bed. I can't take it any longer, and so I say, "Thank you so much for the breakfast. One favor?"

She nods continuously as though the top of her head is attached to an elastic band built into the ceiling. "Sure, spill it."

Which is precisely what I wish to avoid (the regurgitation of breakfast). "I have this anal obsession about clean feet in or on my bed. Can you wipe them? Just use the newspaper that's on my chair."

The look she gives me makes me think I just told her that Santa was really her dad in a rented costume. There is about a thirty-five-percent chance that she will start to cry.

But no! She leans off the bed, picks up the newspaper that only hours ago was in charge of protecting a family picture in the U-Haul. "Oh, sure. No prob. Sorry," she says, wiping her feet.

Where's the catch? Why is this girl so damn nice? I look at her feet. They're now stained with black newspaper ink. This, I admit, is my fault. What could I have been thinking, suggesting a newspaper? (This is how I sometimes get when faced with a dilemma concerning other people's hygiene habits. Flustered. Irrational.) I can't ask her to clean them again, can I? I'll just have to rewash the linen when she isn't around, so she doesn't get offended.

When is she *not* around?

The blue clay bowl on my lap is filled with Rice Krispies and strawberries. Cut-up strawberries. Who has the time or the patience to cut fruit into tiny cubes for the sheer purpose of improving my breakfast experience?

"I didn't want to wake you, but Emma will be here soon."

"What time is she coming?"

"Noon."

"What time is it now?"

Allie looks at her watch. "Eleven-thirty."

Already? "I want to take a shower before she gets here."

"Finish your breakfast first." Yes, Mom. "I can't wait for you to meet her. Did I tell you she looks like a model?"

Wonderful—a model. Isn't that number one on the roommate checklist right before nonsmoker and no pets? When I finish eating, I lay my breakfast dishes on top of yesterday's omelette dishes in the kitchen sink. Apparently not having a dishwasher will be more of a liability than I originally anticipated.

Emma is going to think she's living with two pigs. "Can you wash up while I shower?" I ask.

"Oh! Good idea. No prob."

After an in-and-out shower, I find Allie on the phone and the dishes still in the sink. Terrific.

I get dressed and search for my favorite scrunchie to tie my hair back. Where is it? I always leave it beside my bed. Apparently, in my confusion of living in a new environment I've misplaced it.

I head to the kitchen and begin washing the dishes. A yellow sponge is leaning against the side of the sink. At least it used to be yellow; it is presently part yellow and part decayed brown.

"No, don't do them! I was just getting off the phone. Mom, I'll call you later." She hangs up and rushes over to the sink. "You wash, I'll dry?"

"Sounds fair." Although since she originally offered to do it all, it's not completely fair. "Do we have any extra sponges? This one is pretty grungy."

"Let's see." She pulls out a crisp new one from the cupboard under the sink. "Here you go."

Interesting. Why would one continue using a disgusting sponge when there was a new, clean one under the sink? And what other germs are living on this counter? The thought that we're sharing a bathroom returns, this time frightening me. We're going to require some serious disinfectant.

The buzzer sounds.

"She's here! She's here! I can't wait for you to meet her. You're going to love her!"

Allie leaps to the front door, unlocks it and disappears into the hallway. "Hi!" I hear her say. I walk toward them just as they kiss each other on two cheeks. Double-kiss? Are we movie stars?

Emma pushes her bronzed sunglasses on top of her gold head as she walks into the apartment. Is she Rapunzel? What's with the gold? She couldn't pick a more natural, *normal* color?

"Emma, this is Jodine. Jodine, Emma." She pronounces Emma's name with a flourish. I almost expect her to give a little hand twirl and bow.

"Hello," I say. Emma is at least five-seven. Maybe not quite five-seven. Her brown boots add at least two inches to her.

"Nice to meet you." She saunters into the living room and ogles my head. "You have gorgeous hair. Is that color natural? It's so black!"

"It's natural," I answer, pleased with her flattery regarding my hair yet at the same time exasperated with how willing I am to prostitute my opinions of someone in exchange for a hair compliment.

She reaches out her hand and touches a strand. "And it's so shiny."

"Thanks, I, uh, like yours, too." Okay, so I'm a prostitute.

"Thanks."

Allie claps her hands. "I love it down, too! You should wear it down all the time, Jodine. It's so gorge!"

"I might have to, Allie," I say, and point to the black scrunchie that is perched on the bottom of a braid extending from Allie's head. "If you keep stealing my elastics."

Allie blushes. "Whoops. Is this yours?"

"Yes."

"Do you want it back?"

Yes. "You can use it today."

"Thanks, Jodine!" Allie's smile widens. "I'm so happy!" she squeals. "I have two roomies again. This is totally fab!"

Emma's eyebrows rise, I'm assuming, in amazement of what a cheese ball her new roommate is.

My neck is getting itchy. I want my scrunchie back.

"So what should we do now? When are your movers coming?" Allie asks with a jump. She's back on her imaginary trampoline.

"In about an hour."

"Should we play get-to-know-you games?" Allie asks.

What does she want to play? Pictionary? Hide-and-seek? I'm sure my eyebrows are raised as high as Emma's. (Or at least one of them. That's my one party trick—I can raise each eyebrow separately.)

I visualize the upcoming year as clearly as if I am remembering it: Emma and I hanging out in her room, rolling our eyes at each other every time Allie says something ridiculously cheesy or abbreviates a word. Two's company and three's a crowd, correct? When three people live together, inevitably two will bond and one will end up the odd woman out. It makes sense.

Emma opens her purse, pulls out a hard-shelled sunglasses case, replaces her sunglasses, then slams the case shut. "I have to shit." She throws her purse onto a table and heads toward the bathroom.

Thanks for sharing.

She opens the bathroom door and disappears inside. The door remains open.

She is using the bathroom while leaving the door open.

She has left the door *open*. Open, the opposite of closed. (Actually, wouldn't the opposite of *closed* be *opened* with an "ed" tacked on? I mean, you wouldn't describe a door as being *close* unless it was in near proximity, or unless you were emotionally attached to it, would you?)

A pack of du Maurier Light cigarettes have slipped out of her purse and onto the kitchen table.

She smokes, and she leaves the door open when she defecates. I feel mildly vomitous, as in full of vomit.

Okay, I volunteer to be the odd woman out. I wish Allie and Emma a blissfully happy life together. I am living with a munchkin and a truck driver.

6
EMMA GETS ATTENTION

EMMA

My first thought when I wake up is that I'm on the wrong side of the bed. I normally sleep on the right side and now I'm on the left. Even though I'm in the same queen-size bed I slept in at my dad's, it feels different because I've had to readjust my sleeping position so that I can sleep facing the window.

How long does it take for a new apartment to stop feeling like I have a new guy's tongue in my mouth? How long does it take for the angle the sunlight spills through the blinds, the post-wakeup walk to the bathroom, and my butt imprint in the couch to feel as natural as pulling on my favorite pair of jeans?

My second thought is that my apartment smells like a funeral home. Fortunately not the decaying, rotting, flesh odor (although I've never actually been a witness to that particular experience), but sweet-smelling because of the abundance of useless flowers.

Face it, if the guy is dead, flowers won't help.

Speaking about corpses, I start to think about Nick, my controlling, obsessive deadbeat of an ex-boyfriend. "Allie! Allie!" I shout.

"Yeah?" she yells back.

"C'mere for a sec!"

Two seconds later, Allie knocks on my door.

"One second," I answer for no real apparent reason. She could have just come in, but the fact that she knocked makes me wonder how long she'll wait for me to give her permission to open the door. Two minutes? Five minutes? Will she kill time, twiddling her thumbs or picking her nose, more likely biting her nails, for ten minutes?

Okay. Enough. "Enter," I say.

She opens the door and sticks her head in. "Morning. Do you want some juice?"

"No, thanks. Did Nick have flowers delivered again?"

"Yup. You're not going to believe this. Twenty-one roses."

"What color?"

"Red."

Week one post breakup, he sent seven red roses. Week two post breakup, he left fourteen. Week three, today, his present is about as surprising as my feet hurting after a night of dancing in three-inch-heel boots. So the asshole knows how to multiply, whoopee-do. And red…again? Couldn't he be a little creative with the colors? Why not, say six red, six white, six pink, and what's left? Three? Three purple? Are there purple roses? What about purple hearts? No, wait. I'm the one who's wounded. Forget purple. Seven red, seven pink, seven white. It's not the eighties anymore; he can mix red and pink. He won't get arrested for clashing.

I roll myself in my cream satin sheets like tobacco and weed in a crisp sheet of rolling paper. "I didn't hear the bell."

"Me, neither, I was asleep. I found them outside the door. Our door, not the outside door. I guess the delivery boy rang Janet and she brought them inside."

"Is there a card?"

"As always. Here." She skips toward my bed, hands me the card, and then sits down carefully.

"Love you…miss you…" I read aloud. Blah blah blah. Cry me a river. He should have thought of that three weeks ago. Before I spent twenty minutes doing tongue Pilates with some hot, anonymous bar stud who showered me with compliments and cosmopolitans.

You can't do that when you have a boyfriend, can you?

Maybe you can. It's just not nice.

"Where's the birthday girl?" I ask.

"She went to the gym this morning, came home, and now she's at the library."

"That's the way I spend my birthday, too," I say. "What time is it?"

Allie giggles. "One-ish."

That giggling is going to put me over the edge. It sounds like urine chiming against toilet water at high speed. Be fair, I reprimand myself. Allie's not so bad. I mean, how bad can she possibly be? She admires me, for fuck's sake. She thinks I'm the shit. Just look at her, carefully perched on my bedspread as if she's afraid her ass will wear the bedspread out. She's treating it like it's a shrine, which is totally strange considering what kind of slob she is. I wish I had a couch in here. But there's barely room for me to walk in here. My room is all bed.

"You have the coolest job ever," she says, flipping through next month's copy of *Stiletto,* which put me to sleep last night. I reach across my nightstand for a cigarette. For a moment I consider asking her to open the window, but then I do it myself. Then I wonder if she would have done it, just because I tell her to do it.

I take a deep drag. I wonder what would happen if I told her to get off my bed. Would she ask why? Would she start crying and think I was mad at her?

Can I tell her to get off the couch in the living room if I want to? It's mine.

I certainly did my duty in adding ambience to the apartment—a purple shaggy throw rug under a glass coffee table, purple-and-gray throw pillows to match my purple suede couch and leather purple recliner. All courtesy of AJ's basement. And of course, the dried flowers, gifts from Nick, which I later attached to a metal hanger and hung upside down to dry them out. And dishes. And framed photographs that I "borrowed" from *Stiletto*.

Is there anything in this place that isn't mine?

The table, I suppose. Although that's just a tablecloth covering milk crates. And Allie rolled her computer chair beside it to pass for a kitchen chair. Since I brought everything else, you'd think Jodine could just go and buy a table and chairs.

I exhale toward the window. "My job's not that exciting. It's *Stiletto*, not *Cosmo*. Sure, I get to see celebrities when they come to the office, but they're *Canadian* celebrities. How's that for an oxymoron?"

"Yeah, but you're a fashion editor," she says, emphasizing the word *fashion* as though it was some sort of golden calf.

"A fashion editor's assistant."

She's now lying flat out on my bed, all reverence forgotten. Maybe she's trying to duck beneath the smoke. "You can't start as the editor in chief," she says to console me.

Apparently not. "I don't expect to be promoted after only two months, but how long do I have to search through model cards, trying to find the perfect five-foot-eight, one-hundred-ten-pound brunette with that 'little extra something'? And why does Amanda, my Aren't-I-Crafty-I-Make-My-Own-Jewelry boss, get all the party invites? Last week, she wet her pants because page six of *The Talker* mentioned her as one of the guests at a restaurant opening in Yorkville," I say, getting all worked up. Not that the bar scene in this city is worth the effort it takes me to put on a thong. It's only *Toronto*. But Aren't-I-Crafty acts like every party invite she gets is an invite to the damn Oscars. She acts like my high-school friends who spent years pillaging fashion magazines for the perfect prom dress and then felt devastated when the guys they had their eyes on asked someone else. I used to say it's only high school, dammit, get a hold of yourself.

I need another cigarette.

My cigarette intake has multiplied exponentially since I've moved out on my own. Awful, really, but now that I can smoke without being banished outside, I can't find any reason not to smoke constantly. Besides the whole lung cancer-emphysema thing, of course. And as a plus it drives Jodine crazy.

When I first moved in and pulled out a cigarette, I thought she was going to detonate. But I told Allie from the get-go that I was a smoker, so it's Jodine's tough luck. She tried to be all rational about it, saying I could light up as long as I blew the smoke out the window so as not to pollute the entire apartment.

And she punctuated her suggestion with a cough.

Still, it seems like a fair agreement. But I've decided that the smoking-near-the-window policy will only be followed when Jodine is home. Except for in my room——I can't have it smelling bad, can I?

"Can I have one?" comes a whisper from the horizontal side of the bed.

"One what?"

"Cigarette." Giggle, giggle.

I nearly fall out of bed from shock. The last time I felt this way was when Nick asked me if we could not smoke up one night because he wanted to be able to concentrate on a presentation he had the next day. I hand Allie a cigarette and try not to gawk. "Since when do you smoke?"

She looks like a child smeared in her mother's red lipstick. She doesn't inhale, just puffs in and out like she's sucking on the smoke. "I don't (cough, cough). Just sometimes." She smiles and sucks again.

Halfway through our cigarettes, I hear Jodine's key jingling in the door lock. Allie turns white and stubs out her cigarette in an empty water glass.

We're both laughing when Jodine knocks on my door. She doesn't wait for a "come in." She just enters.

"You're still in bed?" she asks. "Do you know what time it is?"

"One-ish," I say, stretching lazily.

The best part about not being in school anymore is lazy weekends. Spread-eagle days stuffed with omelettes and bacon and home fries and pillows and TV and shopping and restaurants and dancing and *Cosmo*s. I'm capable of sleeping past three on weekends, if left uninterrupted. Which makes me hate my job even more Monday mornings, because I end up falling asleep at 3:00 a.m. on Sunday nights.

Usually, anyway.

Fuck.

I'm supposed to work on a presentation today about shoes for a Monday morning meeting. Is that fair? Why does my boss feel that she's entitled to my weekend time?

Forget it. I'll do it tomorrow. I have too much to do today.

"How about bringing me some juice?" I ask Jodine.

"What, are you crippled?"

"I'll get it," Allie says, and smiles at me. "I need some myself."

Allie has a mild problem with orange juice. If there were an OJA (Orange Juice Anonymous) chapter in Toronto, she'd be its most frequent patron. She drinks it all the time. At lunch. At dinner. With a snack. I'm trying to figure out why she's offered to bring me a glass. Does she really need some juice for herself, to wash away the smoke-stink in her throat? Or is she really the suck I think she is? Or is it possible she's just plain nice?

She scurries into the kitchen and I throw the covers off my body.

"Where are you?" Allie asks, five minutes later.

How can it take five minutes to get a glass of orange juice? I mean, what can possibly happen on the way from my room to the kitchen? "In here!" I call from the toilet.

She walks through my room, into the bathroom, holding a small glass of orange juice. She blushes when she sees me and wraps a strand of her way-too-long hair around her thumb and puts the split ends in her mouth. That girl is always eating various parts of her body. I wouldn't want to be left on a deserted island with her. We run low on food and I'm a goner.

She seems to be debating her next move. Should she leave? Ignore my position on the throne and continue talking to me?

Allie is working out quite well as a roommate, in spite of her obvious flaws. I even let her use my bathroom when Jodine is showering in theirs. And she's a riot. A few days ago, when she was brushing her teeth, I couldn't figure out why she said, "I still have my retainer, too!" Then I realized she must have thought my diaphragm was some sort of orthodontic contraption. It's a good thing she didn't find my vibrator—I wouldn't want the poor girl to start singing into it or anything like that. Or what if she thought it was a hand blender?

"I think Jodine works out way too much," she says to me while her eyes search frantically for something to rest on. They settle on the fuchsia floor mat.

"Every day does seem a bit excessive," I answer, and fart simultaneously. Oops.

Allie giggles and turns bright red. She retreats into my bedroom, making herself at home again on the bed, this time lying vertically. "I think she's anorexic!" she raises her voice to be heard.

"You think? Keep an eye on her at lunch. If she doesn't eat the cake, I'd say there's a pretty good chance you're right."

Allie and I are taking Jodine out for a late lunch, to celebrate her birthday. Her parents booked her for last night, and some guy, Manny, has booked her for tonight.

I'm sure that whatever Jodine doesn't eat, Allie will polish off in no time.

An hour later, the three of us are seated around a table at a downtown Mexican café. "Nothing wrong with a birthday fuck," I comment.

"No," Jodine answers quickly, and condescendingly. "He's an ex. I don't make it a habit of revisiting past errors."

Well la-di-da. "I don't make it a habit of even talking to exes." So there. "And that's because when you go out with an ex on your birthday, you end up fucking your ex."

Allie giggles.

"I don't fuck my exes," Jodine says, emphasizing the word *fuck,* and Allie giggles again.

Allie giggles anytime someone says "fuck."

Allie giggles anytime someone speaks.

"Bet you ten bucks you do," I say.

Giggle, giggle.

"You're on."

I'm on a mission here to remove the pole that is shoved all the way up Jodine's ass. Maybe getting laid will help her.

"How will we know if you're having sex?" Allie asks.

Jodine looks at her sideways. "Isn't my word good enough? Do you want to see the videotape?"

"Oh, you do that, too?" I ask.

Jodine ignores me. "Why do you have to know, exactly?" she asks Allie.

"I meant, so I don't knock and try to come in. We need a warning system."

"First of all, I always make the guy take his shoes off at the front door. Who knows where his feet have been? Consequently, if you see a pair of men's shoes on the front floor mat, don't come in. But you realize all this planning is purely academic. I repeat, I do not have sex with my exes."

"But how will I know if the shoes belong to a guy of yours or Em's?"

"I doubt it would be a problem for tonight. You two are going out after lunch, right? And then later to a movie or something? So you'll know if one of you decides to slip away and bring home a guy of your own. Second, this may shock you, but my long-term plan is to develop a monogamous relationship so that in the future, you'll both be able to identify a pair of shoes with a corresponding man."

"That's not my long-term plan," I comment. "I like the first scenario better. The part about sneaking off with a guy of my own."

"Boys do have more than one pair of shoes," Allie says, obviously still concerned about the logistics behind the plan. "This could get complicated."

"I'll tie a red ribbon around my doorknob or something," Jodine offers.

I think about this for a minute. "Who has red ribbons? Use a scrunchie. We all have scrunchies, right?"

I know Jodine has one. She wears it in her hair every day. I've only seen her hair down once.

So we agree. Scrunchies on doorknobs equals don't knock.

A waitress appears at our table. "Can I get a strawberry daiquiri?" I ask.

"Virgin?" Allie asks.

"No, you?" I say, and laugh.

Allie turns bright red and mumbles something to herself. Uh-oh. She's had sex, right? She can't be a virgin. Can she?

"I'd like a Diet Coke," Jodine says.

Allie stops mumbling to herself. "Do you have any juice?"

"Orange okay?"

"Fab. I'll have a large, please."

When the waitress delivers our fajitas and drinks simultaneously, I laugh at Allie's huge glass of orange pulp. "What is it with you and juice? Don't you ever have soft drinks?"

"No. Pop burns my mouth," she explains, spreading at least a gallon of sour cream over the tortilla. Next, she carefully places the pieces of chicken on the cream, lays out another layer of sour cream, then the salsa, then the cheese, then another large glob of cream. Her meal looks like strawberry pudding. Jodine makes her fajita with a thin film of salsa, a few strategically placed pieces of chicken and a pound of lettuce. I try to keep the ingredients in proportion.

"What does that mean, soft drinks burn your mouth?" Jodine asks. "They're supposed to be cold. You *do* know that, right?"

Allie giggles. "Yes, I know."

I would have been offended by Jodine's comment, but Allie doesn't seem to care when Jodine talks to her like she's missing a few keys on her keyboard.

"I don't like the bubbles," Allie says. "They burn."

Jodine rolls her eyes. "You're not supposed to gargle the pop," she says. "You sip and swallow."

"Sounds masochistic." Giggle, giggle.

"You get used to it. You stop noticing the bubbles."

"What about the first time you tried it?"

"The first time I tried pop? I can't recall the first time I tried pop, Allie." She takes a small bite out of her fajita. She eats everything in small bites. Eating takes her hours. "It's like riding a bike," she says. "Once you do it, it becomes habit."

"I don't know how to ride a bike."

Both Jodine's and my jaws drop in shock. "Unbelievable," Jodine says.

"I don't, really," Allie repeats.

Jodine takes another sip of her Diet Coke. "Didn't your father run behind you, pretending to hold the back of your seat, telling you he would never let go and then let go?"

My father never did that. He bought me a two-thousand-dollar bike and told me to figure it out. Bastard.

"My father tried to teach me, but I was afraid to take off the training wheels."

Jodine looks at Allie with disbelief. "That's absurd. I'll teach you how to ride."

"Uh-huh."

"What uh-huh?"

"Everyone says they're going to teach me when I tell them I don't know how, but no one ever does."

"Do you ever ask them about it again?"

"No."

"Then don't expect them to teach you. Your bike-riding skills aren't everyone's top priority. If you want me to teach you, then ask me. Biking is great exercise."

Not exactly a selling point for Allie. While she seems to have an abundance of energy, she prefers to spend her free time lying in bed reading or watching TV. "Have you ever actually *tried* Coke?" I ask.

"I don't think so."

Impossible! "You've never tried Coke? What do you drink with your Jack Daniel's? What do you have at barbecues?"

Allie stares at me blankly. "Uh, orange juice?"

"If there is no orange juice?"

She appears deep in thought. "Sometimes I pick an orange soda and wait for it to get flat. Then it tastes like that orange drink at McDonald's. They call it a drink but it has no bubbles, did you know? I used to order the small orange juice cartons, but they cost a fortune and they're not always included in the trio meals. Getting orange juice at movie theaters used to be a problem, too, but ever since the whole Snapple craze, they almost always sell juice, any flavor."

Apparently an entire carbonated-free world exists that I am unaware of. Jodine meets my gaze across the table and we both start laughing. "Try it," she says, pushing her glass toward Allie.

"Why? I know I won't like it."

"Just try it. I want to see."

"See what?"

I reach over and take a sip from Jodine's glass. "All the cool kids are doing it," I say.

"Fine, I'll try if it'll amuse you. But, Jodine, you have to try a cigarette."

I almost choke on the so-called offensive bubbles.

"Terrific," Jodine says, squinting her eyes. "But why?"

"Just try one. I want to see."

"But *you* don't even smoke."

"I'll have one, too. We'll all have a drink, and we'll all have a smoke."

"I feel left out," I say. "What do I have to do?"

"You have to close the door the next time you're in the main bathroom," Jodine says, passing Allie her glass.

Allie puckers her lips and sips the Coke as if drinking a glass of straight tequila. And then the three of us crowd by the restaurant bar as I hand out cigarettes.

"You look like a freak, smoking," Jodine says to Allie. "Are you on the StairMaster? Why are you breathing like that?"

Allie blows out the smoke she was holding in her mouth—the smoke she should have been inhaling but was keeping prisoner inside her cheeks—into Jodine's face. "Can you teach us to French inhale?" she asks me.

"That's why they call me Frenchy, you know."

"Sure it is."

"Who calls you Frenchy?" Jodine asks.

"No one."

"It's from *Grease*," Allie explains.

"I've never seen it."

Allie's jaw drops. "No way! Didn't you watch any fun movies growing up?"

"Yes," I say defensively. "I saw *The Wizard of Oz*. And *Annie*. And *Amadeus*.

"I can make smoke circles. Wanna see?" I blow three consecutive Cheerios-shaped ovals into the air.

"Again!" Allie demands, and I do it again. They try, and a few minutes later we're all laughing, watching smoke circles stretch and evaporate into the air.

After lunch, I drive Jodine home so that she can prepare for her nondate and convince Allie to go shopping with me. What better way to spend a Saturday? Shopping and then a movie. Allie claims she doesn't need anything but agrees to come along to keep me company. I drive us to Yorkdale Mall. At Mendocino, I charge three hundred dollars on a pair of pants and sweater. She tries on the same pants, but looks like a stuffed handmade pillow with the cotton balls spilling out.

"What do you think?" she asks, trying to see every angle of herself in the three-sided mirror.

She's not a fat girl; she just shouldn't be walking around in tight pants. Maybe I shouldn't tell her that. Maybe I should tell her she has great legs and that she'd look better in a skirt. But then, won't she know I'm lying? "What do you need to buy those for?" I say. "You can borrow mine." Very good! A most sensitive and appropriate politically correct answer.

She could also use a haircut. She's too short for hair that comes down past her tits. And a few highlights wouldn't hurt. Make that many highlights.

After shopping, I climb back into bed for an afternoon siesta, and Allie climbs into her bed to read. When I wake up, the sun has already fallen below the house in front of ours, and the sky is tinted purple. The phone rings, and a minute later Allie bounces into my room, looking like she accidentally dropped my vibrator down her pants.

"Clint wants to go for a drink! Clint wants to go for a drink!" she says, clapping her hands in excitement.

"Clint? What kind of a name is Clint? Is he a cowboy?"

"Clint is a beautiful name. It's the most beautiful name in the whole world."

Snort. "You are such a cheese ball," I say, laughing. "Does that mean you're ditching me and the movie?" I try to feign indignation, but a bunch of my old school friends already invited me to

meet them for a drink up at Yonge and Eglinton. But seriously—
there's someone a step higher than me on Allie's pedestal? Can I
take this Clint character?

"Oh. Uh-oh." She looks like she's about to cry. "Should I cancel?
Do you want me to cancel? I'll cancel if you want me to." There
is no way she's not praying to herself that I won't make her cancel.
I can practically see her mouth moving.

"Don't cancel," I say, dismissing her with my hand.

She sighs with relief.

After she showers, I help her get ready. "No, Allie, you can't
wear the same top of mine that you wore last time…I know I said
it looked very hot but he's already seen you in it…. Yes, you can
borrow something else."

At one in the morning, when I get home from Yonge and
Eglinton, Allie is sitting on the couch, looking miserable, watching
the end of *Saturday Night Live.* She nudges her chin toward Jodine's
room. I can hear the faint sound of Marvin Gaye coming from
behind the walls.

A black scrunchie is on the doorknob.

7

JODINE HOLDS THE BUTTER

JODINE

I am so angry, my hands are shaking. If I were a cartoon character, gray clouds of smoke would be steaming from my ears, and my face would be the color of Emma's nails, cherry red. It's 3:11 a.m. and someone is making popcorn. Popcorn! At 3:11 in the morning! Why would anyone make popcorn at 3:11 in the morning? It makes no sense.

Every night it's something. Usually it's the giggling. Too often, when I'm trying to fall asleep, Allie is giggling on the phone. I can't decipher what she's actually saying or to whom she is speaking. All I hear is that infernal giggling like a bad echo reverberating through the walls. I would buy earplugs, except that they present two immediate problems. First, how would I hear my alarm clock? And second, whenever earplugs are remotely near my body, I tense with stress. I wore them when I took the LSATs, and now whenever I think of them, my back tenses in an "I am about to sit still for the next three hours that will define my entire future" Pavlovian manner. Since falling asleep requires the absence of stress, I doubt that a stress-inducing object will succeed in blocking out nocturnal distractions.

The first time I heard the giggles I didn't think anything of them, hoping the incident was a one-time thing. The second time, I couldn't stand it. I attempted to ignore them; honestly, I did. I tried to fall asleep, despite the feeling that a pack of flies was buzzing around in my ears, but I ended up tossing and turning, turning and tossing, and eventually I slipped into my black-and-white-and-red Minnie Mouse slippers from Disney World, padded over to Allie's room and knocked three times on the door.

"Come in!" she sang out, obviously unaware of the purpose of my visit. Did she think I was stopping by for a late-night girlie chat? Me? "Hold on, it's one of my roomies," she said into the phone. "Hi, Jay!"

These days, she has been calling me Jay. First she tried Jo, not believing me when I told her that I despised it. Then for some inexplicable reason she tried Jon. Jon? First of all, I despise all male names for females. You know, like Sidney or Michael. But no female has ever even tried using Jon before. I even dislike those ambiguous names that can go either way, like Robin. Although I must point out that I am in favor of names like Carol or Lynn; no matter how many males carry these identifiers, and no matter how they are spelled—Carol/Caroll, Lyn/Lynn—an extra consonant, in my book, does not legitimize the transsexual operation. To me, these names are strictly feminine.

Next she tried Juice, which I thought was utterly ironic, since she's the juice freak in this place. I silenced her with what I thought was a lighthearted "Surely you can come up with something better than that!" glare. She tried Jue, but Emma pointed out that a passerby might take it as a racial slur. She finally settled on Jay, insisting that it was just an initial. I couldn't convince her that Jay is not merely a letter in the alphabet, but is also one of those male names that don't quite pass for female, which I despise. But I have given up. I have decided that being referred to by a letter is far preferable than having to listen to any more options. Hence, to Allie I am Jay.

"Allie, can you lower your voice? I can hear you on the phone and I have a nine o'clock class." I forced a smile, so that she'd think I was a normal, loving "roomie" who needs her sleep, not a tired, irritable bitch.

She corked her giggles, until the next night, when it began again like a bad sitcom rerun you didn't even like the first time it was aired. I was on the brink of sleep—where you're still conscious of the soft, cool pillow beneath your cheek while the peaceful numbness spreads deliciously through your body—and then, giggle. Giggle, giggle.

I felt violated, as I had in the seventh grade when I caught Ronnie Curtzer, the ingrate who sat at the desk behind me in class, peering over my shoulder during a geometry exam. It should not be my responsibility to get out of bed, put on my slippers and ruin my seamless state of sleep, just as it should not have been my responsibility to provide Ronnie Curtzer with the formula for how to calculate the length of a hypotenuse. I screamed, "Alleeeee!"

I heard a muffle and then, "Uh-huh?"

"I can hear you giggling! I'm trying to sleep!"

The following evening, "Alleeeee!" begot an immediate apology: "Sorry, Jay!"

This Pavlovian technique continued the next night: giggle, giggle. "Alleeeee!"

And now it's popcorn. Poppoppop. Popcorn at 3:12 a.m. This is not normal behavior. Wait. I could be wrong. Allie isn't normally up at this hour, even if she does happen to pride herself on her popcorn-making skills. If not Allie, then who is responsible for this charade? Surely not Emma, she who gets Allie to run all her errands, like emptying her trash can, or running to the dry cleaner. If Emma wanted popcorn, albeit it's 3:12 a.m., she would get Allie to do it.

It's my birthday, dammit. Not technically, obviously, since the day ended more than three hours ago. Still, I think there must be some unwritten law that your birthday lasts until you fall asleep. (After all, somewhere in the world, it's before midnight, right?)

Why am I being awakened at 3:12 a.m.—correction, it's now 3:13—on my birthday?

Is this popcorn some kind of karmic punishment for sleeping with an ex? I wasn't planning on sleeping with him. Really. Doesn't intent constitute an integral part of the crime?

My tongue is covered with a thick gummy coat of grossness. I hope my breath didn't taste this way two hours earlier.

When I was having sex with Manny.

I try to remember why, exactly, I had sex with Manny. There are four reasons why this should not have transpired.

1.   I don't like Manny.

2.   I am aware that he has feelings for me, many of them, and it is wrong to have sex with someone for whom you are unable to reciprocate emotion. I am not the type of person to use someone merely for carnal pleasure.

3.   I now owe Emma ten dollars.

4.   As soon as we got to the Italian restaurant on College Street, he excused himself to go to the men's room as he is still a chronic pee-er.

However, the sex did happen, and I am now trying to analyze why. I can only come up with two reasons.

1.   We have four out of five classes together. We sit next to each other and study together.

2.   We finished off a bottle of red wine.

Now, I should mention that of this bottle of wine, I consumed only two glasses, whereas Manny ingested a minimum of three, but because I seldom drink, two glasses for me equals four glasses in an average alcohol consumer. I do not like to drink, because when I do, I become out of control and end up saying inappropriate things, or behaving in inappropriate ways. Case in point, having sex with Manny.

After an evening of candlelight and wine, after we climbed into the cab, I found myself moving my hand toward the already hardened center of his lap, whispering what I wanted to do to him while flicking my tongue against his earlobe.

Okay, so I'm a cheap date. When I told the cabdriver there would be only one stop, there was not much argument from the floppy-haired, erect man beside me whose hand had already found its way up my black silky blouse.

Clearly, my earlier statement to Emma about not being the type of person to sleep with exes needs to be revised.

Allie was home when we stumbled through the door. "It's so nice to meet you after all the wonderful things I've heard!" she exclaimed, making me laugh. I had no idea what "things" she was talking about. I yanked Manny into my room, tossed a black scrunchie on the outside doorknob, popped in my favorite Marvin Gaye CD, hummed "Let's Get it On," lit the apricot candles that were placed sporadically around my room for occasions like this, and let the wine-induced feeling lift me up like helium, up and on top of my sweet Manny.

The plus side of having sex with an ex is that, assuming the sex was pleasant the first time around, the highlights (doing it on the kitchen table, a little fun in the bathtub and the library's eighth-floor men's bathroom) run through your mind like an overplayed porno, escalating your excitement into a full-blown, on-the-brink-of-exploding-and-roasting-the-nearby-villages volcano.

And, of course, we already had a system for the dreaded condom: I reached into the bedside drawer while simultaneously keeping him otherwise occupied. I ripped open the wrapper and slipped him out of my mouth and into the condom in one quick motion. Before he realized and appreciated the switch, he was already inside me.

Since it's an ex, you're not wasting time thinking, Does he like this? Does he think I sweat too much? Why is he touching me there? Instead, you concentrate on *you,* how *you* feel, how good *you* feel, and you wonder why you stopped doing it with him in the first place—oh, what reason could you have had to ever stop doing this, to ever have told this sex-god to stop touching you, not to touch you ever—what, were you crazy? You want him to touch you there and there and *there,* and his musky salty sweat fills your hands, your lips, your tongue, even your lungs, and his hands are in all the right places at all the right times, your back, your breasts, your hair, and don't stop don't stop don't stop—

There's nothing quite like drunken sex. Drunken sex with your drunken ex—it's even poetic.

However, there are plenty of situations preferable to *post-*drunken ex-sex. For example, writing your name with a jagged, rusty nail on a blackboard. Or at a concert, having to use one of the portable bathrooms that don't lock properly and smell like dried urine. Yes, post-drunk ex-sex is far worse. Your mouth is parched. Your inflated, helium high has been replaced with a wrinkled and unevenly colored balloon that isn't even resting comfortably on the ground but instead is hovering two inches above floor level, belly-up, and everyone kicks it when they walk by.

"Where's the bathroom?" he asked, reaching for his baby-blue Gap boxers that appeared to be strangling my reading lamp.

"You can't go now," I blurted out, horrified. What if Emma and Allie were in the living room? It's one thing to have your roommates meet with your sex mate face-to-face prior to the deed, but afterward? God, no. Had they heard us? Probably not—the one benefit of a futon is that it doesn't squeak. For a brief moment, I felt gratitude toward my parents.

A look of confusion crossed his face. He shrugged his shoulders and disappeared under the covers. Uh-oh. Apparently he translated "You can't go now" to mean "Please, darling, stay the night." Terrific. There was no way, no chance, no hope in hell that I was going to spend the rest of the night trapped in some spoonlike position. I wanted him to gracefully leave my bed, my apartment, my mental radar. I had to wake up at nine and go to the library, and the fetus of my impending headache needed to disappear immediately before it would germinate into a full-blown assault on my studying capabilities.

I heard rustling in the hallway and assumed that Emma and Allie were going to sleep. Then quiet. I stepped out of bed and peeked my head out from behind the door.

Allie's door was closed. The glow of a rainbow of colors spilled out from beneath her shut door. Emma, apparently, hadn't even returned home yet. I retreated into my room and gently tapped Manny's shoulder. His open mouth revealed his tongue, slightly protruding over his bottom lip. He didn't budge. I pushed him harder. "Manny, you can go to the bathroom."

"Hmm?"

"Bathroom. Go." I was spared from making running-water noises to inspire him. Not that I thought I would have to. Toilet addicts need only to hear the word *bathroom* and they're off and running. He rolled over, sat up and walked into the bathroom. I reached for my phone and called a cab. Then I went to the kitchen, quietly put a pot of water on the stove. I needed a cup of tea. I needed to buy a kettle. What kind of people use a pot to make tea? It doesn't make sense.

When Manny emerged from the bathroom, I pressed my index finger against my lips, motioning for him to be quiet. "A cab will be here in five minutes," I whispered. "Do you want some tea?"

He looked like a four-year-old watching his parents leave for a two-week trip to Jamaica from the window of his grandmother's mothball-infested apartment. "No thanks," he said, kissing me on the forehead. "Happy birthday. I'll see you on Monday."

Humph. Why didn't he want tea? Why the big rush to leave?

Now this, two hours later. This *popping*. This absurd, ridiculous, horribly inconsiderate popping.

I throw off my covers, stuff my feet into my slippers and march toward the kitchen.

The hallway smells like birthday candles. Have I overreacted? Are Allie and Emma surprising me with another birthday cake?

Am I going to have to eat *another* piece of birthday cake? I've already had to eat *two* today. And one last night with my parents. Are they all conspiring to get me fat?

Why is a red glow cast over the apartment? The walls look like blond hair streaked with semipermanent red hair dye. My armpits feel wet. Why is it so hot in here?

The kitchen door is open, but I don't need to turn on the light.

Shit.

Flames are performing some sort of ritual salsa dance in front of the far wall. The stove and oven are on fire.

Terrific.

8
IRRITATING OMNISCIENT NARRATOR ADDS HER TWO CENTS (WHO *IS* SHE, ANYWAY?)

"Oh, my God, wake up!" Jodine screams. She slams open Emma's door, shrieking, "The kitchen is on fire! Get up! We have to get out!"

Her speech is peppered with far more exclamation marks than she'd ever be proud about using, but if this situation doesn't merit exclamation marks, then what is the point of them, really?

For about four-fifths of a second, Jodine thinks she is going to die. Rationally, she knows she is not in any mortal danger. After all, she can see the door, and it is not blocked by any flames whatsoever. But emotionally—emotionally is always the kicker, isn't it?—emotionally what flashes across the twenty-four-inch TV inside her head is the image of her pathetic obituary, devoid of children, husband or law degree, which instead reads "doesn't bite nails," "took care of stupidities for parents" and "has futon," a futon that, following this train of irrational, emotional thought, is about to be cremated into a pool of ashes.

Emma does not move. Jodine wonders if the carbon dioxide has already made her head fuzzy. If she's unconscious, Jodine will have to carry her out of the duplex, and this might jeopardize her own escape. She's tempted to make a run for it. Should she take off now before it's too late? Isn't it better for one of them to survive than for all three to be destroyed in the travesty? So the others' stories can be told, their memories kept alive?

Thankfully, Jodine comes to her senses. Of course she does. What kind of heroine deserts her crew to save her own skin?

But don't worry about her safety. She's not going to try to martyr herself by squashing the flames with her young body to save them all. She isn't that kind of heroine. And the safety of the world isn't at stake. Anyway, she has lived with these other girls for only a few weeks, dammit. She's not about to give up her life after only one fajita dinner and shared cigarettes.

Emma's having quite a dream and wants to tell Jodine to fuck off. She doesn't say this out loud, of course—not because she's morally opposed to swearing, obviously, but because in her haze of sleep, she can't formulate the words to come out of her mouth. She thinks she's telling Jodine to fuck off. She even visualizes herself mouthing the words, but if she were Veronica in an *Archie* comic book, above her head there would be a call-out without anything inside.

You see, Emma is a deep sleeper and she is in the midst of a pleasant dream where she is about to have an orgasm. She has never been able to have an orgasm in her sleep. She's come close, but no cigar, you know? Emma is making out with a male teacher she had in high school more than ten years ago, someone who would blush profusely if he knew what Emma was dreaming, although he probably wouldn't remember her, because she wasn't as hot back then as she is now and she wasn't exactly a rocket scientist, either—she sat in the back and doodled women's high heels in her notebook and didn't pay much attention to geography, which is what he taught.

Jodine shakes her and she's waking up and although she wants to say, "Leave me the fuck alone, I don't care if there's a fire, I'm this fucking close to nirvana," the news sinks in and she opens her right eye reluctantly.

"Get out of bed," Jodine tells her. "The apartment is on fire." She rips the covers off her body, exposing the butt of a red-lace-thonged Emma.

If Jodine weren't overwhelmed by consuming fears of burning futons, she would find Emma's choice of panties absurd. True, Emma never leaves the apartment in anything but a thong because her pants are tight and there's no way anything but a thong or commando would do the trick in today's panty-line fixated world.

Jodine would wonder, if she were thinking clearly, why Emma would not take off the thong to sleep. She would think that the thong, though seemingly a necessity in light of today's wardrobe, is not a comfortable garment, no matter what Emma claims. As well, even if she loves wearing thongs to bed, why would she choose a lace thong and not a cotton one? It makes no sense.

There aren't too many situations in which Jodine would be required to rip the blankets of her roommate, exposing her in the first place. So it is improbable that she would have ever come to the conclusion that it makes no sense. In any case, Jodine—unlike Allie, who secretly peruses through Emma's things in a vicarious fervor—does not realize that Emma doesn't own any noncotton panties. Emma wears lace exclusively. She's a yeast infection waiting to happen.

Disoriented, Emma sits up and stares. "What happened to your hair?"

Jodine's hair looks like a couple of birds decided to make it their nest. She has post-sex hair. Normally, she would have tied her post-sex hair back into a ponytail or, preferably, washed it, but of course there's no time for that. And besides, her favorite scrunchie was presently on her doorknob. "Get some clothes on," she says.

"All right." Emma, apparently, still does not fully appreciate the gravity of their situation. Instead, she is hoping that her breath doesn't smell as rancid as Jodine's and is wondering, What should I wear?

Jodine storms into Allie's room. "What's going on?" Allie asks. She is sitting up in bed, looking confused but calm nonetheless.

"The kitchen is on fire. We have to get out of here." Jodine tries to keep her voice light and soft, like margarine or spreadable cream cheese.

"Okay," Allie says, as though she's just been told to lower the television because Jodine can hear it through the walls and she's trying to study.

You'd think they would be in the throes of panic, but nothing tonight seems to make any sense (as Jodine would say).

Allie fails to comment on Jodine's bird's-nest hair, not because she doesn't think it looks peculiar, which it does, but because she's not wearing her glasses. Grabbing a sweatshirt, she steps into her running shoes quickly—she ends up stepping on the heel part of the shoe and smooshing it, which is a shame because once you smoosh the heel of a shoe, it never pops back to normal. She picks her glasses up from her night table and limps into the hallway.

Jodine and Emma are frozen, immobile, in front of the kitchen.

The kitchen wall is *still* on fire. How annoying.

"Stop, drop and roll. Stop, drop and roll," Jodine says. She's not sure what part of her brain that comes from. She has a vague memory of a fireman talking to her third-grade class and giving a home-safety demonstration, but that's all she remembers. She might still be drunk, we're not sure.

"We're not on fire," Emma says, rolling her eyes. "You stop, drop and roll when your clothes are burning."

"Maybe we should drop and roll the stove," Allie suggests.

"I'm not even sure it's coming from the stove," Emma says, and coughs. The kitchen is filling with smoke, reminding her of a foam party she went to one spring break in Cancún.

Allie has never been to a foam party, nor does she even know what a foam party is, so she doesn't make the same association. To her it looks like a lot of fog.

Stop, drop and roll. Stop. Drop. Roll. The drill is imprinted in Jodine's mind like red lipstick that stains your lips even though you've already used a half a roll of toilet paper to try to get it off.

"Should we call the fire department?" Allie asks.

Suddenly, Emma snaps into action and heads toward the cordless phone in the living room.

"It's 911," Allie tells her.

"Yeah, I know," Emma sneers, and dials.

"What do we do?" Allie asks.

Stop, drop and roll. Jodine doesn't answer. The stupid expression is doing somersaults in her head. Terrific.

"Maybe we should try to put it out? Jay?" Allie asks.

Stop, drop and roll.

"Jay? Jodine!" Allie screams, shaking her, digging her jaggedly bit nails into Jodine's shoulder.

Jodine snaps out of her reverie, shakes off Allie and lunges toward the sink. She's planning to blast the water, overflow the sink and drown the flames. Ouch. Hot. Too hot. This is not going to work, she thinks, and eyes the fishbowl.

Allie spots Jodine's gaze and smacks her on the shoulder. "You're not frying your goldfish!"

Jodine wants to say that presently, the bowl of water is worth far more than an extraneous goldfish. If one were to weigh the importance of a single goldfish, an unwanted goldfish, an ex-lover's gift of a goldfish (Manny got it for her for Valentine's Day last year), against a kitchen and all its contents, undoubtedly the consensus would be to fry the goldfish, right? But Jodine averts her eyes. Oh, she would just love to pour the contents of the bowl over the burning stove, since at present it is the only water at hand and she doesn't like the fish anyway, but mercifully she doesn't do it.

She must be under a ton of stress if she's now taking orders from Allie.

Allie scampers away from the kitchen, into the bathroom. A few seconds later she runs back, carefully holding the silver bathroom cup, the one that never gets used because Allie and Jodine both gargle with water carried to their mouths with their hands.

Allie makes it all the way from the bathroom without spilling a drop, and Jodine is impressed. If Jodine had been a counselor at sleep-away camp with Allie four years ago (which would have been completely impossible, since she spent her teenage summers as a waitress, scraping ketchup and maple syrup off the wooden floors at Scrambled, a breakfast nook two blocks from her house), she might not be so impressed. Allie has many hidden talents. That summer at camp, she was honored with the position of color-war captain, leading the team to victory with her winning egg-racing skills, which involved racing across the field, balancing a raw egg on a plastic spoon. She now empties the inexplicably soap-streaked cup of water over the stove, and it fizzles.

The fire has now taken over one entire wall.

Finished with her phone call, Emma grabs Allie and Jodine, saying, "They told me to get out of the house, close the doors and wake the neighbors." She closes the kitchen door, closes all three bedroom doors, grabs her purse and leads the others out. She holds Allie's hand, Allie holds Jodine's hand, and the three walk then run in a locomotion-like position. Jodine, the train's caboose, swings her hips and closes the front door behind them.

"I'll get Janet," Allie says. She hopes that Emma will insist that she'll get Janet. After all, Emma has taken care of everything else, so what's one more thing on her to-do list? But Emma just nods in agreement. She does not believe she knows Janet well enough to rouse her out of her bed, even under the present circumstances. Sure, Emma's bumped into their neighbor a few times in the shared foyer, but they've never gotten past the nice-day-outside-isn't-it stage. Allie knows Janet better than the other girls do, so it makes sense (as Jodine would say) that she get her.

By the way, contrary to what Emma and Allie believe, it was not Janet who discovered Nick's twenty-one boring red roses in the hallway, as they had been delivered at 9:55 a.m. Janet was planning to speak to her son before she went out, but her son's answering machine came on and she left the duplex before the flower man even rang the doorbell. Jodine was showering when the flower man rang the bell, but when she left the house, she found them perched on the outside porch, and flushed with excitement, assumed they were for her. This was not an unreasonable assumption, since it was her twenty-fifth birthday. She snatched the mini flower card out of its mini flower-shaped envelope, and was overwhelmed with disappointment when she saw that they were for Emma. Her disappointment caused her further frustration because she figured if she hadn't expected flowers, what reason could she possibly have to be disappointed? She propped the flowers in a standing position outside their door in the foyer. She didn't want to bother unlocking the door after she had just locked it—there was no time for *that*—and headed off to the gym.

You're probably thinking, who cares if Jodine or Janet found the flowers? You're wondering, how is the fact relevant to this story? Because their names both start with *J*? You just don't get it, do you?

The elation Jodine felt when she first saw the flowers, coupled with the overwhelming depression she felt when she realized they were not for her, planted a claustrophobic sense of loneliness that grew in the pit of her stomach.

She wanted someone to send her roses. She wanted a boyfriend to send her roses. This loneliness, this crushing and completely unexpected genuine dread of emotional isolation played a significant role in her decision to breach her NO SEX WITH THE EX rule. Yes, yes, yes, the wine was a factor in this, too. But the point is this: If she hadn't broken the NO SEX WITH THE EX rule, then in all likelihood, she wouldn't have made postcoital tea. If she hadn't made the tea and left the pot on the stove…

Get it?

Allie disappears upstairs to warn Janet, and Emma and Jodine cross the street.

Since smoke is not pouring out of the windows, both girls begin to wonder if they overreacted. Their neighborhood seems too tranquil, too peaceful, too much like the opening clip of the *Golden Girls* for it to be dangerous.

"Should I move my car?" Emma asks, motioning with her chin to her bright blue Jetta, a high school graduation present from her father, parked on the side of the road where they now stood. Their duplex comes with one spot in its garage, and Janet rents it. Emma parks on the street.

Normally, finding a prime spot is unlikely, but yesterday she lucked out with spot primo uno, right across from their place. She isn't keen on the idea of losing the spot, but she has a mental image of a fire truck squashing it into a sheet of blue metal reminiscent of the flattened superpowered bad guys in *Superman II*.

"Just leave it," Jodine says irritably. She does not have the image of *Superman II* in her repertoire; in fact, she has never seen any of the *Superman* movies. Instead, Jodine thinks Emma is being ridiculous for worrying about her precious car when all their belongings, including their clothes, their television, her recently purchased textbooks, her laptop... damn, her laptop and all her carefully transcribed files of case summaries are in a far more precarious situation.

Emma pulls out her cell phone from her purse and calls her father. "Dad? It's me. Can you come to the apartment...? We're having a fire... No, I said *having*. It's still going on... No I'm fine.... They're fine. Well, Allie's still in the building... Yes, she should probably leave... They're coming, I called them... Just come... No, was I supposed to...? Why didn't you tell me...? How was I supposed to know that? I'll ask. Okay." She turns off the phone.

"I don't have insurance," Emma announces to Jodine with a the-dryer-shrunk-my-green-sweater intonation. In other words, she knows the news isn't good, but she's not yet sure *how* bad it will be. Will the sweater just look a little tighter but still be wearable, or will it now make an excellent vest for a Cabbage Patch doll?

The eight-hour-old wine churns in Jodine's stomach. "Neither do I," she says. "Does Allie?"

"I don't know."

"Only the person who caused the fire needs to have the insurance," Jodine says slowly.

"So who caused it?"

"Allie did, if she has insurance." Jodine's head pounds as though it were the planet Krypton in *Superman I,* about to detonate. Stop drop and roll. Tea. Tea! Why did she need tea in the middle of the night? Stop, drop and roll. She must have left the stove on. She must have caused the fire. **What** if the whole place burns down? She'll be in debt for the rest of her life. Panic is racing last night's wine up her throat. "Otherwise, I don't know who—or what—caused it." She pauses. "Do you?"

"No," Emma answers slowly. She rubs her eyes with the palm of her hand, rubbing the crusty remnants of last night's mascara into under-eye circles.

Jodine cringes. Why would someone not take the two minutes to remove makeup? All it takes is a cotton ball and a little cream. She was intoxicated and she still found the strength to make the effort.

"Does that mean if one of us caused it, we'll be responsible for paying for the damage?" Emma asks.

"Yes, legally. But it's possible Allie has insurance. She's lived here for two years. She'll have to say it was her fault."

"Will she get arrested?"

"You don't get arrested for causing an accidental fire," Jodine says. (Jodine hopes.)

"She's taking a long time. I'm gonna see if she's okay." Emma sprints across the street.

Stop, drop and roll. Tea. Stop, drop and roll. Jodine won't admit to the firemen that she used the stove. She can't. Not if Allie's insurance will pay. She'll tell Allie the truth, she'll beg Allie, she'll be Allie's slave for life. She'll be her personal lifelong lawyer free of charge. She'll bite her nails for her. Anything. She just can't afford thousands of dollars of debt.

Allie, Emma and Janet emerge. Janet is wearing a white robe and holding an animal carry-on cage stuffed with a beige cat. Every step Janet takes causes the cat's head to smash into the top of its cage, and the cat to meow its disapproval.

"She doesn't have insurance, either," Emma whispers to Jodine. Allie shakes her head in confirmation.

"Shit," Jodine says. "How can you live on your own for two years without insurance?"

Emma raised her eyebrow. "You're the law student. You should have been more responsible about letting us know we needed insurance."

"How are we going to pay for all this?" Allie wails.

No answer.

Notice that no one suggests faulty wiring. Not one of them insists, "It wasn't me! I demand an investigation!" They're all keeping suspiciously quiet.

"They're going to call Carl," Allie says.

Carl lives in Winnipeg. Carl owns the house. Carl owns houses all over the country. Carl wrote explicitly in the lease that tenants are responsible for taking out accident insurance.

Carl is going to be pissed.

When the fire truck pulls up, the driver sees four women standing on the street, two waving frantically at him. He notices what they're all wearing, but being a man, these are the observations he misses:

The first waving woman, Emma (he doesn't know her name yet), is wearing flip-flops on her feet, the kind you used to buy at a thrift store to wear in the shower at either the gym or European youth hostels, but now come with a designer label stamped on the underside and cost twenty bucks a pair. She's also wearing Diesel jeans and a sleazy thin shirt that isn't done up all the way. (This the fireman does in fact notice.) The combo must be for effect, because really, if she had time to do up her jeans, she'd have time to do up her buttons, wouldn't she?

The second waving woman, Allie, is wearing a sweatshirt and lime-green boxers. They look like an old boyfriend's boxers, the kind he discards in the corner of his bathroom when he undresses to shower, and then forgets about. You wash them for him and then you break up and you keep them either because you're still in love with him and they remind you of him and you sleep with them beside your pillow, as revolting as that seems to you in retrospect, or because you're planning on shredding them in some sort of exorcist ceremony that you never get around to because you meet someone else, someone better, someone who doesn't call you only when he wants to get laid.

Actually, Allie got her boxers at the Gap.

A third girl, Jodine, is wearing fuzzy black slippers that appear to have ears, green-striped pajama bottoms and a navy blue T-shirt. She's not waving.

Next, the fireman's eyes pass over an old woman and a cat. In fact, his eyes basically pass over everything, except for the girl in the open-button shirt. For the next few hours, he'll engage in a bit of flirting with her, a minor amount, nothing his live-in girlfriend should be concerned about. What she should be more concerned with is the fact that they've been living together for two years and he's no closer to popping the question than he was when they first shacked up. Her mother shakes her head a lot and says it's because he gets the milk for free so why would he bother buying the cow, but that's not really it. He wants to get married, just not to her. Want to know what happens to the slimy fireman and his girlfriend? Does she get fed up and ultimatum him? Does she fall in love with someone who deserves her? Does she bump into her ex-boyfriend one random Wednesday in the food court in the mall, start e-mailing him, have an affair, then move all her clothes into his apartment one night while Slimy Fireman is playing squash? Eh? Not knowing is killing you, isn't it?

Moving on.

The first fire truck slams on its brakes smack in the center of the street. Three men dressed in padded vomit-yellow uniforms charge out of the truck. **Slimy Fireman** rushes over to the girls, and the other two firemen **prepare for the** fire-elimination process by pressing large buttons, removing fire extinguishers, pulling and twisting various levers. Slimy unravels a hose at least two hundred feet long, and Jodine imagines how much water the two-hundred-foot hose is about to unleash on her apartment and whether any of her belongings other than her goldfish can swim.

Emma smirks. "That's quite a hose you've got there, honey," she says under her breath.

Jodine ignores Emma's comment. "Does anyone have any gum?" she asks. She has a crappy taste in her mouth, which she would like to obliterate before talking with the firefighters.

Emma has one piece left in her purse but she doesn't want to share it. "No."

Slimy Fireman is now within breath range. "Are you the girls who called the fire department?"

No, they're the other girls who are standing outside at three in the morning. Sheesh.

The girls nod.

"Is everyone out of the building?"

The girls nod again, murmuring "Uh-huh."

"Where did the fire start?" His skin looks as though he's spent too much vacation time in Miami.

"In the kitchen," Jodine says.

"Do you know how it started?"

"I think we left the oven on by accident," Emma says.

Jodine doesn't know why Emma says this, but she's not planning on offering any insight. Maybe they used the stove when she was out. Maybe one of them made cookies before going to bed. Who cares? What is key is that they used the oven, think they might be responsible and don't want an investigation.

"Where is the kitchen?"

Allie outlines the geography of their apartment as two more screeching fire trucks pull into the street. The other firemen organize the hoses and then three of them, including Slimy, charge into the apartment, holding a fire extinguisher and some sort of ax device. A police car and an ambulance have joined the party and sit at the top of the street.

"Mr. Fireman, can I go for a slide down your pole?" Emma asks in a happy-birthday-Mr.-President voice.

"Emma!" Jodine says in a stop-being-so-immature voice. "Punning is the lowest form of humor."

Emma discreetly removes her last piece of gum from her purse, throws the wrapper on the pavement and sneaks the gum into her mouth.

Allie asks to borrow Emma's phone. She calls Clint so she can tell him what happened, hoping that he'll be inspired to come get her and play hero. Excitement races through her, but then she feels guilty for feeling excited when her apartment is burning down, although really, it's a perfect opportunity for him to come take care of her and fall madly in love. He doesn't answer and she hangs up.

Janet consoles her cat.

Emma wonders why it's taking her father so fucking long to get here.

Jodine continues to silently freak out. Stop, drop and roll. Stop, drop and roll. She feels ashamed she lost control. She hates losing control. If she can't control her ability to keep control, how can anyone control anything? Is life a collection of random, uncontrollable events strung together into an existence? But no, she reasons. She was the last one in the kitchen; she must have left the stove on and caused the fire. She was responsible.

She heaves a sigh of relief. Although she is acting libelously and completely irresponsibly by acting libelously, due to the fact that she was, in fact, responsible, she knows that the fire was not random.

Stop, drop and roll.

It makes perfect sense.

9
JODINE NAMES HER FISH

JODINE

Five minutes later, the fireman who asked us the ridiculous amount of questions when he seemingly should have been putting out the fire reappears outside. "It's out," he announces, and I exhale a blowup doll's worth of air. "We're just checking for fire extension," he says.

He's checking for fire what?

Emma articulates my inquiry, "What the fuck is that?"

"We're ripping into the cabinets until we can't see any more damage. We have to make sure the fire didn't spread through the walls. It seems to have started from the oven, just as you girls guessed."

"How can you tell?" Allie asks, and Emma and I shoot her glares of death. Allie doesn't notice.

"Fire travels upward in a V shape. Your fire traveled up from the location of the oven. By the way, I'm Norman," he says, thrusting his yellow-gloved hand toward Allie. Allie shakes it.

At first I'm not sure why Norm here suddenly wants to get to know us, but then I realize he's trying to peer into Emma's absurdly open shirt.

We all introduce ourselves. Wonderful, now we're all friends. Norman can be on my Christmas card list.

Allie nudges her head toward the police cars. "Are they going to investigate?"

What's her problem? We don't want an investigation! Shut up, big mouth! Close your diuretic mouth! I try to silence her with poisoned telepathy.

"Investigate? Why?" Norm asks.

If I continue staring at the spiderweb cracks in the sidewalk, will they solidify into nooses and hang Allie?

"I just thought…uh, why are the police here?" she stammers.

Norm isn't trying very hard not to be distracted by our favorite exposed roommate. "They come in case there's a traffic problem," he offers, his eyes still glued to the valley between my roomie's breasts.

A traffic problem? At four in the morning? Who is even up at four in the morning? "Or in case the fire is not an accident," he adds. "Which this obviously is."

"Oh," Allie says. "Good."

Good. Good? Our kitchen has been zapped into another dimension and this is good?

"Did the fire spread through the walls?" she asks.

"Not as far as we can tell."

"Is the apartment ruined?"

"No. It was a good thing you girls closed the doors. You limited the damage."

There's that word again—*good*. If it gets any better, we can pop open the champagne and celebrate.

"We closed them after we—" Allie says.

"What's the damage?" Emma interrupts. It's obvious that she, too, no longer cares to hear the sound of Allie's voice.

"The kitchen will need some work. The walls are brick, so they survived. But they'll need to be plastered and painted. The cabinets, shelves, microwave and stove are toast." He laughs at his choice of words.

I decide not to share my opinion of puns with him, since he has the power to make me bankrupt. "What about the living room?" I ask.

"You're lucky. We'll ventilate it, and you'll need to get someone to dry-clean the curtains and couch, but it's livable."

"How much will all this cost?" Emma asks.

"Damage-wise? I don't know. The insurance guys will tell you. You won't have to worry about it."

Terrific. I choke on my own saliva.

"Who's your insurance agency?" he asks.

No one answers. He looks at each of us and sighs what I assume is his silly-silly-girls sigh. "You don't have insurance?" We shake our heads, mirroring his solemnity. "Who owns the apartment?" he asks.

Shit. Shit. He's going to call Carl, our landlord. And Carl is going to exorcise our existence from the apartment, then drown us in lawsuits. Drown *me* in lawsuits. Because he's going to want an investigation, and the investigation will reveal that the stove, not the oven, caused the fire, and I'm going to be in debt until my teeth are false, my shoes orthopedic, and I talk to my grandchildren during the prime-time sitcoms they're trying to watch, which I can't hear without my hearing aid.

"I do," I answer, suddenly enlightened with a potentially hugely libelous plan.

The fireman looks up and stares at me. For an elasticized second I am positive he's going to call me on my lie and have me arrested. "Okay," he says, his eyes returning to Emma's exposed cleavage.

What kind of an idiot thinks a barely twenty-five-year-old law student can afford her own duplex? Breast-ogling moron.

Allie's mouth pops open like my goldfish's. Emma's eyebrows rise in eighty-degree angles.

If they ask Janet to confirm that I own this place, I'm as toast as the microwave.

A few minutes later, good old Norm leads us into the apartment to see the damage. Another firefighter brings in a ventilator to rid the apartment of smoke.

Two firemen are still inside. The apartment smells as if Emma smoked four hundred packs of cigarettes and then sprinkled the ashes over the apartment. We gasp at the sight of the kitchen. What was formally known as *The Wall That Had a Stove* is charred beyond recognition. This is what Norm calls "no damage to the walls"? What is left of the cabinets looks like confidential contracts, post shredder machine.

"Oh, my God." Allie's eyes look like two sinks about to overflow.

"We didn't have to use the hose, so there wasn't any water damage." The fireman says. "The fire was pretty contained."

Contained? They call this contained? What is uncontained? This looks like a nuclear wasteland.

"I think I'm gonna puke," Allie mutters, bending forward and balancing her hands on her knees. "I have a really weak stomach." Emma bends over to pat Allie on the back.

Norm gets a better look down Emma's shirt, as I'm sure she is aware. "It could have been much worse," he says gravely.

"We could have been killed," Allie says, dry-heaving. "We are so lucky."

Lucky? Winning the lottery is lucky. Finding the new jacket you were going to buy, anyway, for fifty percent off is lucky. We have no *kitchen*. This is lucky?

"The damage is pretty minimal, considering," Norm continues. "You could have charred the entire place. The majority of the damage is in the kitchen. And if you hadn't woken up—" he nods toward me "—the fire could have gotten all three of you."

Okay, he does have a point. No kitchen is far preferable to no existence. "Thanks," I say. "We appreciate all you've done."

He nods and heads into the living room.

"Mr. Fireman, I'm on fire. Would you hose me down?" Emma whispers à la Marilyn.

"Shh," I whisper back, and roll my eyes. "Look." I point to the fishbowl. My goldfish appears to be on acid. He's swimming incoherently all over his now yellow-tinged bowl of water. "The fish made it. I can't believe it. Why does he never die?"

"The fish? Does he not have a name?" Emma shakes her head in disgust. "Do all law students lack creativity?" She opens the fridge, but no light comes on. "I'm thirsty."

"I don't think you should drink tap water now," Allie says.

"I don't care. Name him anything you want," I say.

"Norm!" Emma calls into the living room. "Do you think the OJ is safe to drink?"

"I don't know. Why take a chance?"

"We should throw it out," Emma says. "It's going to go bad. We have no power."

"Norm?" I ask. "After the fireman? Is that a name for a fish?"

"Norm isn't a name for a goldfish," Allie says. "It's the name of a guy in a bar. You remember *Cheers,* don't you? I think Jay didn't name him because she doesn't want to let herself get attached to him. She knew if she named him, she'd want to keep him."

"You don't have to speak about me as if I'm not here, Allie. But you're right. I'm obviously a petaphobe."

"Or a commitmentphobe," Allie says.

Emma flicks the fishbowl with her nail. "In *Breakfast at Tiffany's* Audrey Hepburn called her cat, Cat."

Allie looks confused. "You think she should call her fish Cat?"

I'd say the fire clouded her brain, but she was just as likely to make a comment like that yesterday. "I think she means I should call my fish, Fish."

"That's silly," Allie says.

"I like it," I say. "There's something unnatural about this creature."

"They should arrest you for attempted murder," Allie says. "You tried to throw him in the fire."

"I was trying to put out the fire."

"Mission not accomplished," Allie says, now giggling. She's pointing to my head. "You look like you have an Afro."

As if the appearance of my hair is of any relevance to the fire *or* my phobias. "Don't we have more important things to worry about?"

Emma smirks and nudges her chin toward Allie. "You don't look much better, Charlie Chaplin."

Allie has a small square soot mustache over her top lip. I snicker. "Or Hitler," I say.

"You can't tell people they look like Hitler," Allie says.

"Why not, Führer?"

"Because it's mean. Anyway, you're one to talk. Your face looks like someone smeared…shit all over it!" Allie emphasizes the word *shit* by putting her hands on her hips and pursing her lips.

"Ew. Not shit!" I say. "That's a bad word, Allie, you sure you don't want to take it back? The language police may come after you. Hey, Emma, whose face is shittier? Mine or Allie's?"

"You're both not looking your best, actually," Emma says, and starts laughing. Allie and I look up at her and suddenly we're laughing, too, soft laughs, like light sprays of rain you don't feel until you touch your hair and it's damp. And then the laughs overtake my body until my stomach feels as if I've done hundreds of sit-ups, and I can't believe this happened. How could this happen? And Emma and Allie are laughing just as hard, laughing until tears streak down our faces, clogging our eyes, our noses, our throats, and suddenly we're crying.

We stand in the kitchen, sobbing, rooted to the ground like gum to the sole of a sneaker.

And then I start laughing again. The bottom half of my salad spinner, perched on a jutting piece of the ravaged cabinet, has been turned into a hyperbola-shaped piece of melted plastic. I point, and Emma starts to laugh again, too.

"That was my one contribution to the apartment," I say.

Allie stands still, staring. "What are we going to do?" she wails.

Excellent question.

"Girls," Norm calls from the living room, "I'm going to install the ventilator in here. It's going to get loud."

"Okay," we say. Allie wipes her eyes with the sleeve of her sweatshirt. She tries to wipe off her mustache, but ends up smearing it across her face.

Norm returns inside what was formally known as the kitchen. "I'm also going to install a new smoke detector. This one is burned to a crisp."

A smoke detector? A smoke detector! "Why didn't the smoke detector go off?" I wonder aloud. Isn't there something wrong with this picture—a smoke detector getting destroyed in a fire?

"A smoke detector without batteries is like a…" He pauses. Obviously similes are not his strong point.

"An empty fishbowl?" I offer. His face lightens up. He's not too swift, our Norm.

"Yeah, that's it," he says. "I should fine you two hundred and thirty dollars."

"Please don't, sir!" Allie pleads, turning mildly red.

I'm curious as to why two hundred and thirty dollars is even vaguely significant in the grand face of the thousands of dollars we'll probably owe, but at this moment, I'm in no mood to analyze Allie's particular idiosyncrasies.

"I won't," Norm says. "I feel bad enough for you girls as it is."

"You're a sweetheart," Emma says, placing her hand on his forearm. "We truly appreciate everything you've done. Is there any way, any way at all, we can repay you?"

Groan.

Norm smiles, exposing a small space between his front teeth. I lower my eyes. Is that a hose or is he happy to see her?

He clears his throat. "Um…you girls…should pack a bag. For a few days."

"Are you taking us somewhere?" Emma asks sweetly. Her hand remains on his arm.

Terrific.

"Do you need a lift?"

"Isn't your father coming to pick us up?" Allie comments, obviously oblivious to Emma's flirting. "Norman, how long will it take to fumigate the apartment?"

Fumigate? Are there bugs? "Ventilate. She means ventilate," I explain.

"A few days. Do you have places to stay?" He eyes Emma.

"I'm hoping something will turn up," she answers.

"Your dad's coming, right?" Allie asks again. "Do you think he'd mind if I stay with you tonight? I don't have anywhere else to go."

Emma rolls her eyes. Allie is clearly cramping her style. "Yes, Allie, you can stay with me."

I just moved out and I'm already moving home. Fabulous. Back home to Mommy and Daddy. I'll be there two hours and they'll have me fixing their VCR, explaining their telephone bill, organizing their taxes—and it's not even April.

I could call Manny. He lives near school. I won't have to tell my parents about this, and he would be more than happy to have me as his guest.

But what does this mean? Are we back together? Are we a couple? Do I have to call him my boyfriend again? I hate that word—*boyfriend*. Lover? Sex toy? My man? I hate "my man" the most. Special friend?

Being together won't be that terrible. The sex is good. Because of our classes, we're obligated to spend a great deal of time together, anyway. Logic follows that since we're spending a large amount of time together, it makes sense for us to be having sex. Since we will be having sex and spending so much time together, we might as well be dating. And since we're dating, and having sex, and spending so much time with each other, we might as well be living together, at least until I have somewhere else to sleep.

There. All settled. Who is Allie to call me a commitment-phobe?

I named my fish, didn't I?

10

EMMA'S BEING SELFISH
AND IS FEELING SORRY
FOR HERSELF
(SURPRISE, SURPRISE)

EMMA

"This could only happen to me," I tell Allie.

"It happened to all of us," she whispers back.

All of us? Please. "I'm the one with a major presentation due on Monday." I don't bother trying to keep my voice down, not that my dad could hear me even if I wanted him to. Which I do. Let's face it, Stepbitch could have taken five minutes to prepare the spare room for Allie instead of staying in bed and sleeping while my apartment was burning down. So *sorry,* didn't mean to ruin her beauty sleep, but why should I have to do this? "A presentation I haven't even started yet," I add. I'm fucked—the design editor is going to be there—and I'm not prepared. How am I supposed to do a presentation about shoes when I'm completely exhausted? I don't think I've ever been this tired. My head feels waterlogged and my neck seems to have morphed into a Slinky. I throw the gray pillows off the couch, onto the floor. "You get to relax all day, so don't whine. Help me pull the mattress out."

"I'll help you with your presentation," she says as she gets her finger stuck between two metal bars. "Ouch."

Foot-fashion help from the girl who wears fluorescent shoelaces in her running shoes. Fluorescent. I'm *de-feeted* even before I begin.

"Let go. I'll do it." I manhandle the mattress into the proper position.

She leans against the wall and closes her eyes. "Thanks."

She gets to nap while I work? I don't think so. I grab a pillow and clean sheets from the closet and toss them onto the mattress. "Can you make it? I need to sleep."

"Don't worry about it. I can do it. Uh, Em, how are we going to pay for the repairs?"

Why are we discussing this now? My brain is shutting down. What time is it? What day is it? I'm beginning to hallucinate about marshmallow-like white fluffy pillows. Soft. I need to sleep. "I'll ask my dad for money tomorrow, okay? Good night."

I collapse into my bed and close my eyes immediately. I'm amazed Stepbitch hasn't turned my room into a toy room or a closet. What a miserable night. After my dad arrived, he took us to the hospital, where we waited for an hour and thirty minutes and then, finally, were locked in a tiny room and instructed to breathe from oxygen tubes. We looked like Darth Vaders. By the time we got home it was 6:30 a.m. The water that pooled around my feet in the shower turned gray. And now it's after seven. Seven o'clock in the fucking morning.

My whole sleep schedule is screwed up. If I sleep my minimum eight hours, I'm going to wake up at three. How will I fall asleep tomorrow night? If I wake up at one, or even two, it might be okay (I usually have this problem Sunday nights, anyway), but I need at least eight hours' sleep! Maybe I should stay awake and drown myself in espresso.

No. Need sleep.

Why did this happen tonight? If it happened during the week then I'd at least get the next day off. I could call in, claiming an emergency. But I can't call in on Monday for a fire on Saturday night, can I?

No.

I have the worst luck.

Need sleep.

"So nice to have you over for dinner, Allison."

We are having a family dinner: AJ, my dad, Barbie, Allie and I are eating hamburgers. Allie and Barbie seem to be competing to see who can drown their burgers in more cheese. They're sitting next to each other, and Barbie keeps telling Allie how pretty she is. They spent most of the day watching home videos while I worked, which I find curious. My father didn't make home videos during his last marriage. Apparently deserting one's family in Montreal is a precursor for becoming Father of the Year in one's next marriage.

I shouldn't be wasting this precious time eating when I should be working—but no, apparently I am not too old to be told when I have to eat.

"Thank you, AJ," Allie says. "It's nice to have a home-cooked meal. Will you be in the office this week?" AJ is an involved alumnus at Ontario University. Allie works for the alumni fund. They got to talking one day, and that's how I got my once crispy-cool, now crispy-cooked, apartment.

AJ thinks Allie is a nice young woman. A good influence. Hah! If I had kept my room in the state she does, I would have been booted out of here years ago.

"Where are you from, Allison?" my father asks.

"I grew up in Belleville."

My father smirks. Belleville jokes are not above his taste in humor. Neither are fat jokes or gay jokes. I'm hoping he's saving his "How many Bellevillites does it take to put in a lightbulb?" joke until after Allie leaves the table. I'd call him a racist, but he doesn't actually make any jokes about any specific race. What is he, then? A differentist? An idiot?

"What do your parents do?" he asks.

"My mother teaches third grade and my father is a dentist."

"I didn't know that," I say. "Smile."

She smiles. Her teeth are white and shiny. Does that mean we'll get free toothpaste and toothbrushes? No, wait. Free bleaching, yes! I spend too much cash on teeth paraphernalia. I always buy the angled brushes that cost twice the price as the plain ones because they claim they can reach spots nothing else can. (So since when do teeth have a G-spot?) Maybe Allie can bring a couple for Jodine. That girl needs some serious breath freshener in the morning.

"Very nice smile," I say.

"Can I go to Allie's dad instead of my dentist?" Barbie asks. She hates her dentist. And her doctor. She doesn't like to be prodded. Last time she went to the doctor she refused to go with anyone but me. I didn't mind because he has a great ass.

"He's in Belleville," my dad says.

"So?"

"We're not going to Belleville."

"Why not?"

Yes, why not, Daddy dearest? Because we're too posh for Belleville, Barbie, you sweet, innocent heart. Only hicks live in Belleville, don't you know that? Bellevillites are good enough to have over at our house for dinner, but not good enough to fix our teeth.

"Because. You were saying, Allie? Go on."

"I moved to Toronto three years ago to go to college."

"And how do you like Toronto?"

"I love it. It took some time to get used to, but I love it."

"Why?" I ask. "This city is awful."

"I hope your enthusiasm rubs off on Emma," AJ says.

The phone rings and my father scowls. It rings again. And again.

"In case no one can hear, the phone is ringing," I say.

"Yes, we can hear," my dad says. "You know we let the machine pick up during dinner."

"What if it's an emergency? Someone's house could be on fire."

"Two fires in two days would be highly unlikely."

"One fire in two days would be highly unlikely," I respond. Allie stares misty-eyed at the phone. Every time it rings, a dopey-hopeful look crosses her face, and when I tell her no, it's not Clint, she looks like a five-year-old girl who dropped her teddy bear in a puddle and watched a minivan run over it.

"I went to Hawaii last year and I ate too much pineapple and I threw up," Barbie announces for no apparent reason except to expose a piece of chewed bun still in her mouth.

"Hon, keep your mouth closed when you talk. And that's not appropriate table talk, is it?" AJ shakes her head at Barbie, and Barbie closes her mouth.

"Emma is still obsessed with Montreal," AJ says, also for some unknown reason. Like mother, like daughter. Do either of them ever stop to think before opening their mouths? "It's time to move on, dear. Everyone else has. The city is dead." She shakes her head. "Have you been there recently?"

"It's not dead," I argue. I hate when AJ starts shitting on Montreal. "Tons of people get jobs there. It has more life in its corner grocery stores then this city has in its entirety."

"Plenty of French people are getting jobs. English people are seeking greener pastures. Enid says——" This is where I tune out. Enid is one of her loser cronies who have an opinion on everything while knowing nothing. She's the type who reads an article on Lebanese cuisine and then considers herself an expert on the Middle East.

"Are you married?" Barbie asks, poking Allie in the shoulder.

Jeez. Married? First she needs a boyfriend. And I'm not putting any money on this Clint character. She speaks to him on the phone all the time——I can hear her giggling and Jodine yelling at her to shut up nightly——but he hasn't made a move. If a guy wants a girl, he makes a move. Period. He doesn't want to be friends. If you ask me, she needs to play a little hard to get so that he'll start chasing her.

I refuse to chase Nick. I don't even want him anymore. His flowers certainly haven't made up for his immature behavior.

I need a *man,* not someone who believes that working for his father means growing and smoking pot all day at home. As for me, I haven't smoked up since we broke up. It's funny how something so much a part of your day becomes irrelevant when it's taken away from you. The truth is, pot doesn't do anything for me, anyway, except make me tired. I mean, I sleep enough as it is. If I still smoked that stuff, I'd be in bed twenty hours a day, and I'm not talking coupling here. I'm talking dead-to-the-world, comatose sleep.

"Just a quick joint," Nick always said, and I'd usually agree, not because it mattered to me, but because it was there. It's like coffee. Even if I've already had two cups, if the waitress fills up the cup for me I'm going to drink it.

Allie giggles. Naturally, obviously. "Married? Not yet. Are you?" She might be a real treat, high. Or completely annoying with all that giggling.

Barbie's face turns halogen-light bright. "No! That's silly. But I have a boyfriend and his name is..."

If my half sister says Ken, I'm going to disown her.

"...Barnie."

Barnie? Who invents a boyfriend named Barnie?

"Barbie and Barnie," Allie says. "How adorable!"

Barbie puts her small, pudgy hand around Allie's wrist. "Mum, can Allie and I go look at photo albums now?" Photo albums, too? Poor Allie. Maybe not poor Allie. She eats this kind of cheesiness for breakfast. She lives on it.

"Let her finish her meal," I say. Although eating only part of her dinner may not be such a bad thing for her....

"I was asking my mom."

Hmm. Maybe I am a bad influence.

"After dinner, I'll look at whatever you want me to," Allie says while picking a stray piece of cheese off her plate with her fingers. She dips it into ketchup and drops it into her mouth. Why doesn't she just lick the damn plate and be done with it?

"Emma," AJ says, "I spoke to Harry and he asked his nephew to do the renovations on your kitchen." Harry is my stepmother's repair-renovation man. Harry arrives after my dad leaves for work and leaves just before my dad gets home. Every day. Week after week. Month after month. How many rooms can AJ possibly need renovated? Suspiciously, my father has never met Harry. Coincidence? I think not. I've met him once, quite by accident, when AJ wasn't expecting me home. He's certainly eye candy, and he wouldn't look twice at me. I didn't exactly set up a seduction scene, but if he wasn't giving AJ the old one-two, why else wouldn't he look at me?

"What if we don't want Harry's nephew to do the work?"

"Then you can find your own repairman. But Harry's nephew

will do it as a personal favor to Harry, so I doubt you'll find a better deal."

"Why can't Harry do it himself?"

"Harry's busy here."

I'm sure. "When will his nephew be coming by?"

"At one tomorrow."

"I won't be moving back into the apartment until six. Can he come then?"

"Probably not. Most people like to work during working hours. Can't you be home at one?"

Am I not most people? "Sure, no problem. I'll just tell my boss I'll see her later. I'm sure she won't mind."

"Good. Then it's settled."

Does she think I can just pop by the office when the mood strikes me? I throw my napkin on the table. "I was being sarcastic. Some of us have to work for a living."

"Emma, you're being silly," my dad says, piling our plates one on top of the other and carrying them to the sink. My mother would have a heart attack if she saw how easily AJ has whipped his ass. In all their years of marriage, we thought he was crazy-glued to his kitchen chair. "I'm sure your boss will understand," he says over the drone of running water. "This is an unusual situation."

"Dad, I can't be home at one." I probably could, actually. Last week one of the editorial assistants left at two to get her bangs trimmed. I bet post-fire renovations qualify as equally work-leaving worthy.

"Do you want me to call and speak to someone?"

He's not even kidding. He obviously thinks I'm still in high school. "No."

"You have to learn to be accommodating," AJ says.

"Am I accommodating?" Barbie asks.

"Yes, sweetheart."

Allie scrapes her fork against her plate to pick up any leftover cheese/garnish she hasn't already devoured, licks it and points it at me in the air. "I can be at the apartment for one. You don't need to be there."

Suck-up. "You sure?"

"Yeah, why not? I work from four to seven. He's just coming to assess, right?"

"That would be wonderful," AJ says, beaming. "Thank you, Allie. You're wonderful. We really appreciate it."

We? What we? Is this AJ's apartment, too? "How long is Hunky Harry's nephew going to take to fix the kitchen?" I ask.

"Who knows?" my dad says.

"I'd think AJ would be an expert on renovations by now."

AJ obviously misses the edge in my voice and runs her hand through her short hair, as though in thought. "Probably about a month."

What? "A month? How are we going to eat for that month?"

"You should have thought of that before you burned down the kitchen," she says.

"I didn't burn down the kitchen."

"Well, who did?"

"We don't know. We left the oven or stove on or something."

"Who's 'we'? All of you collectively left the stove on?"

"Yes. We all held the dial on high until it caught fire."

AJ and my father scowl.

"A month is too long," I say. "Maybe Harry and his relations are genetically programmed to be inefficient. Can't you hire a renovations company to fix it faster?"

"*You* can hire whomever you want. But I know Harry is honest. I've been using him for years."

Oh, I'm sure you've been using him, all right. "Fine. Whatever."

"So how are *you* going to pay for this?" my dad butts in. I hope the emphasis on the pronoun *you* doesn't mean what I think it means. I'm hoping the payment will be more like my backpacking-through-Europe trip. I wanted to go, I didn't have any money, he asked me how I was planning on financing the trip, I told him I was going to get a job, he told me he was proud of me and that he'd pay for my plane and Eurorail tickets, and he gave me three grand.

"I'm going to get a second job."

"You could barely get a first job," AJ says. "I doubt you'll find a second one."

"I'll put it on Visa."

"He doesn't take Visa, dear."

"We'll come up with the money."

AJ and my dad look at Allie for confirmation. She nods uncertainly.

"I hope you don't expect me to pay for it," my dad says.

Well yes, I do. By the look on his face, I can tell that the past tense is called for. I *did* expect him to pay for it. Obviously I can no longer expect this, or why else is he turning purple? "Did I ask you for money?" Maybe if I take the defensive, he'll relent.

Allie is turning slightly mauve. She's actually clashing with my father.

"About every week."

"Well I didn't *today,* did I?"

"No, you didn't."

"So I don't need any."

"Can Allie and I go play now, Mum?"

"Yes, Barbie."

By the look on Allie's face, I hope she's not too nauseous to stand up. She thanks Stepbitch for dinner and follows Bouncing Barbie away from the table.

"That girl is a true sweetheart," AJ says to my father. "She'll make a wonderful friend for Emma." For fuck's sake, I'm three years old and she's setting up a play date.

He nods at her, smiling. "Excellent choice you made, dear."

I drop my glass in the sink and it clanks against the pile of plates.

"Emma, be careful!"

Blah blah blah.

If only my shoe presentation could come to life and give her a kick in the ass.

"Come in!" I say to Allie after she knocks on my door. I want something to drink, but I guess I can't ask her to get me any orange juice in my own house, can I?

She opens the door and slips inside. "How's it going?"

"Fine. I'm almost done. How are the photo albums?"

"Cute. What a cutie your sister is."

"Half sister."

"You two look alike."

"What? You've been doing too much crack." If Allie has ever done crack, I will eat my own shoe. This is the girl who has a hard time with Coke—the soft drink. Actually, I'll eat all the shoes I've alluded to in my assignment. *I've* never even done crack. I've done 'shrooms a few times, acid once, and E twice, but I wouldn't want to fuck with anything too hard.

"AJ's not that bad," Allie whispers. "I don't know why you call her the Wicked Witch."

"I don't," I answer loudly. "She's the *Stepbitch*."

Allie closes the door softly. She has that constipated look on her face. "Can we talk for a sec?"

"About what?" I know what she wants to talk about, of course I do, but do we really have to do it now? She knows I have a huge presentation tomorrow. Isn't this a bit inconsiderate?

"I don't want to lie to Jodine."

"We're not lying, exactly."

"Yes, we are. We didn't tell her that we caused the fire."

I sigh. I had a feeling she was going to give me problems. "Allie, we don't know what caused the fire."

"We don't know *for sure,* but we can make an educated guess."

Yes, I suppose we can. I want to beg her to keep her mouth shut, but I'm not sure if that's the best way to get what I want. She stares out the window and I stare at her socks. They are both black, but one has indented strips and the other doesn't. And she wants to help me with my fashion project? She's wearing two different socks.

"You know it was the cigarette," she says with dread. She leans her back against the wall.

Ah. The cigarette. The cigarette the two of us smoked in the kitchen last night. The cigarette that I threw into the garbage can next to the stove, before we went to bed. The cigarette that probably burned down our kitchen, blackening our walls and lungs all in one shot. "You think it's my fault? That I started the fire?"

"I don't think you meant to start the fire, if that's what you mean. You didn't do it on purpose."

"Gee, thanks. So you don't think I'm a pyro?"

"You did throw the cigarette in the garbage."

"The cigarette I put out." I think.

"Obviously it was still lit."

"Let me get this right. You're saying the fire was all my fault? Let me remind you, you were smoking, too."

"No, it was my fault, too. But not because of the smoking."

"What are you talking about, then? Why was it your fault?"

Her eyes fill and quiver with about-to-overflow tears. "Because…because—" spit it out already! "—because I should have changed the batteries in the smoke detector. If Jay hadn't woken up, we all could have died. And that would have been my fault." Here come the waterworks. Blah blah blah. She blows her nose into the tissue I hand her, and then slides down the wall onto the floor, pulling her knees up into her chest.

I lie facedown on my bed, my neck tilted to the right, facing her. They should really make beds with holes in the center like massage tables, so people don't have to strain their necks. If you like to sleep on your stomach, which I do, you always wake up with a neck ache. Hey, maybe I should get that patented. I could mass-produce the beds and use the money to repair the kitchen. "So what do we do?" I ask.

"We have to tell Jay the truth." She says "the truth" like she's Tom Cruise in *A Few Good Men* and I'm the evil Jack Nicholson shielding himself beneath the military bureaucracy.

"What if she can't handle the truth?"

"That's not the issue. She shouldn't have to worry about all this if she had nothing to do with it."

"You're being too nice. Let me clue you in on a few things. Jodine is in law school. She knows the rules. Why do you think she didn't press for an investigation?"

Confusion overtakes Allie's face. "I don't know. Why?"

"Because she must think she started it." I swear, I'm not just making this up for Allie's sake. It's so possible. "She probably left the stove on."

Allie eyes me doubtfully. "I don't think so."

"Think about it, Allie. If she knew she had nothing to do with it, why would she claim to own the apartment?"

Allie doesn't answer. The computer in her brain is booting, booting…. "I don't know. I just thought she was afraid of Carl."

"But why would she be afraid of Carl if she knew she didn't do anything wrong? She thinks she started the fire, and she thinks that if Carl finds out, he'll hold her personally responsible. Meaning she'd have to foot the bill for the damages."

"But we know she didn't start the fire."

"Do we?"

Allie pauses again. Still booting…. "There was a pot on the stove when we were in there smoking."

Aha! Ding ding! Computer is now on! "There you go. She probably made soup and left the stove on."

"But wouldn't we have felt if the stove was hot?"

"I didn't touch the stove. Did you touch the stove?"

"No, but I think we would have felt it on. We should tell her we know what happened."

"Allie, Allie, Allie. We can't have her calling the police for an investigation, can we?" Except that maybe we'd have to call the firemen again. And Norm…no, remember, money before lust! I've got to save my own ass before I can even consider ogling Norm's. "Think about it," I tell her. "Why else would Jodine claim to own the apartment? So there's no investigator. So she's not found solely responsible. So she can share the cost with the two of us."

Allie kneads through this information, like fingers in a fresh jar of Play-Doh. Poor thing. I honestly hope all this data doesn't cause her head to malfunction. Finally, she nods. "She's trying to screw us."

"Exactly. So why shouldn't we play the same game?"

She looks as though she took off her shoes when she entered a house and then stepped on a thumbtack. "I guess."

"Good. So we're agreed."

She nods.

"You don't say anything about our smoking, and I don't say anything about your knowing that the smoke alarm wasn't working and not telling us or fixing it."

Yeah, I know that's low of me. But drastic times call for drastic measures. And, fuck, this is a drastic time.

"All right." She looks defeated. Her eyes fill with tears again. "Do you think Carl is going to find out and kick us out?"

"No. How can he possibly find out?"

"I have nowhere else to go! This sucks." The tears start rolling down her cheeks.

"Don't cry. Look, it could have been a lot worse. We could all be dead. All we're out is a little bit of cash. How much could it possibly be?"

Maybe Harry's nephew can be persuaded to cut us a discount....

11
ALLIE GETS NAUSEOUS

ALLIE

I notice this guy under a baseball hat, wearing jeans and a navy polar fleece sweatshirt, walking toward me from the opposite end of the street. He stops outside my apartment, looks at something in his hand and rings the bell. Of course, no one answers because I'm still a few houses down. Even though it's only a quarter to one, I assume he's Josh, Harry's nephew, fifteen minutes early.

"Hi," I say, stepping up behind him.

"Hi," he answers, turning around and smiling. "I'm Josh. You must be Emma."

"No, I'm Allie, Emma's roommate."

"Nice to meet you." He shakes my hand with a strong, cold grip. Broad-shouldered, tall, he's exactly as I pictured him. "Sorry I'm early," he says.

"No problem. Sorry I made you wait. The subway took longer than I expected."

I thought Emma's stepmother would offer me a lift, considering she was sitting at home not doing anything, but no. I didn't mind the subway, but walking the rest of the way kind of took the wind out of me. The air has that crisp winter-is-coming-soon feeling, hardening my exposed skin like a clay face mask.

"The walk took less time than I thought," he says, readjusting the Maple Leafs cap on his head.

"Where do you live?"

"Just on the other side of College."

"We're practically neighbors! Did you see the fire trucks?"

"No, but I heard them. It sounded like the entire city was in flames."

"No, just us." I lead him into the apartment and point to the kitchen. "Actually, just *that*. I'll be in my room, if you need anything."

He seems normal. Hopefully he's not here to steal anything. Not that there's much left to steal. Everything should be fine—as long as he really is Josh the repairman, and not Josh the thief/ psycho/rapist/ax-murderer who just happened to be stalking our house when I saw him and invited him inside.

"Josh?" I tentatively walk into the kitchen. He's too cute to be a psycho killer, I decide. Although the guy who played in *American Psycho* was cute and isn't that the whole point? That it's always the cute, normal guy who's the real danger? Actually, I didn't see the movie, but I saw the trailer. I don't like movies I know will give me nightmares, and that one seemed a likely contender. I saw *Silence of the Lambs* on a plane and spent the next two weeks dreaming about men eating me, and not in the good way. (I have done that— I'm not a total prude. Once. I did it once. Or, more accurately, I had it done to me once.) Anyway, I have enough nightmares already, like figuring out how I'm going to pay for this whole mess.

What if Josh—what if his name isn't even Josh?—is hiding in some shadowy crevice, waiting to repeatedly stab me with carving knives? His own carving knives, obviously, since we don't have any working ones anymore. Okay then, what if he's a pervert and is presently in the process of installing hidden cameras in our showerhead?

"In here," he calls from the kitchen. He's on all fours beside the stove, his head tilted toward the ceiling, an expression of concern covering his face. His jeans are faded in the rear, but no butt cleavage, not that I'm looking.

"You okay?" I ask.

"I'm fine. Better than your kitchen."

Crisis averted. He seems like the real thing. "Let me know if you need me," I tell him, and return to my room.

Time to call Clint. I haven't spoken to him since the fire. I left a message at his apartment yesterday, but I didn't want to scare him with the details, so I simply told him to call me back at Emma's. Which he didn't. But that's okay, he was probably too embarrassed to call me there because…well because he doesn't know Emma's family, does he? Anyway, he's probably been busy with work. If I had told him it was an emergency, he would have run over to make sure I was okay.

That's what I should have done. I should have used the word *emergency*. He would have come and taken me back to his place to comfort me. As I cried in horror on his couch he would have gently soothed me while rubbing my back with soft, feathery, loving strokes. Or maybe he would have tucked me under his sheets and like a gentleman offered to sleep on the couch, only to be later awakened by my screaming caused by nightmares of burning toasters. He would have rushed in and asked, "Allie? Are you okay?" And as he wiped the streaming tears off my cheeks I would have said, "Hold me," or something that didn't sound so cheesy even though they always say that in the movies. And then we would have had sex. And fallen madly in love.

I dial his extension. Ringing. Ringing. Ringing…

"Hello, you've reached Clint Webster—" Allie Webster sounds so natural, doesn't it? "I am in the office but away from my desk at the moment. Please leave your name and number and I'll call you back as soon as I have a chance." Beep.

"Hi, it's me. I guess you're still at lunch. I…um…my apartment burned down. It's better, though." Am I a moron? "It was just the kitchen. Anyway, I'm back at the apartment. So call me here. Bye." I hang up the phone and sniff my room, searching for potential smoke damage until Josh calls me into the living room.

"I'm estimating ten," he says, and I'm pretty sure I'm having a heart attack. Really. My right arm gets cold and everything. That's a sure sign of a heart attack, isn't it? Or maybe it's the left arm. Or maybe the arm gets hot. Whatever. I'm breathing all over the place and my heart is doing a bongo thing on its own. I know Norm said it could be up to ten thousand, but that can't be true.

"What? You mean ten hundred?" What is ten hundred? Who says that? I'm not only a moron having a heart attack, I'm a moron having a heart attack who can't count. Please make Josh the repairman mean one thousand.

When he laughs, his eyes crinkle until you can barely see them. Is this funny? Is my heart attack funny?

"Ten thousand," he says. He must realize I'm not kidding, because he flattens out his smile.

"Dollars?" This time I *am* kidding and he smiles again. I can't believe it's actually going to cost that much.

I moan and steady myself on the almost clean-smelling couch pillows. Yesterday, Emma's father sent some sort of specialists into our apartment to dry-clean the couch, the curtains and possibly the air. Twelve hundred dollars later we were allowed to breathe in here without inhaling toxins. Twelve hundred dollars. Twelve hundred dollars plus ten thousand, not ten hundred. And I still have twelve thousand in student loans outstanding. I don't have to know how to count to know that I will never be out of debt. I will spend the rest of my life owing money.

"Are you sure?"

"A hundred percent. You're going to need a new refrigerator, stove, oven, linoleum for the floor, counters, cupboards. And I'll have to replaster the walls and ceiling.... Are you okay? You look like you're going to pass out. Do you want a glass of water or something?"

My breakfast is quickly moving its way back up my digestive track. Josh must notice this happening, because his forehead is all scrunched up with concern. "Okay," I answer in a faint voice that doesn't really sound like mine, but more like one of the singers on *Alvin and the Chipmunks*.

"Okay meaning you're okay, or okay you want water?"

"Water. Please."

Josh disappears into the burnt abyss and I ask myself, how did this happen? Two months ago I lived with my two best friends in a whole apartment, and now I live with scheming crazy women who have burned down my kitchen.

It's coming back up. Breakfast, you've met my mouth before, haven't you? I swallow it back down.

"I'd pour it into a glass," he calls out from the kitchen, "but I don't think you have any left. You'll have to drink from my bottle. I only had one sip from it, so don't worry. I'm healthy. Is that okay?" He walks back into the living room and hands me a bottle of Evian. Fab, no more dishes. That'll be what...another thousand bucks?

I take a long sip of the water. But what's this? The water seems to be going the wrong way. Why is the water going back into the bottle?

"I'm going to throw up," I say, and cover my about-to-explode mouth with my hands. Don't do it. Stop right there. Where do you think you're going? Get back down there! Is it a sign of my insanity that I'm talking to my puke? At least I'm not talking out loud. Am I? If I'm insane, how will I know if I'm talking out loud?

This is so incredibly embarrassing. At least Josh isn't Clint.

He puts his hand on my shoulder and gently holds me up. "I think you should go to the bathroom," he says. He guides me through the hallway, opens the bathroom door and lifts the toilet seat.

The bagel and strawberry jam I ate for breakfast end up in the toilet. Ew. My new best friend Josh is holding my hair, telling me I'll be okay. I haven't thrown up since I got drunk two years ago at a frat party. I hate throwing up. My body feels like an orange being transformed into freshly squeezed juice.

I may never drink orange juice again.

And here's more. Ew.

At least when I do this drunk, I'm not aware of my surroundings. If I were hammered now, I wouldn't care that some strange boy is holding my hair, his hands warm against my neck. I wouldn't care about anything because I'd be too out of it to notice. The worst part about this is that there's no reason for my sickness. None whatsoever. I didn't drink and I didn't eat anything sketchy. In other words, I didn't have a good time. So why am I being punished?

"I'm done." I sit down next to the toilet on the fluffy floor mat. Some of the puke-spiked water is dribbling onto the sleeve of my red sweatshirt, making a dark blue stain on the thigh of my jeans.

"You sure?" he asks, and lets go of my hair.

So. Isn't this an interesting way to get to know one's repairman? I analyze the grout between the floor tiles, to avoid meeting his eye. "I'm sure. Sorry I ruined your water."

"What do you mean? It's still good," he says, his eyes crinkling again.

I try to keep my mouth closed while I laugh so that my puke-smelling breath doesn't gross him out any more than he already is.

"You have a cute laugh," he says.

I pretend to scratch the bridge of my nose while I talk so that my hands can serve as a breath-buffer. "I hate my laugh. I sound like a hyena."

"No. It's cute."

Is he flirting with me? Am I sitting on the bathroom floor covered in puke while a repairman is flirting with me?

"This fire really got to your stomach, eh?" he says, looking at me with wide, concerned eyes.

I think he's flirting.

"I guess. Or maybe I have the flu." I should just stand up and brush my teeth.

"You're not pregnant, are you?"

I'm pretty sure you still have to have sex these days to get pregnant, but you never know. Maybe it is morning sickness and I'm carrying Jesus II. "Hope not," I say so he doesn't think I'm some sort of virgin freak. "There's not too much space for a baby in this apartment, in case you haven't noticed. Especially an apartment with no kitchen." I'm now rubbing the skin between my lip and nose, in order to appear to have an excuse to buffer my disgusting breath.

"Ouch. Let me see your hands."

Why is everyone so obsessed with my nails? Woohoo, I bite my nails, big deal. Now what? Do I hide my fingers behind my back and let him smell the grossness emitting from my mouth, or do I let him see my disgusting bloody hands? No, wait. Faulty logic!

Either way, I'm leaving my mouth exposed, so I might as well hide my hands behind my back.

"I used to bite mine," he says. "Then I joined the NBA."

"I don't follow basketball."

He laughs. "No, I mean Nail Biters Anonymous. And I'm kidding. Hello, my name is Josh and I'm a nail-biter? Give it a try. It works."

I unhide my hands and stretch my fingers. "You really stopped?"

"Yeah."

"How?"

"Polish."

"French manicure?"

"No smart-ass, the clear, bad-tasting kind."

"Been there, done that."

"Didn't work?"

"No, it did. For about two months. Then one broke," I tell Josh, "and it was over. It's like when you're on a diet and you break it with one piece of cake. You figure you might as well eat the whole thing. After I broke one nail, they all looked uneven, so I figured I'd bite them all just a little bit, to make them more the same length. I bit a little off one, and a little off another, and a little more off another one…maybe it's easier for guys because your nails are supposed to be short." Suddenly I sniff and remember where we are. "I think we can go back to the living room now."

"You sure you're okay?"

"Yeah." I hold up my hand for him to pull me up.

He looks at me peculiarly.

"It's not contagious," I say. "Help me up."

He grabs my hands and pulls, and I nearly smash into him. Smiling, he returns to the living room. I brush my teeth and then join him. As I plop down on the couch, I find myself staring into the blackened kitchen.

He sits down next to me and folds his hands behind his head. "Repeat after me, it's just a kitchen. It's just a kitchen."

"It's just a kitchen. A ten-thousand-dollar kitchen. Ten thousand dollars we don't have."

Josh suddenly looks uncomfortable. I suppose it's not good practice to tell your repairman you can't pay him. That's like a manicurist telling her client she's run out of nail polish. He readjusts his cap. It has one of those perfect arcs on the rim. How do guys get it that perfect?

What are we going to do? How are we going to pay him? I feel the need to reassure him. "I'm sure we'll come up with the money. Not sure how, though. Any ideas how we can repay you?" I look up at him and he's squirming and fidgeting with his cap. Why does he look so weirded out? All I asked was how we could repay him—

Oh, God. He thinks I'm prostituting myself for the kitchen. "I so didn't mean that the way it came out. I don't mean that I'll pay you in…I mean…we just don't have the money right now. But we will. Have the money. To pay you with."

Moron prostitute who can't count.

His eyes crinkle again. "You scared me for a minute." Now he looks flustered. "Not scared me because the idea of you and me…I mean…" This is getting worse by the second. "Not that I was thinking of sleeping with you." He laughs. "Yes, I'd like some salt with that foot. Thanks."

I laugh and relax. "I'm not a bartering type of girl, anyway."

"No, but my job would certainly be more interesting if all the pretty girls I did work for offered to pay me with sexual favors."

I feel my cheeks turning a shade of fuchsia. I'm not sure one should be having this type of conversation with a strange man in an empty apartment. Too bad Emma isn't here. She'd enjoy this kind of thing. I bet she'd like his broad shoulders, his tall, lean, muscular body, although I'm not sure if he's exactly her type. Nick has a lot more gel in his hair. As far as I can remember, anyway, from the one time he came with Emma to the apartment and from that picture Emma has hidden in her panty drawer. Not that I was snooping. I never snoop. I just ran out of socks and she has so many cool ones in different designs and colors and I knew she wouldn't notice if I borrowed one pair.

I never realized handcuffs came in so many colors and sizes.

Forget Emma. Josh doesn't seem like the tight black pants, black silk shirt, black leather jacket in the summer, purple-tinted sunglasses at night type of guy. But who knows what he wears when he's not fixing kitchens?

Maybe Jodine will like him. Not sure what the story is with her and Manny.

I'd probably be interested in Josh myself, if I weren't already in love. I'll tell you one thing, though. I bet that my unbroken hymen is worth a lot more than theirs, if we *were* in the bartering business.

"Thank you," I say. He *did* call me pretty.

"You're welcome. I gotta tell you, you don't look like you're old enough to drink, never mind barter yourself."

I get this a lot. Not the bit about bartering, but the drinking part. Not sure if it's my height or my baby fat, but I get carded at every bar I go to. And the drinking age in Toronto is nineteen. "How old do I look?"

"Seventeen?"

"Great. Thanks. I'm twenty-two."

"Close."

"What close? It's a huge difference."

"You'll appreciate it when you're older."

"And there's an original line. Where did you read that, in *Clichés Unlimited?*"

Josh laughs, and I ask, "How old are *you?*"

"How old do *I* look?"

I study his skin for signs. It doesn't look old-leathery or anything like that. No laugh lines around his brownish-greenish eyes. No hair in his ears, either. (A sign of age, though not entirely accurate. If it were a true sign, my dad would be a gazillion years old. Honestly, a person could make braids from the growth in his ears.) Josh is under thirty for sure. No zits, either, so that takes him out of the early twenties.

"Take off your hat," I say.

"Why?"

"I have to check for gray and balding, just to be sure my assessment is correct."

A light brown curl flops onto his forehead as he removes his hat. He lifts his fist to his chin in a mock pose. "See? No balding. There've been a few gray strands, but they've been appropriately dealt with." His thick hair curls just above his ears, which look shiny. Shiny probably because they've been under a hat all day. But no hair inside these ears. Definitely no hair.

"If you pluck them, they grow back in pairs." I'm referring to the gray, of course.

"What pluck? Men don't pluck."

"Of course not. I'm sure your grays fall out naturally." I take his hat and play with it in my hand. "How do you get the arc so perfectly bent?"

"Do you mean the beak?" he asks, looking at the rounded sun visor.

"Is that what it's called? A beak?"

"I think so. That's what I call it. I bend the beak into a circle—"

he demonstrates for my benefit "—and then stick the beak between the strap and the semicircle for a while until it's set."

"Twenty-seven," I interrupt.

"Twenty-six." He adjusts his cap yet one more time and puts it back onto his head. "Not bad. You have excellent age-estimating skills."

"Thank you. Now, if I can develop my moneymaking skills, we'll all be good."

"We meaning you and Emma?"

"Me, Emma and Jodine. Three girls living on three meager budgets." Why am I telling him all this?

"What about your parents? Can't they help?"

No way. They'd give me the money, I'm sure. They've never said no to anything I've ever asked for, but that's why I try not to ask for a lot. For one thing, they're still paying off my brother's wedding. Besides, they didn't want me to come to the big, bad city to begin with. How can I admit they were right? "I don't want to worry them," I say. It's not that I don't want to fill him in with family history, but even if he's not a thief/psycho/rapist/ax-murderer psycho, he doesn't need to know that my parents are a viable option, even though, as far as I'm concerned, they're so definitely not.

"Are you still in school?" he asks.

"I graduated last year."

"What do you do now?"

"Telefundraise."

"Tele-what? You're a telemarketer?"

"No I am most certainly *not*. I call alumni and ask for donations to OU."

"You sell steak knives, don't you?"

"Fifteen dollars a piece," I joke. "And they were all in my kitchen drawer." Actually, their blades are still there, but the handles have disintegrated. "So what school did you go to?" I ask, and then feel instantly horrible. He's a repairman. He probably didn't go to school. What a snob I am, assuming everyone went to college.

"I'm still in school."

"Really?" Okay, so now I'm a snob for assuming all repairmen don't go to school. "Where?"

"OU. In May, you get to sell me steak knives."

"What are you studying?"

"Philosophy."

"Part-time, I guess?"

"Yeah."

"How long have you been at it?"

"About seven years."

"Wow. How come you wanted to stretch it out?"

"After high school, I traveled for a few years and then—"

"Where did you go?"

"Australia. Asia."

"Lucky. And after that?"

"I did a semester at school, but I decided I wanted to work, too. Harry offered me a part-time job, so now I work for him three days a week and take classes Tuesdays and Thursdays."

"Good for you. So tell me, what do you want to do with your degree?"

"What do you mean?"

"What do you want to do for a living?"

"I like what I do for a living."

Open mouth, insert sock with hole in it. "Of course. But you don't exactly need a philosophy degree to hone your skills, do you?"

"No, you don't, but I'm not going to school to help me get a job."

"That's probably a good thing, considering I've found it doesn't help."

"What, you don't want to sell steak knives forever?"

"Not quite."

"What do you want to do?"

Marry Clint? Is that a career? "Not sure," I answer. I have no idea what I want to do to make money, and it's starting to make me nervous. "Why don't you open your own repair company? I'll cold-call strangers and get you clients."

"Sounds like a plan. What did you study?"

"Humanities," I answer. "A little of everything. A little history, a little literature, a little philosophy." I'm a well-rounded person, I almost say but don't. I don't want to draw any attention to my few extra pounds. "I have to tell you, I'm not crazy about philosophy. I think philosophy is like a novel without the good parts."

"How's that?"

"It's so dry. A good book tries to get across the same message, but jazzes it up a bit. Like when I was younger and I couldn't swallow pills. My mother would crush them up and mix them with jam."

"Got it," he says. "You're funny." He laughs and shakes his head.

Funny, eh? The telephone rings, interrupting the conversation. Clint! It's Clint! "Excuse me for a sec.... Hello?" I say while holding my breath, and let me tell you, it's no easy feat to do both at the same time.

"Hey! You okay?" a deep male voice asks.

Clint! It's Clint! "Hi, Clint!" About time! He probably just got back from lunch and was so concerned, he called me right away. "I'm fine. It was a bit nuts, but everything is going to be fine. I was at Emma's yesterday while they cleaned the apartment."

"Crazy girl! You should have called me earlier."

I knew it! I knew it! If I had left him a message, he would have instructed me to come over right away so he could take care of me. Right now I could be lounging in a pair of his jogging pants. Hmm, I did call him, didn't I? Maybe not. Hmm. Idea! Maybe I should tell him I still can't stay here. Forget idea. I already told him everything was fine. Stupid, stupid, stupid.

"Sorry," I say. Why am I telling him I'm sorry? Never mind, I have another idea. "The repairman is here now doing an estimate. Maybe I'll come over for dinner? My kitchen is still off-limits."

"Oh. Uh, okay. Meet me at my place after work."

"Great. Your place at seven. Thanks. Everything all right with you?"

"I had a pain-in-the-ass day. Really awful. I'll tell you all about it later."

Dinner at Clint's! "Can't wait. See you later."

"Bye." He hangs up the phone.

"Sorry," I say to Josh, who is still sitting on the couch next to me. "Back to the kitchen."

"Yes, back to the kitchen."

"Is it still ten thousand?"

"Unfortunately."

"Okay. I need to discuss options with my roommates. When can you start once we've figured out how we're going to pay?"

"I can start on Wednesday. First I'm going to need to order some parts."

Parts? He needs to order an entire culinary mall. "That sounds fine. Can we pay you in installments?"

Dinner at Clint's dinner at Clint's dinner at Clint's...

"A hundred percent. But I'm going to start with the floor so

I'll need at least two grand up front to start ordering the parts." He shrugs his shoulder apologetically. "Sorry."

Two grand! I hope the other girls have some Houdini money. My account is as well-rounded as my education, only in the former case I mean one big, fat zero. "Why don't I call you tomorrow with an update?"

"Sure. It was nice meeting you, Allie."

"Hmm? Oh. You, too." I'm glad we have such a nice guy working with us. "Bye." I'm about to close the door.

"Don't you want my number?"

Right. Earth to Allie. I grab a piece of paper and a pen, and hand it to him. He puts the paper against the wall and starts to write out his number. Halfway through, the ink runs dry. "I hate when that happens. They should make pens that work upside down. Can I use your back?"

I turn around and bend over. The pen tickles through my sweatshirt.

"Allie?"

Dinner at Clint's dinner at Clint's dinner at Clint's…

"Yes?"

"Until your kitchen is ready, you're more than welcome to eat at my place. I live pretty close by. I'll write down the address. Invitation's open. Anytime."

Dinner at Clint's dinner at Clint's dinner at Clint's…

"Thanks. I appreciate the offer. Have a good day."

"You, too."

I close the door and look at the paper. He wrote his name, number and address all in caps. I drop the paper onto the table.

Dinner at Clint's dinner at Clint's dinner at Clint's…

12

TUESDAY 7:00 A.M.:
NOTE TAPED TO INSIDE
OF FRONT DOOR
(NOT TO REFRIGERATOR
FOR OBVIOUS REASONS)

Who: Allie and Emma

What: House Meeting

When: Today 8:00 pm

Where: Living Room

Why? To discuss following agenda

> *1. What new appliances need to be purchased/rented*
> *2. How to best utilize our remaining apartment space*
> *3. Plans on how to raise the enormous amount of*
> *money we now owe*

Food: Pizza to be ordered

Don't be late.

Jodine

13
JODINE WORKS IT

JODINE

Five more minutes on the treadmill. That's it. Then I must stop. There are fifteen minutes left on the timer, but I have to stop with ten minutes left or I'll be late for my own meeting. I spent the morning preparing for this meeting. I researched prices for kitchen appliances, drew loose floor plans and brainstormed moneymaking schemes.

Who knew Emma would have been the go-getter of the group and close the kitchen door—while I fell apart? I'm a total embarrassment.

1.   I am an embarrassment to the field of law. What kind a lawyer am I going to make if I fail to follow the terms of my own lease? It specifically states that I am responsible to purchase insurance. And did I get insurance? No. Did I even remember that it was in the lease? No. How am I going to succeed if I can't even align myself with the right side of the law? I'm a driving instructor who blows past a stop sign. An aerobics instructor who trips over her own steps. A Weight Watchers employee who weighs three hundred pounds.

2.   I am an embarrassment to humanity. What kind of person doesn't take responsibility for her actions and makes her innocent

roommates struggle to pay for her crimes? A terrible kind. An awful, disgusting, horrendous person.

Right foot, left foot, right foot, left foot. Breathe in. Breathe out. Three minutes left, then I go. I increase the incline and add a touch of oomph to my arm swing. This is painful. But I deserve pain.

Beep. Beep, beep, beep. The treadmill hums as it creaks and tilts vertically. I should be doing a full forty-minute workout. I'll have to jog around my apartment to make up the lost time.

One minute left. Or eleven, technically, but I can do only one. Left foot right foot left foot right foot. My extra-long shoelace has unraveled and is now a bright white snakelike blemish against the black-faced fake rubber treadmill mountain. They're white because they're new—I buy a new pair of running shoes every six months. You're supposed to. Running shoes lose all their support when they're at the mature segment in their life cycle. When I was in college I earned an aerobics instructor's certificate, so I know these things.

I didn't get certified so I could *teach* aerobics. Do I look like I could be an aerobics instructor? Do I have Farrah Fawcett hair or *Flashdance* leg warmers? I don't think so. I got certified, one, so I could understand what I was doing with my body, and two, so I could be well-rounded (mentally, obviously) and get into law school. Thirty more seconds.

I grab onto the handlebars, step off the moving floor, retie my laces and jump back on in one quick motion. But my assigned workout time is over! I wasted too much time! I can't stop now. My legs will inflate into masses of flab.

Three more minutes. And then I'll quit. When the timer flashes seven minutes left, I'll step down. There won't be time for a cool-down. Who cares about the cool-down, anyway? You barely burn any calories in the cool-down. When I used to do the Jane Fonda videos, I would fast-forward the warm-up and skip the cool-down, using the saved time to do the high-impact segments twice.

I increase the incline another level. The soles of my shoes squeak against the rubber.

The cold air feels like a car air conditioner on full blast against my sweaty skin. It's five past eight. I sprint toward the house. I'm late. I'm always late. Not horribly late, but late. But there's always too much to do. How can someone who makes constant lists be so terrible at managing time? But how is my whole day supposed to fit into a measly twenty-four hours? It makes no sense. And why did I say eight? I could have asked to meet at eight-thirty, or nine, but I randomly chose eight. I suppose if I had said eight-thirty, I would have arrived at eight-forty-five. If I had said nine, I would have arrived at nine-fifteen, and so on. Definitely, I should have made the meeting for later on; I wouldn't have had to cut short my workout. Besides, I don't even have plans for later this evening—Manny, of course, tried to book me up, but I think I'm Manny-ed out for the next few days. Possibly for the next year. Although…I make a mental list of why having Manny around is not as terrible as the apocalypse.

1.   This is not permanent. I will be moving back to New York in May.

2.   Being back together will positively influence my grade-point average and ensure that it does not drop below a B.

3.   If he dislikes me I will have to make new friends to sit with in class. There is no time for that.

4.   Summer is over. It is too late to find another warm body for the winter.

5. He thinks I am the sexiest woman in the world. He says that. Constantly.

6. I had nowhere to sleep while my apartment was toxic. It's only for a few months. What's a few months?

By the time I reach my apartment, I'm hot and sweaty and mildly out of breath. It's eight-fifteen. As I turn my key in the lock I hear laughing inside. "So sorry I'm late," I say, running into the living room.

"No prob," Allie says, and bends her head backward over the back of the couch. Her hair touches the wooden floor and picks up a dust bunny. Disgusting. She needs a haircut. "We ordered already. We got a large half plain and half pepperoni. Is that okay?"

No, it is not. I like vegetarian pizza. Why would anyone prefer plain? There's nothing healthy about plain at all. And pepperoni? Do they know how many grams of fat are in a single slice? They couldn't wait an extra fifteen minutes to order? They had to order precisely at eight?

I smile. Grimly. "No *prob.*"

Sniff, sniff. I smell smoke. Emma is sprawled on the couch, her feet resting across Allie's thighs. A cigarette floats in a glass half filled with water. Is that my bathroom cup? A gray ash is polluting the vessel I drink out of. Disgusting. Unbelievable. She'd better plan on giving that glass a solid detox.

She looks far too content in her position to have just recently sunk her tush into the pillows. My bet is that she has recently violated the stand-by-the-window-while-smoking agreement as she has many times before.

"What is *that?*" I ask, pointing to a large silver microwave perched on the coffee table. "It looks like something beamed out of *Star Trek.*"

"It's a cooking mechanism used to warm up food," Emma says, and Allie giggles.

"Yes, thanks. And where did it come from?"

"I bought it," Emma says.

Bought it? Bought it? Who said she could buy it? I have a list, dammit, a list! A microwave was not number one on my list! "Is this its home? It seems somewhat out of place blocking the television, don't you think?"

"Do you have a better idea?" Emma asks, shrugging her shoulders.

"The kitchen table, maybe?" The kitchen table, or more accurately, the living room table, is still a pile of milk crates. And we still have no chairs.

"The plug is too far from the table. We tried it," Allie says. "Anyway, it doesn't block the TV when you're sitting on the couch."

Great. Now we have a kitchen table in the middle of the living room that we can't even use because we have no kitchen chairs, and we can't even dump things on it that come equipped with a wire since there's no outlet nearby to plug anything in. "Did anyone think of an extension cord? Hello?"

They look at each other as if I'm talking Swahili. When did they become best friends, exactly? Did I miss something? "It looks kind of awkward," I say.

"So does our kitchen," Emma says. "The microwave is fine here. It makes making popcorn convenient."

Well, fine then. "Where's Fish?"

"On the television," Allie says.

Yes. Yes, he is. He's swimming around in circles totally unaware that his surroundings have changed. I slide into the recliner and bend my legs to the right in a side crunch. I remove my notepad from my schoolbag. "Okay. The first issue I'd like to discuss is appliances. I see a microwave has been taken care of." I tick off the word microwave in number two. "How much did you spend?"

Emma pauses in thought. "Two-fifty."

For that price, there'd better be at least three other microwaves hiding somewhere. And it should at least transform into a freezer when a combination secret code is typed in. "Why on earth was it so expensive?"

"Because I didn't want to get a cheap one," she says, flipping her hair. "If it's our only workable kitchen appliance, it should probably be top quality."

I am positive that a one-hundred-dollar microwave would have nuked our frozen leftover food just as well. "I think we should return it. I saw perfectly acceptable microwaves for a hundred dollars on the Net."

"It was on sale. I can't return it."

"Two hundred and fifty dollars and it was on sale? Is it a magic microwave? Did Elvis use it?"

Allie runs her fingers through her dust-bunny-infested hair. "I don't think Elvis was alive when microwaves were created."

I ignore her and return to my list. "I found an agency that rents kitchen appliances to students." I take the carefully folded rip-off phone number out of the zippered compartment of my schoolbag and place it on top of the microwave. "I saw the flyer on a bulletin board at school. I was going to suggest we rent a mini fridge and microwave, but you seem to have taken care of the microwave—"

"So how are we going to raise this money?" Emma interrupts.

"We'll get to it. It's on the list," I explain. Why isn't she letting me go through the list? I should have made photocopies so that they could follow along without continuous interruptions.

"I think we should talk about money," Allie says to Emma.

Emma nods.

I roll my eyes. "Okay. Let's talk about money." Breathe in. Breathe out. One foot at a time.

"Are we going to get kicked out of the apartment?" Allie asks, frowning.

"I thought you wanted to talk about money!" What's wrong with these people?

Allie wraps her arms around herself. "I just want to know if you guys think we're going to get kicked out. Because I have nowhere to stay in Toronto and getting kicked out would really suck."

Emma pats Allie's arm. "We're not going to get kicked out. Carl doesn't know what happened. Carl is never going to know what happened. We're going to design the kitchen to look exactly like our old kitchen. I'm good with designing, remember? I'll make a sketch for Harry's nephew. We're not getting kicked out."

"Stop worrying, Allie." I'm worried enough for the both of us, anyway. I feel like a deceitful parent telling a child, yes dear, the tooth fairy exists only if you believe in her. "Back to money. What do we owe Josh?"

"Two thousand," Allie says. "And that's just the deposit."

"And we owe twelve hundred to my dad." Emma closes her eyes as though she's visualizing each dollar. "Oh, and you two owe me two hundred and fifty for the microwave."

"What are you talking about?" I ask, and her eyes flutter open.

"My father paid to have our apartment dry-cleaned. You know? So we could sit in here?"

Fine. Although I'm sure her father in his Rosedale mansion can wait a few months for his twelve hundred dollars. But the Special Edition microwave? "You think we're splitting the two-hundred-and-fifty-dollar microwave with you?"

"We're all going to use it," Allie points out.

"But who keeps it afterward?"

"We'll worry about afterward, *afterward*," Emma says. "Did Josh say how long the construction would take?" she asks Allie.

Does she have ADD? Why does she keep jumping from one idea to another?

"He can't order the parts unless he has at least two grand up front. So it depends how long it takes for us to come up with the money."

"We're going to need to buy insurance, too," I say. "That'll be a few hundred dollars at least."

Emma shakes her head. "That's a waste of money. What are the chances we have another fire? That money could be better used—"

I silence her with an icy look. "We're buying insurance. End of story."

"Okay, big shot, what kind of money do you have put away?" Emma asks me.

My savings? I don't think so. "I have enough to cover my rent for a year. That's it. What about the two of you?"

"Forget it." Allie shakes her head. "I'm barely covering my living expenses."

"I don't have any extra cash, either," Emma declares.

Then why did she come home with two new bags of clothes last week? "What about your dad?" I ask her.

"What about *your* dad?"

My dad? Please. Her father lives in a Rosedale palace, and my parents haven't paid off their mortgage. "I'm not asking my parents. It's our problem."

"And I'm not asking my dad," Emma says. "Allie?"

"My parents? No way. I'm not even telling them about the fire. They'd drive up tomorrow, kidnap me and take me home."

"So what do we do?" I ask.

Silence. Emma's eyes are closed again and it's driving me mad.

"Come up with ways to make the money?" Allie looks to us for confirmation. Eyes closed, Emma blindly nods in agreement.

"And how do you propose we do that exactly?" I ask.

"Bake sale?" Allie suggests. Seriously. That's what she says.

I rub my hands over my eyes in despair. "Brilliant idea, Al. At fifty cents a piece we only have to sell twenty-four thousand cookies."

Allie flushes. "I was kidding. Get it? We have no kitchen."

A joke. Allie is making a joke. "Sorry."

"Whatever." She inserts her thumb into her mouth. "What about a garage sale?"

I can't watch her bite her nails right now. I just can't. It's too disgusting. Her teeth grip onto a piece of raised skin and she rips it off. No, I can't watch. I'm going to be sick. "Can you not do that?"

Allie's teeth freeze in mid-chomp. "Not do what?"

"That. Bite. Disfigure yourself. It's disgusting."

Emma snorts and opens her eyes. "Why do you care?"

I shake my head. "It sickens me. I can't help it."

Allie flushes bright red and places both her hands behind her back. "I'll stop. I want to stop, anyway. I don't even realize when I'm doing it."

"How do you not realize?" I ask. "I can't focus on anything but it." I rub my eyes as though trying to wipe away the sight of Allie's fingers. Actually, it's Emma's cigarette that has made my eyes itchy.

"Okay, okay."

"I think you should get a tongue ring," Emma tells Allie.

Allie looks horrified. "Why?"

"Because then you'll play with it instead," she explains.

What does that have to do with anything? "I don't think it's healthy to play with your tongue ring," I say. "A tongue ring would look ridiculous on her. Nothing about Allie says tongue ring."

Emma nods. "But that's what would make it so cool. She looks innocent, but then she opens her mouth and wham-oh. Plus supposedly it leads to great blow jobs."

Allie looks slightly less horrified. "Does it hurt?" she asks.

This is ridiculous. Allie in a tongue ring would be ridiculous. "Can we discuss mutilating Allie's extremities another time, please?"

Emma closes her eyes again and takes a deep breath. "I don't think your garage sale idea is that bad."

"It's not that great, either. We don't have too much stuff worth selling." I pick up the pen and paper. "Okay, number one. Garage sale. What do we have to sell?"

"I have books," Allie offers, raising her fingers into her mouth again. Awareness sparks on her face, and she pulls her finger out before she can do any real damage and, mirroring my movement, raises her hand to her eye and rubs. "Uh-oh."

What now? "What?" I ask.

"I think I just rubbed my contact off," she says, prodding her index finger into the inside corner of her eye. "I can't see out of my right eye. I hate when this happens."

"Where is it?" Emma asks, searching between her couch-matching purple throw pillows.

"In my eye." Allie blinks and shoves her face toward me. "Do you see it?"

"Where am I looking? What am I looking for?" I place one hand on her cheek and one on her nose.

"In the inside corner, I think. I can feel it. Do you see it?" She spreads her eyelid with her index and thumb fingers and looks downward. All I see is white eyeball.

This is absolutely revolting. "I don't see anything, Al. I'm not even sure what I'm looking for. Why don't you let it sit for a few minutes and then maybe it will go back to normal."

"You think?"

"What do I know about contacts? I have perfect vision."

"It will come out by itself," Emma says with authority. "I once lost a condom inside. I swear I thought it had disintegrated, but the next morning, plop, there it was, on my inner thigh."

"You think it's the same thing?" Allie asks.

"I can sell old clothes," Emma says, returning us to the more pressing issue. "Clothes I don't wear anymore. Jodine?"

I don't have extra clothes. I can't just start giving stuff away. Maybe my parents have some extra stuff. I shrug. "We can sell Fish. I don't know. Let me look through my parents' house."

The buzzer rings.

"Pizza!" Allie jumps off the couch, her right hand over her eye. What if she needs to get an eye patch? Will men find it sexy? It would certainly dilute her innocent look. It would match with the tongue ring. "Ten bucks each, please," she says.

A thirty-dollar pizza? Is the crust laced with caviar? We exchange money for food and place the pizza box beside the microwave.

I unsuccessfully try to locate a source of napkins. I run into the bathroom for toilet paper. I pick up a slice of plain and blot the pizza.

"What are you doing?" Emma asks.

Blot, blot. "It's too oily." The blotting isn't working. I remove the cheese and deposit it on my napkin.

"Really? I think it's de-lish," Allie says.

At least she's eating something besides her fingers.

"What's our next idea?" I ask, attempting not to make oil fingerprints on the paper. "Come on. Let's brainstorm. No idea is a bad idea," I say, mimicking Mr. Polanski, my tenth-grade English teacher, who wore thick blue undershirts under his translucent white shirts, which was most definitely a bad idea.

"We should start a delivery service," Allie says, still playing with her eye.

"We only have one car. We wouldn't get a lot of business," I remark.

I pull a wrapped chocolate pumpkin from the pizza bag and an idea hits me. "Maybe we can carve Halloween pumpkins?" I toss the pumpkin at Emma's lap. "You're an arty person. You can come up with the creative designs."

"I'm allergic to pumpkins," she says. "Pumpkins and the cold."

Pumpkins and the cold? What kind of person is allergic to pumpkins and the cold? How is one allergic to the cold? We live in Canada. What does that mean? She's a walking hive from November to March? Sorry, October to May? "Speaking of which, it's boiling in here," I say. "Can we open the window? Maybe we can get rid of the smoke smell."

Allie jumps up and opens the window. "What if we offer to take kids trick-or-treating? Like a baby-sitting service for Halloween?"

"Speaking of tricks, what if we become call girls? We can turn our apartment into a brothel," Emma says.

Allie and I are silent. We stare at her openmouthed.

"Relax, I'm kidding."

I don't truly believe her.

"Although we could make about three hundred dollars a pop. How are you girls at lap dances?"

"No," I say.

"Bikini car washes?" Emma suggests.

"Next idea?" I say.

"I thought no idea was a bad idea."

"None except that one. Anything else we can do for Halloween?"

"I know!" Allie says, her left hand fluttering above her and her right hand pushing on the inside of her eye. "A Halloween party!"

"I love it!" Emma squeals.

Not a bad idea. Everyone likes a good party. I write "Halloween party" and underline it in red in my notebook. "Where? Here?"

"Here? No. Think big or get out of the kitchen," Emma says. Allie laughs.

Is that even an expression? "How much can we make? If we can get two hundred people to come and we charge five dollars a head, we'll only make a thousand."

Emma starts snapping her fingers in excitement. "So we'll charge seven dollars a head. And get four hundred people to come."

"That's less than three thousand dollars. We need at least twelve thousand."

Emma's beat is getting faster. "So we'll have four parties. One at Halloween, one at Christmas, one at New Year's and one on Valentine's Day. And maybe one on April Fools. We can use that money to go to Greece or something."

"I'm not sure if April Fools is a national holiday," I comment.

Allie claps her hands. "Who cares! Think of the crazy decorations. We can hang everything upside down."

Are they starting a band here? Should I start humming? "Who do we suppose is going to pay to come to our party?" I ask.

Allie picks up another piece of pizza. She's eaten more than both Emma and I put together. "Our friends," she says, exposing chewed cheese and tomato sauce.

"What friends? You're going to charge Clint a hundred and thirty-three times?" I ask slightly viciously, and then feel responsible for the wounded expression on her face.

"I have other friends," Allie answers, looks at Emma and rolls her eyes.

Are they rolling their eyes at me? I'm exasperating them?

"Don't be a bitch," Emma says to me.

My neck muscles tense. I need a massage. Where's Manny when I need him? "Fine. I'm speaking solely for myself," I say. "I don't think I have a hundred and thirty-three friends to invite."

Emma squints at me. "How many people are at your law school?"

I see where she's going and I don't like it one bit. They're going to make me invite people I go to school with to this party. "I don't know."

"Over four hundred?"

"I suppose so. I'd estimate the total count at around four hundred and fifty."

"Then all you need is to convince a third of the students to come. And if that third each brings a date or a friend, we meet most of our goal."

Allie takes another bite of her pizza and claps with the slice still in her hand. "And you know what? If the undergrads hear that the law school kids are going, they'll for sure want to come."

Did she just say law school *kids?* Should we ask our parents to sign permission slips before attending as well? Will there be milk and cookies?

"Okay. Tomorrow we need to find a bar to hold these parties. Who's coming with me?" Emma asks.

Allie bounces in her seat. "Me! Me! What time?"

"I'd say the best time is around seven. The manager of the place

I have in mind will be there, but there won't be any customers, so he can talk to us. We have to find a cool place that will let us keep the cover."

Disappointment clouds Allie's face. "I'm working. Can't we go tonight?"

"I don't feel like going tonight," Emma says.

I shake my head in disbelief. "You're going to convince a manager to let us take the entire cover?"

"I'm an excellent presenter. Yesterday I somehow convinced the editors to do a two-page spread on thigh-high boots."

"Was that your presentation?" Allie asks, blinking frantically. "How were you?"

"Brilliant, obviously."

"Obviously," I say. But I've seen some of Emma's techniques for persuasion and they are often borderline whorish. "I'd better go with you."

Allie fidgets with the corner of her eye. "I think I'm going blind."

"You're not going blind," I tell her. "If that's it for tonight, let's meet again tomorrow. I want to finish my workout."

"I'm going out for a bit," Emma says. "Anyone wanna come?"

"I do." Allie frowns. "But I can't put in another contact until I get this one out. And my glasses are hideous."

"Okay. See you guys later." Emma rolls off the couch.

"Wait, guys?" Allie whines.

"Yes?" I ask.

"So you're sure we're not going to get kicked out of here, right?"

"Stop being annoying, Allie," Emma says, kisses Allie on the forehead and then disappears into her room.

I decide to ignore her as well. "It's freezing in here," I say. "Allie, can you close the window?"

"Why don't you just start the microwave? That should warm us up."

An appliance that heats up a room and makes popcorn simultaneously? It should, for two hundred and fifty dollars.

14
ALLIE GOES NUTS

ALLIE

It's eleven-thirty and I've been standing in front of the bathroom mirror, my neck awkwardly tilted toward my reflection, my butt sticking out behind me, trying to get this stupid, frustrating contact out of my eye for the past two hours. I can feel it in the right corner, thick and jarring, and what if I can never get it out, what if I have to feel this horrible annoyance forever and can never put in another pair of contacts? My eye is blotchy from the constant prodding and I'm trying to squeeze it out as though it's the last drop of conditioner in the bottle and I've already left it upside down for ten minutes and still nothing is coming out. I'm squeezing my eye I'm squeezing I'm squeezing, and is that it? Did I get it? I think I see something! Rats. It's gone. I lost it. I want to go to sleep. But what if closing my eyes drives it to the back of my brain? What if it pierces important veins and makes me blind and I wake up feeling like I'm wearing one of those eye masks people wear on airplanes, except I'm not on an airplane, I'm blind in my bed and I can't ever watch TV again and I have to read books that have been translated into braille? Why did I rub my eyes when I'm wearing contacts? Why, why, why? Is that it? Did I feel it? I think I felt it. I think it was some sort of bump in the left corner. It's moved! It's migrated! This is it! This is not it.

My neck hurts, my arms hurt, my back hurts and my head hurts from being able to see only out of one eye and I'm getting dizzy. Can't one of my roommates help? Or at least watch to make sure I don't fall down from dizziness, knock my head on the corner of the counter and bleed to death? Is this ever going to end? Am I going insane? Why can't I find it? I want to sleep. I hate this. Where is it?

Is that it? I think it is. Careful…don't want to scare it. I'm touching it. Got it. Moving it to the left. Gently. Gentle. There it is, a thin piece of plastic-ish material all squashed and mangled in my eye. I pick it out with my thumb and index finger and drop it into my hand. It un-crumples as I squeeze solution on it, like the white wrapper that comes on fast-food restaurant straws that I squish off and then watch expand as I aim a drop of orange juice on it.

I dump the offensive contact in its case.

Thank God Clint won't have to see me in my glasses. Although he was wearing his glasses when I went for dinner yesterday. And sweatpants and an old sweatshirt. But he still looked cute. He looked like he was ready to cuddle. But his roommate hung out with us the entire night, so there couldn't be any cuddling. I bet he was planning a night alone for us, and then his roommate showed up unexpectedly and ruined everything. Oh, well. Next time.

Bedtime!

I tiptoe into my room because Jodine is already asleep and she gets really pissed off when I wake her up and——

A small gray blob scurries along the hallway, into the burnt kitchen.

Could it be I've damaged my eye and now it's playing tricks?

The small gray blob is squeaking.

Ewwwwwwwwww.

15
EMMA DEALS

EMMA

"Do you know what a blind spot is?" Miss Know-it-all asks after a blue BMW honks when I cut him off.

I'm going to kill Jodine. Fuck. I'm afraid I may swerve into a brick wall in order to squash my passenger side. I wish I had a James Bond car and could eject her. She's been at this all day: "I don't think that stop sign was a suggestion" or "Are you aware that there's a speed limit here?" Blah blah blah.

"Yes, I know what a blind spot is," I say.

"Do you know you're supposed to look at it? To make sure there are no other cars coming?"

"We should have taken the subway," I tell her.

She purses her lips, looks like she's about to say something and changes her mind.

Good idea. It's the first smart thing she's said all day.

Five minutes of beautiful, peaceful, pleasurable silence pass and then she shatters the quiet like a fist through a window. "You're right. We should have taken the subway. We're going to have to pay for parking."

Eject. "We might."

"It's impossible to find parking around Jergen Street. We're going to circle for hours."

Blah blah blah. Nothing is more annoying than someone who whines about parking and doesn't even drive. It's worse than a Torontonian who says how decrepit Montreal has become when she hasn't been there for two years.

I turn onto Queen Street, and two blocks later pull into an empty spot.

"Lucky," Jodine mumbles.

I snort. "Ready? You're going to let me talk, right?"

"If you say so. But I do study litigation, you know."

I can just see her jumping in with an objection and screwing everything up. "Just don't say anything."

The wind blows through the sweater jacket I'm wearing as we walk toward the bar. It's almost time to buy a new winter coat. I'm thinking about something in brown leather.

The bar is called 411. Not because it gives out information but because its address is 411. My friends and I used to hang out here on Thursday nights. I open the heavy metal door and Jodine follows me inside.

And here goes nothing.

"Hi, is Steve in?" I ask the back of a young girl with cropped red hair, black leather pants and a silver tube top. She's standing behind the coat check, seemingly organizing leftover jackets.

She turns to face us. "Yeah, he's in."

The question wasn't meant to be rhetorical. "Can I speak to him?" I ask.

"One sec."

She disappears behind the coats and returns with the tall, goateed Steve, who looks like Mr. Clean.

"Yes?" His eyes scan my plunging neckline. "Can I help you?"

"Hopefully," I say. "Do you remember me? I used to hang out here."

His eyes slowly scan upward, slowly...and rest on my face. "Hey! How the hell are you? Where've you been hiding?"

I hear Jodine gasp. Hah! She didn't think he'd recognize me!

"You know. Been busy. I have a business proposition for you."

"What sort of business do you have in mind?" He smiles, exposing the space between his two front teeth.

"I'd like to organize a party for the Saturday night before Halloween. This is my friend and business partner, Jodine." I motion to Jodine.

"Hi," she says, a bit awkwardly.

Steve nods in her direction. I wish she'd worn the tighter shirt I suggested.

"Halloween Saturday? That's a busy night," he comments, yielding his head from side to side as though it's a seesaw.

"It will be a busy party," I say, trying to sound overly convincing.

"How many people can you bring in?"

"At least four hundred."

Jodine gasps again. At least Steve's not paying attention to her.

He rubs the top of his shiny bald head with the palm of his hand. "How? Is this a group thing?"

"Yes. We're from Pi Alpha Pi. It's one of the OU sororities."

"A sorority, eh?" He laughs. "You girls going to be dressed in nighties when you throw around your pillows?"

Ha ha. Hilarious. "If you comp us enough booze, we will."

He smiles, seeming to like that idea. Perv. "What do you want, part of the door?"

"Yes. You charge five on Saturday, right? How many people do you normally bring in?"

"About two hundred. I'd say an extra hundred on Halloween weekend."

He's completely full of shit. I've been to this bar on a Saturday night and the only way he'd pull in two hundred people was if all the bathrooms in the city were blocked and someone slipped Ex-Lax into everyone's margaritas.

"How about we'll do all the promoting, and charge ten at the door, which we get to keep. You make the bar."

He laughs. "That's quite a risk for us. What if you girls can't get anyone to come? Why should we take a loss? Maybe, and I mean maybe, we'll consider letting you charge five over our five. And we keep the bar."

Aha! He's interested! Jodine's eyes widen in an I-can't-believe-he's-giving-us-shit-all expression. I'd agree with the option, but the thing is, if it was his suggestion, it can't be good for us. I shake my head. "I don't think that's worth our while. How about this—the cover is ten, we keep seven and you get three? And you still keep the bar."

Jodine cringes.

Steve muses it over. "What if our regulars don't want to mix with your guests?"

"Even if that happens, which it won't, it is a sorority party—" I enunciate the word *sorority* with extra tongue so he'll create visions in his head of breast-flashing crazy coeds licking tequila salt off his bare chest "—we'll still bring in two hundred more people than you count on. So even if all your regulars for some completely improbable reason decide to veto your bar, you'll still make twelve hundred dollars, which is two hundred dollars more than you would make. Not including the booze. And that's if *none* of your regulars come. And I think you have a bit more faith in your loyal customers than that, don't you, Steve?"

He crosses his arms across his chest. "Maybe."

"It's a win-win situation. You're going to make a killing."

He nods. "We're an eighties bar, eh? Only eighties music."

"Bring on the Michael Jacksons."

He smiles and motions to the bar. "You girls want a shot?"

"I can't believe you pulled it off!" Jodine exclaims, shaking her head. "Are we going to have to wear sorority outfits?"

"Probably." We both start giggling. "I was pretty good, wasn't I?" Well, I was.

"You were amazing!" Since the compliment is from Miss Smarty-Pants herself, it must be worth something.

"Have you thought about law school?" she says. "You'd be a wicked litigator. Why don't you come to class with me one day? Maybe you'd like it."

Can you say *boring*? I'd be asleep in four and a half seconds. "No thanks. I don't think it's my style."

Jodine slides into the passenger seat, pulls out her hair elastic and then ties her hair back again. "You know, your calculations weren't exactly accurate. Steve claimed he could get three hundred people on Halloween night, not his regular two hundred. So if nobody from his regulars showed up, he'd be out three hundred dollars."

Blah blah blah. I check my blind spot for Jodine's sake and then pull into the street. "It's not my fault he can't remember his own bullshit, is it?"

We pick up drive-through at McDonald's. A grilled chicken burger with no mayo, no cheese, no special sauce and a Diet Coke for Jodine; a Big Mac, large fries and a chocolate shake for Allie (not going to help her in the hips department, but who am I to comment?); a Quarter Pounder, a medium fries and a soda for me.

The fries and drink are all gone by the time we get to the apartment. You know how it is—you say you're just going to have one fry, one sip, and before you know it it's all gone.

"Thanks, guys!" Allie says from the couch when I throw her the bag and hand her the shake. "I just got home two secs ago." She takes a deep sip as though it's water and she's been camped out in the desert.

It's not soda, but at least she's making progress. She's graduated from orange juice.

Jodine and I sit down on the couch. "Good?"

"Fab. Thanks." Allie takes another long sip, her cheeks indenting. "I think I saw a mouse yesterday."

Jodine and I lift our feet off the floor. "Are you sure?" I ask.

"No." Confusion spreads over her face. "I think."

Jodine's eyes narrow and she puts her hands on her hips. "Yes or no. There's no middle ground here. You don't understand. I hate mice. I mean hate. Despise. Loathe. I don't like regular pets, imagine how I feel about uncivilized ones."

"I don't know. I saw a blur of gray."

Jodine's eyes scan the apartment. "Were you wearing your contacts?"

"No. I finally got them out. It took me forever. I was up until—"

Jodine looks at me and shakes her head dismissively. "She was probably seeing things."

"You think?" I ask uncertainly. I don't want to put my feet down just yet.

"I hope." She shudders.

Allie takes another sip out of her shake. "If you guys think I was imagining it, then I probably was."

We all slowly place our feet back onto the floor.

Allie claps her hands. "How'd it go?"

Jodine throws her hands in the air in amazement. "You wouldn't believe. Emma is a superstar."

I bow. "He's letting us take seven dollars off the door."

"I can't believe it! That's what you said we'd get!"

"I don't lie, darling." Well, only sometimes. "We're in business."

"Fab! Oh, by the way, Nick called."

Of course he did. He calls every day. "What did he want?"

Jodine puts her burger in the microwave. "Are any of yours cold? I'm nuking mine."

I shake my head.

Allie takes a bite of her burger. "Mine's fine." A trace of special sauce drips down the corner of her lips. She rams a handful of fries smothered in ketchup into her mouth. "He didn't believe me when I said you weren't home," she says, exposing the fries.

Chew, swallow—then talk. Chew. Swallow. Talk. Maybe I should buy her those poetry magnets, spell the words out and magnetize them to the fridge. Oops. We don't have a fridge, now do we? "He's such a loser," I say.

Jodine sets the timer for thirty seconds.

"Are you going to call him back?" Allie asks.

The hum of the microwave is a bit distracting. Maybe in front of the television wasn't such a brilliant idea. Every time someone turns it on, little squiggly lines run across the screen. I raise my voice to be heard. "Should I?"

"Maybe. I feel bad. He keeps calling. And sending stuff."

"Don't call him," Jodine interjects. "It's over."

Allie nearly chokes on her food. "Big talker," she says. "You call having Manny over, over?"

Jodine laughs. "Good point."

"So what's up with that, anyway?" I ask, facing Jodine.

She's staring distractedly at the microwave that says two seconds left. At one second left she presses cancel on the keypad.

I point an accusing finger at her. "So you're the culprit!"

"Didn't your mother teach you it was rude to point? And why am I a culprit?" She takes a bite of her chicken burger, chews and swallows. Take note, Allie. Study the order.

"You're the one who always stopped the microwave before it was ready," I explain. "Every time I went into the kitchen, I noticed the timer said ten seconds, five seconds, one second, whatever. I couldn't figure out what was going on."

"Guilty as charged. I didn't realize my impatience was being monitored numerically."

"You need to develop patience," I tell her. "It's like acquiring a taste for sushi."

She shakes her head. "There's no time for patience."

"You don't even like Manny, but you let him take up a ton of your time."

She shrugs. "But it's not as if he's taking up any extra space. He's there, anyway."

I laugh and finish my burger. "He's there? That's a great reason for a relationship. It's right up there with good looks and charisma. What is 'he's there'?"

"He's always there. It's a hassle to not be together."

"That's the worst reason for a relationship I ever heard," Allie comments.

Jodine snorts. "Since when are you the resident expert on relationships? Have you ever even had one?"

Allie turns bright red and stuffs another handful of fries in her mouth. "Of course I've had relationships! And sometimes I've ended them because we were staying together for the wrong reasons. And 'he's there' is definitely a wrong reason."

"What's the harm? It's only for a few months. I'm off to New York this summer, anyway."

"A few months?" I ask. "That's more like a year."

Allie sighs and takes a final sip of her shake. "You're never going to meet The One when you're stuck in a dead-end relationship."

"What One?" Jodine asks, rolling her eyes. "There's no such thing as The One."

"Of course there is," Allie argues. "You don't think you're ever going to meet your soul mate?"

"One day, I hope I'll meet someone and fall completely in love—yes. But soul mate? Someone that I'm destined to be with? One single person who's the lid to my pot? That's idiotic."

"So I'm an idiot?" Allie asks, and I don't think there's any good outcome for this conversation. It should just stop right here.

"I didn't say you're an idiot," Jodine says. "I said the concept is idiotic."

"So I'm an idiot."

"If you believe in soul mates, maybe."

"I do believe in them."

"And I assume you believe Clint is your soul mate?"

Allie's blush deepens. "I think he might be."

"How do you know?" I ask.

"Because…did I tell you that he's from Belleville? We were in nursery together. Our mothers did carpool together. We're sitting next to each other in the class picture, holding hands. He was wearing the cutest little pair of OshKosh jeans. And once I was crying for no reason and my mother was trying to get me to stop, and she asked me if I wanted ice cream, and I said no. And then she asked me if I wanted to watch TV, and I said no. And then she asked me if I wanted to play with Clinton and I said yup and my parents drove me over to his house and I stopped crying. In my baby book I wrote I love Clint. My brother and his friends were into making home videos and they decided to tape our wedding. I was wearing a puffy dress and he was wearing a suit and his hair was all fluffy and my brother pretended to be the minister and they invited the whole neighborhood and I made myself a minibouquet out of red tissue paper and we got married. Isn't that cute?

"And then that summer his father got a new job, and they moved to Toronto. I cried for the first few days when he left, but then of course I forgot about him. Not forgot-forgot, of course, I always wondered what happened to him, but I hadn't really thought about him in years until it was my first day of Psych 101, my freshman college year and he sat down next to me. Come on. There were twelve hundred people in that class. What are the chances that he would have not only enrolled in that class but that he would sit down *right next to me?*"

I nod. "It does seem pretty unlikely," I comment. I'm still amazed that she turned down the offer for ice cream.

"Of course we didn't recognize each other right away. But during the boring parts we started talking and he said he was born in Belleville and blah, blah, blah—"

Don't I say blah, blah, blah? Is she mimicking my expressions? Can you say *Single, White Female?*

"—and then we couldn't believe the fact that we were sitting right next to each other. *Right next to each other.*"

Right next to each other. Yes, we caught that the first two or three times.

"And we became friends. We started hanging out all the time. He had a girlfriend then, and after that I was seeing someone and he had a girlfriend, and after that he was seeing someone when I had a boyfriend. Or kind of a boyfriend, anyway. Anyway. And now we've both been single for over a year. And I just know it's going to happen. I can feel it. We're like Harry and Sally. Or Dawson and Joey. Or Kevin and Winney. Or Ross and——"

"Yes, Allie." Jodine rolls her eyes. "Every television series has a pair of best friends who are destined to be together unbeknownst to them."

"Did I mention he's a Taurus and I'm a Pisces? Those are like perfect signs together."

"It sounds pretty soul mate-y to me," I say.

"So you believe in soul mates, too?" Allie asks me.

Is it too late to back out of this conversation? I'm going to get an argument from either side. "I don't know. I'd like to believe in it. I don't think it's so crazy. I'm waiting for a man who idolizes me, who thinks I'm the best person who ever lived, who thinks I'm gorgeous, brilliant, funny, completely awesome. There must be someone out there who recognizes my wonderfulness. But soul mate? Do I even have a soul? What's a soul? I don't know. Sure, probably. No. Okay, maybe."

Allie smirks at Jodine. "So I guess you're living with two idiots."

Jodine shakes her head. "Tell me, Allie, what happens if a person has one perfect match for him or her? And he lives in a different century? Or what if you had a soul mate but he died in a car accident when he was twelve? Or what if you were standing next to him in the elevator, but you didn't know it was him and now he's married to someone else?"

Allie blinks repeatedly.

Or what if you were dating your soul mate and then you dumped him believing he wasn't your soul mate but then you realized he was? "This is a stupid conversation," I say. "We don't know, so what's the point in arguing about it? Do we want to argue about if there's a God, too? Or about what happens when we die?"

Jodine shrugs. "There's no God and we rot."

Allie looks like she's about to cry.

Oh God/no God. Fuck. All this talk is giving me a headache. "I think maybe Allie could be right. There is a soul mate for each person, but I'm not waiting around. What if you finally meet your soul mate and you find out that he has a small cock? I'm not taking any chances. I'm going to call Nick back."

Ah, Nick. How could a guy who gave me multiple orgasms every night not be my soul mate? What more do I want? Flowers? He does that, too!

I walk into my room, close my door, lie on my bed, pick up the phone and dial his number. Why is it that it takes one call to memorize a number and five years of not calling to forget it?

The phone rings. And rings again. And rings. His machine picks up.

Why am I calling? And where the hell is he? It's Tuesday night. Why isn't he answering the phone? Bastard. I slam down the receiver. Forget it. He doesn't deserve a message. Not if he's out gallivanting with his friends or out with some slutbag. If he wants me back so badly, or if he is actually my soul mate, he should be waiting at home for my phone call.

Do I go outside and continue the dumb discussion about soul mates or stay in my room and watch TV?

I hear Allie's whining voice ask from the living room: "Jay, I promise I won't ask you this anymore, but you don't think we're going to get kicked out, do you?"

An even more annoying conversation. I'm going to stay in my room and watch TV. With a cigarette. I open the blinds and pull back the window screen and light up, letting the mixture of night-time air and smoke flush against my face.

Who the fuck needs a soul mate, anyway?
What the fuck is that gray thing on the floor?
It's a sock. Just a sock.

16
THE POSTURIZATION
OF ALLIE

ALLIE

"Hang out here often?" I whisper, sliding behind the wooden rectangular table into an empty seat facing Jay.

Jay looks up and then back down at her book. "Hi. Hold on one second. I have one more page."

What am I supposed to do while I'm waiting? There's nothing for me to do in the law library. Law is even more boring than philosophy.

La la la. What should I do, what should I do? Don't bite. I am not going to bite. I will not put my fingers into my mouth. They are slowly starting to grow into humanlike fingers and I will not destroy them.

I'm bored.

Not as bored as Josh must be all day. Since I'm the only one home during working hours, it's become my responsibility to keep him entertained. Can you imagine working on a burnt kitchen by yourself, all day? I'd go nuts. I'd start to hear the tiles talking or something. I'd even talk to the goldfish, if it were still in the kitchen instead of swimming around in the living room. To prevent this from happening to Josh, I moved my CD player into the kitchen so he can listen. He wasn't crazy about my *Rent*, *Les Miserables* or *Beauty and the Beast* CDs, so we borrowed Emma's Lenny Kravitz. And now, when he doesn't think I can hear him, he sings in this low, completely off-key voice. It's kind of cute, and I have to admit, it's nice to have someone around during the day. He's almost finished the floor. Emma drew him an awesome picture of what the kitchen looked like before so he can copy it as close as he possibly can. Thank God Jay loaned us the cash. Grudgingly. But she didn't have much choice, since she's the only one with any of her own money in the bank. We're going to pay her back right after the party, of course. As she has reminded us. Repeatedly.

"I'm bored."

"I'll be two seconds, Allie."

"Okay." Didn't she say one second? I could swear she said one second.

One…two. That was two. "Are you done yet?"

"I'm going to kill you."

"Where's Manny?"

"Bathroom. Obviously. He goes to the bathroom every—"

Manny returns to the table. "Hi, Allie. How are you?"

"Fine, thanks. You?"

"Good. Working, as usual."

I peer into Jay's open textbook and shake my head. "I'm pretty sure I'd fall asleep reading that stuff."

Manny's jaw drops in mock amazement. "Asleep? But it's so riveting!"

Jay rolls her eyes and swats him. "Oh, shut up. You love this stuff."

He blushes. How cute is that? "You can't find it that boring," I tell him. "I hear you're the brains behind this study-group operation."

He runs his fingers through Jay's hair. "Is that what she says about me when I'm not around?"

"Only when you behave," Jay says squirming as though her pants are too tight. I'm not sure if she's more uncomfortable with him touching her hair or him touching her hair in public.

"Are you coming postering with us?" I ask him.

He looks questioningly at Jay. "Posturing, as in assuming a pose?"

I giggle. "No, postering, as in plastering the campus with posters."

Understanding registers in his face. "You're putting up the absurd posters you made for your Halloween party. Where are you going?"

Last night we had too much wine and too much fun creating posters on Jay's computer. Actually, Emma and I sat in our fave couch positions, and Jay sat perched with her laptop on the recliner. She seems to really love reclining.

We used Jay's "No idea is a bad idea" approach, which apparently means no idea is a bad idea unless I suggest it.

Jay turns off her laptop and slams her textbook closed. "You don't have to come."

Manny continues playing with Jay's hair and she continues to squirm. "Where are you guys going?" he asks.

I flip through the posters. "The law school, the business school, the med school, the arts department, the Greek association."

His eyes light up. "Greek as in sorority?" he asks. "Do you really want me to come?"

Jay fake-smiles. Or at least I assume it's a fake smile. I can't a hundred percent tell the difference between her fake smiles and her real smiles. If it was a real smile, her eyes would smile, too, right? "Your call," she says. "I'm sure they'll be having naked pillow fights right about now."

"Oh, come with us!" I say. "It'll be fun. It won't take us more than half an hour and you need a break. Oh! And then you guys will come back after and I'll make you dinner!"

"Make dinner?" Jay asks. She turns to Manny and shakes her head. "Her many hours on the phone have obviously made her forget our present cooking situation. She must mean *order* dinner."

"No, look what I bought!" I pick up a plastic bag and pull out my new appliance.

"Don't unpack it here," Jay whispers at me. "We're in a law library."

Does a sandwich-maker make noise? Would it be okay to take out a sandwich-maker in the med library? Why not the law library?

I put it back in the bag. "Rebecca, my last roomie, used to have one of these and I used to make wicked pizza sandwiches."

"What's a pizza sandwich?" Manny asks.

"You'll find out if you come postering and then come for dinner. You might as well. You have to eat, right? And then you guys can go back to the library and be losers and study."

"Losers, eh?" he asks, laughing. "But I only got here an hour ago."

"Your eyes are already drooping. You need a break."

"If Jodine doesn't mind."

"Why would Jodine mind? Of course she wants her boyfriend to help. Right, Jay?" Well, I would want my boyfriend to help. But Jay's eyes are slitting into mini cantaloupe slices and I'm getting the feeling she might not feel the same. Oops.

"Sure, if you want to," she says.

"Only if you really want me to," he answers.

Why is he being such a girl? No wonder Jay gets annoyed with him. C'mon, Manny, be a man! Say you want to go postering!

Jay throws her arms up into the air in exasperation. "I don't see what the big deal is. We're just going to hang up silly posters. If you want to come, then come."

Manny smiles as though his first-grade teacher just gave him a gold sticker for having the neatest desk in the class. "Okay…"

Way to go, Manny! Be assertive!

"…if you're sure."

Oh, for the love of God.

17
POSTER MANIA

Looking for Summer Employment?

THE VERDICT IS...

THE ULTIMATE
HALLOWEEN GET TOGETHER

Hosted by
THE NEW YORK ASSOCIATION OF LAW FIRMS

Where: 411 JERGEN

When: SATURDAY, OCTOBER 27
         9:00 UNTIL MIDNIGHT

Cost: $10 AT THE DOOR

Rules: DON'T OBJECT...JUST BE THERE.

Halloween Bash

brought to you by the

INVESTMENT BANKER ALUMNI CLUB

STRENGTHS	WEAKNESSES
• classy bar • interesting people • wonderful drinks • low cost - only $10	• it happens only once

OPPORTUNITIES	THREATS
• make business contacts • find a summer job • meet attractive women dressed in skimpy outfits • have a great time	• if you don't come some other guy will schedule a game of golf with the CEO of Nike • if you don't come you'll have to ask for your old job back at McDonald's this summer • if you don't come the potential love of your life will fall for some other schmuck

LOCATION 411 JERGEN

DATE SATURDAY, OCTOBER 27

TIME 9:00 TO 2:00

work diagnose eat sleep study work diagnose eat sleep study

NEED A LITTLE FUN?

Rx PARTY WITH US ON HALLOWEEN

WHERE? *411 Jergen*

WHEN? *Saturday, Oct 27*

from 21:00 until

whenever your beeper

drags you back to hell

get back to saving people

study work diagnose eat sleep study work diagnose eat sleep study work diagnose eat sleep study work diagnose eat sleep study work diagnose eat sleep study work diagnose eat sleep study work diagnose eat sleep study work diagnose eat sleep study work diagnose eat sleep study work diagnose eat sleep study work diagnose eat sleep study work diagnose eat sleep study work diagnose eat sleep study work diagnose eat sleep study work diagnose eat sleep study work diagnose eat sleep study work

WHAT DO

POEMS,

THE

CIVIL WAR,

AND

ABSTRACT
THOUGHT

ALL HAVE IN COMMON?

THEY ALL MAKE LOUSY COSTUMES

GENERATE SOMETHING BETTER AND REVEAL IT AT OUR

Halloween Party

FOUR HUNDRED AND ELEVEN JERGEN

SATURDAY, OCTOBER TWENTY-SEVENTH

NINE O' CLOCK

TEN DOLLARS

CRAZY PARTY

LOTS OF BEER AND LESBIANS
WHO WANT TO EXPERIMENT

411 JERGEN
SATURDAY,
OCTOBER 27
9:00 TILL
YOU WAKE UP WITH
A HANGOVER AND
A NAKED CHICK
IN YOUR BED!

ONLY 10 BUCKS AT THE DOOR!

ΑΠΟΛΑΥΣΕΤΕ ΛΕΣΒΕΣ

18
ALLIE! YOU'RE BEING AN IDIOT! HE LIKES YOU!

ALLIE

"This is the best pizza sandwich I've ever had," Manny says, popping the last remaining bite into his mouth.

"And the first," Jay comments, patting his knee.

What is this? Affection? She's touching him, in public, when they're on the couch and I'm only a foot away on the recliner? Has an alien spirit sneaked in through the open window and polluted Jay's emotions?

Manny licks the fingers on his left hand as his right one casually rests behind her shoulder. "Yes," he says, and smacks his lips. "But the best."

"What did I tell you about smacking your lips?" Jay says, squeezing his side.

I hate having my sides squeezed. My brother used to wake me up in the morning by sneaking into my room and pinching both sides of my waist. It drove me absolutely crazy. The only other thing that drove me as crazy was when he'd lift me up by my feet and carry me around the house. I don't understand why he didn't believe me when I said I didn't *like* it.

Isn't tickling strange? It must be the only thing that forcibly makes you laugh and makes you miserable at the same time. A lot of other things give you pleasure and make you miserable a few seconds later—shooters on an empty stomach, drive-through fast food, a liter of chocolate brownie ice cream—but I don't think there's anything other than tickling that does it simultaneously. Unless you can feel your stomach growing while you're eating the ice cream, which sometimes I think I can.

"What did I tell you about tickling my stomach?" Jay says. "Quit it."

Manny complies graciously by bending over and sticking his fingers under her armpits.

"Stop it!" she yells, wriggling and laughing. "We're eating. This is completely inappropriate dinner behavior. And you're making me sweaty!"

"I like you sweaty!" he giggles back.

Are they flirting? Jay can flirt? I guess she's not as cold as Fish, after all.

Manny grabs both of her hands above her head and leans her back against the couch cushions. He sits on her, all the while continuing to smack his lips.

Are they playing?

I think they are!

I wish I had someone to play with. I have Emma, I guess. She watches *Seinfeld* and *Simpsons* reruns with me after midnight while eating chips and other nonperishable snacks. And when she wakes up on weekend afternoons, she does her nails while I flip through old copies of *Stiletto*.

But a guy is probably more fun to play with. I know that doesn't sound PC at all, and I know you're supposed to be happy about being single, and I am, really, but I'm pretty sure a boyfriend would make everything a lot more, well, interesting. Why doesn't Clint realize what he's missing? My life feels like a piece of scrap paper all colored with crayon markings without distinct black lines to guide me where to go. Should this triangle be green, this octagon maroon, this…what other shapes are here? Circle, square, rectangle, oval…there must be more. What's that shape with five sides called? Six sides? Seven sides? Hexa-what?

I was never any good at geometry. Or math in general, for that matter. That's why I didn't go into business. Although if I'd gone into business, I'd probably have a real job and not be floating down the I-have-no-clue-what-I'm-doing-here river of post-college. Maybe I'll become a chef. Why not? I'd get paid to cook all day, and I love to cook! I jump off the recliner and pick up Manny's plate. "Do you want me to make you another pizza sandwich?" I ask.

The lip-smacking finales with a loud kiss on Jay's lips. "That would be great. Would you mind?"

"My pleasure. I'm going to make myself another one, too. How about you, Jay? Do you want me to make you something else?" Except for a missing mouse-size bite (I shouldn't even joke about that), her sandwich is completely intact.

"I'm fine, thanks," she says.

How can she be fine? If I ate only one bite of dinner, you'd hear my stomach grumbling in California, as at least a five point five on the Richter scale. "I can make you one without cheese, if you want," I tell her. "Sorry about that. I forgot that you don't like cheese…bread…meat…" I forgot she doesn't like, um…to eat.

"Well…all right."

Will surprises never end? First she displays emotion, in *public,* and now she wants to eat. Oh-oh. She appears to be hesitating. Why is she hesitating?

"Can you make my pizza without the cheese? And without the bread? Just vegetables?"

What's a sandwich without bread? Manny must be as puzzled as I am, because he's shaking his head. "That's it?" he says. "Just some vegetables? You're going to waste away. You know I like you with a little more bread on your body."

She pokes herself in the stomach. "Yes, well I don't."

Hmm. Neither do I, on my body, that is. If there were any more bread there, I could open up a bakery.

I probably shouldn't have had the *mmmm* potato skins today before work.

Or the *mmmm* chocolate bar on the way to the library.

Or the *mmmm*—forget it. I probably shouldn't become obsessed with food intake, mine or anyone's else's. "I'll make you whatever your heart desires," I say.

Jay lies her head on Manny's thigh and looks up at me. "Thanks." Manny kisses her on the forehead and she closes her eyes.

"You two are ador! Really the cutest couple ever," I say, "It's so nice to see. I'm so happy for you guys." Who are these people on our couch?

Manny laughs. "What is *ador?*"

"She means adorable," Jay explains.

I spread the tomato sauce over the bread for Manny's sandwich. I know people claim tomatoes are fruits, but *come on.* Can it be more of a vegetable? I pick the ingredients off my previously created stations on the crate table and place them carefully on the sandwich for Manny. Tomatoes, cheese, green peppers, red peppers, pepperoni. Two pieces of pepperoni for the pizza, one piece of pepperoni for me. Okay. One more piece of pepperoni for me. Mmm. One more. That's it. Enough. One more. Now that's really it.

Now cheese. I pick up my newly purchased cheese cutter and begin slicing the mozzarella into strips. I love mozzarella. It's my all-time favorite cheese. One piece for the pizza, one piece for me. Maybe it's my second-favorite cheese. I love old cheddar. Maybe that's my favorite. Mmm. Old cheddar. I like Havarti, too. I wouldn't want to leave Havarti off the list. And what about goat cheese? Oops. I almost just sliced my finger off. No one (except maybe Hannibal) wants a finger in his pizza. My fingers are almost healed, too; I wouldn't want to ugly them all up with a gash across them. They're not perfectly healed, obviously; it's only been a few weeks, but they do appear less mangled. One piece of mozzarella for the pizza and one for me. Mmm. I should have bought goat cheese for the pizza! Why didn't I think of that? Tomorrow I'm getting goat cheese. One slice of mozzarella on the pizza, one for me. That one was a bit skinny, actually, so two for me.

I hate when you slice the cheese and the block ends up lopsided. The once-perfect square or rectangle always turns into a hexa-something. Why is that? How does one side become three times the size of the other? Unacceptable. I'll cut just one more piece to even it out. That should do it. Nope. Mmm.

This reminds me of the time I tried to cut my own bangs. First the left side, then the right. Then the left to balance the right. Then the right to balance the left. So who wanted bangs, anyway? Wisps are always in style, aren't they?

Maybe I shouldn't become a chef. I'd probably turn into a per-fectly round ball. Symmetrical or not, being round is far worse than being bald. Hair, at least, is easy to grow back, and it's easy to cover up with a scarf or a wig. But it's hard to find an outfit for a ball. "Do we have any plastic wrap?" I ask.

From my aerial view, I can see Jay shrug her shoulders. "Did you buy any?" she asks.

"No." Oops. That was stupid. Now I have no other choice. I'll have to, uh, dispose of the cheese.

"Rewrap it in the original packaging and put it into the fridge." Our mini rental fridge got delivered today and is now plugged in beside the table.

Hmm. There won't be any room left in the fridge if we fill it up with morsels of leftovers, symmetrical or not. I guess I should do my roomie-civic duty and eat the rest of the block. No need to be accused of fridge hogging.

Fab! The slits of sky I can see through my blinds are the color of blueberry yogurt, and patches of exposed sun are casting splashes of lemon over my walls and bedspread.

Mmm. I'm hungry.

Good morning, world!

You know those days when you wake up smiling for no specific reason? There was no late-night telephone call from the guy you like, no reading about how Tom and Mary finally confessed their love for each other in the last paragraph of a seven-hundred-page romance novel, no knowing that you have fresh bagels and lox and whipped cream cheese in your fridge ready for your breakfast—but you feel great, anyway. You inhale the happy, beautiful air, and your room looks soft and golden, and you're excited to get up, get out of bed, and just be.

That's how I feel right now. There's no reason, except what's not to be happy about? I have two great roomies and we're having a party. Fine, we have no kitchen and we could get kicked out of the apartment at any time because of it, but Jay and Emma keep promising that we won't. Okay, so here's the real reason for my good mood: I called Clint last night and told him about the party, and he's coming! I haven't seen him in over a week. And he hasn't even met my roomies yet, isn't that crazy?

Clint is coming!

I'm supposed to tell Josh about the party, too. He must have repairman friends that we haven't advertised to yet. I gave him a key so I don't have to wake up every morning to let him in, and I can already hear him scurrying around in the kitchen. I slip on my slippers, pull an oversize sweatshirt over my T-shirt and sweatpants and totter into the kitchen. "Morning!"

He's leaning forward on his knees, a tape measure stretched from what was once the stove, to that space between his legs where I'm not exactly looking. He looks up and smiles. "Morning, Sleeping Beauty."

Ah, if only I had my prince to kiss and wake me! "It's not that late. What time is it?"

He sits back on his legs (I'm still not looking) and looks down at his watch. "Ten-thirty."

"Ten-thirty? I don't think that makes me Sleeping Beauty." I yawn and cover my mouth so he doesn't get a whiff of my morning breath.

"You're normally up at ten."

Hmm. How long has he been studying my sleeping habits? Is this significant? This must be significant. "Were you getting lonely?" I ask. It's so easy to flirt when you don't mean it. It's good practice for Clint, anyway.

"My job is a lot more fun when you're around. I brought you breakfast."

"You did? That's so sweet."

He holds up a carton of eggs and a mini bag of cheese. "We're going to make omelettes in the sandwich-maker."

"I can't wait to put something solid inside me." Uh-oh. Did I just say that? That could be interpreted in a very different way than intended. "Um… Did I tell you I've been making pizza all the time?"

"I bet you want to make it every night."

Oh, boy. "Yup," I say. "I do. Use the sandwich-maker, I mean. Not make out. Make it."

He looks at me weirdly.

Quick! I have to make a recovery so he doesn't think I'm a shameless wannabe slut! "And now you say it can make omelettes, too," I mumble, trying to sound mundane. "Can life get better than this?"

Now the look on his face says he thinks I'm a lunatic. If given a choice between having someone think you're a shameless slut or a lunatic, slut is probably the wiser choice. Maybe. "Is there anything that thing can't do?" I ask.

"It doesn't refrigerate very well."

"The sandwich-maker freezes food, too?"

"I was making a joke."

"Oh." Now he's looking into my eyes as if there really *is* nothing there. "Uh, we have a fridge now." Dumb, dumb, dumb.

"So I see. Hopefully in a few weeks you'll have a human-size one."

"To refrigerate human-size meals," I say with a wink. See? I can flirt properly.

"Is there something in your contact?" He stands up and I swear, his head is less than two inches from mine as he looks into my eyes, squinting and searching for the intrusive offender. "Nope, nothing there."

"How much do I owe you?" I ask.

"For the larger fridge or the eye exam?"

I give him my fake smirk—the one where I open my lips all the way and squint my eyes. "Both. I'll just get out my corporate charge cards. Is AmEx Platinum okay?" My brokenness has become a favorite source for our jokes. "No, silly, for the eggs."

"My treat."

"Oh, come on, you bring me something every morning and you never let me pay you back."

"When your kitchen is fixed, I will one hundred percent let you make me an extravagant meal that encompasses baking, frying and freezing. I'll let you buy all the ingredients."

"Okay, but at least let me make the omelettes."

"No, I'll make them. There are techniques one must be aware of before attempting such a complicated task in the sandwich-maker."

Hmm. It's a good thing he's charging us by the job, not by the hour. "What can I do to help?" I ask.

He walks out of the kitchen and into the new cooking area. "Just remember to unplug the sandwich-maker so you don't set the rest of your apartment on fire."

Ha, ha. "Okay, but let me shower before we eat."

I walk into the bathroom. The toilet is unflushed. Jay never remembers to flush it in the morning, and every morning I'm greeted with a diluted bowl of yellow.

Would you look at my hair, please? I can't believe I just talked to a guy with sleep in my eyes, my hair in random knots, and one of the legs of my sweatpants rolled up to my knee. How does this happen when you sleep? Why am I only wearing one sock? Did one foot get hot in the middle of the night?

After my shower, I dodge back into my room to get changed so Josh doesn't think I'm trying to seduce him from my towel.

"Hello," I say, reappearing in the area-where-we-now-eat.

"Hello," he says, smiling and exposing his dimple. He has one on the left side of his cheek. I, too, have only one dimple, on my right side. (Not being symmetrical might explain my obsession with trying to symmetrize food.) Isn't it strange that both Josh and I suffer from the same simple-dimple affliction? How sweet, together we make up one complete duo-dimple duet.

Speaking about being unsymmetrical, my right foot is a half size bigger than my left, which makes shoe shopping really annoying. The last time Emma and I went to the mall, she snuck me two different sizes, but I felt too guilty to rip off the shoe store like that. I mean, it would have been okay if they could sell the leftover shoes, but what were the chances that a customer would come in asking for the exact opposite?

Emma did a similar kind of switch at the Mermaid Bikini shop. She bought a medium top and a small bottom. She claimed it was the store's fault for only catering to averages. She pointed out, while not able to look directly at me, that there were plenty of women out there with medium bottoms and small tops, so she would be doing someone a favor. I could understand that, but what evaded me was why she needed a new suit in October. "Just in case," she said, which was ridiculous because how can she afford a winter vacation given the dire situation of our finances?

My gaze drops from Josh's dimple down to his legs. Strange how my eyes keep going back down there, to that general area, only now they drop to the floor. Maybe Josh's feet are asymmetrical, too? Wouldn't that be crazy? Nope. I think they're the same size. Although he is wearing shoes. And most people do buy the same size shoes for both feet, otherwise they'd be advertising their deformity for the whole world to see instead of trying to mask it so—

Sniff, sniff. Mmm. Up, up my gaze travels, slave to my nose. Josh is laying out pieces of cheese on the grill. I grab one in midmovement from his fingers. "It smells fab," I tell him. "Is that salsa in there?"

"Hey—let me see those nails! You stopped biting, eh?"

I nod happily.

"They look great."

"Thanks you." My goal is to have perfect hands by the party. Did I invite Josh to the party? "Did I tell you about our party?"

"Nope."

"You have to come."

"I do? Why?"

"So you can contribute to the Save-Our-Kitchen Fund."

"I think it's too late to be saved."

"Okay, Heal-Our-Kitchen-Fund."

"Aren't I already contributing?"

"Yes, but you have to come. We need your spirit as well as your brawn." And your money. "And you have to bring your friends." And your friends' money.

"When is it?"

"Next Saturday. It's a costume party so you have to dress up."

"Okay. So does that mean I will soon be able to order you girls some more parts for your kitchen? You could use new counters."

"We will hopefully make lots of money so you can order lots of parts. So you have to come."

"How come there are all these things I have to do?"

"Because you are very important."

"Suck-up. What are you dressing up as?"

I steal a leftover piece of cheese from the plate and pop it into my mouth. "I don't know yet. Em and I are going shopping tomorrow."

"Is that Clint guy your date?"

That Clint guy? How does he know about Clint? Did Clint call while I was out and leave a message with Josh? This is not good. No, wait, this could be very good. Clint will be jealous. Is Clint jealous?

Josh takes two plastic plates out of a bag and places them onto the table. "You just turned bright red. So what's the story? Are you two involved?"

Involved? Emotionally—yes. Imaginary—yes. Physically—no. "He's only a…" No, I won't say it. I won't say "friend." Should I tell him the truth? Why not? Maybe he can give me advice. The male perspective. "He's more of my Harry."

"Your who?"

"As in When Sally Met?"

"Ah." He opens the sandwich-maker and pokes at the square of food with a fork, looks at the utensil, then closes the appliance. "So the gallant Clint is your best friend and soul mate?"

"Kind of. He hasn't realized it yet, though. We're still at the point in the movie when they spend all their time together but haven't slept together and he hasn't freaked out yet."

"Does he know how you feel?"

"No…not quite. Maybe. I guess not. I kind of mentioned something once, but then I took it back and now we're really good friends, best friends, but I'm not sure if I should tell him and risk ruining our friendship, in case he's not interested."

Josh stares at me and seems to be contemplating something. "Tell him."

"Really?"

He smiles. "How could he not be interested? He probably has no idea you'd even consider being with him. Guys aren't great at reading women's signs. You have to flirt with him. What does he do? Does he touch you a lot?"

"Um…a little." He touched my hand when we split the check at the restaurant the other night. "I have to be obvious? I thought I *was* being obvious."

He scratches his head. "Uh-oh."

Uh-oh is not good. How many times have you ever heard "Uh-oh, I just won the lottery," or "Uh-oh, the professor just made the final exam optional"? "What do you mean, uh-oh?"

"I suppose it *is* possible he knows you're interested, and he isn't responding because he's not interested in you—although highly unlikely." Josh averts his eyes when he says the word *unlikely*.

"Why unlikely?" I ask. If given a choice, I prefer to go with *unlikely* rather than *uh-oh*.

Josh doesn't answer. Maybe he's afraid of hurting my feelings. Maybe Clint did call here and Josh answered, and the two of them had a big fat laugh at my expense. Maybe Clint shakes his head with amusement/pity every time he leaves my house, except that lately, Clint hasn't been leaving my house at all because he hasn't even been coming over.

Uh-oh.

"No guy cares about jeopardizing the friendship," Josh says finally. "Not if he wants something else. At least, most guys."

Clint knows. He knows and he doesn't feel the same way. He knows and he thinks I'm an idiot. He knows, finds me physically repulsive, doesn't like me and thinks I'm an idiot.

Josh looks up at me and stops his hand in mid-put-food-on-plate motion. "Or maybe I'm wrong. I could easily be wrong. Don't freak out. Maybe he doesn't know. He might not have a clue. He's probably been secretly pining over you for years, thinking he doesn't have a chance. You? Like him? Never! Not in a million years! I bet that's what he's thinking. I know that's what he's thinking."

I force a minismile. Clint doesn't think that. Josh saw the horrified look on my face and is trying to make me feel better. He pities me. Oh, God, he *pities* me.

Or maybe he doesn't. Maybe there's truth to what he said. "Has anything like that ever happened to you?" I ask.

He blushes. "Sort of."

"So what did you tell her?"

He uses a plastic fork to scrape the omelettes off the grill and onto the plates. "It was the other way around. I was the interested partner."

It happened to him! If it happened to him, it could happen to Clint! Maybe Clint does like me and is too afraid to tell me. "So why didn't you tell her?"

He fidgets with the handle of the sandwich-maker. "Sometimes the timing is off."

"What, did she have another boyfriend?"

"Not exactly."

"Was she getting over a breakup?"

"No—"

"Was it when you were traveling? Did you have to leave her behind? Was it a doomed love affair? Did you say goodbye at the train station? Did you run beside her car as she waved from the window and blow kisses?"

"Not quite." Josh looks up at me and smiles sadly. "I'm working with her and I don't want to put her in an awkward position, since I see her every day."

Uh-oh.

I open my mouth to say something and then close it. Open. Close.

He laughs softly and shakes his head.

"But I don't want to say anything because she seems to be interested in some other guy. And I don't want to risk our developing friendship. Or my employment. But I hope the other guy realizes how lucky he is."

I open my mouth and close it again. And then open it. "Thank you," I say. I'm not sure what else to say. What's the protocol when your repairman tells you that he likes you? And not in a hey-baby-let's-break-in-the-new-Formica-countertop type of way? "Men confuse me more every day," I say.

"Women confuse me."

I get goose bumps whenever guys use the word *women* and include me in it. Isn't that strange? I'm so used to being called a girl, I find it really sexy when they call me "woman."

Do I find Josh sexy? Am I attracted to Josh?

He seems to be waiting for me to say something, but instead I stand here contemplating the chances of being transmitted to another room by merely blinking my eye. To my room in Belleville. There has to be a remote possibility of that happening, doesn't there? Even a small chance? I stay quiet and he shakes his head. Maybe he'll say he has to leave early today. Like right now. Or maybe he'll excuse himself to use the bathroom. Or maybe he'll—

"That's what you women should do to raise some money. Offer a course on understanding women," he says, deciding to toss a random observation into the tension-heavy burnt kitchen.

Actually, that idea isn't half bad. "You know, I bet we could make a lot of money." Will he notice if I start walking back to my room?

He laughs. "You're going to teach it?"

"Me? No. What do I know? Emma, maybe." One mini-step back. Two.

"You have to teach some of it, or I'm not going to come." He smiles at me and I smile back.

Three, four. "Okay, okay, I'll teach part of it, if the girls like the whole idea. I really love it. I think I'm going to e-mail them immediately."

"Immediately? You're sure you're not suddenly uncomfortable around me and now you want to dash off at the first available opportunity? What about breakfast? Aren't you hungry?"

My stomach grumbles at the word *hungry*. "Yes, I am hungry." I can be normal. So what if my repairman has a crush on me? No biggie. I sit down on the couch. "And not at all uncomfortable. See?" I put my feet up and lie back. "Would I be making myself so at home if I was uncomfortable?" I can do this. And I'm not that uncomfortable. It actually feels kind of nice. Like climbing under fresh sheets after laundry day. He *likes* me. I'm *likable*.

"Good. Get ready," he says. "This is going to be good."

"Are you still going to come to the party?"

"A hundred percent."

I open my e-mail account and see "New Messages: 7."

The first message, regarding the Halloween party, is from Jodine579@Ontariouniversity.ca. I click on it. And wait. And wait. And wait. Why does it take so long? It's so slow. This is worse than watching paint dry. Not that I've actually ever watched paint dry. Or even painted.

Here it is!

> *We're throwing a fantastic Halloween party.*
> *And you're invited.*
> *Where?*
> *411 Jergen*
> *When?*
> *Saturday, October 27, 9—2*
> *$10 at the door (proceeds go to charity)*

We're a charity? Ten other people are on the "to" list. Who are all these people? Noah, Cindy, Jeremiah (the bullfrog?), Natalie, Mohammed, Manny... Manny! I know Manny. Manny495@ Ontariouniversity.ca must be the Manny I know. How many other Mannys can Jay know? I wonder if he got to choose that number or if it was assigned. What could 495 possibly stand for? I'd take 1407 if I had a choice. Both my parents were born in January, my mother on the fourteenth, my father on the seventh. None of us thought 0101 would be an appropriate code for anything—too obvious—so 0714 became our alarm code at home until the neighbor's delinquent kid broke in and stole our stereo (but we couldn't prove it since he hasn't been seen since), and then we changed the code to 1407. And now I've been using it for pretty much everything since being in Toronto. What's the point in coming up with more codes if I already remember that one, right?

Wait a minute. Where am I? Why aren't Emma and I on Jay's "to" list? We must be on her "blind carbon copy" list. Why are we on her BCC list? Are we closet roommates? Does Jay tell people she lives alone?

I should forward this e-invite to all my friends. Hmm. It doesn't help if they live in other cities and can't come, does it?

Forward to...Clint! There's a start. Who cares if he already said he'd come. He hasn't received an *official* invite yet. Everyone likes to have things on paper. Or on virtual paper. There are also my friends from work. Jill. And Raf. That's two. Who else? I can't send an e-invite with only three names on the e-mail. That just looks pathetic.

I could make up a bunch of addresses, but what if Clint uses my database to forward ads for his Cobra shoes or something? His messages would come back undelivered and then he'd know I'm a fraud. I could just use all my out-of-town friends. He'll figure

I'm confident that even out-of-towners want to attend my party. And then he'd wonder why I put him in my out-of-towner "to" list, adding a little mystery to our otherwise predictable relationship.

Or maybe he'll just think I'm a weirdo.

Ah. BCC. I think "blind carbon copy" was made for situations like this. I put my own e-mail address in the CC section and then put Clint in the BCC section. There we go. It's perfect. Brilliant. Now he has no idea how many people I invited. Now he thinks I'm mysterious, after all.

Message number 2 is called "Luck," forwarded from my former roomie Rebecca. It's a poem!

> *If you send this e-mail to ten people, you'll have good luck.*
> *Otherwise, you're going to be royally fucked.*
> *Send it along and don't ask why.*
> *Otherwise, you will surely die.*

Hmm. Six people. Who should I send it to?

One new e-mail! Oh. It's my e-invite. From me. To me. Right.

Who should I forward the chain letter to? I know I'm not going to die if I don't send it out, obviously, but isn't there a small, zero point zero, zero, zero one-percent chance that I will? And if there is a zero point zero, zero, zero one-percent chance possibility that I will, why take a chance?

When I was a kid, I loved chain letters. I loved going through the mail and seeing my name written in thick cursive letters on specially purchased square pastel envelopes decorated with glittery star-shaped stickers. I wanted pen pals. I wrote blurbs about myself to all the teen magazines, praying they would print them in their pen-pal section and that I would get hundreds of fancy square envelopes stuffed through my mail slot—kind of like that scene in *Harry Potter* when all the envelopes fly into the house and there's nothing Harry's uncle can do. Of course I hadn't seen Harry Potter back then, obviously, although it's too bad because I bet I would have loved it even more as a ten-year-old. I get sad sometimes in toy stores when I see Millennium Barbie or a doll that can eat on its own or something like that, because I think about how much I would have loved it when I was ten. I suppose I could buy it now, but it's not really the same, is it?

Where was I? Right. Anyway, one day I got a letter. Not a chain letter, mind you, but a pen-pal letter. I was about to leave on a road trip to Toronto with my family, and just as we were locking up the house, the mail came, and I saw that there was a square fancy pink envelope with a return address to somewhere in Philadelphia, and it was for me, me, me! Inside was a piece of folded stationery with small pink balloons that floated up the left side of the sheet. The letter was from a girl named Dana. She wrote that she had seen my pen-pal blurb in *Pop,* she liked to read a lot, especially *Sweet Valley High* and *The Baby-Sitters Club,* and her favorite TV shows were *Facts of Life* and *Family Ties,* her favorite subject in school was English, and her favorite color was pink. My hands trembled as I read the letter because this girl was exactly like me. Exactly! Then it hit me: my blurb was in *Pop!* When my parents stopped to get gas I ran into the convenience store to buy the magazine. But when I found the issue and scanned the pen-pal page, there was Nancy's blurb and Mandy's blurb and Samantha's blurb, but where was mine where was mine where was mine?

So then I thought maybe it was in *Seventeen* or *Teen* or *Tiger Beat* or one of the other ones and that Dana had been confused, so my mom and I spent an hour in the convenience store, probing every teen magazine. But we couldn't find it. I figured I'd see it eventually. Sometimes Canada gets the new magazines a little bit after they come out in the States. I bought a special set of rainbow-tinted stationery, and while my father drove, I wrote a twelve-page letter to Dana about everything I could think of, while trying not to get carsick since reading or writing while in motion always makes me carsick. I adorned the envelope with both sets of stickers—shiny moons and fuzzy pink hearts—that I'd also bought at the store.

When we got home a week later, I thought my chest might explode as I ran to the mailbox, expecting to find it stuffed with other letters from other pen pals who craved seeing their names on stationery envelopes as much as I did. But the box only held two credit card bills for my dad. Every day for the next month, I hurried home from school to check for mail, but no pen-pal letters came, and a wave of melancholy would overwhelm me. And I never got a response from Dana.

Years later I brought up the incident with some friends, and Jennifer, my once-childhood best friend I'm still in touch with, clapped her hand over her mouth and admitted that she had written the Dana letter as a joke.

Great joke.

The letter I mailed to Dana never came back to me. I wonder if anyone ever read it. Maybe it went to slush-pile heaven with all those Santa letters I sent when I was six years old to Mr. Claus, North Pole, Canada.

The other five e-mails in my in-box are from people I've met over the Net. I love chat rooms. A lot of cool sites have communities and you can meet normal people from all over the world. It's not the same as feeling a letter in your hand, but I think it's still pretty good. I have two pen pals in Australia, one in Scotland, one in Miami and one in New York. Maybe I should have put them on the "to" list when I sent that e-mail to Clint. Like I said, a little mystery might do our relationship some good.

What relationship?

Never mind that now. Who should I send the chain letter to? Hmm. Four of my foreign pen pals, Jay and...Manny! Why not? He could use some luck. Send.

Now for the message that I was originally intending to write.

Hi, Jay. What do you think about offering seminars to clueless men on how to pick up women, for twenty dollars an hour? Luv, Allie

Too bad a group of guys didn't burn down their apartment and offer the same course in reverse. Men 101: how to get a man to fall in love with you. Men 201 (no prerequisite mandatory): how to seduce your best friend.

"Allie?" Josh's voice breaks my concentration.

"Yup?" I call out.

He pops his head into my room and starts to laugh.

"What?"

"It's the way you're sitting. You're going to kill your back."

I'm on my stomach, my knees bent at a ninety-degree angle, my feet hooked at the ankles, my head propped up by my elbows. It's the reverse of my Phone Concentration position. "You think? Is this why my back always hurts?"

He laughs again. "Yeah, I'd say so."

"What's up?"

"I'm taking off for the day."

Josh works here only in the mornings. He has another project at school in the afternoons. I prop my upper body up higher. "'Kay. See you tomorrow. Thanks for the breakfast."

"See you soon."

What to do for the rest of the day? Play on the Net? Watch TV?

Read? What I should really do is put together a résumé. I need to find a job. Or at least figure out what I want to do. I don't mind what I do now, I'm actually good at it, but how much better would it be to have an office and a salary and benefits and work from nine to five instead of being stuck in a tiny open space, get paid by the hour and work during prime time TV?

Maybe I'll watch TV. Can I get a job in TV?

I once wanted to be a singer. But then I sang a Celine Dion song at the school talent show and thought I was going to make a high note—I could do it—I'm almost there—I'm going to hit it—and then smack! It was as if I had jumped off a diving board and hit my head on the cement at the bottom of a pool. I stopped the song midway, burst into tears, ran off the stage and never signed up for another talent show.

Ooh! Clint's online! He's on instant messenger.

Clint says: *Do I have to dress up?*

Does he have to dress up? Does that mean he's coming? Of course he's coming. Why wouldn't he come? He already told me he would come. Has he been considering changing his mind?

Allie says: *Yes. What are you going to be?*

That isn't a very flirty response. How come I'm able to flirt with Josh but not with Clint?

Clint says: *What are you going to be?*

And he's not talking about my career dilemma. Okay, here goes nothing.

Allie says: *What do you want me to be?*

Did I just write that?

Clint says: *I'll have to think about that one.*

Allie says: *You should never think about things too long.*

As in us! Get it? Get it?

Clint says: *An angel?*

Allie says: *Aw, hell.*

Clint says: *A devil?*

Allie says: *Don't you know it.*

Did I just write that? DID I JUST WRITE THAT?

Clint says: *You'd look cute as a schoolgirl.*

Did he just write that? DID HE JUST WRITE THAT?

Ooh, kinky! He's flirting with me! Will my old tunic still fit?

Allie says: *Wanna be my teacher?*

In the art of love?

Clint says: *What costume does that involve? Just a suit?*

Only if it's your birthday. Get it? Birthday suit.

Allie says: *I was kidding! A teacher isn't a costume for a boy. Maybe you can be a schoolboy and I can be your teacher.*

There are some things I'd like to show you.

Clint says: *Only if you promise to tell me how naughty I've been.*

Omigod.

Allie says: *I'll bring my ruler.*

Oh. My. God. There *is* a God. See? See?

After all these years, it's finally going to happen! If my lips were any more spread into a smile I'd be a cartoon character.

Clint says: *You know what? Maybe I'll be Troy Cobrint. Great promo op for the Cobra shoes. Gotta go.*

Pfffffffffffffffffffffffffffffffffffff. My balloon of happiness just let out all its air and did its zigzag I-give-up dance around the room.

Actually, it's more like that talent show, when I took a nosedive onto the invisible concrete floor of the pool.

Splat.

Oh, look. One new e-mail. Click. Slooow...so slooow... It's from Manny!

Hi, Allie. Thanks again for dinner last night. Can't wait for your party. Hopefully your new "luck" will make sure it goes well. So all proceeds are going to charity? You guys are hysterical. Take care, Manny

How sweet! How nice is a guy who makes nice with his girlfriend's roommate? Jay had better not screw this up.

How awes would it be if Manny and I became friends? Every day could be like yesterday, with the three of us hanging out on the couch!

Hi, Manny! Dinner was my pleasure! I'll cook for you guys whenever you want! Happy costume hunting. Allie

Two new e-mails and they're both from Jay. The first one is labeled *"Re: Moneymaking Idea." Allie, the seminar idea definitely has potential. We'll discuss later. Jodine*

The second one is labeled *"Re:Fw:Fw: Luck." Please do not forward chain letters. I find them extraordinarily annoying. Thank you.*

Couldn't she have combined the two e-mails into one? Is it lunchtime yet?

Yup.

Pizza sandwich?

19
EMMA LOOKS SILLY

EMMA

"I still think we would have made gorge Pink Ladies," Allie says, fiddling with the tuner on my dashboard. "We could have all worn pink jackets and puffy skirts, and you could have worn your leather pants and been Rizzo."

"I'm not going to my own party dressed as a cheesy Pink Lady," I repeat. "And we don't have pink jackets and puffy skirts."

"I just don't understand what makes Pink Ladies cheesy and Charlie's Angels cool."

"Pink Ladies were cool—in 1985."

"But you said the bar plays eighties music! And Charlie's Angels are from the 1970s! Why are Charlie's Angels cool?"

"They just are. When Cameron Diaz stars as Sandy, then we can dress up as Pink Ladies." Why does the song playing sound like elevator music in slow motion? "What are we listening to?"

"Love Songs, Eight-Eighty."

"Can you change to another channel? Preferably one that won't put me into a coma?"

We have just come from last-minute costume shopping

downtown. We needed three sets of hoop earrings and some other last-minute Angel accessories. When I suggested we go as Charlie's Angels, Jodine agreed, mostly because I promised to be on costume detail, and that the costumes would be cheap and not look at all whorish.

A tall command, I tell you.

I tried to convince them both that we all needed new leather pants to perfect the outfit, but they didn't go for it. It's too bad, because I saw the perfect chocolate brown pair on Queen Street only last week. I also envisioned us wearing water pistols strapped to our thighs and tube tops. Now, that's sexy.

Jodine said it wasn't in our best interest to waste a few hundred dollars on pants or on unnecessary sex paraphernalia when the money could be better invested in dishes.

Somehow Allie has managed to find a *Grease* remix on the radio and is bopping her head in tune to it. "Where to now?" she asks. "Home? Are we going to get ready? It's only two. We still have time, right? We don't have to be at the bar till eight, right? Are you going to shower now? What if no one comes? Are we going to look stupid? Are we going to have to pay the bar? Why are we going uptown?"

I should have allowed the elevator music to stay on and lull her to sleep. I pull into a parking spot. "I have a surprise for you."

Allie's face scrunches in confusion. "You do? What?"

I think I should be nominated for the world's best roommate award for what I'm about to say. "I've noticed that you've been really good about not biting your nails. And I'm proud of you." On pilot, Allie spreads and extends her nearly healed fingers. "So I'm treating us both to a manicure at Suave," I continue. Suave is my favorite salon in Rosedale.

Allie jumps in her seat and claps her hands together. "Omigod!

That is so nice! I can't believe you're doing this! This is the nicest thing ever!"

See how easy it is to do a nice thing for someone? To make someone think you're the best person ever? I was planning to get my nails done, but I hate going alone, and then I thought of taking Allie. "My pleasure."

I park the car. "We're a little early," I say as we walk toward the salon. I hold open the door and Allie walks in. "Hello," I say to one of the two receptionists. If I were a salon receptionist I bet my hair would fall out. They change their hair color so often they remind me of mood rings. Last week they were both blondes and today one is a brunette with black streaks and one is a cherry redhead.

"Hi, how are you?" the brunette says. Her hair looks like the jar of swirled peanut butter and chocolate spread that I've noticed Allie eats with a spoon while watching TV.

"Fab, thanks. You girls?"

"Wonderful. Any chance you can get us in a bit early today?"

"I'll see what I can do for you, sweetie." She analyzes the names in her reservation book. "All right, I have someone for your friend." She points Allie to the nail room. "You can go right in, honey." Allie shoots me a what's-going-to-happen-to-me, are-they-going-to-take-off-my-fingers look and then timidly walks through the door. "Now let me see who can take you," the brunette says, flipping through pages.

I survey the reception area. Did they paint the walls? They used to be light beige and now they're lilac, a much classier choice. I think they change the colors on the wall as often as the reception-ists change the color of their hair. If I want to be a designer, I should probably be somewhat more aware of my surroundings, shouldn't I?

Jesus Christ.

What the fuck is he doing here?

Nick is at Suave.

Why the fuck is Nick at Suave? Is he waiting for some slut to get her hair highlighted? Is he waiting for some whorebag to wax her bikini line? Is that what he's doing here? I hope the waxer is causing severe pain and I hope the slutbag sprouts ingrown hairs all over her bikini line and looks like she's having a severe pubic acne outbreak next time she puts on a thong.

"Hey," he says. He's leaning back on a metal chair, his arms crossed in front of his chest, his legs spread open.His eyes are bloodshot and glazed. A wide smile looms across his face. Why is he so fucking sexy?

Fuck fuck fuck.

"Hello," I say, trying to force my voice to have an icy quality. My stomach feels like it has morphed into a garbage compactor and is in the process of squeezing the French fries that recently passed into my digestive system into a small hard cube in the pit of my abdomen. "What are you doing here?"

"Waiting for an appointment." Aha! That would explain his wet hair and the black smock.

No question about it, I definitely should be somewhat more aware of my surroundings.

"It's good to see you," he says.

"I'm sure."

"I hear you're having a party tonight."

"I am."

"Am I invited?"

I sigh loudly. "Do you want to come to my Halloween party?"

"Maybe."

Why do I put up with this? Why is he here? It's my fucking fault. I'm the one who made him book an appointment here and now he loves this place. What was I thinking? What kind of moron am I? How can I escape to the hairdresser/manicurist for makeover therapy when my ex also visits the same salon?

"Harriet will do you," the brunette says, motioning to a woman with swirly hair, who is wearing a long black cape.

"So will I," Nick-the-prick says from his chair and laughs.

Ha ha. I give him one of those you're-so-immature looks and follow Harriet/Swirly into the nail room. I'm not sure if her cape is part of her nail-doing getup or if she's in the Halloween spirit. Swirly's lips look as though they've been infused with air, and they're absurdly lined with a thin black pencil. I certainly won't be asking her to do my makeup.

"Did you know that guy?" she asks as I slip into the seat across from her. To my right, Allie is already having her cuticles cut.

"My ex," I answer, and take my rings off.

"I get it. And you just ran into him?"

"Unfortunately." I relax my fingers into the soapy hot water bowls.

Allie leans her body to the right and then to the left, trying to get a glimpse of him. "He's here?"

Does she think she's going to be able to see through a closed door? "He's in the reception area."

"Is he getting his nails done, too?"

"He's coiffing his prized hair."

Swirly whistles. "When did you guys break up?"

"End of August."

"Why?"

"He's a prick."

"Can I get a French manicure?" Allie asks the small Asian woman filing her nails.

She shakes her head. "They're too short. Next time. Do you want them round or square?"

"Round?" Allie asks, and looks at me.

"Square," I say.

"So why is he a prick?" Swirly asks.

I take a deep breath. "Because he's too intense for me. And controlling. And possessive."

"He sent at least a hundred roses to our apartment," Allie interjects. "We're roomies."

Why does she have to use the word *roomies* at the salon? Can't she pretend to be even a little bit cool?

"What are the chances that he'd be here the same day and the same time as you?" Swirly asks.

"Pretty unlikely," I say. Absurdly unlikely.

What a fucking ass. He planned this. He planned on seeing me. He could have come any day for the past three months. It's not like he does real work during the day. But instead he made an appointment for a Saturday. This Saturday. He must have called and asked when I was coming in. It's so obvious. And is that his Mustang parked right in front of the window? Is there any way it wasn't parked *directly* in front of the nail room on purpose? "I bet he set this up."

"Really?" Allie's eyes widen. It seems like they're always widening. Why does everthing I say amaze her? "You think he knew we were going to be here?"

We? What we? What does he care about seeing her? "He knew what he was doing."

"Why?"

"So he could casually see me. And so he can stop by on his way out to say how good it was to see me and ask me to get a drink or something. He's so predictable. He'll just hang around until I'm done, you'll see."

Allie nods. "You're terrif at reading people. Have you thought about becoming a psychologist?"

As if I want to listen to other people's problems all day. As if mine aren't enough. "Not really."

"Em, what color should I get?" Allie asks.

"Red."

"Really? You think? Not pink?"

What is it with her and pink?

"Get whatever you want, Allie. They're your nails."

"No, I like red. Red, please."

Twenty minutes later, when Allie positions her hands under the nail dryer, smiling gleefully at her polished red fingernails, and Swirly is painting on my topcoat, Allie asks, "Is that Nick getting into his car?"

Swirly's head spins and we both watch as a newly coiffed Nick unlocks the driver's side of his car, a cigarette hanging lazily from his lips. He climbs inside and slams the door behind him.

And now he's purposefully making me look like an idiot.

Bastard.

20
JODINE GETS READY

JODINE

I don't understand why Allie can't remember to change the showerhead from the mist setting back to localized pressure. Really. It makes no sense. She's obviously aware of altering the setting—she does it every time she showers—so why can't she remember to alter it back? There is no time for mist, and it doesn't get the shampoo out. It's about as effective as spraying my head with a water pistol.

Allie knocks on the door. I can hear her giggling on the other side.

What is so funny? What does she want? Can't I have ten minutes of privacy? Ten minutes. That's all I request. Ten measly minutes.

She knocks again. Repeatedly. Can I ignore her?

She's still knocking. Now she's calling out my name with each knock. "Jay!" Knock. "Jay!" Knock. "Jay!" Knock.

"WHAT?" I holler over the pounding water. "WHAT, WHAT, WHAT?"

She creaks open the door and slithers inside. "Sorry! I just need to get my brush."

Terrific. Now she is humming. Why is she still in here? Does she have to brush her hair in the bathroom?

"Are you almost done?" she asks. "We have to go soon."

"It's only seven," I say. "We have plenty of time."

"But you said you were going to be home at six."

My gym workout took slightly longer than I expected. "I'll be ready on time. We're not leaving until eight."

"Okay!" she sings, "but hurry up!" She disappears back into the hallway, leaving the door slightly ajar behind her.

Why did she do that? Do I really want to get out of the hot shower and into cold, steamless air?

"Allie!" I scream. "Al-lie!"

She pops her head back into the bathroom. "Yup?"

"Can you close the door, please?"

"Sorry!" Slam.

Fifteen minutes later, after I've shaved my legs and brushed the leave-in conditioner through my hair, I exit the bathroom, wrapped in my bathrobe. Madonna is blasting from Emma's room, I'm assuming to get us into the spirit.

I close my door behind me and survey the clothes spread onto my bed like cut-out paper dolls. Emma insisted I borrow a pair of her slinky satin black pants. Why not? It's Halloween. I also borrowed a bright red tube top.

She's wearing her silver one. Allie's wearing her black one.

Why does one girl have so many tube tops?

The phone rings and I see on the call display that it's Manny. Why is he calling now? Doesn't he know I'm getting ready? I spoke to him at five and told him I'd see him later. I let it ring again. The machine will pick up. I'm going to see him shortly, anyway.

"Hi, Manny!" I hear Allie say in her room. Why why why? Why didn't she contemplate, for one single second, that there was a reason I didn't pick up? Now I have to lie and pretend I didn't hear the phone ring. How annoying.

Why hasn't she called my name yet? It's been at least a minute. What are they talking about?

This is getting ridiculous. Really. It's been five minutes and the red light on my phone still signals that they're yapping. What are they talking about? They barely know each other. What could they possibly be discussing?

I am not going to wait for them. I'm going to get dressed, and they can talk for as long as they want. I couldn't care less. If they want to be best friends, they can be best friends. Allie sure has that market cornered, as far as male best friends go, and as far as I'm concerned, she can keep it. A woman's best friend should not be male. In fact, a woman's only true friend is herself.

"Jay! Manny's on the phone!"

No kidding. They've only been chatting for twelve minutes. What could they have possibly been discussing for twelve minutes? Were they talking about me? What else do they have to discuss besides me?

Maybe I just won't pick up. Or I'll just let him wait. He made me wait, so I should make him wait.

And I would, if I thought for a second that it was his fault. He obviously didn't call to talk to Allie. She probably just didn't shut up.

"Hello," I say coldly.

"Hi!"

"'Bye, Manny!" Allie says.

"'Bye, Allie," I say, allowing an edge to creep into my voice.

"Just called to see if you were all ready for tonight."

"What was that all about?"

"What was what about?"

"I was just wondering what you and Allison could possibly be talking about for twelve minutes."

Manny laughs. "Are you jealous?" he asks hopefully.

I *don't* think so. "I'm just not sure I comprehend what you and my roommate could have been discussing that was so lengthy."

"I was just teasing her about her e-mail chain letter."

"She sent you an e-mail chain letter?"

"Yes—she sent it to you, too. We were on the same list."

I never have time to look at lists. Upon receiving chain letters, I simply press Delete. "Did you e-mail her back?"

"Of course I did."

Is something going on here? Is Allie after my boyfriend? Is the whole sweet naive thing a complete facade? Am I being played? Are they having an affair? "Why would you e-mail her back? Isn't it customary to forward a chain letter, not to reply to the person who sent you one?"

"Because she's your roommate. And I care about you. And I want to feel at home when I'm at your place."

Interesting. "But why is she e-mailing you to begin with? Does she like you?"

"Not like *that*. She's your roommate and she wants to be a part of your life, maybe?"

"Does she have to be a part of all aspects of my life? She can be so annoying."

"She's not annoying. You have to give her a chance."

Terrific. This is exactly the problem. One of the main perks of having a boyfriend, or a "special friend" or whatever Manny is, is that it's his responsibility to listen to me complain about my roommates. And it's my roommates' responsibility to listen to me complain about my boyfriend, "special friend" or whatever. If my boyfriend and roommate become friends, then their respective responsibilities cancel each other out, don't they? Plus, since I'm their shared interest, I will undoubtedly end up as the frequent lead topic in their conversations. I do not care to be rehashed in this way.

And what about once I move to New York and no longer speak to either of them? Are they going to go out for coffee to discuss how much "I've changed"? I hate that. You know, when ex-boyfriends and ex-friends tell you how much "you've changed"? What does this mean? Usually it means you no longer have time for them and it would break their fragile egos to consider that you have outgrown them, so instead they have to imagine that you've morphed into some kind of insufferable being whose morals have become horribly out of whack, when in reality you just don't pick up when you see their name on call display. "I don't see any reason why you two should be friends. Can you not encourage this?"

"Okay," he says, sighing. "If that's what you want."

I tell him I'll see him at the party, and I continue getting ready.

"Jay!" Allie screams from the hallway.

"What?" What? What does she want now? It's only seven-thirty. She can't be hurrying me already.

"You forgot again!" she screams.

"I forgot what?" I scream back. What is she rambling about?

She knocks on the door.

"Come in."

She opens the door and sits down on my bed. She's already in full Charlie's Angels regalia. She's wearing the tube top and tight black pants. Black sunglasses are perched on top of her head. "Hi." She smiles sheepishly. "Sorry. But you never remember to flush the toilet." She hands me a powder-blue scarf. "Can you tie this around my neck for me?"

Absolutely ridiculous. First she tries to steal my boyfriend, then she criticizes my hygiene, and now she wants me to help her get ready? I tie the scarf in a knot around her neck, resisting the urge to twist it tighter...tighter... "There you go. And I did flush the toilet."

"Come look if you want." She giggles. "I just went into the bathroom and there's pee in the toilet."

Absolutely ridiculous. I follow her into the bathroom and she lifts up the toilet seat. Indeed, there is urine is the toilet bowl.

Oh. "You know what?" I say. "I run the shower water first to get it to warm up. And while I'm waiting, I usually use the facilities. I don't like to flush because it makes the water cold." My face feels as hot as if it's been rammed into a toaster oven turned on broil.

"Do you think you could try to remember? I don't care that much, but Josh comes by in the mornings and he gets to the bathroom before I do. He probably thinks it's a little weird that someone keeps forgetting to flush."

How horrifically embarrassing. Our repairman thinks I'm a pig.

"I'll try to remember."

"Maybe we should put up a sign?"

"What would it say, Allie? Please flush? Would that be less embarrassing?"

"No, I mean a hidden sign to secretly remind you to flush. Maybe something yellow? Like a banana candle or something?"

"Can we discuss this another time?"

"Okay. Are you going to straighten your hair?"

"Why?"

"Emma thinks you should blow it out fluffy like Farrah Fawcett."

"Well if Emma says I should, then I guess I have to. Emma is the boss."

"Okay, good."

My sarcasm apparently just glides right over her head.

"So hurry up!" she sings. "Not much time left!"

I cannot take her anymore. I must put my foot down about something. Since there are numerous issues to step on, I chose the Manny concern. "Allie, I want to discuss something with you."

"Yup. What?"

"I think it's a bit weird that you're e-mailing Manny."

She appears mildly confused. More so than normally. "Really? Why?"

"I just don't understand *why* you'd e-mail him."

"Because...because I want to be friends with him?"

"Why? Why do you need another male friend? Don't you have Clint? You know I'm not that serious about him. So why develop a relationship with him? Are you planning on going after him when I move to New York?"

Allie looks horrified. "What are you talking about? Of course not! How could you think that? What kind of roomie would that make me? I just thought it would be nice to be friends with him. That's it."

"I think it's weird."

"You're being nuts," she says, shaking her head. "But I won't e-mail him again if that's what you want. Don't freak out."

I am hardly freaking out. "Thank you."

"Now, get ready. We're late."

I hear her knock on Emma's door. "Em? Are you ready? Can you show me how to wear the water pistol? And can you do my makeup?"

Can't that girl do anything on her own?

Truthfully, I was planning on wearing my hair down, and possibly fluffy, but now I don't want to do it because it will seem like I did it just to please Emma. But isn't not performing a task for the sake of not pleasing my roommate just as ridiculous as performing a task to please her?

Once the satin pants **are pulled** up, the tube top squeezed into, the hair fluffed, the sunglasses perched on top my head, the water pistol strapped to my thigh, the black scarf tied around my neck and the hoops strung through my ears, I set off for Emma's room to see how they're doing.

Allie has rearranged the bottles of hair spray and mousse to clear a spot for herself on the counter beside the sink in the bathroom off Emma's room. The mirror is against her back. As Emma applies foundation with a small triangular sponge, Allie's eyes raptly follow her fingers as though they're a bouncing red ball moving from word to word, encouraging Allie the five-year-old to sing along.

Allie lifts her chin with her fingers to show off her recently made-up face.

Her complexion has always been smooth, but now it's glowing. Her eyes look about twice as large as they normally do, due to heavy black eyeliner, mascara and multilayers of blue eye shadow. Her lips are stop-sign red. As are her nails. Her nails?

"Allie! Your nails look gorgeous!" I grab her hand to get a better look. "But why did you pick red? You should have picked a color that won't exaggerate your still-healing cuticles."

"Emma took me. She surpithed me. Ithn't thee the betht?"

I feel a pang of roommate jealousy. Why didn't I think of doing that? Allie stopped biting in the first place because of my encouragement.

"Did you pluck your eyebrows?" I ask.

"We certainly did," Emma says. "She was looking a bit like Bert."

Allie swings her tiny feet. "Do I look too surprithed? Are they too arched? Do you like them?"

What is wrong with her mouth? "Why are you lisping?"

Allie shrugs. "Listhping?"

"Yes, lisping!"

She shrugs again. "I think ith becuth of the lipthtick."

I breathe a sigh of relief. For a moment I actually thought that Emma made her get her tongue pierced. Which is ridiculous, since Allie was speaking normally only a few moments ago. Unless Emma did it to her just now. "Stick out your tongue," I say.

"Ahh…"

Satisfied that she has not been mutilated, I say, "I don't understand. The lipstick is making you lisp? If you're allergic to it, take it off."

"No, it'th juth that…" She stretches open her lips and then closes them. "I'm afraid of getting it on my teeth."

"Why would you get it on your teeth? You're not going to get it on your teeth," I tell her. "Women all over the world wear lipstick and they manage not to get it on their teeth."

She shakes her head. "I alwayth get it on my teeth."

Ridiculous. "So don't chew on it." I cannot spend the whole evening listening to her talk like a five-year-old whose mother hasn't made the time to take her to speech therapy.

Emma puts down the lipstick brush and lifts her right index finger into the air. "You have to do the finger trick. Stick your finger into your mouth—no, Allie, your finger has to be dry. Don't wipe it on your costume. Use tissue."

Allie dries her finger on the tissue and then sticks it between her lips.

"No, Allie, move it to the center of your mouth and wipe your teeth."

Allie moves it to the center and wipes her teeth.

"Now slowly pull it out. Pretend you're giving Clint a preview."

Allie slowly pulls it out.

"Not bad. If I were him, I'd let you give me a blow job."

Allie looks at her red-smudged finger.

"Now anything that would have been on your teeth is on your finger. Wash your hand and you're ready."

Allie turns her head toward the mirror and smiles into it. Un-smiles. Smiles. Un-smiles. Smiles. "Thanks, Emma! You're the best!"

You're the best. You're so amazing. Suck up.

Allie appraises my outfit. "Your hair looks terrif, Jay! Completely gorge! And Manny's not going to be able to take his eyes off your butt in those pants." She smiles dreamily to herself. "Do you think Clint will think I look hot?"

I lock eyes with Emma in the mirror. "Yes, Allie, Clint will think you look hot."

Emma carefully applies her seventies' baby-blue eye shadow and does a model pose in front of the mirror. "Are you Angels almost ready?" she asks. "Aren't you going to do your makeup, too?" This last question, obviously, is addressed at me.

"I'm not a huge fan of makeup," I say.

"It's Halloween. Not wearing makeup on Halloween is like not telling someone you love them on Valentine's Day."

"I don't think I've ever told anyone I love him on Valentine's Day."

"You know, you're allowed to tell friends you love them on Valentine's Day. It doesn't have to be a guy." Emma laughs. "My new goal is to get you to tell me you love me by Valentine's Day. But for now, give me your face and I'll do your makeup."

I'm not the type of person who tells friends I love them. I sign my birthday cards "fondly" or "best wishes," and I always sign my last name, even on family cards, which for some reason has always amused my parents.

"No time for my makeup," I say. "We're running late as it is."

"Not really," Emma counters. We turn the clocks back to Eastern Standard time tonight, remember? So we gain an extra hour."

"That only happens at 2:00 a.m.," I say.

"Everyone I know does it at midnight. Can we do it now? We might forget later. So can we? Now?" Allie pesters.

I sigh. "Fine. We'll do it now. But I think we should get to the bar an hour earlier, just in case the rest of the world doesn't know the new rules."

"At least the VCR clock will be right again," Allie says.

"It's so stupid," Emma says. "Maybe we should protest by not changing them. The whole clock-changing phenomenon seriously makes no sense. It's going to get dark at five. Why should it get dark at five? So farmers in Nebraska or wherever can have an extra hour of sunlight at six in the morning? No one else is up at six in the morning."

Allie looks at her blankly.

"Actually, Emma," I say. "Daylight saving time has nothing to do with farmers in Nebraska. Farmers hate changing the clocks. Daylight saving time was implemented during the world wars to cut energy costs."

"It's still stupid," Emma says, applying mascara. "Let's boycott."

"I'll change all the clocks in the house while you do Jay's makeup, just in case we forget to do it later," Allie says. "This way for sure, we can sleep in an extra hour." She smiles widely and leaves the bathroom.

Two red smudges glisten from her two front teeth.

21
OMNISCIENT NARRATOR TRIES TO GIVE UNBIASED MULTI-PERSPECTIVE ACCOUNT OF PARTY

You want a tour of the bar, don't you? Fine. It's still empty. But you'd better pay attention or you're going to get all confused when the action takes place later on.

It's eight-thirty. Emma is parking. Jodine told her she should leave the car at home and they would split a cab. But Emma doesn't go anywhere without her car, so she promised she wouldn't have too much to drink. Which of course she does.

Don't worry. This isn't going to be a story where a drunken Emma drives into a tree and beheads her two roommates. She's not going to have to live with overbearing guilt the rest of her life. They're not going to make her life into an after-school special. Hate to give it away, but there are no car accidents, not even a fender-bender, in this entire story. Truth is, it probably wouldn't be the worst thing in the world for Emma's character if while intoxicated, she totaled a parked car. As long as no one was hurt, of course.

But this doesn't happen.

Oh, well.

Come on, come on.

The first thing you see when you get to the bar is the bouncer. He doesn't talk much. He's six foot two and weighs two hundred and fifty pounds, and he's wearing a puffy jacket, black pants and a look that says, *Don't fuck with me.* He has on one of those headphone walkie-talkies. He's not wearing a costume. Spoilsport.

("I didn't say that, sir. It wasn't me, sir. It was that guy." Now point and run.)

Behind him is a heavy steel door. On the other side of the door is a woman dressed as a cat (furry tail, yellow pantsuit, blackened nose and whiskers). She's perched on a wood table, waiting to collect the partygoers' money. Behind her is a geisha (painted white face, hair held together with chopsticks, a tight shiny black Asian-style dress) guarding the coat check. To the right of her a hallway leads into a large square navy room, lit with carefully positioned spotlights and mirrors. Two bars line the room. The one on the right is the main bar; the other bar is on the left. Cheryl and Tiffany tend the main bar. Right now they are dancing to a George Michael song while they set out the proper materials for the evening. Steve is pacing up and down the floor. He's on his cell, arguing with his wife.

Two other bartenders take care of the left bar, but they won't be described to you, because to be honest, only two characters in this story ever make it to that bar and they're too busy groping each other to notice the bartenders, so why should you be bombarded with the details?

The bathrooms are located to the left of the room. Whoops, those should have been pointed out first thing (in case of emergency). Regardless, the bathrooms are not overly important to this story, although each of the principal characters does use the facility at least once, some (Manny, for instance) more frequently.

Beyond the two bars is the dance floor. It's not a huge dance floor, and dancers usually end up spilling into the main bar area, but it has a solid polished hardwood floor and blaring strobe lights above it. Behind the dance floor is a small staircase that leads to a second level. On this second level, there are booths set into the walls and one more bar.

And one more bartender.

This is no ordinary bartender. This bartender is Tom Cruise, Brad Pitt, Kirk Cameron, John Travolta as Vinnie Barbarino come back to haunt us, every other guy you or your older sister ever did or ever will think of as hot, rolled into one supercharged sex god. Do you know what would happen if you cut and pasted all the best characteristics of every man you've ever fantasized about into one blank palette? You would either get a horrendously disproportional cubist painting, or, if you did it correctly, this bartender.

His name is George and he takes over the entire second floor whenever he's behind the bar. Every movement he makes shouts confidence, power, sexuality. He is Sex in a pair of black pants. He's also wearing a tight black T-shirt that perfectly illuminates his arm and chest muscles. And he's not just a body...look at that face! His perfectly square jaw and piercing blue eyes look like they could cut through any last-minute jitters you might have about sleeping with a man you just met a half a second ago.

Tonight he's wearing a cape and white gloves because he's Dracula. I doubt there is one single woman in the entire world who would turn down having him suck her neck.

He hums the tune to "I Want Your Sex" and gets his shot glasses ready.

You just know that he's getting mixed up with our heroines somehow, don't you? Did the elongated description of him give it away?

Here come our heroines. Finally. It's already eight-forty. They were supposed to be here ten minutes ago, but Jodine's makeup prep took longer than expected. She made Emma repeat it three times.

They reintroduce themselves to Steve and then realize that there is nothing for them to do, so they hang up their jackets and head over to the main bar.

Emma sits down on a bar stool and pulls out a cigarette. She only has five left and she's wishing she had bought a new pack.

Jodine sits down, too, and scrutinizes Cheryl's sculpted body. Cheryl is wearing a black leather bustier that cuts off above her stomach, and silver stretch pants. Her arms are perfectly sculpted. What exercises does she do to get them like that? Jodine wonders. Just push-ups? The rower? She wonders if it's appropriate to ask the bartender what gym she goes to. And why isn't she dressed up? It's Halloween. If Jodine dressed up, surely the bartender could have found something in her closet besides her regular attire.

Allie repeatedly looks at her watch and then bounces on her toes. "Why ithn't anyone here yet?" she asks. After Jodine pointed out the new red marks on her teeth, the lisp made a comeback.

Yes, Allie is nervous. You see, she's the type of girl who after receiving an e-invite, RSVPs within the first five minutes. Since "fashionable" and "late" are both foreign concepts to her, putting them together is like speaking to her in Japanese. And she doesn't speak Japanese. Wouldn't you be floored right now if you found out she actually did speak Japanese? And Polish and Portuguese? Would your whole perspective of her change dramatically? What if you found out that at night she sneaks out of the house and is an international spy for the Canadian government? Would you reread the whole story to see what you must have missed?

Don't worry. No crazy curveballs. She only speaks English and a little pig Latin, and needs too much sleep to be a covert spy. Does the Canadian government even have spies?

"Allie," Emma says. "You've got to relax. Do you want a smoke?" Secretly, Emma hopes that Allie will not say yes, since that will only leave her with three.

"No. Maybe. Will it ruin my lipstick? What if no one comes? What if it's just the three of us? What will we do?"

"You're stressing me out," Jodine tells her.

"I think we need some shots," Emma says.

"Good idea," Jodine says.

Emma props herself up onto the bar. "Excuse me, can we get nine kamikazes?"

Jodine's mouth drops open. "Nine?"

"Nine is some." Emma pulls her credit card out of her purse. "I want to start a tab," she tells the bartender.

"What's a kamikaze?" Allie asks. "Will I like it? Is it fruity?"

Emma puts her index finger on Allie's mouth. "Shh. Just drink."

"Is it carbonated?"

Jodine tears her eyes away from the bartender's forearms. "Allie, sit down. You're driving us crazy."

Allie's face flushes the color of her nail polish and she hoists herself onto a bar stool.

Cheryl pours the concoction into nine shot glasses that were already lined up on the bar.

"Ready?" Emma asks.

"Ready," Allie bellows back.

The three girls pick up their shots.

"To making a shit-load of cash tonight," Emma says. They clink their shot glasses and down them.

"Mmm. That's good," Allie says. "It tastes like Kool-Aid."

Jodine raises another glass. Allie and Emma follow. "To one day in the not-so-distant future, coming home to an intact kitchen," she says. They clink their shot glasses and down them.

Allie picks up the next glass. "To having terrif roomies, being happy and finding The One," she announces, and giggles. They clink their shot glasses and down them.

The girls' heads feel a tiny bit lighter, the music sounds a tiny bit louder, and the flashing strobe light looks a tiny bit strobier.

"Who's going to man the door?" Jodine asks.

Emma cringes at Jodine's choice of the word *man*. "Can't you choose a different verb than 'man'? That's so sexist."

Jodine rolls her eyes. "I didn't realize you were breaking the glass ceiling in that outfit," she says.

Emma readjusts her tube top. "These outfits aren't antifeminist. Feminism should be about women using what they've got to get what they want."

"I'm pretty sure that's not the definition of feminism," Jodine responds.

Come on, is this really the time or place for a political debate?

Emma stretches her arms above her head and brings them back down in a circular motion. "Blah blah blah. I call first shift."

"Okay," Allie says. "But I want second."

"Why do we need to stand by the door at all?" Jodine asks. "They're paying Cat-Lady to do that."

Emma opens her purse and pulls out her round tube of lipstick and a lip brush. "I don't trust Pussy for one second. If we're not watching, we'll never see any of the money. I'm going first."

Jodine vehemently shakes her head. "No way. Why should you get the first two hours when no one's having fun, and Allie and I get stuck with the two hours when the party's in full swing?"

Emma dabs the lip brush against the tube and applies it to her lips. "It's a fair trade. The first two hours are the busiest."

Jodine crosses her arms below her tube-topped chest. She hates the thing. It keeps falling. "No way. We should rotate every half hour. This way, all three of us have a good time, and none of us want to kill ourselves."

Emma mulls this over. "Okay. But I start."

"Fine," Jodine says.

"When is my turn, then?" Allie asks. Her cheeks are already flushed.

Maybe three shots before the party even started wasn't the best idea, Allie, dear.

"In half an hour," Jodine says.

Guess who is the first guest to arrive? Manny. Obviously. He actually felt bad for getting here this late (keener). He hoped to arrive at eight-thirty when Jodine was supposed to, but accidentally smashed his hook in the door of his car and had had to return to his apartment for more aluminum paper. In addition to the aluminum hook poking out of his sleeve, he has a patch over his left eye, a feathered hat, tight black pants, a purple shirt and a black vest. He pays Emma ten dollars and enters the bar.

"You girls look gorgeous," he says to Jodine and Allie.

Allie's not sure if she's supposed to ignore him or not, so she half smiles and fidgets with her tube top.

"Thanks," Jodine answers. "Do you know what we are?"

"J.Lo's?"

"Come on! Why would we all dress like Jennifer Lopez? We're Charlie's Angels," Jodine says.

"Is that why there's a water pistol strapped to your thigh?"

"Uh-huh."

Allie is keeping her mouth shut. She doesn't feel like being told she's acting like a boyfriend stealer, thank you very much.

"Are you a pirate?" Jodine asks.

"Either that or a construction-site victim," he says.

Allie giggles. She can't help herself.

Manny puts a twenty-dollar bill on the counter. "Do you girls want a drink?"

Emma takes two ten-dollar bills from two giggling girls in playboy-bunny outfits. She's thinking about starting a pool for the most-creative-way-to-announce-you're-a-slut costume.

"Is anyone here yet?" one bunny says to the other as they hop over to the coat check.

Three guys wearing Greek letters on their chests are next in line. Goateed-Guy turns to Blond-Buzzcut-Boy, points to the bunnies and says, "Do you think those girls are lesbians?" Crewcut-Cad nods and smirks.

Emma smiles. Yes, little frat boys, I'm sure these lesbians have decided to dress as male fantasies just to attract other women. And what are they dressed as? she wonders. Mockeries of themselves?

She decides to charge them twenty dollars each, and pockets the extra.

Let the good times roll.

By eleven, the party is in full drunken swing and Allie is on her second round at the door. Jodine is sitting on the same bar stool she was sitting on earlier, but now standing next to her are Manny and Monique. Monique is in law school with Jodine and Manny.

Jodine likes her, but finds her a bit strange. The first time they ate together, Monique pulled out baby food—in a packaged baby food jar. Crushed peas. She claimed she found the jars easily transportable and the taste of the food delicious.

The second strangeism, according to Jodine, since strange, like beauty, is in the eye of the beholder, is that she wears clothes that look as though they have been pulled off a runway. Have you ever watched a fashion show and thought, Oh, I wish I had that in my closet? No, right? The thing is, most of the stuff would look highly inappropriate in the real world, since much of it looks like material draped over the body of a twelve-year-old with pelvic bones sticking right out of her body. Moreover, Monique's body is nowhere near similar to a supermodel's. She's tall (fine), but has reasonable hips, thighs and at most B-cup breasts. Anyway, not only does she wear these getups around town, but she wears them to school. Must one wear a fur-lined mauve sweater jacket, beige leather pants and three-inch black boots to Property Law at 9:00 a.m. on Monday?

Tonight Monique is wearing fishnet stockings, red heels, hot pink shorts and a silver bra.

"What are you, exactly?" Jodine asks.

"A call girl." Monique laughs. "An expensive one."

Not leaving much to the imagination, are we? Jodine thinks, and wonders, Where has the art of subtlety gone?

Monique takes a big gulp of her drink. "So how are you, Jo? Did you have a good summer?"

Has she not spoken to Monique since last year? Jodine doesn't remember. That's too bad. Monique is fun to study with. They should ask her to join them in the library one of these days.

Monique isn't particularly fond of Jodine. The truth is, she thinks Jodine is a bitch who treats Manny like crap. She's sure he would be much better off with someone nicer, someone with a bit more flair…essentially, her.

Here's the scoop: after Monique broke up with her college boyfriend in her first year of law, she decided to get to know the cute brown-haired guy who sat in the front row, doodled people's faces in his notebook instead of taking notes and still managed to ask at least one perfect question per class. You know the kind of question, the type you wonder about but can't really articulate, and then he asks it, and the teacher explains, and everything the teacher has been rambling on about all hour finally makes sense.

That spring exam period, Monique sat next to him at the library, monitoring his breaks so they would coincidentally bump into each other at the vending machine. But then exams ended and nothing. No phone call, no plans to meet over the summer, nothing.

Monique just happened to pick the same five classes as Manny for second year, which meant they'd spend all day together. Monique thought everything was smooth-sailing; they were laughing and whispering during classes, passing jokes, studying in the library until closing time, until one day in October Monique noticed that instead of doodling their professor, Manny was doodling Jodine, the serious-looking girl who always came five minutes late to class and laid out two pens and three different color highlighters on her desk as soon as she sat down. Manny and Jodine were dating by the first week of November.

Monique decided to go the friend route and the three of them studied at the library all year.

But then Jodine took off for New York, and whom do you think Manny called every night to pull him out of his depressive state? That's right, Monique. She was the one who had to take him to movies, who had to nurse her glass of wine while he analyzed why Jodine didn't call him, why Jodine didn't love him, why Jodine couldn't commit to him. It was enough to drive a normal girl insane.

But Monique had a plan! She figured she'd nurse Manny back to emotional sanity and then, wham-oh! He'd fall in love with her. And the plan was working. By the first week in September, Jodine's name came up only once an evening instead of once every second sentence. Monique figured she'd bide her time, waiting until Manny was fully cured, and then she'd make her move. She didn't want to be a rebound. She wanted them to spend this Halloween as M&Ms. (Get it? Monique and Manny!)

But then Pole-Up-Her-Behind returned and slept with him again.

And now what was Monique supposed to do? She decided she wasn't going to hang around in the wings this time, begging to be re-trampled on. So she is here tonight, not to be chummy with Manny and Jodine, but because everyone she knows is going to be here and she wants to pick up.

Of course Jodine is completely clueless about all this. She's still clueless about a lot of things. She still thinks Allie has the hots for her man, but the truth is Allie doesn't have even one hot for any man except Clint.

Jodine feels a big wet kiss on her cheek and sees Emma smiling wildly.

"Shit, I just got lipstick all over you," Emma says, smearing it off with her hand. "Allie and I just switched again."

"How are we doing?"

"We're making a fucking fortune. I should have volunteered to do the door all night. I got to check out the selection as they came in. And let me tell you, there is one seriously fuckable guy floating around in here."

Monique's eyes do a tour around the dance floor, looking for this fuckable guy. She has not had sex in thirteen months and has decided that this is ending tonight.

"Monique, this is my roommate Emma. Emma, Monique."

Emma eyes the whore costume. "That's what we all should be doing," she says, nodding her approval. "Letting it all hang out.

Instead of wasting time with Charlie's Angels. No one gets it. Someone just asked me if I was Lara Croft."

Emma leans over to give Manny one kiss on each cheek. "Having fun?"

He takes a swig of his beer. "A blast. Good party."

"Emma, look to your left. I think that's Nick." Jodine has never met Nick, but she has seen a few of the pictures that Emma hasn't destroyed.

Emma's eyes narrow. "I don't have to look. I know what Nick-the-Prick looks like."

"You saw him already?" Jodine asks, still trying to get the lipstick off her cheek. Why would Emma kiss her on the cheek when she was wearing lipstick? Does that make sense?

"He walked right up to me and handed me ten bucks. I almost told the bouncer to throw him out, after what he pulled this morning. But I didn't want him to think I give a shit."

Of course, Nick had no idea that Emma was going to be at the salon this afternoon. He was happy to see her, yes, but he's getting a little bit fed up with all the dramatics.

But he decides to give Emma one last chance. Eyes glazed, he picks his drink off the bar and squeezes his way over to the group. He obviously considers himself too cool to wear a costume and is wearing his usual black pants, black shirt, downtown getup. He pats Emma on the shoulder. She doesn't turn around.

"Em, can I talk to you for a sec?"

Her mouth tightens. She's still mad at him for making her look like an ass in front of the manicurist. "Now's not a good time."

"When is a good time?"

"This afternoon would have been a good time, when you couldn't even manage to say goodbye at the hairdresser." Emma's voice rises with every word until she's louder than the "I'm

Walking on Sunshine" track swirling in the background. "Why do you think we always have to go by your schedule, Nick? Does the whole world revolve around Nick, Nick, Nick, Nick?"

Jodine, Monique and Manny stare at the floor.

Jodine is annoyed that Emma is making a scene at their party. Monique is wondering why Jodine's roommate is blowing it with such a stud. Manny is thanking God that he's not *that* guy. No guy ever wants to be *that* guy.

Nick puts his hands on Emma's bare shoulders. "Can you stop freaking out for two secs so we can discuss this like adults?"

Emma picks up his hands and throws them off. "I have stuff to do," she says, and storms away.

Great, Jodine thinks. Now it's Monique, Manny, Nick and me. Which one in this list is not like the others? Yes, Nick! You win! Too bad Nick is not Mick. Then there would be perfect alliteration.

No one speaks for at least two minutes. Finally Jodine realizes that she is required to be the grown-up. "Hi, Nick, I'm Jodine, Emma's roommate."

"Jo?"

"No, Jodine. This is my friend Manny," she says, motioning.

Monique almost wants to punch Jodine for not introducing him as her boyfriend. On the one hand, she's happy that maybe Manny will see the light and leave the bitch, but on the other hand, she hates to see her sweet-smooch treated in this manner. But Manny doesn't even notice because he's still basking in the "I'm so happy that she wants to be with me" glow.

"And you're…Emma's other roommate?" he asks, eyes appreciating Monique's costume.

"No, I'm Monique. I just met Emily for the first time." She flips her hair behind her head and smiles.

He smiles back.

"It's Emma," Jodine says.

Manny wraps his arm around Jodine's waist.

Nick shakes his head. "Emma's always been crazy."

Monique smiles. "Is she your girlfriend?"

"Ex-girlfriend," he answers. Their gazes lock.

"She's not crazy," Jodine comments, suddenly defensive. "Just expressive."

"Can I get anyone a drink?" Nick asks.

Jodine shakes her head.

"No, thanks," Manny says.

Monique smiles and links her arm through Nick's. "I'd love one."

Uh-oh.

Jodine feels her armpits dampen. She probably shouldn't be fixing up her roommate's ex-boyfriend with a woman dressed as a prostitute, should she?

Emma is dancing on top of the left bar when she sees the fuckable guy she let in earlier, standing below her.

When he had paid for his ticket and handed her a twenty, their hands touched, and a surge of heat penetrated her fingers and spread through her body. When she handed him his change, his huge smile made her legs feel like she was melting.

For someone who was almost burned to death, she sure uses a lot of fire imagery.

"Enjoy the party," she told him, noticing he was alone. Which meant no girlfriend.

He smiled his movie-star smile. "I plan to."

And she planned on enjoying it with him.

Now here he was, still alone, on the market all right, and Emma is primed to snatch him up. And it won't bother her slightly if Nick-the-Prick watches the whole event unfold.

He is no longer wearing his coat, and she can see his costume, a baseball uniform with a Blue Jays cap on his head and a baseball glove on his hand. She bends toward him and he helps her off the bar. "I was looking for you," she tells him.

"Were you? That's what you were doing up there? Looking for me?"

"I was in the perfect position to dance and scout. Nice costume, by the way. Basketball player?"

He laughs, exposing those perfect, big white teeth she noticed earlier. He fills out that uniform in all the right places, and she feels the heat run through her body again.

"Wrestler, actually," he says, and his eyes smile down at her.

"You're going to have to take off some of the layers if you're trying to be a wrestler."

He takes a swig of his beer. "Is that an invitation?"

"Buy me a drink and we'll see."

"What'll you have?" he asks, his eyes skimming over the invitation standing before him.

Clint doesn't know who this woman in the tight leather pants is, but he figures she'll tell him when she's good and ready. And he has a feeling that when she's ready, she'll be good.

Uh-oh.

"Josh! You came!" Allie exclaims, pulling him into a hug. He's wearing a cowboy hat, blue jeans and a worn-in white T-shirt. He looks like a young Marlboro Man.

"Of course I came," he says, rubbing his hand on her back. "Let me look at you." He pulls away from her and whistles. "You look hot."

"I do?"

"Boiling. I brought two of my buddies. Allie, this is Danny and this is Jordan. Meet Allie, by far the hottest woman in the whole place."

Allie blushes. "I bet you say that to all the Angels."

Danny looks over at Jordan. "He doesn't, actually."

All three of them hand Allie their ten dollars and go to the coat check. A few minutes later, Josh returns to Allie's side. "I thought I'd keep you company." He sits beside her at the table.

"I'm fine, don't worry about me. Go have a drink with your friends. I'm sure you don't want to sit by the door all night."

"I'll sit wherever I want to sit, as long as I'm not interrupting. Where's Clint?"

Allie looks around anxiously. "I don't know. I haven't seen him. I'm not sure if he's here yet."

He's a moron, Josh thinks. "Are you making me a lot of money?"

"Tons." Allie pats the mound of money in the metal box she's holding.

"I'll keep you company until he gets here."

Allie smiles. "Thanks. I appreciate it."

"I'll be two seconds," Manny tells Jodine. He removes her hand from under the back of his shirt. "I just want to run to the bathroom."

If Jodine were her sober self, she would probably be thinking, *Again? This is the fourth time in two hours.* But since she's completely plastered, all she's thinking is, *When can we go home? I want to have sex.* Do you remember the effect alcohol has on her when she gets drunk? She's like a librarian in a porno movie. One second her hair is back in a tight bun, her eyes magnified behind small granny glasses. The next second the hair is a-flyin' and the glasses are somewhere under a polyester couch.

Manny disappears into the bathroom, and within three seconds, Jodine forgets that she's supposed to be waiting for him.

She pushes through the dancing couples. One of them is Emma and Clint. Not that she notices.

"'Scuse me, 'scuse me," she says, attempting to be heard over the music. She climbs the steps and tries to count how many people are here. One. Two. Three. Stop moving! How can she count them when they're moving? She feels a bit like a queen surveying her kingdom. Who are all these people? Look, there's Sonny and Cher! And there's a tree! There's a woman with a white mustache and a Got Milk sign! Who are these clever, creative people? Hello people! Hello! She waves. She decides she needs another drink and that's when she sees him.

The Hottest Bartender in the World. Gorgeous George.

That isn't a man, she thinks. It's Zeus. She is pulled toward him as though she is a piece of magnet and he is a fridge. The fancy, expensive kind that has a built-in water system. She finds an empty seat at the bar and steadies herself onto the stool.

How is it, she wonders, that the masses of single women in the world are so unaware of this treasure hidden away on this island?

"Hello," Jodine says.

"Hello," says George/Zeus. "What can I get you?"

I love you, she thinks. She's surprised how easily the word *love* comes to mind when usually she scorns it, but there it is, all shiny and fluffy. "What do you recommend?"

"That depends on what you like." He smiles at her and she falls into his eyes and falls and falls and falls and she feels like she's a tiny piece of lint and he's an industrial-size vacuum cleaner.

She can't speak. She can't do anything but stare into Zeus's face. For at least a second, time seems to stop and she feels like she's at home, staring at the cover of an issue of *People* magazine, this luscious man on the cover, and at present, she has no immediate plans to stop.

But Zeus must get on with his job. He has other customers who require watering, and they are waiting for him to finish serving Jodine. "How about a cosmopolitan?" he asks.

Jodine, in a trance, nods. Three minutes later, she is still in a trance as he hands her the drink.

"Quite a party, isn't it?" he says to her.

"It is." She decides to attempt to impress him. "It's *my* party."

"Really? You organized it?"

"Yes." She nods repeatedly.

"Impressive. Good for you." He leans over and puts his elbows against the bar. He smells like a mix of alcohol and musk. "Try the cosmo. Tell me if you like it."

Jodine briefly wonders if maybe she has had enough to drink, but takes a sip regardless. "Perfect," she says.

"Good. It's on the house."

"It is? Why?"

"Just because." He smiles his godlike smile again and walks toward another customer.

Manny appears behind her and wraps his hand around her waist.

Jodine's public affection alarm goes ballistic. Ah! Ah! Why is he touching her in front of Count Zeus? Go away! Go away! This is why she doesn't want a boyfriend—how will Zeus continue to offer her free drinks when some strange man is manhandling her right in front of him?

"Can you not touch me in pubic, please?"

"Pubic or public?" Manny asks.

"Both. It makes everyone uncomfortable," she whispers.

Projecting a little, are we?

Manny pales. Or maybe the strobe light hits him at that exact second. Who knows? "Okay, sorry," he mumbles. "Do you want to dance?"

"Fine." She hates dancing, but she'll do anything to avoid Zeus seeing her with another man.

It's midnight and here's the panoramic view:

The place is packed. No one knows who all these people are, but there are hundreds of them.

Emma's body is pressed against Clint's. Their actions are completely inappropriate due to the Milli Vanilli dance song blasting, but who's going to stop them?

Manny is trying to press his body against Jodine's. She backs away and ends up dancing alone around the room, looking like a cross between a ballerina with bunions and a break-dancer with arthritis. If she could see herself from an external perspective, she'd never dance again.

Allie is still at the door. She's been there since eleven and is annoyed that neither of her roomies have come to change places with her. Josh is still sitting beside her, keeping her company, but he's starting to feel as though he has to check on his buddies, since he was the one who insisted they come. But no way is he going to leave her there by herself.

Monique and Nick are sitting in a booth on the upper level, deep in conversation.

Bartender George is still really, really gorgeous.

By twelve-thirty, Allie has had it. Who do her roomies think they are that they can desert her to watch the door the whole night? "Would you hold down the fort while I look for my roomies?" she asks Josh. And where is Clint? How could he not come? He promised he would come. Why didn't he come?

She searches through the room. Where are they? She looks up and down the two bars. Nope. She pushes through the dance floor. She sees Jodine with her hands above her head doing what looks like some sort of fertility dance.

"Jay!" she screams. She bites her lip and prays she doesn't look like that when she dances.

Jodine doesn't hear.

"Jay!" she screams again.

Manny appears by her side. "She's completely hammered," he says.

"Well, it's her turn to watch the door. It's been her turn for the last hour."

"Sorry, Allie, she must have forgotten. Can you get Emma to do it? Jodine is not in much of a money-counting state right now."

"Fine. Where is Emma?"

"I saw her dancing somewhere down there," he says, pointing at the bathroom.

Allie makes her way through the dance floor, looking for her roomie.

Uh-oh, this has potential crisis stamped all over it. She's going to run smack into Emma and Clint making out on the dance floor. She'll start screaming or something and make a huge scene and she'll start crying and it'll be one of those moments that is appallingly embarrassing for everyone.

Allie spots Clint, standing outside the men's bathroom. By himself.

"Clint!" Allie squeals, skipping toward him.

"Allie," Clint says, showing off that movie-star smile. "I was looking for you."

Allie is too thrilled that he's here, he's here, he's here, to wonder why he didn't look around more thoroughly.

Just then Emma walks out of the women's bathroom. She looks around, misses Allie and Clint, and starts walking back toward the dance floor.

Allie reaches out and grabs her by the arm. "Em," she says. "There you are!"

Emma turns around and looks momentarily confused. "Oh, hi," she says.

"Em," Allie says again, grabbing onto Clint's hand, "I want you to meet my Clint."

Shit, Emma thinks. Shit, shit, shit.

Clint smiles at Emma. "Oh, we already—"

"Nice to meet you, Clint," Emma interrupts, extending her hand. "I'm Allie's roommate."

Clint shakes Emma's hand. "Nice to meet you, too."

22
EMMA GOES NUTS

EMMA

"How did you not know it was him?" Jodine asks me, hands flying in exasperation. "How many Clints can there be? The possibility that there was only one Clint at the party didn't occur to you?"

She pushes all the way back in the recliner and sighs. I inhale and blow a smoke circle over the couch; she ogles the cigarette now dangling from my fingers.

I'm pretty sure the reason she hasn't yet told me to get off the couch and smoke by the window is that she feels bad for me. This is good, since there's not a chance in hell I'm standing up just so that I can pretend I actually keep the apartment smoke-free. She knows I smoke inside, I know she knows, she knows I know she knows, and so on. Who the fuck cares if I smoke inside, anyway? There are far worse things that happen. Like finding out that the first guy I've been attracted to in a million years is off-limits.

"No, I didn't make the connection," I say. "It didn't occur to me that Allie's soul mate may be hitting on me. What was I supposed to do? Wear a sign that says Off-Limits to Allie's Soul

Mates? And anyway, why was Allie's soul mate hitting on anyone in the first place?"

"Maybe because Allie's soul mate doesn't realize he's Allie's soul mate?"

I blow another circle into the air. "So tell me, what do I do? I made out with Allie's soul mate."

Jodine, eyes fixated on the cigarette, looks as if she's dying to say something but is trying to restrain herself. Does she have the nerve to reprimand me for smoking in the house when she's aware of my inner mayhem?

Apparently she does. "Em, I have to know, do you normally open the window when you smoke? I know you're upset now, so it's okay, I won't get upset, but I'm just wondering, if I'm not here do you smoke out the window or just smoke from the couch? I won't get upset, just tell me the truth."

Like I said, I know she knows. So what is this, true confession time? I choose to ignore her question entirely. "Maybe dating him would be good for her. *Me* dating him, I mean, it would help her get over it. It could actually be beneficial to her in the long run. I'd be saving her from a lifetime of heartache."

"And of course, it would be a supreme sacrifice on your part. After all, what are friends for?"

She looks at me as if I'm a vibrator that's two sizes smaller than what I promise I am on the box. "Forget it," she says, grimacing. "But you should tell her that he hit on you."

"I'm not going to tell her if I'm not even allowed to date him! What's the point in that? She'll mope around here for weeks. If she's going to feel miserable anyway, why can't I date him?"

"Because you can't. She has to realize that he's a complete scumbag in order to get over him. How can she come to this conclusion if the person she admires most in the world is dating him?

If you date him, you tell the world he's worthwhile—see what I mean? You send her an unconscious message that he's too good for her and that he's perfect for you. Do you really want her to start eating her fingers again?

"She needs your support," she presses on tactfully. "She needs you to help her see him for what he is."

"She needs a haircut. Maybe that's why he doesn't like her. Maybe one night when she's sleeping we can cut that braid off. That might help."

Jodine chooses to ignore me. "She needs your help. And she won't be angry with you. You didn't even know who he was, although I'm not sure how." She mutters that last part under her breath.

"Do you really not think her hair is too long? Impossible. You must."

"Can we move past the hair?"

Groan. "This is so Romeo and Juliet. He's probably my soul mate and I'll never know."

"Spare me. You spent two hours dirty-dancing with him and now you're talking duo-suicide?"

"But he was *sooooo* cute."

Jodine shakes her head. "Not my type at all. Too done. Highlighted. He reminds me of processed cheese."

She doesn't even eat nonprocessed cheese.

She pulls on the lever so that the recliner is at a ninety-degree angle again. "Speaking of soul mates," she says, "your *other* significant other left the bar with Monique last night."

Monique? Significant other? What? "What are you talking about?"

An oopsy expression spreads across her face.

"Nick. I'm pretty sure I saw him leave with Monique, a friend of mine from law school."

I inhale furiously on the cigarette, look around frantically for an ashtray, can't find one and drop my half-smoked cigarette into a glass of water. "Fuck."

"I just bought those glasses today, you know. They were actually for drinking purposes."

"How dare he? How dare he come to *my* party and then leave with some fucking slut? I'm going to kill him. We are never getting back together now."

Jodine waves her hands in front of my head as though trying to wipe away a mesh of cobwebs. "Hello? Clint? Soul mate? Remember?"

Clint? Who? "What do I do?"

"What do you mean, 'What do I do'? Nothing! You and Nick are over, remember? I even heard you tell him you didn't want to talk to him. You can't not talk to him and then tell him he can't go out with other women."

Why not? "I can't?"

"No!" Jodine laughs.

"Maybe I want to get back together."

"You have to get a grip."

I'd like to get a grip—around Nick's neck. I light up another cigarette and inhale.

"Where's Allie now?" Jodine asks.

"At work." *Monique was the one dressed as a prostitute.*

"Why did she go so early?" Jodine asks.

Allie's Sunday shift starts at six and it's only five. "Because she forgot to change her clock. I wanted to talk to you privately so I didn't remind her." *Nick went home with a prostitute.*

Jodine laughs. "I can't believe you let her go to work an hour early!"

"I needed to talk to you about Clint." *He went home with a disgusting whore.*

Jodine sighs and reclines her chair again. "So do I. I met someone at the party."

Why are we talking about her? She has a boyfriend. She shouldn't be meeting anyone. "Don't you have a boyfriend?"

"Manny's not really a boyfriend. I was at the bar and—"

"I have to call him," I interrupt Jodine, who for some reason is babbling about Greek mythology or something. *How dare he go home with another girl! How dare he! He comes to his ex's party and goes home with another girl, a prostitute, a disgusting whore!*

"You have to call who?"

"I have to call Nick."

"Nick? We're not talking about Nick. We're talking about Count Zeus!"

Can't her problems wait for two seconds? Aren't mine a little more pressing at the moment? "Why doesn't he miss me?" I say out loud, more to myself than to her. "Didn't I look good last night? He chose a whore over me, can you believe it? What is he, blind? I have to call him. I have to tell him what a prick he is. I have to tell him that he misses me." I hurry into my room and close the door.

"She's not a real whore, Emma! She's a law student!" Jodine hollers from the living room.

I dial his number. Pressing the familiar buttons sends streaks of regret through my arms. It rings once. Twice.

"Hello?" he answers.

"Nick." Thank God he answered. "Hi."

"Emma?"

"Yeah."

"Oh. Hi."

What is this? What is *oh*? "I need to talk to you," I say.

"Talk? Now?"

What, he's deaf now, too? "No, I called now, but I want to talk tomorrow," I say, immediately regretting my choice of words. "Yes, now," I amend in what I hope he recognizes as my deep, throaty voice.

"Now isn't a good time." His voice, however, is tense. Not the reaction I was hoping for.

"Why not?"

"Well…"

"Well what?"

"I have someone…someone is here."

Someone is there? Oh, my God. "Is it the call girl? Is it? Is that whore in your apartment?" I shriek.

"Emma, calm down." His voice takes on a condescending crescendo. "Don't call her a whore. Her name is Monique. She's a law student."

Congratufuckinglations. "*Why* is she there?"

"We're hanging out."

Hanging out? Is that what law students are calling it these days? "Let me talk to her," I say. I should be allowed to talk to her. If she wants my man, let her fight it out with me and not just sneak behind my back.

"No, you can't talk to her."

"Why not?"

"Because you can't." This is the second time in two minutes that someone has said "No you can't" to me. "Can I go now?" he asks before I have time to reflect on this.

Go? Does he think I'm letting him off the phone so he can go "hang out"? I don't think so. "Did she just get there?"

"Not exactly."

Oh, my God, he *did* fuck her. "You fucked her!" My low, throaty voice has reached an octave that until this moment only opera singers have reached.

"Emma, that's none of your business. We've been finished for months now. Get over it." The next thing I know there's a dial tone blaring into my ear.

He hung up on me. HE HUNG UP ON ME?

I storm into the living room. "Get up. We're going."

Jodine jumps off the chair. "Going? To 411? You think Count Zeus will be there?" she asks, her face brightening.

What is she rambling about? Why would we be going back to 411? "We're going to Nick's. Come on."

Jodine sits back down. "We're not going to Nick's. You're crazy and I have a headache."

"We're going to Nick's. I need to talk to him. Take an aspirin and drink a glass of water to flush the alcohol out of your system. I need you to come. I really, really shouldn't be alone right now. I don't ask for much, but I'm asking you to please, please come with me."

"Why do you close your eyes when you talk?"

"I do?" What the fuck is she talking about?

"Yeah. Only when you get upset."

"Who cares? Let's go."

"All right," she says, not moving.

"What is it?"

"Nothing," she answers. "It's just that…"

"What? WHAT?"

"Your eyes," she says with awe. "Are those tears?"

Hello? I'm human. I have feelings. Which is more than I can say about that piece of shit who left me for a fucking whore. No doubt about it, any man who can do this to his soul mate has to be a complete scumbag.

* * *

"Emma, can you slow down? You're scaring me."

I turn right onto Eglinton Avenue and make a sharp left onto his street.

"Have you ever gotten any speeding tickets?"

"A few."

"How borderline are you to losing your license?"

"As borderline as you can get."

"Don't close your eyes when you drive."

"Sorry. I'm trying to think but you keep talking." I pull up two houses behind his duplex.

"He lives here by himself? How does he afford it?"

"His father pays for it."

I turn off the ignition. We stare at the house. Here I am. What do I do now? "Do I just ring the door and yell at him?" I ask Jodine.

She considers this and shakes her head. "You'll look petty."

"I want revenge. Can I key his car?"

"If you're caught, you'll have to pay for the damages. I'm not sure if no-fault car insurance covers felony."

We snicker. What am I doing here again? Have I gone crazy? I need a smoke. Where are my smokes?

A two-hundred-watt idea pops into my head. "Wait here." I get out of the car and close the door before Jodine can ask me what I'm doing. I walk toward his duplex and follow the path into his backyard. The fence lock is broken, just as I remember.

And there it is. His prized possession. Ah. The sweet, sweet taste of revenge. It's a good thing this fall has been so warm or he would have moved it inside.

"Let's go," I say when I get back to the car.

"Where?" she asks wearily.

"You'll see."

I take off down the block. "I think there's a twenty-four-hour hardware store open on Mount Pleasant Road."

"Hardware store?" Jodine sounds mildly alarmed. "What do we need at a hardware store?"

I start laughing uncontrollably. "It's a surprise," I say.

I slam into Park in the hardware store parking lot. "I'm leaving the car running, so don't go anywhere."

"Where am I going?"

I run into the store. "Hi!" I say to the hardware man. He's wearing overalls and a baseball cap. It's Tim the Tool-Man Taylor!

"Can I help you, doll?"

Help you can. "Can I get an ax?"

"An ax?" He looks at me with surprise. Do dolls not buy axes? I follow him to aisle eight.

He pulls out the mother of all axes. "This what you want?" he asks me.

"How about something a tiny bit smaller?"

He scratches his head. "You mean a hatchet?"

Whatever. Not sure what a hatchet is. Sounds like something Ma and Pa Hillbilly would bury after a feud with them-there neighbors. "Sure, a hatchet."

Tool-Man Taylor hands me the perfect-size mechanism of destruction.

I'm not sure if being seen in the middle of the night with a mechanism of destruction is a good thing. "Uh, could you wrap it, please?"

He ties a plastic bag around the handle. Now the thing looks like a hatchet with a bandage.

"That's it?"

"You want a bow and ribbons, go to the Gap," he says.

I take off the bag and wrap it around the blade. Now it looks like a giant lollipop, but it'll have to do. I go to the car.

"What's in the bag?" Jodine asks.

"You'll see." I throw the car into Reverse and head back toward Nick-the-Prick's. I stop the car two houses down from his place and turn off the engine.

"It's too bad we're not wearing our Charlie's Angels costumes for effect," she says. "Am I waiting in the car?"

"No, I need your help. Follow me. And shh!" She follows me and the lollipop-hatchet back to Nick-the-Prick's, through the fence, into the backyard.

She crouches against the house's brick wall. "He should really fix that lock," she whispers. "So what are we doing? Tee-peeing his backyard? What's in the bag? Shaving cream and toilet paper?"

I point to the six-foot plant that is slightly hidden beside the fence. "You see that?"

"The tree? That's what you want me to cover in toilet paper?"

"That baby is coming down." I pull the bag off the hatchet and grin wildly. "It's the perfect revenge. He loves that plant!"

Jodine gasps. "What is that? What are you talking about? We can't just cut down a tree. I'm not a tree murderer! Why would we cut down a tree?"

"It's not a tree," I giggle. "It's a marijuana plant."

Jodine's mouth opens in shock. "We...it's..."

"Close your mouth. You're acting as though you've never seen one before."

"Not everyone has led the illustrious life you have," she hisses at me. "How can he grow this stuff here? What about the people who live upstairs? Isn't this problematical?"

"Don't be ridiculous, Jodine. They're a hundred and eighty

years old. They don't steal any—they don't smoke dope. Now, get ready to catch it. I'm going to start chopping."

"Catch it? But...but..."

"Shh. Just catch."

I plunge into it. This baby is going down.

A quarter in...halfway in...three quarters in...a light bursts on in the upstairs bathroom.

I freeze. I can see Nick-the-Prick's face clearly. He's in the upstairs bathroom.

"He can't see us," Jodine whispers. "It's too dark out here."

"I know," I whisper back. "But you know what that is, don't you? It's the after-sex pee. I can't believe he did it again, especially after our conversation."

"Fucker."

"I can't believe Monique is such a ho." I try to keep my voice at scratch level. "I'm calling her Mo-Ho from now on."

"What's a Mo-Ho?"

"Like J.Lo? Jennifer Lopez? Get it? Mo-Ho?"

"You're insane."

Nick-the-Prick sticks his index finger into his nose.

"Don't laugh," I whisper, giggling. "Shh!"

He turns the light off and I go back to work. A few more strokes and the plant starts falling. "Timmmmmber!" I whisper.

"Ouch!" Jodine mutters. "I got it. Let's go." She lifts the front end and I pick up the back.

"I can get disbarred for this," she says, kicking the fence open with her foot.

"You haven't even been barred yet. But if you do, you can always get a job as a drug dealer."

"Too much manual labor," she grunts as we trudge out the yard.

"Yeah, but think of the benefits." I motion down the street. "I'll get the car," I tell her. "You wait here."

Her eyes widen. "You can't leave me with this thing!"

"I'll be two minutes. If anyone comes, pretend it's a Christmas tree."

I make a mad dash for the car, start the engine and drive toward her with the door still open.

We try shoving the plant across the back seat, but about a quarter of it sticks out of the car.

"Let's put it through the window," I suggest.

"Are you nuts? There must be some kind of law against driving with things hanging out the window. What if we get stopped? One more ticket and you might lose your license."

This woman is going to be a lawyer? And she's worried about my license? I look at her face and realize she's kidding. "Do you have any other ideas?"

She turns the plant around and places the end with the jagged edge on the back seat and props up the end with the flowers on the dashboard. "Violà!"

Now, why didn't I think of that?

"Where's the hatchet?" she says.

"Don't you have it?"

"Why would I have it? It's *your* hatchet. I'm just here for company."

She's starting to annoy me. "I don't think so. Once you got in the car you became an accessory to the crime."

"We have to go back and get it. It has our fingerprints on it."

"Think, Jodine. Nick-the-Prick isn't exactly going to call the police. 'Hi, Officer, someone stole my marijuana plant?' We've committed the perfect crime. Besides, we don't have time to go back. We have to make another stop."

"What now?"

"The pharmacy."

"We have enough drugs," she says with a straight face.

Jodine made two jokes in one night! Alert the media!

"I'll stay here," I tell her as I pull into the pharmacy parking lot. "Go in and get a pack of garbage bags so we can cover the plant."

"Okay." She opens the door.

"One more thing."

"What?"

"Get a pack of rolling papers."

"Rolling papers! Why?"

"For papier mâché. Why do you think? To roll with."

"They're not going to sell them at a pharmacy."

"I promise they will."

"How do I know what they look like?"

"Just ask for them."

"Isn't that illegal? Won't they know what we want them for?"

"If they ask, which they won't because they sell about a million packs of them a day, tell them you're rolling your own cigarettes."

Jodine looks as if she's going to have a heart attack.

"Go on," I urge. "The longer I sit here with a six-foot marijuana plant sticking onto my dashboard, the more chance we have of being spotted."

Three minutes later, Jodine rushes back into the car. "I can't believe how easy that was!"

I reverse out of the parking lot onto the road.

"Can you please, please slow down now?" Jodine asks. "Getting a ticket right now would be really, really bad."

I cross my fingers for a male cop.

23
ALLIE CONTEMPLATES
THE FUTURE

ALLIE

"Sure, I'd love to donate fifty dollars to buy a library book," Mrs. Connington says.

"Wonderful!" I press Script Two on my screen. Wohoo! My third today! I'm defying all laws of averages! It's a bird, it's a plane, it's Telemarketing Girl!

"I think my daughter-in-law's nephew wrote a book about whales. Can I buy that book?"

The targets don't always get that the buying of a book is a theoretical deal. I readjust the headset on my hair. "While I can't guarantee that the library will purchase your selection, I can certainly jot down your recommendation."

Sometimes the targets are pretty nice. It's sad that this surprises me, but it does. I guess it's because most people are so mean. I don't know why this is so; I've never hung up on a telemarketer when he/she calls me, even if he/she is selling steak knives. (We need steak knives, actually. And forks and spoons. Hello? Telemarketers? Call us!) Even if I know I'm not going to buy anything, I would never be rude. It's someone's living.

Phone surveys are my favorite. Pre-fire, someone from the Ontario government called and asked me four gazillion questions, which I didn't really mind because I love the idea of being included in provincial statistics. ("That's me! I'm a college graduate! Look!") He asked me if I was in sales and I said yes. I tried to explain that I was in phone sales, as in telesales, not the sale of phones. But phones would be a stupid thing to sell, via phone. If someone answered, then he already had one, right? Anyway, the Ontario research guy said, "Thank you for your time, but I'm afraid that people in sales are not eligible for this survey," and hung up. Huh? Is there something wrong with people in sales? Are we not researchable? Am I even in sales? And what about the four gazillion questions he already asked me? They weren't part of the survey? It took four gazillion questions to get to the point where he could realize that I wasn't even survey-able?

Script Two is blinking on my screen like a flashing red stoplight. I'm not talking about an eight-sided stop sign; I'm talking about a converted traffic light, you know? When I first got my training driver's license, my parents had the dumb idea that my brother was the ideal instructor candidate. On our first driving excursion, he told me that stop signs with white borders were optional. I believed him and almost ran over an old lady walking her poodle. I would have lost a ton of points for that one. Instead, I swerved and took off my dad's side mirror. I tried to explain to my parents that it was my brother's fault, but they claimed I should have known my brother was teasing and if I wasn't sure, I should have checked the manual. As Jay would say, does that make any sense? What was I supposed to do? Pull out the manual while I was driving? Would that have been any safer?

I don't like driving. I'm not great at it. I've been in three accidents and they've all been in the parking lots of shopping malls.

"Hello? Dear?" Mrs. Connington interrupts my thoughts.

Oops. Where was I? Right: "Would you prefer to make your donation using Visa or MasterCard?"

Isn't that clever? It's a trick I developed. The script says, "Would you prefer to make a credit-card or check donation?" but I deduced that when you offer people this choice, people usually choose check, and half the people who promise to pay by check, when they get the invoice in the mail, don't. If you offer only credit-card options, there isn't much to choose from. Tricky, aren't I? Did I forget to mention that we get a five-dollar bonus for every credit-card donation we solicit?

They call me the credit-card queen. Usually. But tonight I've gotten only two. Normally I pull in at least six or seven. If I don't pull in a certain number of credit cards every shift—and I have five shifts a week—I'll be missing a fraction of my rent. If I don't make at least three donations a shift, I'll lose my shifts. And then I won't be able to make a larger fraction of my rent, a larger fraction meaning all of it, which also means not a fraction at all, since a fraction means "a part," doesn't it? (How can 2/2, or even 1203/1203, be considered a fraction when it means one entire thing?)

I forgot what I was talking about.

Oh, yeah.

I never thought I'd be the type of person to live from paycheck to paycheck. I just assumed that my first year post-college I'd have some snazzy job that required me to wear cute tight Ally McBeal suits and carry around leather clipboards and have drawers full of gold engraved pens, you know the kind of pens I mean, the kind your uncle sends you for graduation.

Telemarketing—sorry, *telefundraising*—isn't a career. It's a time-passer. A commercial in the sitcom of life. It was my summer job. And now it's November.

The job search starts tomorrow. I have to find the perfect career, or the truth is, I'm going to have to go home.

My mother runs a day care and she wants to give me a job. I love the day care. I do, really, but I also love Clint. And if I go home to Belleville, what are the chances that our paths will ever cross again? Of course if we're *really* soul mates then we'll end up together, no matter what.

But what if we're supposed to be soul mates and I screw it up by moving away? Remember Jodine's elevator analogy? I'm not taking chances. I'm staying here for two more months, until the end of December. I'll give fate two more months to get its act together, and then that's it. After two more months, if nothing happens, I can only deduce that Clint and I are *not* meant to be. Wait—make that the end of February. I have to give Clint a chance to figure it out and then work up the courage to talk to me. Actually, make that the end of March. No one wants to move in the middle of winter. March 21. The first day of spring. That's his deadline. He either realizes he loves me or I'm out of here.

Mrs. Connington pauses. A paralyzing fear that she's changed her mind—she doesn't want to make a donation now or ever—briefly overtakes my mouth and neck. "Visa, please," she says, and I exhale.

"What is that?"

There is a six-foot plant by our TV. Jodine is immobilized on the recliner staring at it, and Emma is cutting off some of the leaves.

"A marijuana plant," Emma explains. Snip, snip.

A what? Huh? "It's so big!" Massive, actually. It looks like it might rip open our ceiling.

Emma shrugs. "They grow big."

I drop my bag and coat on the couch. "But why is it in our living room?"

Jodine eyes my stuff like it's a sick person's used tissue that didn't make it into the garbage pail. "Can you not leave your stuff all over the living room?"

"Sorry." Oops. I can never remember to put stuff away. Why is that? Am I genetically predisposed to be messy? I think it has something to do with my basic need to procrastinate. I mean, why do something now that can easily be done later? I pick up my jacket, hang it up in the front closet and head to my room. I drop my bag onto my bed. My clock glares that it's ten o'clock. Another oops. Meant to change that last night. How come I forgot to do that, too? I went to work an hour early like an idiot. Luckily, my boss was there and I helped her put away some files and got paid for the hour, but still, I could have been home watching TV.

I should change the clock right now. It'll only take two secs.

Never mind. I'll get to it later.

I close my door on the way out. I always keep my door closed. No need for everyone to gawk at my unmade bed and panties hanging out of the drawers.

I'll get to that later, too.

"You shouldn't write off the idea so quickly," Emma says to Jodine as I sit down on the couch.

"What idea?" I ask.

Jodine shakes her head emphatically. "No way. Not a chance. That's the worst plan I have ever heard. Plan dismissed."

What are they talking about? "What plan? Why is it the worst? What are you talking about?"

"But we could make a fortune," Emma insists.

Hello? Hel-looooo? Am I wearing an invisible cloak of some sort? "How can we make a fortune? Can someone answer me, please?"

Jodine is shaking her head at Emma. I wonder if she's getting dizzy.

I, on the other hand, am getting fed up. This invisible cloak has more power than I originally thought. Apparently it also blocks out all sound, but I can fix that:

"CAN SOMEONE PLEASE TELL ME WHAT IS GOING ON? WHY IS THERE A MARIJUANA PLANT HERE AND WHAT ARE YOU TALKING ABOUT?"

Emma and Jodine both look at me, startled.

There. Much better.

"Relax," Jodine tells me.

She's telling *me* to relax? The girl who two seconds ago thought my coat and bag were contagious?

Fine. I'll relax. I cross my arms above my chest. See? I'm relaxed. I wait for them to fill me in.

Emma returns to her clipping. "We went to Nick-the-Prick's," she says, "and we cut down his marijuana plant. And now I think we should sell this stuff to pay off the kitchen."

The head-shaking resumes. "No," Jodine says. "We're not becoming drug dealers."

"It's not drug dealing. It's exchanging pot for a new fridge."

"No," Jodine says again.

Although I am in the market for a new career, drug trafficking isn't exactly what I have in mind. I've smoked a few times with Clint (three times, actually), but I've never seen *the plant*. I've never even seen *the pot*. All three times, I was sitting in someone's room and someone pulled out a joint and I just smoked it because, well…everyone else was doing it.

Can't you get into a lot of trouble for selling it? What if we only sell it to people who claim they don't inhale? If Emma thinks it's a good idea, it might not be such a terrible plan.…

Wait a sec. Didn't Rebecca tell me a few months ago that Thomas Modcin, the guy who sat in the back of our grade-nine geography class, got arrested for drug-dealing and went to jail?

And that she saw his mother at the Sunshine bakery and she was wearing all black and crying?

And that his father was so distressed that he couldn't concentrate on his surgery (he was a surgeon) and he killed a patient during a routine gall bladder operation and was now being sued for malpractice?

Maybe it *is* a terrible plan. "I agree with you," I tell Jodine.

"You do?" Jodine's eyes widen in surprise. "If Allie agrees with me, it must be the worst idea known to man. She always agrees with *you*," she says, motioning to Emma.

"No, I don't. Do I, Emma?"

"Yeah, you do."

"Okay, so maybe I do."

The phone rings and no one makes a move to get it.

"If it's Nick-the-Prick, tell him I've moved to Australia," Emma says. Emma and Jodine stay rooted to their spots.

I guess I'm getting it. I'm not sure why. It's probably Manny, anyway. And then Jodine will probably give me looks for saying hello.

The call display says "CLINT." It's Clint! Fab!

"Hi!" I say.

"Oh...Allie." He coughs into the phone. "Hi. I thought you'd be at work."

"I just got home! What's up?"

"Not much. Um...what are you doing?"

"Hanging out with Emma and Jay."

"Everyone's there?"

"Yup."

"I was thinking of coming by."

Here? Tonight? "Great!" I have to shower. I have to change. I have to clean my room. "Come over whenever you want."

"Okay. Thanks."

Thanks? He's thanking me?

"When are you coming over?" I ask. I need a work-back plan.

Emma stops clipping. She turns to me and mouths, "Who is it?"

"Clint," I mouth back and give her two thumbs-up.

"Um...half hour?" he answers.

Only thirty minutes? No, no! I need more time! I picture my unmade bed and hanging underwear and remember why I keep vowing to break my procrastination habit. "Terrif," I tell him. "See you then!"

I hang up the phone and jump up and down. "He's coming over! He's coming over! Do you think this is it? Is he finally coming over because he realizes that everything his heart desires is right here in this very apartment?"

"Allie," Jodine says, and shakes her head. "I think you might be right."

24
JODINE'S DRUG
INDUCED EPIPHANY

JODINE

"Does my butt look big in these jeans?"

If Allie asks me one more question about how she looks, I'm going to murder her. "Your butt looks fine. It looks the same as it did in the last two pairs of jeans."

The truth is, her butt looks the same in all three pairs—round. But if one tells a roommate that, one risks laying the foundation for a severe eating disorder.

"Thanks," she says cheerfully. "But which does my butt look the best in?"

"These." I simply do not wish to watch her try on one more pair.

"Em, what do you think?"

Emma looks up from her clipping. "Definitely those." She puts the clippers down on the table. "I think I'm going to take a quick shower."

She avoids my gaze as she walks into the bathroom. Feeling guilty about the reason why she suddenly wants to freshen up, perhaps?

Twenty minutes later, Clint buzzes, and Allie leaps to the door from the couch.

"Hi, Al," he says, and takes off his shoes. His crisp jeans and tight black jersey are a mite too snazzy than one might expect for hanging out at a friend's place. In fact, he looks almost like a throwback to disco. Case in point: as usual, his hair looks overly processed. Does he use a whole tube of gel in there?

"Hi, Clint," I say. "Nice to see you again." We met at the party, but unlike Emma, I did not molest him. Instead, I simply told him it was nice to meet him.

He looks into the kitchen. "Shit. Wow. This is a disaster. When is it going to be fixed?"

"We raised a little over two grand at the party," Allie says. "So we're about one-fifth of the way there."

He sits down on the couch and looks around the room, I assume in search of the one roommate who isn't here.

"So," I say. "How nice of you to come by. How unexpected." Apparently there's something in my tone that gives me away as being in-the-know as to his clandestine escapade, because he turns a shade of pink and smirks.

"Yeah well... How are you? Hungover?"

"Not at all." Who told Don Juan here how much I had to drink last night? "Did you have a good time at the party?" Two can play at this; if he's going to harass me, then I'm entitled to do the same as well, correct?

"I had a great time, actually." His gaze peruses the room. "Just the two of you? Where's Angel Number Three?"

"I'm here," Emma says, appearing in the doorway, in her well-rehearsed Hollywood-star-making-an-entrance style. She's got on her black stretch pants, a low-cut, breast-hugging white tank top and bright red lipstick.

Come on, Emma. You could have at least given Allie a shot.

"Hi," says Clint, his eyes obviously imagining her without said tank top and stretch pants.

Allie is still too busy basking in the happiness of his arrival to notice where his eyes are roaming. Or on whom they finally rest. She takes his coat and heads to the front closet to hang it up.

Is it possible I finally have her trained?

"Hi, Clint," Emma says, sashaying over to us.

Interesting. Where is she going to sit? I'm on the recliner, and the couch seats two comfortably, three squished. Clint is sitting on the right side of the couch. Is Emma going to have the audacity to go for the middle?

But no, she drags Allie's computer chair from the pretend table into the TV area and places it next to me, beside the television facing the couch.

What is this? She gave the proximity to Allie without a fight? Just like that? You can sit next to him and I'll sit by the television? What kind of strategy is this? Has she decided to be a good roommate and give up? Unlikely. She must have another plan in mind that I'm not privy to.

Clint is still following Emma's movements, and his vision can't help but stumble over the six-foot plant to the left of the television. "Why is there a marijuana plant in your living room?"

Allie sits down on the other end of the couch. Oh, come on, Allie! The middle was wide open! You're not going to win if you can't even sit next to him!

"It doesn't fit in my room," Emma says.

Clint looks at her uncertainly.

"It was a gift," she explains.

What's that, Em? You don't want to tell the guy you're trying to steal from your roommate that you broke into your last lover's backyard and axed his prized possession?

Allie looks confused but keeps quiet.

"That's some gift," Clint says. "So do you share?"

"We certainly do," Emma says.

I assume they're talking about smoking the plant, and I am not thrilled. They're going to smoke it here? Right now? My hangover is finally starting to wane and it's dawning on me that I was an accomplice to the crime. Do stores keep a record of people who buy rolling papers? Was I on camera? Is that indiscretion going to come back to haunt me?

Allie's eyes widen. "We're going to smoke? Now?"

"Why not?" Emma asks.

Because it's illegal, because Janet will smell it and call the police and they'll storm our apartment and we'll be thrown in prison and I'll be squashed in a cell—without a kitchen—with the two of them for the rest of my life.

Emma picks up a leaf and studies it. "They're too wet. We have to dry them out."

"How do you do that?" Clint asks.

"A friend of mine used to do it in the oven," she says.

A friend? Who's that, Emma? "Too bad we don't have an oven," I say. "Oh, well, no drugs tonight, then."

She looks at the microwave. "We can try nuking it." She takes a paper towel, scatters a few leaves on it and places her concoction in the microwave.

"I don't believe this," I say, "but if you're so intent on doing this, do it right. I think this plant is a hermaphrodite, which means it's both male and female. Use the flowers on top. They're female, and more lethal."

Emma looks at me with new respect.

"I wrote a paper on marijuana for Criminal Law," I say.

"Are you going to smoke?" Allie asks me.

Are they on crack? "No, I'm not going to smoke. I've never smoked and I'm not going to start now."

Emma laughs. "Spoilsport." The microwave dings, and she opens the door and fingers the material. "Looks good. Smells good, too. Who wants to roll?"

"I will," Clint says. "Do you have papers?"

"Jodine has the rolling papers," Emma says.

Clint and Allie both look as though they're going into cardiac arrest.

"You've caught me," I say, motioning to the plastic bag that contains the paraphernalia required for this illicit endeavor. "Yes, I'm a pothead. Law student by day, joint roller by night."

"And a crazy drunk on the weekend," Clint adds.

"How come you never told me?" Allie asks.

Hello? Earth to Allie? "I'm kidding, Allie. What about you? Are you going to smoke?" Not that anyone could tell the difference if she did; sometimes I think she's permanently stoned.

Allie looks at Clint and Emma. "Sure. Why wouldn't I?"

Maybe if you had a mind of your own and didn't follow what everyone else did all the time?

Ten minutes later, after I've forced the three of them to stand by the window to smoke—I'm still sitting in the recliner—Allie says, "I can already feel it." She giggles and passes the joint to Emma, who ignores the window and blows the smoke in my direction.

How can Allie feel it already? She inhaled only four and a half seconds ago. "You made it all wet, Allie," Emma reprimands. "Don't slobber all over it."

"Sorry. It's just that I feel so relaxed. You should try it, Jay."

Why, just because Allie says so? Just because someone tells me to do something, I should do it?

"It's no big deal, Jodine," Emma says, again blowing the smoke at my face. "If you don't want to, it's cool. No pressure."

"Thank you." Whenever she says it's cool not to do something, I know what she's really thinking. She's thinking I'm going to give in and do it because secretly I really think it's not cool to not do it.

What did I just say? I didn't say anything. What did I just *think?* Why are there cobwebs around Emma's head?

"I'm just surprised you've never tried it before," Emma continues, blowing more of that disgusting stuff my way. "People like you normally love this stuff."

"What do you mean, people like me?"

"People who have trouble relaxing. People who are high stress. People who are a little anal."

Anal? I'm not anal. "I'm not in-all," I say. Did I say "in-all"? Why did I say that? What does that mean?

Emma and Allie smile at each other.

Allie giggles. "Whatever you say."

"I'm not."

"Okay," Emma says. "You don't have to explain anything to us."

"I am not *in-all.* I am in-all at all." I giggle. Why am I giggling? I never giggle. "Pass it to me."

"Pass what?" Emma asks. "The spliff?"

Allie starts giggling. "Spliff? What kind of a word is *spliff?* That's the funniest word I've ever heard. Say it again."

"Spliff," Emma repeats solemnly, and Allie doubles over in giggles.

"Yes," I say. "The spliff." Why is Allie laughing? *Spliff* makes perfect sense to me.

Now Clint and Allie are laughing, too.

It's not that funny.

Is it?

Emma passes the spliff to me. "You don't have to prove anything to us."

"I'm not trying to prove anything. It's obvious I'm getting stoned just sitting here, so I might as well experience it *in-all*." There's that word again. Is there a dictionary in the house?

I abandon my post on the recliner to join the others at the window and carefully remove the joint from her fingers and inhale. Exhale. "I don't feel anything," I tell her. "I feel *no-thing*. No-thing in-all."

"Amazing," she says. "You're like a sponge. You'd probably get stoned just talking about it."

I inhale again. And again. And again.

"Don't hog it," Emma says. "Now you're supposed to pass it to Clint."

Pass it? But I just got it! "I notice you took three long hauls, but who's counting?" I say. This entire procedure makes no sense. Why waste time with passing? "Why didn't you make four mini ones so that everyone gets his own instead of only one big one that we all have to share?"

"Because it's a social activity," Emma explains.

Clint laughs again and Emma joins him.

A few minutes later the spliff is passed back to me. Finally. I inhale a large amount in an attempt to maximize my smoking time. "I think I just inhaled a piece of plant. Is that supposed to happen?"

Clint and Emma shrug. I pass it to Allie.

"It's too short," she says. "I'm going to burn my lips."

"Anyone want a zinger?" Clint asks, looking at Emma.

"I don't think so," Allie says, looking bewildered. She obviously has no idea what a zinger is.

"I do," Emma says.

Clint turns the remaining joint inward. Emma puts her lips about a fraction away from his and inhales as Clint blows out.

What are they doing? Are they making out in front of Allie?

"I want one, too! I want one, too!" Allie shrieks.

Clint and Emma stay rooted in their positions for a few seconds. Then Emma pulls back and Allie leans over and inhales from Clint.

What is this? A drug-induced orgy? I need to sit down.

Clint collapses on the couch and Allie follows. "Let's watch *Seinfeld*," she says.

"Good idea." Emma clicks on the television, then casually sits right between Allie and Clint. "I couldn't see from where I was sitting before. This is much better. Allie, can you scoot over?"

I start laughing uncontrollably.

Two hours and two bags of nonperishable salt-and-vinegar chips later, Clint leaves, and the three of us are lying comatose in our usual spots. I'm in the recliner, they're on the couch.

I am a disgusting pig.

Tomorrow I am skipping all my classes and spending the entire day strapped to the StairMaster. Right now I need something sweet. "Do we have anything sweet?" I ask.

"I have a banana," Emma says.

"Banana? What kind of junk food is that?" I want something shameless—which means fattening.

"I can make us the perfect snack," Allie says. "I'll make us s'mores." She gets a bag of marshmallows and a bag of chocolate cream-filled cookies. She opens three cookies, sandwiches a marshmallow in each, closes each cookie, then places them on a paper towel and pops them in the microwave.

What, only one s'more each?

We all stare silently, watching the marshmallow expand.

Twenty more seconds.

"I think they're ready," I say.

"Almost," Allie says.

Ten more seconds. "It's enough," I say. "Turn it off."

"Almost," she repeats.

The marshmallows explode all over the inside of the micro-wave.

"Oops," she says, pulling out the paper towel covered in goo. "It's still good," she says, and hands it to me.

I dip my finger into the melted chocolate. It *is* good. It has a bit of a marijuana smell to it.

"I think he wanted to kiss me when we were doing that zinger thing," Allie says.

I decide to ignore this insight and focus on the food I am now licking off my fingers. Yum. Sticky.

Emma apparently has another notion. "Really? What makes you think so?"

Why would she say that? What is wrong with her? Why does she get so competitive for every guy she meets? She needs some serious help.

Allie has that dreamy look on her face. "Just a glitter in his eye."

I resist the urge to snort. Yeah. A glitter of the reflection of Emma's breasts.

"So you're still sure you two are soul mates?" Emma asks.

Why is she torturing the poor girl? Does she get some sort of perverse pleasure from taking what someone else wants?

"Yes," Allie nods. "I'm sure. He's gorgeous, he's smart, he has the nicest, most caring eyes…he's…"

She'd better shut up. Telling the mistress how worthwhile the guy is doesn't normally help one's case.

Emma nods. "And you're sure he's the one, even without having ever slept with him?"

This is extremely painful.

"Yes," Allie answers, still in la-la land. "What does sex have to do with it?"

"What does sex have to do with it? Are you kidding? What if he's lousy in bed?"

Allie dismisses the idea with her hand. "You can learn that kind of stuff."

"Wow." Emma shakes her head in amazement. "You've obviously never had a bad fuck."

"I..." Allie looks slightly flustered. "No, I haven't."

Emma narrows her eyes. "How many people have you slept with?"

"How many people have *you* slept with?"

"A lot," Emma answers.

"How many people is a lot?" I ask. What would I classify as a lot? Anything with double digits, I think. Ten is a lot. Up to nine, you're just a normal, nice girl with a healthy sex drive, but as soon as you pass number ten, that's it. You are automatically reclassified as a slut.

Emma looks at me, amused. "What's *your* magic number?"

"I'll tell you if you tell me."

"All right."

I am struck with a brilliant idea. "Let's each write down the number and see if the others can guess which number belongs to whom."

"Fun! Allie, get us some paper and pens."

Allie, of course, does as she's told.

"Are we writing out the names or just the number?" I ask.

"Ooh, how fun!" Emma says. "Forget the guessing part—let's just do the names. It's a memory game!" She starts scribbling immediately.

Okay, there's Will and Jonah and Manny. Can't forget Benjamin. And Manny, of course. No, wait, Manny only counts once.

That's it. This is pretty pathetic. Only four? I think five is a nice, round number. I need one more. Count Zeus, maybe? Can I start a wish list?

"Can I have another piece of paper?" Emma asks.

What?

Allie hands her another piece. She is holding her own paper against her chest.

"If it was only once, and it was under a minute, does it count?" Emma asks while writing.

"I would think so," I say.

"Really? We used a condom and I didn't feel anything. Should he really be on my permanent list?"

"Yes!" Allie and I both answer.

Emma scribbles for a few more seconds and then puts her second piece of paper down. "Okay. I'm done. I figure if I can't think of them within the first five minutes, they obviously weren't that memorable and shouldn't make the list. Allie, you first."

Allie looks as if she's about to cry. "Does it count if you were in separate rooms when it happened?"

I'm not even going to ask her to explain. "No, Allie. You definitely had to be there at the time."

She holds up her paper. It's completely blank. "I've never…I've never actually done it."

What? She's never had sex? Ever? Not even for a second? Her face is slightly flushed so I decide to attempt to act nonchalant. I take a deep breath. "Really?" There. That was well done. That sounded pretty calm.

Emma starts laughing. "Get the fuck out of here! You're still a virgin?"

Way to go, Emma.

Allie turns a deeper red. "Yes."

"Shit," Emma says through her hysteria. "That's insane!"

"It's not insane," I intervene. "A lot of people save themselves for marriage." Which makes no sense. If you don't have sex before you're married, when *do* you have sex?

"But I'm not saving myself for marriage," Allie says. "I've just never had anyone to do it with yet."

"We need to get you laid," Emma decides, nodding her head.

We could probably do that if you'd stop feeling off the one guy who might actually want to sleep with her, Emma dear. I knew what your hand was up to under that blanket. "How many people are on *your* list?" I ask her.

"Twenty-seven."

"Twenty-seven?!" Allie and I shriek in unison.

"It's not that many, considering I've been sexually active since I was fifteen. That's ten years. That's two point seven guys per year."

"You lost your virginity at fifteen?" Allie asks.

"Yeah. So? It's not that young. Everyone I knew was doing it."

Twenty-seven?

"I hadn't even kissed a guy at fifteen," Allie says.

Twenty-seven?

"We grow up faster in Montreal. Jodine? You?"

"Me?" I hold up my piece of paper. "Nothing too interesting. I lost my virginity at eighteen and I've been with four guys in all." I let out a little giggle. I think it has something to do with the words *in all,* but I can't remember.

Emma rolls her eyes. "I expected something more from you. Boring."

Twenty-seven?

"Why do you think you sleep with so many guys?" I ask her.

"Why? I don't know."

"Did you have feelings for all of them?"

"No."

"You were just attracted to all of them?"

She thinks about this for a second. "No. I wasn't attracted to most of them."

Allie looks confused. "I don't get it. Do you just really like sex?"

"Not especially. Besides with Nick-the-Prick, that is. Yum."

"You've slept with twenty-seven different guys and you don't even like sex?" I ask. "Why did you do it?"

"I'm not sure. When I was younger, I was scared of giving head. Sex was easier. You don't have to do anything. You can't really be bad. And I was afraid of being called a cock-tease."

Allie hugs her knees to her chest. "What's so bad about being a cock-tease?"

"You get a reputation," Emma explains.

This makes no sense. "You'd rather have a rep for being a slut than for being a tease?"

Emma nods emphatically. "Absolutely. I wanted people to know that I'm not shy to be sexual. I'm not a prude like most girls out there."

That is the most ridiculous thing I have ever heard. "But then men sleep with you not because they like you but because they hear that they can. They'll never get to know you."

"Not true. Once they sleep with me they'll get to know me and they'll realize my greatness and then they'll like me for who I am. And then I'll be the girl that got the sleazeball to change."

The sleazeball who got the sleazeball to change. "I think you have serious self-esteem issues."

"I agree," Allie says. What is this? Allie is thinking that Emma isn't Ideal Woman? "I think ever since your dad left, you've been craving male attention, and this is how you choose to get it," she says.

Emma looks at her in bewilderment.

I look at her in awe. "That was pretty insightful," I say. "It makes a lot of sense."

Allie shrugs. "It's a textbook case."

But Emma shakes her head. "That's not why I sleep around," she says.

Allie and I both stay silent.

"It's not."

We wait.

"Is it?" Emma asks, and starts laughing. "You see? I told you my dad fucked up my life. Bastard. So, Dr. Allie, tell us, why is Jodine so screwed up with men?"

Me? "I'm not screwed up with men."

Allie and Emma both giggle.

"I'm not."

"You're a human Popsicle with Manny," Allie says. "And with us, half the time. I think you're afraid to get close to people."

What is she talking about? I am not afraid of intimacy.

Allie looks at my face searchingly. "Did you get hurt when you were younger? Did someone break your heart?"

I've never been dumped, how could anyone have broken my heart? "No one broke my heart."

"You have to have a heart for it to get broken," Emma says. "Didn't you say you've seen *The Wizard of Oz?*"

Allie ignores her. Allie ignores Emma? "Did you have a best friend who moved away when you were younger?" she asks me.

"Nope," I say, shrugging. "Sorry." Sorry I've never had a best friend? Why is it I've never had a best friend?

"Nothing bad has *ever* happened to you?"

"Of course bad things have happened to me! What do you think, I've led a perfect life?"

"You tell us," Emma says. "I told you about my twenty-seven guys and Allie told you she was a virgin," she says. "You have to give us something."

"No one has a perfect life," Allie says. "Do you want to talk about it?"

Why should I tell them? Do I want to tell them? My head feels light and heavy and smoky. I close my eyes.

Why not?

"My mother had breast cancer."

Allie sighs. No one speaks.

"Shit," Emma says finally. "That must have been awful."

"It was. But she's okay now. She's in remission. They were able to remove it."

"The lump?"

"Yes. And her breast."

Allie gets up and then sits on the chair beside me. She rubs her hand against my knee. "I'm so sorry. When did it happen?"

"When I turned seven. She was in surgery on my birthday. She told me she was going to be in the hospital for a few weeks, but I was sure she would be home in time for my birthday cake. How could she miss my birthday? I sat and waited for her on the porch stairs and when it was night, I thought that she had to be dead. And that my brother and father just didn't want to tell me. They didn't want to ruin my birthday, so they were going to wait one more day to tell me the truth. Why else wouldn't she come home?"

"But she did come home," Allie says.

"A week later. And I was pissed off at her. Isn't that ridiculous?

I was pissed off at her for deserting me. But it wasn't just that. For the first time I realized that she *could* die, that she could leave me forever. There were some things she just couldn't make better, do you know what I mean? It's like she lied to me. I wouldn't talk to her for a month. I wouldn't even look at her. Isn't that horrible?"

"No, it's perfectly normal," Allie says. "You were terrified of losing her."

"I used to be terrified of losing my mother, too," Emma says.

Can I have one moment when it's just about me, Emma? I sigh. "I'm still terrified that it'll come back. And I'm also terrified that it'll happen to me. I'm in a high-risk group. I do everything to try to reduce the possibility."

"So that's why you work out so much and monitor everything you eat," Allie says.

My mouth is dry. I pick up my glass of water off the floor and take a long sip. Have I rendered them both speechless? Is it possible?

Apparently not. "So that's why you're a bitch to Manny," Emma says.

"She's not a bitch," Allie says. "But she's not the warmest, either. I think you're afraid of being deserted, Jay. You don't want to fall in love."

"Or maybe Manny just doesn't do it for me," I counter.

"Maybe," Allie says, and shrugs. "He might just not be your soul mate." She gets off the kitchen chair, presumably to walk back to her spot on the couch, and knocks over my glass of water.

"Allie! Be careful!"

"Sorry. I'll clean it." She bends down and wipes the puddle with the sleeve of her shirt.

What is she doing? "I'll do it. Just pass me the paper towels. You're making even a bigger mess." Fine. Maybe disorder scares me. Maybe I need to be in control to feel safe. "Are people always introspective when they're stoned?" I ask.

"Sometimes," Emma says. "And sometimes you just end up eating everything in your fridge, watching *Rushmore* for the four-hundredth time, passing out on the couch, waking up the next morning with drool hanging out of your mouth, and generally feeling like an ass. It can go either way."

I think I'm hungry again. "Any more marshmallows?"

25
EMMA'S ILLICIT PHONE CALL

EMMA

"Hello?"

"Hi, Emma?"

"Yes?"

"It's Clint."

"I know."

"You do?"

"We have call display."

"Crazy. So why didn't you let Allie pick up?"

"Did you call to talk to Allie?"

"I...not really."

"I didn't think so. Anyway, she's at work."

"I know."

"So you called to talk to me."

"Yes, I did."

"What do you want to talk about?"

"What do you think I want to talk about?"

"I bet the last thing you want to do is talk."

"Can I come over?"

"Are you crazy? No! Allie will be home soon."

"I want to see you."

"Why?"

"Why? Because…I want to continue where we left off last week."

"Where is that? Allie closing the door behind you when you left here?"

"No, I meant the night of the party."

"Ah. You mean our dance."

"Is that what it's called these days?"

"It's actually called two people hooking up who should not be hooking up."

"I don't get it."

"And you *won't* get it, not from me. My roomie thinks you belong to her."

"What if I disagree?"

"Do you?"

"What do you think?"

"I think Allie has done everything but pissed all over you to mark you as her territory."

"I'm interested in a different kind of bodily fluid, and from someone else."

"What fluid would that be?"

"Why don't you let me come over and show you?"

"I told you. Allie is going to be here any minute."

"So come to my place."

"Your place? I can't."

"Why not?"

"Because Allie will freak out."

"We won't tell her."

"That's not very nice."

"Come over."

"Not tonight."

"Another night?"

"I didn't say that."

"You didn't have to."

"So now you can read my mind?"

"It wasn't your mind talking to me the night of the party. Come over, Emma."

"Hmm. Convince me. What would we do?"

"First I'd pour us some wine."

"I like wine. What would I be wearing?"

"Not much."

"I have great lingerie. Do you want me to be wearing my black garter?"

"I like black garters."

"Good. Because I have one on. But it's under my red dress. Would you mind unzipping that for me?"

"I can do that. Should I do it with my teeth?"

"*Ooo*, good. That feels nice. Your tongue feels hot against my skin."

"Where do you want my hands?"

"I want them…hold on. I just want to close my door."

26
JODINE COUNTS DOWN

JODINE

Twenty days until exams

"What are you doodling?"

"Nothing." I suspect that this is probably one of those things a boyfriend isn't supposed to see.

Manny slides my spiral notebook across the library table toward him. "Why are you drawing Dracula?"

"I like Dracula."

"Really?" Is that a gleam in his eye? Can he put that out, please? "I didn't know that."

"You don't know everything about me."

"I guess not." That gleam just got brighter. "Maybe I'll bring over a cape and some fake fangs tonight. Rrrrrrr."

Manny is poisoning my perfect image of Count Zeus. Time is also doing a number—not on me, but on my newly found fabulously fanged friend. I need to return to the bar and refuel his memory. I need to go as soon as I finish exams. I need to have another party. When? When's the next appropriate holiday?

New Year's.

"I think we're going to have another party for New Year's," I say, pulling my notebook back toward me.

A strange expression overtakes Manny's face. It's almost one of constipation. "New Year's?" he asks. "I need to talk to you about that."

He's not going to suggest something absurd like a romantic weekend in cottage country, is he? "What is it?"

"I was wondering if you wanted to…well…" Spit it out, constipation-face. How can anyone who pees so often be constipated? "I was wondering if you wanted to come home with me."

He's asking me to sleep over at his place? Is he that bothered that I always make him come to my apartment? "Whatever. I don't care where we have sex after the party."

He shakes his head. "That's not what I meant. I mean *home*. Ottawa. I promised Mom I'd come home for the holidays and I'd like you to come with me. To meet her. And Dad, and my sister, and her husband, and their kids."

Meet mom? And dad? And sis, hubbie and kids? Already? We've only been dating for…fine, we've been dating for a year and a half, but not *seriously*. What about a romantic weekend in cottage country? How about that? "I can't go away for the holidays. My parents need me here. And we have to have the party. To make money. To pay for the kitchen." Thank goodness for the kitchen. Love that kitchen.

His face has fallen like an up-do at the end of a night of dancing. "Do you have to be at every event?" he asks.

"Yes, I do." Terrific. Now I have to be at every event.

"So we're going to spend the holidays apart, in different cities."

Yes, exactly as we've spent every holiday before this one. "I guess so. Unless you want to come back for New Year's." Actually, I would prefer if he were here for Christmas and gone for New Year's. This way, I can spend the party hitting on Count Zeus.

"I can't. My sister is at her in-laws for Christmas, so she's going home for New Year's. Will you be upset if I don't come to the party? Will you be mad at me?"

A whole night alone with Count Zeus? I'm sure I'll get over it. "Well, if seeing your sister is more important than being with me…" His face drops. Uh-oh. Why did I say that? Did I go too far with this guilt-reversal thing? What if he changes his mind? He looks so serious. He's about to speak…five, four, three, two, one…

"I really want to be here, Jodine, but I can't. I just can't."

"It's okay. I forgive you."

Happy New Year!

Seventeen days until exams

"We can't have a party when I'm not here!" Allie whines, irately crossing her arms over her chest. "It's not fair."

I shrug and push back the recliner. "So don't go."

"I haven't seen my family in ages. I have to go home."

"What can I tell you? You can't have everything. We need this New Year's party. We can't give up the opportunity just because you choose to see your family."

"Easy for you to say, Jay. Your family lives here." She uncrosses her arms and pouts. "Can we do something else before I leave? I don't mean instead of New Year's, I mean in addition to it. How about the How to Pick Up Women seminar?"

Emma opens the window and lights her cigarette. "We could. Besides the moneymaking thing, a room filled with men dying to find out what women really want does have possibilities. When would we have it?"

"We need at least two weeks to advertise it," Allie says.

"And a day or two to plan it," Emma adds.

"No way," I say. We're not doing it in two and a half weeks. "I'll be right in the middle of exams."

"So you won't come," Allie says. "We don't all have to go to every event."

"Terrific. Plan away." Fine. I'd rather not take part in the seminar from hell, anyway. Don't they realize that only women—women thinking that the place will be filled with men—will bother to show up? All I care about is being at the New Year's party with Count Zeus.

"Fun!" Allie exclaims, and claps her hands. "We'll make a fortune! It'll be packed! Where should we go to have it? Oh, I know! I can rent a classroom at school. Even better, an auditorium. I can get it cheap. It'll be like a real lecture."

Allie giving a lecture on how to pick up women? Will she just be repeating after Emma? This might be too amusing to miss. "Why don't you have it on the sixteenth?" I suggest. "I have an exam that afternoon and then not another one until the next Monday, which is my last exam. I'm too tired after writing for three hours to concentrate on anything, anyway."

"Perfect," Emma says.

Damn right it is. I have an excuse for not planning this travesty but I still get to watch.

"It looks like I'm the only one who'll be missing anything," Allie says. "Will you girls keep an eye on Clint for me at the party?"

Emma nods. "What are friends for?"

Twelve days until exams

"I want you," Count Zeus says, and lays me down onto the bar.

He pulls himself on top of me, his hard, perfect body pressing against mine. My Charlie's Angel costume is ripped and lying on the bar next to my throbbing body.

His fingers run up and down my exposed skin, and I tingle with anticipation. He lowers his lips to my neck. He's licking and kissing, licking and kissing—

Something wakes me up. I open my eyes. My dream terminated as though it was a movie and the reel suddenly broke. If I were in a theater right now, I'd be hissing and booing and throwing popcorn at the screen.

Is someone tickling my neck? I scoop my hand below my ear and feel something soft and furry.

It squirms.

"AAAARRGGGH!" I scream, and shoot the vampire-creature across the room.

Omigod, it's a flying mouse. There is a mouse flying across my room. Omigod omigod, there was a mouse in my bed. There was a mouse on my neck.

Allie bursts into my room. "What is it? What's wrong?"

"There was a mouse. On my neck." Stop, drop and roll? That's definitely wrong.

"For heaven's sake, it's only a mouse," she says. Since when is she so brave? "Where is it?"

"I don't know. I shot it somewhere that way." I point in the direction of the wicker basket. "I think it landed in there."

"Don't move," she says, and disappears. Move? I am never moving again. I am never sleeping again.

It's two o'clock in the morning. Why do horrible things continually happen to me in the middle of the night?

Allie comes back with a broom. I'm surprised she knew where the broom was, as she has never volunteered to use it. I'm also curious as to why this is her weapon of choice. Maybe she finds sweeping scary, but somehow I don't imagine that unwanted house pets would concur.

She takes the broom and pushes the basket out of the room as though it's a hockey puck and she's guiding it into the net.

I hear Emma giggle from her room. Why is she not commiserating? She giggles again. She must be on the phone. Who is she talking to at two in the morning?

I follow Allie out of the apartment. When we get outside, she tilts the basket. All my sweaters tumble onto the pavement. A little gray mouse covered in a pink sweater makes a mad dash into the middle of the street. I hope he gets run over.

"All done," Allie says. "Back to bed."

"I'm not going back into my room. What if he has friends in there?"

"It was probably the same mouse I saw a few months ago."

"So he's been hanging out in the apartment since then? Planning the perfect attack? That was so very vile. It was on my pillow."

We reenter the apartment. Emma is still giggling. I'm fine, Emma. Thanks for asking. I hope she's not talking to whom I think she's talking.

"Good night," Allie says.

My legs feel like wooden sticks, my body cold and clammy. Maybe Allie was right. I am a human Popsicle, only the way I'm feeling has nothing to do with how I feel about Manny. It's all about mice. Any kind of mice—Mickey Mouse, Minnie Mouse, including that device attached to our computers. Even the mousse I wear in my hair is threatening, just by word association. Am I actually going to be able to put my head on that pillow tonight? Not a chance.

Allie witnesses my immobilization. "You okay?"

"No, I'm too revolted to sleep." Why am I paying for an apartment that has mice in it? Someone is going to get a nasty letter about this occurrence. "Do you have Mr. Carl the landlord's address? I'm going to write him a formal complaint."

"Yes. I'll find it for you tomorrow. Right now you need sleep. I have an extra pillow. You'll sleep in my room tonight."

I must be extremely emotionally disheveled, because this sounds like an excellent plan.

Eleven days until exams

"Thanks, Josh," Allie says.

"No problem." Josh is bent over my radiator, sealing all potential openings. Apparently there are numerous superfluous punctures in the wall. "It'll take me ten minutes tops."

"Thank you, thank you, thank you," I say, my legs curled underneath me on my bed. Allie is sitting next to me, her back against the wall. Without having been asked, she wiped her socks clean with a paper towel prior to sitting.

"Anything for my favorite roommates," he says. Although he has used the plural, his gaze follows Allie wherever she moves and I'm pretty sure he meant the singular. Only a smitten man would have insisted on dropping all his plans to come here tonight bearing anti-mouse artillery. When he's coming back tomorrow morning for work anyway. The floor is done and he's now working through the cupboards.

"Hello?" I hear Emma's voice from the entranceway. "Anyone here?" How nice of her to notice us. Last night while we were under attack by alien vermin, she was far too preoccupied to notice. "What's going on?" she now asks, her jacket casually hung over her arm. She spots Josh bent over. "Just what I like to see. A guy on his knees."

How cheesy. I hope a mouse jumps out from the radiator and bites off her feet. Aren't mice attracted to cheese?

Josh tilts his head toward the door. "Hey, Emma."

"Hi. What are you doing here? Did I forget to change the clocks and come home too early, à la Allie?"

Allie turns bright red. That was nice, Emma. Embarrass her for no reason.

"No, you're right on time," he says. "I'm trying to get rid of your rodent problem."

Emma looks down at the floor and climbs onto my bed. "We have a rodent problem?"

The only rodent around at the moment is Emma. I want to ask, So who were you on the phone with last night while we were battling a mutant mouse? "I was attacked last night," I say instead.

Emma shakes her head and her perfectly combed hair fluffs from side to side. "Ewww. You saw it in here?"

"Unfortunately."

Her arms twitch in an attempt at commiseration. "I'm glad it was in your room and not mine."

"Aw, thanks."

"You know what I mean."

Not really.

Josh is holding a trap. "This should do the trick," he says.

Emma gasps. "We're going to murder mice? That's horrible!"

For someone who's only showed up for the last round, she has a hell of a lot of opinions. "You can keep them as house pets in your room, if you'd rather," I tell her.

"Snap, clap, and it's over with," Josh says. "As clean as a guillotine. He won't feel a thing."

Revolting. "Won't there be blood?" I ask. "Disgusting mouse blood? Isn't there some other way?"

"I also brought these ones." He picks up a piece of cardboard. "Now, don't touch this. If there's a furry gray thing within twenty yards, it'll attract him, and then glue it to the surface. The other way is more humane, but at least this way, he has a chance. If he's still alive when you find him, you can set him free. It might not even hurt him that much. Kind of like ripping off a bandage that had been stuck to a hairy arm. You can use whichever you'd like."

But then I'll have to...touch it.

"Josh?" Emma asks.

"Yeah?" He turns around and faces us, a wad of white tape in his hand.

The corners of Emma's mouth turn up and she looks a bit like a female Jack Nicholson. "I never realized just how sensitive you are. You ever been in a bedroom with three girls before?"

What is she doing?

Josh looks down at the tape. "Can't say that I have."

"I bet it's your biggest fantasy. Three girls?"

Is she hitting on him? Why does she have to sexualize every guy she meets?

"My fantasies aren't that exotic. All I need to make me happy is one loveable woman." He looks up at Allie and smiles, exposing one perfect dimple.

Did I just see what I think I saw? Did this adorable man just shoot down Emma for little ol' Allie?

Emma storms out of the room.

One rodent down.

Six days until exams

The Count smashes the cocktail glasses off the bar and pushes me on my back.

"I have a boyfriend," I protest, even though the heat is searing through my body. "I shouldn't."

"You want it," he tells me. He slides his hands up my shirt and cups my breasts. I moan. He rubs his thumbs against my nipples. I moan again.

He takes my wrists and grips them above my head. He lifts my shirt and exposes my breasts. So gently, he takes my nipples—both at the same time—into his mouth and commences sucking.

"I can't," I repeat. Moan, moan, moan.

"You can't, or won't?"

He grabs the elastic of my panties with his teeth and pulls them down. He sets my wrists free and I slip my fingers through his thick strands of hair, panting as he kisses and licks me.

"I want to fuck you," he says. "Spread your legs."

"Fuck me!" I scream.

He grabs my wrists with one hand again and secures them above me. He pushes inside me, hard and huge and pounding, hammering, throbbing.

"Harder!" I scream, his breath hot in my ear. "Faster! Fuck me fuck me fuck me!"

He's pulsating into me, his heart is frantic against my breasts, and then he combusts.

Sigh.

"I have to go to the bathroom," Manny whispers, lifting himself off of my wet body and out of my bed.

One more day until exams / Omigod only eight hours left to study / I'm going to sleep through my alarm and be late / I'm going to fail

So tired. Need sleep. Why can't I find my keys? Where are my keys? Found them. Must do other things. What other thing must I do?

1. Insert key into keyhole. Check.
2. Turn key. Check.
3. Open door. Check.

4.   Inhale overwhelming revolting smell. Check.

Allie and Emma are sitting on the couch watching a *Sex and the City* rerun. Apparently, their noses are immune from smelling the worst aroma ever to hit mankind.

"What is that stench?" I ask, closing the door behind me.

"What stench?" Allie asks.

"You don't smell it?"

"I don't smell anything."

"Me, neither," Emma says.

"It smells like death and manure and garbage rolled up in rotting seaweed. It's revolting. I can't believe you don't smell it."

I hang up my jacket and follow my nose through the apartment. "Don't bother getting up. I'll find it."

"It's probably just the garbage," Allie says. "I didn't change it today."

If she can concede to the possibility that garbage might cause such a disgusting odor, then why not take it out? Oh, no, let Jodine take care of it when she gets back from the library at one in the morning the night before her first exam.

The overflowing pail has been rammed with numerous cartons that obviously were supposed to be recycled. I tie the bag and toss it into the green garbage container outside.

Don't bother to help, Al. Don't get up, Em. I have nothing else I need to be doing tonight. You guys just sit. Relax.

Sniff, sniff. It still smells.

"Where's the marijuana plant?" I ask suspiciously. It no longer takes up the space beside the television. Maybe it has been hidden in some deep corner of the apartment and is now growing pungent fungus.

"I dried the leaves and put them into jars. I'm giving them away as Christmas presents to all my friends back home."

Tell me that Emma didn't put marijuana in the mail. "How did you send it?"

"A friend of mine was driving in. Don't worry, I kept some for us."

Do I look worried? As if I'll ever smoke again. After that experiment, I found myself rereading the same sentence in my textbook, over and over. Which was really confusing, since a person can only be tried once for the same crime.

Plus, I put on at least a hundred pounds that night.

And I talked too much. There are some things that should remain private.

Where is the smell coming from? Sniff, sniff. The bathroom? No. Sniff, sniff. I'm standing outside my room. I'm noticing an increasingly excessive aroma. I open my door. "It's coming from my room," I moan.

"That's probably a sign to change your sheets," Emma calls out.

Vile, vile, vile. It's coming from the radiator. Omigod. It's coming from the mouse pad. There's a dead mouse stuck to the mouse pad.

I run into the living room, hysteria rising through my body like shampoo being squeezed through the nozzle. "There's a dead mouse in my room! There's a dead mouse in my room! What do I do?"

Neither of them budges. They are both glued to the television screen, as tight as the mouse is to his cardboard coffin.

"Did neither of you hear what I said? There is a dead mouse in my room!"

"I heard," Allie says. "That's really gross. Come sit down for two minutes and we'll discuss at the commercial."

"If it's dead," Emma adds, "then what's the problem?"

"There is a dead mouse next to my radiator, and first you let the smell fester in my room, and now you refuse to stop watching an episode for five minutes—an episode that you've already seen—to acknowledge my trauma?" I pick up one of the recently purchased garbage bags and storm toward my room.

I take a deep breath, roll up my sleeve and pick up the sticky cardboard, my hand brushing against the gray corpse. Terrific.

I will lose all control if any part of me gets stuck to this paper. I'm in no mood for this.

"Don't forget to wash your hands before you touch any of our stuff!" I hear Emma call out from the living room.

Thanks.

27
PAY ATTENTION, ALLIE!

ALLIE

"Can you all quiet down, please?" Emma asks.

The measly seventeen of us in the room hush.

Not the world's greatest turnout. I would have suggested canceling, if we hadn't already paid the fifty dollars for the room. And another fifty for placing an ad in the school newspaper. At forty bucks a pop, we're only making five hundred and sixty dollars, since the three of us didn't pay.

This sucks.

Fourteen men look up at Emma expectantly.

I bet the pathetic turnout is because it's the middle of exams. "This disaster is all your fault," Emma pointed out to me as we waited at the door for more people to show. She also said, "Nothing I could say will ever work on these losers. They're hopeless."

"What did you expect, the football team? Did you think the school studs would be the ones to sign up for a How to Pick Up Women seminar?" Jodine practically spit. Ever since her run-in with Mickey, she hasn't been sleeping well and hasn't been in the best of moods. "And would a guy with any brains skip his library time to come hear your theories on dating?"

"At least they're making an effort," I point out. "And they paid their fees, didn't they? The party will have a better turnout. We'll make up the money then." We're hanging up posters for the event, right after this.

Emma sits on the desk in front of the room and crosses her legs, flouncing her stiletto camel boots and brown leather pants (which I'm pretty sure are new even though she insisted she had them before. I would have noticed those before). "I don't think I'm going to need that," she says, and pushes the microphone to her left. "Hi, boys."

"Hello," they answer back.

She smiles. "I'd like to welcome everyone to our How To Pick Up and Impress Women seminar. There is a complimentary notebook and red pen on each of your chairs for taking notes. Also, feel free to interrupt me with questions. Just raise your hand." She wiggles her hand to demonstrate, and the room gets an extended view of her cleavage.

"The dating scene is a jungle. Today I'm going to teach you how to navigate it and end up on top. No pun intended." She giggles.

"Why aren't you up there?" Josh whispers to me. He's sitting beside me in the last row. Clint is on my other side. Jodine and Manny are sitting in front of us.

"Are you kidding? What do I know? Em's the sexpert."

"I'm more interested in what *you* have to say."

Did Clint hear that? I wonder if Clint heard that. He seems to be very immersed in the lesson. I have some advice for him—all he has to do to pick me up is say, "Let's go."

Isn't it possible that he came here because he's trying to learn the best way to admit how he feels about me? Who would know more about how to pick me up than my roomie?

Emma continues. "There are two types of women to pick up. The first type is the woman you don't know. You may find this overwhelming, but you shouldn't. The truth is, women don't want to be alone. They want to meet men. They want to meet *you*. But here is the contradiction—women want to be picked up, but don't want to feel as though they're being picked up. In technical terms, that means that your job is to pick her up while giving the impression it's the last thing you're trying to do. Everyone follow so far?"

Nods from the audience.

"This is why bars are terrible places. You can't pretend you're not trying to pick up. So forget bars, and focus on less-obvious meeting places. Video stores, movie theaters, car washes, any place you can pretend you're not there to pick up works."

Josh leans toward me. "Didn't you tell me that she met her ex-boyfriend at a bar?"

I swat him on the arm. "Shh. I can't hear."

Emma uncrosses and crosses her legs. "If you sense that the woman is reluctant to give you her phone number, it may be because she's not a hundred-percent sure you're not a serial killer. To placate her, hand her your business card, tell her you'd love to take her out for dinner later in the week, and tell her to call you. This obviously works best if you have an impressive job."

Josh groans. "These guys are all students!"

"Shh." I swat him gently on the head. That's two swats in less than a minute. Does Clint see us flirting?

"The second type of pickup is the acquaintance. She doesn't think you're a serial killer, because she already knows you. First, accidentally on purpose brush against her. Skin contact is very important. If she's interested, she'll flirt back. If she's not, she'll joke it off and won't think any less of you, because as a man, you're expected to flirt shamelessly."

Josh fake-yawns and drops his arm against the back of my chair.

"You're too much," I say, slightly louder than necessary.

Clint doesn't notice. Is he having that tough a time with women that he has to pay such close attention to the lecture? Yoo-hoo? Hello? The real thing? Right here?

Emma continues. "If she jokes it off, all hope is not lost. Try this. Women want what they think other women want. Continue to flirt with her, but program your cell to ring when she's nearby and then say, 'Hi, Tara,' and walk away to talk. Here's another tactic. Tell a mutual acquaintance about the stunning bathing-suit model/rocket scientist you've been casually dating. Don't tell your crush about the pickup yourself. Women hate men who brag."

Josh leans forward and whispers to Jodine, "Did I tell you about the date I went on last night? She's a brain surgeon and in her spare time she makes cookies."

Emma has moved on to dating. "Don't invite a new girl to an activity involving water without giving her a backup option. This includes waterslides, hot-tubbing and pool parties. Many women are uncomfortable with their bodies and will say no, not because they don't want to go out with you, but because they don't want you to see them in a bathing suit on the first date."

Jodine flips her head to face me. "Why do I have a feeling Emma's never said no to a hot tub?"

Emma apparently sees Jodine talking, because she casts her a dirty look. "Say you're all at a bar," she says, all serious, "and even though I have explicitly pointed out that this is not an ideal mating ground, you meet someone who just happens to get a rise from you, if you know what I mean. Now, pay attention. This is very important. If she introduces you to two of her friends, offer to buy them each a drink. This is tricky, but it scores huge points when done correctly. If she concludes that you're generous, she'll likely go home with you, but if she thinks you're hitting on her friends, it's just you and Mr. Hand. So keep your eyes focused on your date. I can't stress this enough."

Josh taps Jodine on the shoulder. "Allie's friend, would you like a Life Saver?"

Did Clint see that? He must have seen that.

Nope. Still paying attention. Funny, he was never this attentive in school. Apparently he's far more interested in this kind of subject matter. Where does Emma come up with all this stuff?

"Okay, boys. This one's *really* crucial. It's regarding your bathroom. Once you have her in your apartment, she's going to visit the bathroom, and if you fuck it up, she'll be out of there before you can even say 'blow job.' First—If it's grimy, she's not going to want to stay over. So clean the urine off the floor. You're not at war, you're allowed to miss, but she doesn't have to know about it. Second—Hide the porn. She knows you jerk off, but she doesn't need to see the evidence. After all, she's there because she believes you believe she's the sexiest thing on earth, so why would you need outside stimulation? Third—Make sure there's toilet paper. For some inexplicable reason, men always forget to take out a new roll after they've finished the old one. Wiping may be optional for men, but do you really want her drip drying? I didn't think so. Fourth—Throw out all boxes of tampons. It doesn't matter where they're hidden. She'll go through your cupboard, find them and then there's no sex for you. Even if they are your sister's, she won't believe you. Throw them out. Fifth— Contrary to popular conviction, leave the toilet seat up. Although leaving it down would seem to be the polite thing to do, it may be viewed as a feminine trait. Women like *men*. Women also like uncharted territory and a challenge. The toilet seat up says, No he's never let another woman train him, and the door, or seat, is wide open for you."

"I've never even seen your apartment," I whisper to Josh. "Do you leave the seat up or down?"

"Neither. I have a urinal in every room. Very useful. Also doubles as a beer basin."

Emma slides off the desk and pulls down a projection screen. She turns on Jodine's laptop and clicks on a file.

Uh-oh. Jodine and I both sink into our seats. We were at the dress rehearsal. We know what's coming next.

"This," Emma says, "is the woman's vagina."

"Terrific," Jodine mutters.

"This," she says, and suddenly the vagina's clitoris turns pink, "is where you should be focusing your attention."

Jodine groans softly.

"I'm not sure why so many of you keep missing it, but there it is. Find it. Make friends. You can play with it with your fingers or your tongue.

"If she's doing this—" Emma breathes in and out quickly "—that's good. If she's not making any sound, move around a bit and keep trying." She pauses to take a sip of water.

Clint is taking notes.

Josh is shaking his bright red face.

A buzz-cut boy with glasses raises his hand. "Excuse me?"

"Yes?" Emma asks, smiling.

"Why do women always act so squeamish about receiving oral sex?"

"That's an excellent question. Most women love getting head. Why wouldn't they? It's similar to the bathing-suit issue—they're embarrassed. They think they taste bad. It comes from all those jokes about fish. My recommendation, and I'm sure all the women in the back of the room would agree with me, is to constantly reassure them that you love the taste. That you're hungry for it. That you wish there was a perfume that smelled like her pussy."

The fourteen men turn around to look at us. I attempt to smile. Jodine covers her face with her hands.

Did she just use the *P* word?

An hour later, Emma is summing up. "Please write out your e-mail address, home address and phone number on the paper being handed around the room. Oh! One more thing. Easy on the cologne, okay? One of you out there smells like an overdose of maple syrup. Remember, you want to attract the woman, not give her diabetes. Happy hunting, and thank you all for coming."

28
OMNISCIENT NARRATOR RINGS IN THE NEW YEAR

"Ten! Nine! Eight! Seven! Six! Five—"

Let's freeze for a second, shall we? It's New Year's Eve and once again they're at 411. The girls have decided to have their second party at 411, where they held the Halloween bash, for multiple reasons. One: They were too lazy to search around for a new bar. Why fight the familiar? Two: Steve, the manager at 411, was so thrilled with the first party, he is willing to charge twenty dollars at the door (everything gets exponentially expensive on New Year's) and give our favorite roommates fifteen dollars per person. Three: Jodine wants to see Count Zeus again, and since she doesn't know his real name and can't look him up, 411 is where they've gotta go.

Allie is in Belleville. Right now she's sitting on her parents' couch, looking at Times Square on television. Her mother is with her, her father is with her, her brother and his wife are with her, her grandparents are with her, and they all shout "Hurray!" when the clock turns twelve. They kiss, they laugh, they love, la-di-da-di-da, and that's all you're going to hear about Allie's New Year's.

Ibid for Manny in Ottawa.

Nick and Monique were supposed to spend the evening at a friend of Nick's house party. Monique said there was no way in hell she would spend New Year's with Nick's psycho ex-girlfriend at some stupid party. She calls her psycho not because she knows that Emma axed the marijuana tree (she and Nick are not actually aware that Emma is responsible. Nick did not check on the condition of the tree until a week and a half later, when the temperature dropped below zero, and therefore did not associate Emma with its demise. Instead, he assumed a bandit in search of free pot was the culprit), but because she heard Emma screaming at Nick on the phone, and Monique being the refined kind of person she is, didn't appreciate being called a whore.

But then here's what happened. Monique had been wearing a red see-through silk dress (she had seen the dress on *Fashion TV* and knew she had to have it), and Nick had screamed, "Why aren't you wearing a bra under that?" She'd answered that you weren't supposed to wear a bra under a dress like this, that what he saw were just nipples after all, and who cared if other people saw a hint of them? Deaf to her "but-it's-New-Year's-protests," he'd screamed that none of his friends were ever going to see her nipples, and had insisted she either change into pants or she'd be spending New Year's alone. She'd told him to have a good night. Apparently, there was a small way in hell, because Monique ended up stopping by 411 because she knew of nowhere else to go, but when she saw Emma and some new man and Jodine but no Manny (the one person she had hoped on seeing) she decided she'd be better off at home.

Josh is at a pub with his buddies. As much as he wants to contribute to the Fix-the-Kitchen-Fund, in his opinion the first party's only saving grace (besides the fact that it made a hell of a lot of cash for the girls) was Allie, and since Allie is in Belleville, a pub and his buddies is the preferred choice.

Who else is there? **Not Janet**, but you don't care about her, anyway. You probably **don't even** remember her. (The next-door neighbor?)

And of course, there's Clint. Surely, you remember him. He's at the party with Jodine—and Emma, obviously.

So. The party. You can skip back to the last party if you want a description of the bar. It's pretty much the same, only minus the costumes—unless you count the sparkled outfits and body glitter everyone seems to be wearing, and the sleazy bartenders who were there last time. Including Count Zeus, too, only sans fangs and cape.

The girls arrived at the party exactly as you'd imagine: they got dressed, Emma drove, they did some tequila shots, they took turns watching the door for an hour, but then decided they trusted the doorwoman not to steal their share. Then Jodine did a little more tequila, Emma a lot of on-the-bar dancing, both a lot of hi-how-are-you-so-glad-you-could-comes, and they both lip-synched a lot of Culture Club. There are only a few important scenes, however, which should be presented in detail before we return to the countdown, so here goes.

SCENE ONE

[Jodine is in the bathroom, adjusting the water pads in her bra, hoisting up her breasts so that they appear to be overflowing from the plunging red tank top Emma insisted she buy at Mendocino the week before. She turns around to check out how her butt looks in the clinging gray pants she bought there as well. She reapplies her red lipstick and uses the water from the bathroom sink to revive her hair, which is being worn festively down. She sucks in her stomach and walks toward the VIP bar. Because it is only nine-thirty no one is at the bar except Count Zeus, who without his fangs and cape is still stunning, even in a button-down silver shirt.]

JODINE: Hi.

COUNT ZEUS: Hello, what can I get you?

JODINE: *[Looking somewhat unsure of herself.]* Can I get a kamikaze? *[Emma ordered a kamikaze last time, so Jodine figures it must be a sexy drink.]* Can I have two?

COUNT ZEUS: *[Pours the drinks and sets them down on the bar in front of her.]* Sure, doll.

JODINE: *[Raises her left eyebrow in an attempt to be suggestive. She can raise it, no problem, she's just not sure it comes across as suggestive. The drink's not bad actually.]* One's for you.

COUNT ZEUS: *[Smiling.]* You have both. I'll have a drink with you after midnight.

JODINE: But my outfit may turn back into rags after midnight.

COUNT ZEUS: I could always use some rags to clean the bar at the end of the night.

JODINE: *[She has no idea what he means, but imagines him removing gray dish towels from her body and dropping them onto the floor. She does the two shots.]* That calmed the nerves. *[She's hoping he'll ask, "Why are you nervous?" This will lead to "Because it's my party," which will lead to "Oh, I remember you, you threw that incredible Halloween party. Weren't you the angel?"]*

COUNT ZEUS: Don't worry, you look hot.

JODINE: *[Leans into the bar to accentuate her cleavage. The pink shimmering powder that Emma sprinkled over her breasts glimmers.]* Thank you.

COUNT ZEUS: What are you nervous about? Trying to impress some guy?

JODINE: Perhaps.

COUNT ZEUS: Your boyfriend? *[Lines up various alcoholic concoctions in preparation for the long night ahead.]*

JODINE: *[Tries to look coy.]* No.

COUNT ZEUS: Who is it, then? Some guy you've been stalking from afar?

JODINE: Perhaps. *[A couple is climbing up the VIP stairs toward them. 411 is starting to fill up. Jodine realizes she might not have the count's undivided attention for the rest of the evening. The kamikazes have given her courage.]* He's you.

COUNT ZEUS: *[Looks at her strangely.]* Me?

JODINE: Yes, you! *[The couple sits down on Count Zeus's bar stools.]* Maybe we'll have that drink later?

COUNT ZEUS: Come find me. I'll get someone to cover the bar for a while.

JODINE: *[Smiles as she sashays Emma-style down the VIP steps and over to another bar for more fornication-fortification, i.e., alcohol. Count Zeus appreciatively watches her walk away.]* And you can cover me, big boy. Anytime. *[These last words aren't actually spoken; she just thinks she says them.]*

SCENE TWO

[Clint and Emma are sitting on stools at the bar on the right side of the room. Their legs are pressed against each other's, trying to force their pants to disintegrate with the pressure. Both are holding cigarettes. He inhales, she exhales, and vice versa.]

CLINT: I like your knees. *[He caresses her left knee.]* I like your thighs. *[He caresses her right thigh.]* I like your breasts.

EMMA: Whoa. I get the idea. This is a public place, remember?

CLINT: You didn't complain last time.

EMMA: Last time I didn't know you were someone's soul mate.

CLINT: I love it when you say the word *mate*. What do you say we get out of here?

EMMA: Down, horn-dog, down. We can't leave. It's my party. Are you going to behave yourself tonight or not?

CLINT: *[He moves his hand **toward the** inside of her thigh.]* Oh, I'm going to behave, all right. Only not in the way you mean.

Now back to the countdown. *"Four, three, two..."*

Hold it! One more freeze and that's it.

There are three hundred and thirty people in the bar. When the corks start popping, they're all going to go for that New Year's kiss. Two hundred and six of these people are going to go for the lips. Can you guess any of their names?

Unfreeze.

Freeze.

Tee-hee.

Did you ever play freeze at summer camp? The counselor calls "Freeze!" and the first person who moves has to stack up the plates and clean the table. Remember when you were pouring the milk into your cereal and someone screamed, "Freeze!" and the milk continued to pour? It spilled out of the bowl while the Rice Crispies crackled and popped all over the table, and not only did you get stuck with kitchen duty that day, you never did get to eat breakfast.

Unfreeze.

"One! Happy New Year!" Corks pop, people cheer, Madonna's "Holiday" plays.

La-di-da-di-da.

Clint and Emma can no longer resist the delicious temptation of the forbidden. Their lips are irresistible to each other, like a new white shirt and a spilled glass of fruit punch. Their tongues follow suit.

Jodine, tequila at work, has made sure she is standing next to Count Zeus behind the bar during the countdown. Because she couldn't figure out where the latch to the door was, this involved climbing under the bar to get there limbolike, and she might have sprained her back, but who cares? She's there and he's there and now he's popping champagne, and as the bubbly drips down the bottle, Jodine thinks it all looks pretty phallic. She takes the bottle and laps the sweet liquid into her mouth and then passes it to him. After he's taken quite a guzzle, she removes the bottle from his hands, grabs hold of his collar, pulls him toward her and pushes her tongue into his mouth.

She's hot and bubbly and celebratory and sexy, and he's more than happy to be the one to bring in her New Year.

'Course, he has no idea who the hell she is.

29
JODINE HAS A HANGOVER

JODINE

My head feels like a sink. Someone forgot to turn off the faucet above it and a constant stream of water is dripping into my brain. Is this Chinese water torture?

What time is it?

I glance at the clock on my nightstand and realize that my arm is covered with mini goose bumps. It's 7:00 a.m. and freezing in here. Where is my duvet? I see it in a lump next to me and attempt to cover myself. It doesn't budge.

Is someone in there? Is there a man in bed with me? It must be Manny. Who else would be in bed with me? What day is it? Isn't Manny away? A memory of tequila and Count Zeus's lips grows in my brain like an infected mosquito bite. Is he here? Did I bring him home? I unwrap the duvet, fearful of what I might find. And there's a…pillow. No man. Just feathers wrapped in cotton. Phew.

I'm alone, with nothing but a hangover to keep me company.

After the kiss, I was waylaid by law-school friends and Count Zeus went back to serving drinks. At two a.m., when our guests began to disappear home, I followed Emma and Steve into the back room to count the money, and when I returned, Count Zeus had already closed his bar and gone.

How could he have left without saying goodbye? Did he think I would go home without saying good-night? Why didn't I have a glass of water before I went to bed, like you're supposed to, to avoid the pounding-head syndrome? My mouth feels as dry as the dishes of potpourri my mother used to place sporadically around the house.

My mouth.

Zeus's tongue in my mouth. Was it a dream or did it really happen?

Need water.

I gently lift my legs out of bed and head toward the mini-fridge. Someone left the light on in the hallway and it spears through my brain. Agh. I need water. Where are the glasses? We bought six. You'd think that once in a while someone else could pitch in and remember to clean them. I cup my hands under the newly installed sink in the kitchen and lap up the water. Ah. Better. Need more. Need to lie down again. Must sleep. I head back to bed.

I am already engulfed in the blankets when suddenly I realize that there was a scrunchie on Emma's door. Why was there a scrunchie on Emma's door?

Terrific.

I pull the covers off again and return to the scene of the crime. The newly ingested water makes a swishing sound in my stomach. Yes. That is definitely a scrunchie on her doorknob. A red velvet scrunchie. I walk back to the front hallway. Black leather loafers. I pick them up. Size eleven. I've seen these shoes before. Why do they look so familiar? Whose are they? Why does my body feel as if I fell while waterskiing, refused to let go of the rope and was dragged behind the boat for hours while being made to swallow gallons of water?

I was sitting in the back of the car last night when Emma drove us home. Who rode shotgun?

"My roommate is having a party at our place tonight. Is it cool if I crash on your couch?" he had asked.

I hadn't even known Clint had a roommate.

The brand-new soles of my running shoes slam against the wooden floor as I jog through our apartment. They were a Christmas present from my parents. Each lap starts next to Allie's unmade bed, continues through the hallway, toward the window in my room, into the bathroom, out of the bathroom, past Emma's shut door (scrunchie still there), into the front hallway where Clint's shoes used to be and are now gone, circles around the dust balls in the living room, delves as deep into the kitchen as I can get without tripping on some sort of tool, and then repeats in reverse back into Allie's room.

Why would the scrunchie still be on Emma's door if Clint's shoes are gone? Is there another guy in there with his laces still done up?

Sixteen laps later, Emma screams from within her scrunchie-protected fortress, "What are you doing?"

"Jogging!" I yell back.

"Why?"

"Because I'm disgusting!"

"Why are you jogging here?"

"Because the gym is closed today!"

"Why aren't you jogging outside?"

"If you ever got out of bed you'd see there was a blizzard!" I trot toward Emma's door. "Are you alone in there?"

"I am."

I push open the door and jog inside. The covers are pulled up to her neck. Beside her bed are six glasses and two—no, three—ripped condom wrappers. "Clint stayed over?"

"Yes."

That settled, I debate whether I should resume my lap. I am resolved to remain as neutral as possible in this impending disastrous situation.

"Wait!" Emma pleads. "Don't you want to hear about it?"

Can I also have hot wax dripped onto my eyelashes and then ripped off? I shake my head. "No."

She sits up, holding the sheet against her body. "Oh, come on! It's your job as a roommate to listen."

And it's your job as a roommate not to have sex with your other roommates' believed soul mates. In spite of my disgust, I remain in her room, but I continue jogging on the spot as though the action can somehow make me appear less interested. "Where did he go?" I ask nonchalantly. I sincerely hope he pulled a *wham, bam, thank you ma'am* and disappeared to whatever sports bar men who sleep with women and then never call go.

"He's watching football with his friends this afternoon, but he'll be back at four. We're going to spend the entire weekend right here!" She motions with a flourish to her bed. She pats the empty spot beside her. "Can you sit down? I can't talk to you when you're moving."

So don't talk. "I can't sit, I have to be aerobic for forty-five minutes."

"Fine, keep jogging, but you have to listen. He was pretty good—"

Terrific. Details.

"I had an orgasm, too, which is always an unexpected bonus.

And he wasn't that big, so we were able to experiment more with positions...."

Do I need to know this?

"Nick was long and thick, so sometimes random positions were uncomfortable. Clint is smaller, so we were able to try some alterations on doggie style and..."

Why is my Discman never around when I need it?

"Allie! Hi!"

Allie's voice screeches back at me from inside the telephone receiver. "Hi! I'm so glad I caught you at home!"

Emma covers her lips with her finger, I assume to warn me not to tell Allie that Clint is lying next to her on the couch, in his boxers, with his hand resting on her stomach. You don't say, Emma!

"Hi!" I repeat, because I don't know what else to say. If I'd seen her name on the call display I would never have answered, but I couldn't resist "Anonymous." What if Count Zeus located me and was calling to ask where I disappeared to last night and could we get together for a drink?

"Happy New Year!" she says cheerily. "How was the party? Did you have fun? Did people come?"

I look at Emma's hand caressing Clint's head. "People did."

"How much did we make?"

"About forty-five hundred."

"That's amazing! I don't believe it! I must have missed the best party ever. We're almost there! Did you give the money to Josh?"

"Yeah. He finished the cupboards, the sink, is working on the counters and ordered the fridge, stove and oven. But he said they're going to take at least three weeks since we want them to replicate our old ones."

"He's awesome. So what have you guys been up to?"

Um…Emma runs her fingers down Clint's chest. Can't we keep discussing the kitchen? "We've been keeping busy."

"Do you miss Manny?"

Who? Right, the man I used to sleep with. He called me on the first to wish me a happy New Year, his voice dripping with hope and expectation. I should have told him about the kiss. I should just break up with him. I *have to* break up with him.

Still…it is nice to have him around…sometimes. Especially at school. And do I really want to sit alone all semester? But doesn't that make me the world's most horrible person? Although we never agreed to be exclusive. He might be with someone else in Ottawa. I've never told him he couldn't. In college he was pretty serious about some girl. I bet she was home for the holidays. He easily could have kissed her at midnight. It was just a kiss. At New Year's. It's bad luck not to kiss someone at New Year's, isn't it?

Maybe I didn't do anything wrong.

Allie's high-pitched voice interrupts my pathetic attempt at rationalization. "Did you see Clint at the party?"

Maybe I should just say no. "Yes."

"You did? And? Did he say anything about me?"

"He didn't do much talking."

"I called him to wish him a happy New Year, but his roommate said he hasn't been home much. I wonder where he is."

Ah, so Clint really does have a roommate. He might be a cheat and a rat, but apparently he's not a liar. "When are you coming home?" I ask, in a lame attempt to change the subject.

"On Sunday, around nine."

Clint and Emma will surely have sex at least seventy times before then. "Come home soon. Do you want to talk to Emma?"

Emma emphatically shakes her head *no!*

No way should I be feeling guilt for this on my own. I hand her the phone.

"Um…hi, Allie… Yes, I'm having fun…. Yes, he was there… No, I didn't get much of a chance to *talk* to him." Clint's hand reaches under her shirt to tickle her and she giggles. "No. I didn't see him with any *other* girls."

Well, I have to give her credit. Like Clint, she's no liar.

Squeak. Squeak. Squeak.

Today is the last day I can sleep in late, as my final law school semester starts tomorrow.

What is that noise?

It had better not be another disgusting rodent. I check the mouse pad beside the radiator. Nope. Maybe one of the pads in the living room caught one. Nope. They're all clear.

The squeaking is emerging from Emma's room.

They're having sex at eight-thirty in the morning. Who has sex at eight-thirty in the morning? How are they having sex at eight-thirty in the morning? Emma's not even up at eight-thirty in the morning. And they were locked in the bedroom all last night. And all yesterday afternoon. And the entire day before that. When I returned from dinner with my parents, I found Emma's black lace bra lodged between two pillows on the couch, leading me to believe that when I am not around, they have sex in other areas of the apartment as well.

Last night I had a nightmare that they do it on my bed whenever I'm out.

Maybe they're trying to squeeze in as much sex as possible

before Allie returns home tonight. They'll have to stop their bunny performance when Allie's here, right?

Right?

Maybe I should do laundry now that I'm up. It wouldn't hurt to throw my duvet in there, would it?

30
ALLIE IS OBLIVIOUS

ALLIE

I'm home. Finally. First my train was delayed two hours because of rail problems, and then the trip took twice as long because of a snowstorm. And then there were no taxis and I had to wait forever. I should have just taken the subway and streetcar, but my bags were heavy and I've been up since six this morning. I know it was extravagant to spend all this money on a cab, but really, I'm so very, very tired.

I should have arrived this morning, and here it is already two o'clock in the afternoon. I feel as if I've wasted the whole day— I was planning on making my roomies breakfast in bed, but it looks like that will have to be some other morning.

I missed them. It was great to see my family, of course, but sometimes the people you live with become your family.

Where did I put my keys? Here they are. "Hello? Anyone home?" I ask, and push open the door.

Are those Clint's shoes?

Jay, on the recliner, and Emma, head popping up from the couch, turn to me in surprise.

"Allie!" Jay says. "I thought you were coming back at nine!"

I swear those are his shoes. I know what his shoes look like. "Is Clint here?"

I see the tip of Clint's head crop up from behind the couch like a chocolate Pop Tart emerging in slow motion from a toaster. "Hi," he says.

I can't believe it! Clint is here! "Hi!" I exclaim. "You're so sweet! You've been waiting for me to come back since nine this morning? I'm sorry I kept you waiting. My train was delayed and delayed and delayed. You must have been so bored. Thank you so much for waiting!" I am not crazy! He must be a little bit in love! He's been waiting here for hours.

"I…yeah. Crazy."

I drop my bags onto the floor with a thud, throw my coat on the edge of the couch and squeeze between Emma and Clint on the couch. I lean over and give him a big hug. Mmm. His hair smells like shampoo, as though he just got out of the shower.

You know how you feel after you've eaten just the right amount and you're not hungry anymore but you're not too full, either? Perfectly content is how I am right now. Perfectly happy. "What should we do today?" I ask.

After two hours of television, Clint stands up and yawns. "I have to go."

Emma leaps off the couch. "I'll drive you," she says.

I stand up, too. "I'll come keep you company!"

"Actually, Allie, I'm sleeping at my dad's tonight, so I'm just going to drop him off on the way."

Sleeping at her dad's? The only time I've ever known Emma to voluntarily stay at her father's was when our kitchen burned down. And even then she contemplated staying at a hotel. "How come?" I ask. "Don't you have to go to work tomorrow?"

"I…my dad and AJ have a party tonight and I promised I'd baby-sit."

I follow Emma into her room and watch her dump clothes into a black mesh bag. "Here, you forgot this," I say, picking up her red scrunchie from the floor. A thought occurs to me. "Why don't you just bring Barbie over here?" I ask. "We could all hang out. I bet she'd love to see your place." It amazes me that Emma hasn't invited Barbie here once. If I had an older sister who lived in her own place, I'd want to be there twenty-four seven.

Emma picks up the bag and I follow her toward the door. Clint's gray wool coat is already zipped up. He pulls her coat off the hanger.

"I…no," she says. "AJ wants me there."

I really think Emma should insist on showing her sister this part of her life, but I know it's none of my business, so I keep my mouth shut. "All right. Your call." I kiss Clint on the cheek. "Thanks for surprising me."

Once the two of them leave, I plop back onto the couch. "What do you want for dinner?" I ask Jay. "Pizza sandwich?"

She stares ahead at the *Simpsons*. "Okay. No bread or cheese for me."

Since when does Jay watch the *Simpsons?* "Sure."

I cook and watch simultaneously. "When we get an oven, I'm going to make some amazing dishes. My mom taught me how to make a turkey."

"What, you can't make a turkey in the sandwich-maker?"

"Ha ha. We should probably buy a regular toaster, eh?"

"We can almost afford it. We've raised a large chunk of the money already. I think we only need one more party on Valentine's Day."

I nod in agreement and sneak a piece of mozzarella.

Jay swirls the chair to look at me. "So did you speak to Josh when you were away?"

One more piece of cheese and that's it. "Yup."

Jay raises an eyebrow. How does she do that? I try to raise mine. I don't think it's working.

"What are you doing with your face?"

"Nothing." I take another piece of cheese. "He said he's pretty much done the counters. And as soon as the fridge, oven and stove are delivered he'll be done. Did you see how nice the cupboards are? I like the glasses you got. I think tomorrow we should get plates and cutlery. A few days ago he told me he'd be done by the beginning of February."

This time she raises her other eyebrow. "You spoke to him from Belleville?"

"Yup." I put Jay's vegetables in the grill and close the handle.

"He called you?"

"Yup."

"Why?"

"To wish me a happy New Year."

"How did he get your number?"

"Looked it up, I guess?"

"He likes you, eh?"

"We're friends."

"No. I mean he *likes* you."

"You mean he likes-me likes-me?"

She looks confused.

"It's a line from *The Wonder Years*." She has heard of *The Wonder Years*, hasn't she?

"What's your problem?" she asks, suddenly angry. "Why won't you go out with him?"

Whoa. What's my problem? What's *her* problem? Why does

she suddenly care who I date? "I can't date one guy when I'm in love with someone else."

"You won't date him because of Clint?"

I nod. "How can I date Josh when I confide in him about Clint? He'd know that my heart wasn't in it. He's a great guy—I couldn't let him be the runner-up prize."

"That makes no sense. What if you and Clint don't happen? You're never going to date another guy again?"

The problem with Jay is that she doesn't know what it's like to have a dream. If people gave up on their hopes at the first road-block, think about how many dreams would go unfulfilled. "I think Clint and I are going to happen. I can feel it."

She looks at me with doubt. I hope she's not ruining the karmic energy.

I sigh. "But if it doesn't happen soon, I'll give up. Okay?"

"Set a date," Jay says. "Be specific."

"April first." I take a deep breath. "The truth is," I say, and then suddenly feel the whole story begin to pour out, "I only stayed in Toronto because I was afraid that if I left, Clint and I would never have a chance, and my parents want me to come home because they think I'm wasting my life here, and I can't be a telefundraiser forever but there's nothing else I can do, and then just when I think he doesn't care about me after not even calling to wish me a happy New Year, he shows up at my house to surprise me. So what do I do?"

Jay stares at me, her mouth wide open. "Where you live should not be about him. What do *you* want?"

Suddenly, the room feels watery. Everything I want is confused and fuzzy and the room around me looks like a watercolor I did in art class that slipped out of my mittened hands and into a puddle. The colors and lines are swished and blurred. What do I want? What does anyone want? I want a job that makes me want to get up in the morning. I want the person I love to love me back. I want to know what is in the air that is making my eyes itch.

Oops. I forgot about the vegetables. I open the sandwich-maker and reveal burnt broccoli.

I shake my head. "I want real kitchen appliances."

31
EMMA TAKES A PILL

EMMA

"Get up. Allie's going to be home from work soon. You have to get off me."

Clint kisses my throat. He smells like a mixture of sweat and the sundried tomatoes that were in the ravioli we ate earlier. "Can't we just tell her?"

"Why don't we just stay like this and wait for her to find us?"

"You're a real comedienne." He runs his thumbs down my body and then lifts himself up and out of me. "Shit," he says, hanging a foot above me.

Shit? That's not what you want to hear a man say as he pulls out of you. "What is shit?"

"Look."

I lift my head and follow his eyes. The condom is hanging like a peeled banana at the base of his dangling penis.

Shit, shit, shit. "It broke?"

"Exploded." He tugs at a piece of the shredded latex.

Shit, shit, shit. "But how?"

"I don't know."

"You couldn't tell this was happening?"

"If I could tell would I have kept going?"

Do I really need sarcasm right now? "Did you come inside me?"

He looks back down at his wilted penis. It looks a bit like the center of a sunflower with the broken bits as its leaves. "Yeah."

Hysteria flows through my body alongside millions of unobstructed sperm. "Why would you come inside me?"

"I always come inside you."

"Well you're never going to again! How could you not tell it was happening? You constantly bitch that I make you wear condoms, that you can't feel anything, that it's like wearing a raincoat in the shower, and now when you're not even wearing one YOU CAN'T TELL THE DIFFERENCE?"

"You're going a bit crazy, I think."

I push him off and roll onto my side. "What do we do now?" I will not cry, I will not cry. I will not get pregnant, I will not get pregnant. Can you will yourself not to get pregnant? For some insane reason, I think about the cowardly lion in *The Wizard of Oz,* when he repeats over and over, "I do believe in spooks…I do believe in spooks…" as though saying the words will make the spooks go away.

Clint lies next to me and wraps his arm around my waist, his breath tingling my ear. "Are you on the pill?"

I elbow him in the stomach. How does he not know whether I'm on the pill? "Have you ever seen me take a pill?"

"Different girls take it at different times. I don't know your schedule by heart."

"If I were on the pill, would I be FREAKING OUT?"

Does he not listen to me when I talk? I told him I used to be on the pill, but it made me irrational.

"What are we going to do? Are you going to get pregnant?" He runs his hands over his face as though he's the one with the problem. "I can't believe this happened, I can't believe this happened, I didn't realize, I didn't know…"

I'm the one who might turn into a whale and he's hysterical? Should I slap him out of it? Suddenly, I remember the alternative. "Stop blabbing. I can take the morning-after pill."

"The what?"

I feel as if I'm in a sword-and-sorcery fantasy movie and I've just remembered the magic potion. "The morning-after pill. You take it so you don't get pregnant. A friend of mine in Montreal took it."

"Do they have them in Toronto, too?"

"No, they only sell them in Montreal." He stares at me blankly, and I say, "I'm kidding, stupid."

"Do you have any here?" He takes off the shredded condom and drops it in the garbage.

"No." Am I a pharmacy? Do I have a sheet of pills stashed behind the spare rolls of toilet paper? "We have to go to the hospital and get them."

He scrunches his nose. "I hate the hospital."

Is there someone who likes going to the hospital? Ooh, what should we do today? I know, let's inhale odors of decay and urine! It's not a vacation. You go when you're sick or when you break something. Like a leg or an arm. Occasionally a condom. "Get dressed. Let's go."

"Now? We have to go tonight?"

"When did you want to go? In nine months?"

"You said you're supposed to take it the morning after. Cobrint is opening his new bar tonight. I have to go. It's business."

Business or not, if he chooses to go to some sports-bar opening instead of coming to the hospital with me, Allie is welcome to him. "Fine. I'll go by myself. I don't need you."

He sighs. "Don't go alone. Can't you ask Jodine to go with you?"

What a prick. What kind of man chooses work over his woman in need? "Nick would never bail on me like this."

He blanches at Nick's name. "Why are you bringing him up?"

Because no guy likes to be compared to another guy and come up short. "Because he'd come with me."

He steps into his jeans. "I'll come with you."

I wrap my arms around his neck. "You will?" His pants are hanging around his calves.

"I will. Maybe if we go right now we'll be able to make the bar opening later."

Five fucking hours later, the pills are in my purse, the party has started and ended without our presence, and I pull up in front of his apartment.

He puts his hand on my shoulder. "Aren't you coming in?"

All I want to do is take a hot shower and go to sleep. "Not tonight. I've been sleeping at my dad's a lot. Allie is getting suspicious."

"So let's tell her."

"Super. Something else I have to deal with."

"So we won't tell her. Why are you so moody all of a sudden?"

I shrug. "I'm pregnant."

He smirks and shakes his head. "Not funny."

"You better not have AIDS or anything."

"I don't. Do you want me to come back to your place?"

"No. We'll tell Allie, okay? Just not tonight."

I return home. It's pitch-black in my apartment and on my way into the kitchen I stumble over a piece of an appliance. Couldn't they have left one measly light on for me? Does no one care if I trip and break something? Just what I need, to break my arm and have to go back to the hospital. What was that, anyway? Probably pieces of the new stove and oven. I heard rumors of them being delivered the other day, but I hadn't really paid attention. I definitely heard something about a fridge arriving.

I turn on the lights, look for a glass, can't find one and pull the pills out of my purse. "Take two pills immediately," the instructions say. "Take the next two pills twelve hours later. Warnings: You might experience nausea. You might experience break-through bleeding. You might experience lower abdominal pain. You might experience diarrhea. You might experience an ectopic pregnancy."

This is too much experience for my taste.

When the alarm goes off at 7:00 a.m., I decide to call in sick. I barely slept, I'm tired and I feel nauseous. Fine, I don't feel nauseous right now, but I'm sure I will, and do I want to be at work when I start puking? I don't think so.

I go back to sleep.

Giggle, giggle. Deep male voice. More giggle, giggle.

I cover my face with my pillow. How inconsiderate! I'm almost nauseous and she's giggling all over the place. "ALLIE!"

The giggling stops and there is a knock on my door.

"Come in," I say groggily.

She opens my door and peeks in. "What are you doing home?"

What are you being so loud for? "I'm trying to sleep. I'm sick."

"You are? I'm so sorry I was so loud! I didn't realize you were home! Do you want some juice? Let me get you some juice."

Allie disappears into the kitchen, leaving my door opened.

Couldn't she close the door? I don't want Josh to see me lying in bed. Or maybe I do. He was looking pretty cute at the How-to-Pick-Up-Women seminar.

Nah.

It's one o'clock. I have to take my pills again. I'm not supposed to take them on an empty stomach. "Allie?" I call out.

"Yeah?"

"Can you get me a bagel? Grilled in the sandwich-maker?"

"Okay! But guess where I'm grilling it."

Who cares? "Where?"

"On the stove! Josh finished it! And he installed the oven! The kitchen is done! You have to come see! Everything is ready!"

Wohoo. As if suddenly I'm going to start cooking.

Moments later, she returns to my room with a tray. "Don't worry about anything," she says, fluffing up my pillows. "Allie's going to take care of you all day."

Jodine picks up the water bottle, takes a sip and sits down on the recliner. She eyes my pajamas. "Early night tonight?"

"I'm sick." I wrap Allie's spare comforter tighter around me.

She scowls at the water bottle. "Did you drink straight from the bottle? I don't want to get sick."

She's such a complainer. "It's not contagious. The condom broke and I took the morning-after pill."

She eyes my stomach. "Are you okay?"

"Just nauseous." Well, not as nauseous as I thought I'd be, but it could start at any time, can't it?

"What did you do all day?"

"Allie rented some movies for me."

Jodine heads into the kitchen and opens the new fridge, I'm assuming in search of another bottle of water. "Allie stocked the fridge!"

"She did?" I hadn't looked. She's been bringing me food all day.

"I wish we had taken pictures of the kitchen before it burnt down so we'd have something to compare it to now."

"I drew it out for Josh. I am a designer—I know how to draw."

She continues rummaging around in the new fridge. "Whose sandwich is this?"

"Allie made it for me. Can you pass it?"

She tosses it. "Why?"

"Because I'm hungry."

"No, I mean, why did she make it?"

"Because she was worried about me." Unlike you, apparently. "She wanted to take care of me."

Jodine snorts. "Don't you feel guilty letting her take care of you while you lie about why you're sick?"

"Can't I ever just worry about *me?* Why should I have to feel bad for Allie right now, when I'm the one who might be nauseous?"

"I want you to tell her. Soon."

Do this, do that. Blah blah blah. "Fine. When?"

Jodine crosses her arms in front of her like a judge about to pass sentence. "You have two weeks to tell her, or I'm going to."

"Whatever." I storm out of the living room and into my room, slamming the door behind me.

Why does no one care about how I feel?

Fuck. I forgot the sandwich.

"Calling all roomies! Calling all roomies!" Something is shrieking loudly from the other side of the apartment.

"What?!" I holler.

"We have to make a toast. I brought a bottle of wine!"

I wrap my blanket over my shoulders and wander into the kitchen. It looks almost exactly the same as it did pre-fire. Not that I can remember what it looked like pre-fire that clearly. Now that I think about it, the stove was actually a lot more to the left....

Too late.

Allie is sitting on the counter, pouring pink zinfandel into what must be newly purchased wineglasses.

Jodine is leaning against the fridge.

"Thanks, Allie," I say as she hands me a glass.

"Is that good for your nausea?" Jodine asks with a smirk.

Fuck off. "I'm sure I'll be fine. But thanks for caring."

Allie raises her glass in the air. "I just want to take this opportunity to say how much you two mean to me. Really. We went through a really tough time, but instead of cracking, we stuck together and overcame the obstacles. We did some amazing fund-raising—and I know fund-raising—and I'm proud of us."

"Don't we still owe Josh money?" I interrupt.

"A little," she says, and dangles her legs. "But who cares? We have a fab kitchen! And an even fabber friendship!" She leans over, clinks her glass with Jodine's, then with mine, and then drinks.

Jodine lifts her glass to mine. "To true friends," she says, glaring at me ever so slightly.

We clink and drink.

I'm getting the feeling that Jodine's toast wasn't that heartfelt.

32
JODINE GETS CHOKED UP

JODINE

I can't believe the nerve of that woman! It's preposterous. Allie has been running around after her like a human crap-shovel, and last night Emma told her, for the fiftieth time this month, that she's sleeping at her dad's. It's ridiculous. Absurd. And to top it all, Allie has been counting down the days until today, the day of the Valentine's Day party, because she's convinced that today is *the* day.

Manny stretches his arm around me and nuzzles my face against his chest. I can't breathe when he does this. It constricts the fresh air from heading into my lungs and all I can smell is his laundry softener and my own breath. I need space to sleep. I twist my body so that I'm facing the window instead of him, and he wraps his arms around my body so we're spooning. There is no way I'm going to be able to fall back asleep.

The sky looks a little lighter than it did a minute ago. Why didn't I realize it was getting lighter while it was happening? It's odd that even though I was staring right at it, I didn't even realize that the sun had begun to consume the blackness. Have I been so conditioned to abrupt endings and beginnings, to opening credits rolling, to final exams being written, that I can no longer discern a subtle difference?

I turn back toward Manny and lightly run my fingers over his soft, damp long forehead, his tilted-up nose, his wide, flat cheeks. His eyes flutter.

Why did I kiss Count Zeus? Why didn't I tell Manny?

"I love you," he murmurs, and pulls me closer.

I stop breathing. My face, my hands, my legs feel cold and stiff and empty.

I roll back around. The sky is already a few shades brighter.

"You're late!" Allie tells me, and I feel an odd sense of déjà vu. She is sitting on the couch, watching a *Cheers* rerun, wearing black pants and one of Emma's red shirts.

"Sorry, sorry, I was at the gym."

"You have to hurry up! We're going to be late!"

I shower, dry my hair and put it into a ponytail. I don't feel like wearing it down. I put on the little red dress that Emma insisted I wear for this occasion. The phone rings. Allie answers and quickly calls out, "Jodine! It's for you! It's Manny!" Since that time I told her off for speaking to him, she has never spent more than six seconds talking to him. I think I may have overreacted.

"Hello?" I say.

"Hi," he says, sounding ice-covered and far away.

Did someone see me with Count Zeus? Does Manny know? Do I want Manny to know? "Where are you?"

He doesn't say anything.

I wrap the phone wire around my thumb. "Manny? What's wrong?" He knows. Someone told him. A mixture of sadness and relief wafts through me.

I hear him take a deep breath. "My grandmother collapsed. She's in the hospital. I'm at the airport. I'm going to take the ten o'clock to Ottawa."

His grandmother? What? "I'm so sorry."

"I'm going to miss the party."

"Don't worry about it. Are you okay?" *Is there something I can do?*

"I'm okay. I can't tell you how happy I am that I came and saw her at Christmas. My mom is pretty messed up."

I remember how my mom wouldn't get out of bed for three weeks after her mother had died, and how I forced her to get up and take a shower and change her sheets because their room had started to smell and my father didn't know what to do. "I'm really, really sorry," I say. *Do you want me to come with you?*

"I'll call you in a couple days," he says.

"Take care of yourself." *Do you need me to be there with you?*

I hang up the phone and stare at the phone wire still wrapped tightly around my thumb. I unravel it and plan for the evening ahead. Just me and Count Zeus.

33
DID YOU HAVE TO KEEP
LEFTOVERS, EMMA?

EMMA

"Can we go now?" Allie yells from the living room. "Aren't you guys ready yet?"

I'm going to kill her. That voice is driving me nuts. Why does she want to be there so early when she's just going to spend the first hour freaking about why no one else is there yet?

"Calm down!" I holler from my bathroom. I apply my lipstick and pout into the mirror.

"I'll be two minutes!" Jodine screams from her room.

It's always two minutes with Jodine. If I got a dollar for every time she promised she'd be ready in two minutes, we wouldn't be having this party.

The buzzer rings.

"Are any of you expecting someone?" Allie yells.

It had better not be Clint. I specifically told him to meet me at the party. Not that he listens to what I say. I tell him to star-six-seven his phone when he calls me, but does he remember? No. Allie picks up every time he calls and then he has to talk to her for at least ten minutes. Either I have to wait for him to call back, this time using star-six-seven, or I have to call him and remember to call someone else right after so that his doesn't remain the last-called number on the display. "I'm not expecting anyone!" I holler.

"Me, neither!" Jodine screams.

I reapply my lip liner and pout one last time at the mirror. Perfect. I squeeze my lipstick into my purse, turn off my lights and close my door behind me.

Allie is sitting in the living room next to a skinny man with a mustache and faded jeans. I have no idea who this man could be. Allie's dad? Surprising her on Valentine's Day? That seems something cheesy enough for a member of Allie's family to pull. "Hi," I say.

Why is Allie trembling as if it's minus ten degrees in here? "Emma," she says. "This is Carl."

Carl? What is a Carl? Is this Allie's Clint-replacement? She needed to find another guy with the first initial *C*?

"Carl," Allie repeats, while making strange eye motions toward the kitchen. "As in Carl, our landlord. Carl, this is Emma, one of my roommates."

Oh. *That* Carl.

"Hello, Emma. It's a pleasure to meet you." He thrusts his hand toward me and I shake it. "I'm in Toronto on business and I thought I'd drop by and see how that mouse problem is coming along. Your other roommate told me that she had hired someone to take care of it, but I thought I'd come by and make sure the situation was under control."

I smile tensely. "Thank you for coming by. I'll go get Jodine." I excuse myself with a wink and smash open Jodine's door.

"Are you an idiot?" I resist the urge to disengage her face from her head.

She is organizing the contents of her purse on the bed. "What are you talking about?"

"You called Carl about our mouse problem?"

"Why shouldn't I have called Carl? Josh should be reimbursed for all those mouse-killer contraptions. Legally, Carl is supposed to pay for pest control."

"Did he?"

She nods triumphantly. "Yes, he did."

"Wonderful. Now he's come to make sure the situation is under control."

The color drains from her face, leaving it as pale as a toilet bowl after it has been flushed with Drano. "Uh-oh."

"Uh-oh is right. If he notices our little renovations, we're going to get booted."

Jodine follows me back into the living room. Carl is on bent knees beside the television, peering at the radiator. "Whoever did this, did a bang-up job. No way a mouse can get in through here."

I catch Allie smiling as if she did it herself.

Carl stands up, cracking his knees. "Have you seen any more mice?"

"No," we declare simultaneously.

"It's all under control," Jodine says. "Thank you for coming. We shouldn't take up any more of your time."

"It's my pleasure," he says. "I'll check out the kitchen and then be on my way."

Allie whimpers, "The kitchen?"

He nods. "I should check behind the stove. That's often the source of the problem. There's always an opening around the stove."

Shit, shit, shit. How can I stop him? Should I yell fire? No. Allie might not get that I was trying to distract him, and would probably break down and confess. The three of us stand immobilized in the entranceway. He's going to notice. How can he not? The appliances are glistening like overbleached teeth. We're going to get kicked out. He's going to sue us. We're going to go to jail for signing a lease without insurance. We're going to be convicted of pyromania. I don't want to go to jail. I can't live the rest of my life with women.

Allie's face is scrunched as though a nurse is about to give her a shot in the arm.

Jodine looks as though she belongs in a wax museum.

I hold my breath.

Carl whistles as though he's a construction worker and I have just walked by in my deepest plunging shirt. "Oh, my," he says.

Shit shit shit.

"You girls keep the kitchen so clean," he says.

I look up at my roommates. Allie giggles. Jodine's face starts to melt.

We did it. We're in the clear. We've just got the results back from the doctor and they are NEGATIVE, baby! He's an oblivious idiot. I'm not going to have to offer him sexual favors, after all.

He moves the stove and looks behind it. "All clear."

Allie giggles. "Fab!"

"Thanks for coming," Jodine says, exhaling.

Carl pushes the stove back against the wall. "Let me just check under the sink," he says. He bends down, cracking his knees again.

Under the sink?

He opens the cupboard doors under the sink.

Shit. Shit, shit, shit.

The next scene happens in slow motion. Like when Bruce Willis is chasing after the evil Russian mercenary and trains are exploding behind him and you can see the veins in his neck bulging.

Carl opens the doors. Carl sees the stack of minijars. Carl picks up a jar. Carl looks at one of the jars quizzically. Carl unscrews the lid off the jar. Carl smells what's inside the jar. Carl's eyes grow about ten times the size as they were a moment ago. Carl puts down the jar and stands up. Carl opens his mouth. "Are you girls selling pot?"

Jodine's face gets de-Drano'ed.

Allie looks as though the nurse missed her arm entirely and is repeatedly jabbing her in the head.

I, however, rise to the occasion. "That's not pot," I say. "It's oregano."

He waves the jar in front of my face like a father finding a pack of cigarettes in his thirteen-year-old daughter's schoolbag. "Do you think I'm an idiot? I know what pot smells like."

Aha! He knows what pot smells like. I wink at him. "Well, then we won't tell anyone if you keep the jar."

His face turns a shade of blue. "I want all of you out of here by the end of the month."

"But, Carl," I say, gently running my hand over his scrawny chest. "Isn't there anything we can do to get you to change your mind?"

He gasps. And so do Allie and Jodine. "I want you all out by the end of the week."

Prude.

"B-but, s-sir!" Jodine stutters. "You can't do that! You can't kick tenants out on a whim. We have a lease! I'm a law student, I know these things!"

"If you are not out of my apartment by noon on Saturday, one week from today, I'm calling the police and telling them that you're running both a drug ring *and* brothel out of this apartment. Now give me a bag."

Jodine hands him a shopping bag from the grocery store. "It's recyclable," she says inanely. He picks up my jars and packs them into the bag. "I am confiscating all of this."

Sure. I bet he smokes it all.

34

'TWAS THE NIGHT BEFORE VALENTINE'S DAY, AND THINGS GOT A LITTLE GORY, SO POUR YOURSELF SOME CHARDONNAY, WHILE THE ANNOYING OMNISCIENT NARRATOR RECOUNTS THE STORY

Again, and for the final time, they're at 411. The girls chose 411 for all the reasons stated at the last party. (Again, you may skip back to the first party should you require a refresher of the bar decor.)

It's ten o'clock and the bar is packed with prowling singles in search of provisional nighttime bedmates, as well as drunken, gyrating couples. Time Warp is blasting through the speakers and some of the less inhibited guests are spinning to the beat. Except for the major characters—namely, Allie, Emma and Jodine—the principal actors are all here. So where are the girls?

They're waiting in the line outside.

At the last two parties, the girls were able to find parking spots directly in front of the building. This time, however, Emma circled the block three times before pulling into a parking lot four blocks away. The temperature had dropped to below freezing, and even though they were wearing their proper winter coats, none of them had on hats, scarves, mittens or any another winter paraphernalia. When they saw the line of fifteen or so other nonwinter-clothed partygoers, they tried to walk straight past the bouncer and into the bar.

The bouncer did not accept their plan of attack. "Where do you think you girls are going?" he asked.

"Sir," Jodine said. "Don't you remember us? This is our party. We have to get inside." Jodine is not in the mood for this one bit. She is still in the process of freaking out regarding the apartment travesty. She assumes she's going to have to move back home. She can't believe she's going to have to move back home. She is really, really dreading moving back home. What a terrific evening this is turning out to be, she thinks. Absolutely fucking terrific. What else is going to go wrong?

"We're not letting anyone in right now," he said, looking straight ahead.

Why do bouncers do that? They always look right above the waiting-in-line heads.

"Sir," Jodine repeats. "This is our party!"

He motions for them to move to the back of the line.

Emma folds her arms across her chest, not in defiance, but because she's not wearing a bra and her nipples are freezing. "I'm allergic to the cold. Can you walkie-talkie Steve, please?" She is furious about having to wait in line and even more furious about getting booted from her apartment. This would only happen to me, she reasons. Why don't bad things happen to anyone else?

The bouncer continues looking straight ahead. "Steve is unavailable right now. If you don't get to the back of the line, you're not going to see the inside of this bar."

Emma tries calling Steve on her cell, but the line is busy. Steve is on the phone screaming at his wife, as usual.

Allie's toes and fingers are numb. She wishes she had chosen to borrow a thicker pair of Emma's socks. She exhales little puffs of breath to watch them crystallize and wonders if passersby will think she's smoking.

Five minutes later, when Jodine decides she's had enough, she returns to the bouncer. "Excuse me. The bartender is a friend of mine." She's kissed him, hasn't she? Shouldn't that allow her into the bar?

"Which bartender?"

Now, this presents a problem. She can't refer to him as Count Zeus, can she? She'll just have to trick the bouncer into admitting them into the bar. "The one who works the VIP bar?"

"You mean Leslie?"

Leslie? His name is Leslie? Jodine is furious. There is no way Count Zeus's name is Leslie. How can the hottest man in the world be named Leslie? The hottest man in the world should have a macho name like Tom or Brad, not one of those he/she names that she has already complained about. She supposes that since his parents didn't know he was going to become the hottest man in the world when he was born, they couldn't have known not to call him Leslie. But wouldn't naming him Leslie be some kind of jinx? Some kind of prophetic fulfillment?

Jodine resolves that Count Zeus being named Leslie makes no sense. "His name cannot be Leslie," she says with conviction.

"Get to the back of the line."

Jodine shuffles her way back through the crowd. Does Count Zeus no longer work the VIP bar? What if she can't find him? She attempts to calm herself with labored breathing. The bouncer probably just didn't know who worked where. Breathe, breathe. Too cold to breathe. She is about to freak out completely, when Steve pops his head through the window, spots the girls, gives them a What-are-you-waiting-in-line-for hand motion and shouts to the bouncer that the girls can come in.

"That'll be ten dollars each," the woman at the door says in a monotone tone.

"No fucking way. Steve!" Emma screams, and grabs the arm of Steve's shirt before he can evaporate. "Tell them it's our party. Tell *everyone* it's our party."

"It's their party. Put your coats in the office and then I'll buy you each a drink at the VIP lounge. You look as though you could use a little defrosting."

The VIP lounge sounds good to Jodine. She holds her breath as they approach the bartender. Why is there a blond woman in a black-lace bustier (it doesn't matter what pants she's wearing, does it? You can't see them from the other side of the bar) smirking at them?

The blond woman in the bustier asks, "What can I get you?"

"Where's the Count?"

"The who?"

"The..." Jodine's heart sinks like a seven-hundred-pound man in the Dead Sea. "Are you Leslie?"

"Yeah, why?"

Jodine is now unconfused. "Never mind. Can I have...twelve shots of vodka and lime, please?"

"Are you insane?" Emma asks.

Allie throws her hands over her head in amazement. "I can't do four shots of vodka! I can barely do one." She sits down on a stool.

Jodine sits down beside her. "Who said I was sharing?" She looks at Allie's wide eyes and sighs. "Relax. Just kidding." When the shots arrive, she divides them into three equal shares. Each roommate lifts one into the air.

"To paying off Josh," Allie says, and they all clink glasses and then drink.

"To having nowhere to live after next week," Jodine says, and they all clink glasses and drink again.

"To worrying about it tomorrow," Emma says, and they all clink glasses and then drink.

Allie's gaze wanders around the strobe-lit room and she hops off her bar stool. "Someone else can have my last shot," she says. "I want to go find Clint."

Emma picks up her last shot with one hand, and Allie's glass with the other. "To finding Clint," she says. She clinks both glasses together and downs Allie's, then hers. "I need to reapply my lipstick," she says, hopping off her bar stool. (Actually, Emma isn't much of a hopper. She's more of a slinker.)

Jodine looks up. "Where is everyone?" she says aloud, realizing that she has been abandoned. She downs her last shot. "Four more," she tells Leslie.

One. Two. Threee. Fooouuuuuuur.

Hiccup.

Now, where is her Count? Why isn't he waiting for her, lips puckered, cape afluttering? Can vampires be flashers, using their capes like raincoats?

She leans over to the bartender. "'Scuse me. What happened to the Leslie who used to work this bar?"

"What?"

Right. She's Leslie. Or was he Leslie? She's confused again. "The bartender in the cape?"

"None of the bartenders are wearing a cape, hon."

"He's gorgeous. I mean gorgeous."

"You mean George?"

Yes. George. Isn't George a more appropriate name? Can't you see perfect white teeth belonging to a man named George? Nodding, Jodine repeats, "George."

"He's off tonight."

"Off?"

"Yeah. But I just saw him a few minutes ago heading that way." She points toward the main section of the bar.

He came to the bar tonight even though he's not working? He must have heard about the party. He must be here to see me, Jodine thinks, nodding to herself. It makes *sense*.

What *do* vampires wear under their capes?

Allie and Clint are sitting at Cheryl and Tiffany's bar. (You remember Cheryl and Tiffany, don't you?)

Allie is describing Carl's visit in a lighthearted and quasi-amusing manner while sipping from a glass of cranberry and vodka.

Logically, Allie should be extremely disconcerted by recent events. Unlike the other two girls, whose parents live in the city, she has nowhere to go starting next week. But all hope is not yet lost for Allie. Just the contrary. It was just a little too convenient, too coincidental, that this catastrophe happened on the night before Valentine's Day. No, it wasn't coincidence at all; it was fate. She's known all along—she's felt it in her bones—that tonight will finally culminate (and consummate, giggle giggle) into a relationship with Clint.

But *when* tonight? When she tells him she's moving back to Belleville and he realizes what he'll be missing and he tells her he loves her and that he's always loved her but didn't realize it until just this moment and can they go home (*home* to be defined at some later date, as right now the concept is kind of up in the air)?

Allie wipes her tongue across her teeth, hoping that any lipstick smears on her teeth have been wiped away.

It's now or never. Unfortunately, that's the way fate works.

"Since I have nowhere to live," she says, trying to appear coy by squinting, "I'll have to move back to Belleville." She sighs deeply, exhaling about the same amount of air that has enlarged Clint's head in recent months.

Back to Belleville? Clint has to physically restrain himself from screaming "Yes!" and punching the air with glee. This is the best news he's had all year. No more sneaking around! "That's too bad," he says. "Nothing can convince you to stay?"

"I'm not sure."

"Aw, Allie." He wraps his arms around her and pulls her into him. "I'm going to miss you. Can't I convince you to stay?"

Be careful, Clint. A little too much of a performance might work against you.

Allie pulls back a fraction and stares at his lips. They are perfect lips. They are soft, red, moist, plump, watermelon lips, and they are less than two inches away (albeit two inches away from her forehead, but this can be remedied). "Yes," she says, and in one swoop reaches for him on her tiptoes and kisses him. She knew his lips would be delicious and they are, and now he'll have to tell her that he can't live without her, that he loves her, and all those other things mentioned earlier.

Clint doesn't pull away immediately, as surely he should. Instead, he's thinking that maybe Emma set this up, that maybe Emma wants to have a threesome and this is her way of getting the ball rolling.

When the kiss starts to get a little bit sloppy, Allie pulls away. "Wasn't that perfect?" she asks, staring at him with wide Little Mermaid eyes.

Uh-oh, he's thinking. Maybe Allie has something else in mind. YOU THINK?

"Wasn't that wonderful?" Allie swoons. "I knew you had feelings for me! I knew it!"

"It...I..."

Emma swaggers out of the bathroom, lipstick freshly applied, and moves toward them.

"I... It..." Clint has begun to look a bit dazed and confused.

Emma of course, has no idea what has just taken place and places her arms around both her good ol' chums. She kisses Clint on both cheeks and pats him on the crotch where she knows Allie can't see. "Did Allie tell you about the eviction?"

Clint thinks *eviction* sounds a lot like *erection*.

Emma continues to pat. "I don't know what the fuck I'm going to do," she says, "but I figure I can worry about it tomorrow, right?"

Allie tries to catch Clint's eye and tell him telepathically that she wants to be alone with him.

"Did you check out some of the outfits here tonight?" Emma nods at someone's black cat suit with red hearts all over it. "You'd think it was Halloween. Look at that one." She gestures at a woman wearing a translucent red dress with nothing on underneath. "Not leaving much to the imagination, is she?" Although, she is wearing gorgeous red heels. Why doesn't she have a pair of ruby shoes?

The woman in the not-leaving-much-to-the-imagination dress sees Emma pointing. She hasn't heard what Emma has said, but she knows instinctively that she is being talked about. Their eyes lock.

Emma thinks the woman looks familiar. "Shit," she mumbles as the woman purses her lips and proceeds toward them. Clint and Allie take a step back as Emma and the not-leaving-much-to-the-imagination-woman face off.

"Is there something you'd like to say to me?" the woman asks.

"Excuse me?" Emma says, glaring.

All the drunken couples and singles around them freeze and turn to watch. All the men hope they'll start rolling around on the ground, hissing and ripping each other's clothes off. "Since you seem to enjoy talking about me, I'd like to know what you're saying."

Suddenly, Emma remembers where she's seen this woman's face before. "You're Mo-Ho."

Saying that aloud probably wasn't Emma's best move.

Monique stabs a finger at Emma. "And you're psycho. First you call me a whore on the phone and now you're calling me Mo-Ho in public? What's a Mo-Ho? I'm going to sue you for slander."

Emma remembers her telephone call to Nick the night of the Halloween party. This girl was begging for a name-calling after the costume she flounced around in that night. You can't dress up like a prostitute and then whine when you're called a whore can you? "Do you want a piece of me?" she screams, her eyes squinted shut.

Allie and Clint both cannot believe that Emma just said that. Did she think she was a drunken fifty-year-old four-hundred-pound man at his neighborhood pub? Who says that?

Emma feels a rush of adrenaline. She's always wanted to say that! Wohoo! That felt fucking amazing! She opens her eyes and clenches her fists in front of her breasts. Bring it on!

Mo-Ho has never been in a bar fight and doesn't want to start now. She doesn't know why she approached Nick's psycho ex in the first place, except for the fact that she has just spotted Nick and the sight of him has enraged her. She had come to this party because bringing in the New Year on her own had been too depressing and she was determined to find a guy, any guy, to go home with tonight. But now she is starting to doubt her decision to be here. She's also wondering how to get out of this situation intact. "No," she says. "Sorry I yelled at you like that."

That'll do it.

Everyone sighs. The explosive scene appears to have been diverted. You know in those action movies when the villain is about to blow up the train station but the hero shoots him and he falls on his back? And the music softens? That's what happens here.

"And I know you don't want Nick, anyway," Monique says. "I saw you with your new man."

And then the villain pops back up, Freddy Kruger style.

Don't say it don't say it don't say it…

Mo-Ho motions at Clint and half smiles. "I saw you guys making out at your New Year's party."

She said it.

Meanwhile…

Jodine spots Count Zeus from afar. He ducks into the office. Excitement, fear and nausea all dance through her as she maneuvers her way through the crowd. She's not sure exactly what she's going to do, but she's determined to corner him alone. Through the room's window, she can see his back. He seems to be sifting through a stack of papers. She sneaks through the opened crack of the door and closes it behind her.

"Hellooo," she says, employing her raised-eyebrow seduction trick.

"Hi." He raises an eyebrow back.

She feels herself being pulled toward him. "I've been looking for you."

He smiles.

He's so hot, she thinks. "I'm not letting you get away this time." She motions to him to come closer with a Marilyn Monroe finger curl.

"You're not?"

She pushes the strap of her dress off her shoulder. "Would you mind taking off the rest?"

His musk cologne overwhelms her as he unzips the back of her dress, and for a moment she feels like fainting—no, make that swooning. The dress falls in a heap onto the floor.

He runs his palms over her black bra and matching thong, spins her around and leans her back onto the desk, hungrily attacking her lips. One hand pulls at her hair; the other squeezes her butt. She untucks his shirt and feels his skin against her fingertips.

"You're amazing," he whispers. "Who are you?"

She laughs. He doesn't know who she is. He doesn't remember her. Somehow this makes it all the more exciting. Soft tongue, warm skin, hot body—someone who won't expect anything of her tomorrow, because he doesn't even know her name.

And once I do this, she reasons, once I go through with it, once I have sex with this stranger, I'll have to break up with Manny.

What kind of person would she be if she didn't?

Manny is not at the airport where he's supposed to be. Manny, instead, waited at the airport for hours, attempting to fly standby to Ottawa. At a quarter to ten, when he was told that he could get on the ten o'clock, he called his father's cell phone.

"Go home," his father said. "She's okay."

"She is? What happened?"

"She decided to join a step class at the Y. What seventy-year-old woman tries a step class?"

"She fell?"

"No, dehydration. Anyway, she's fine. Go home."

Exhausted and emotionally drained, Manny was in a cab on his way home when he decided to drop by the party. After waiting in line for twenty minutes, then paying ten dollars to get in and another two to check his coat, he sees Jodine head toward the office. Pit stop at the bathroom and then I'll go find her, he thinks.

* * *

Count Zeus unhooks her bra and tugs on her nipples.

Now she has a reason to break up with Manny, she reasons. But why is she thinking about Manny? This isn't about Manny. It has nothing to do with Manny, nothing to do with Manny at all.

"I want to come inside you," the Count says while biting the side of her neck.

This was what she has been fantasizing about, isn't it? This stranger fondling her in the dark? But what is that strange thing he's doing with his tongue? Until this moment, she never realized that a tongue could be pointy.

"Oh, Count," she murmurs. Wait. He has a name. Leslie? No way. Greg? Gary? George. "Oh, George."

He squeezes her nipple again. Ouch. Watch those nails, Count George! If she'd wanted her nipples pierced, she would have gone to a professional.

The panic sets in. Why is she lying practically naked on a desk in an office, with a strange man sticking his tongue down her throat and painfully tweaking her nipples?

Maybe if I think about other things, it will go faster, she thinks. Like she used to do with...what was his name again? Benjamin? Why did I break up with him again? What was wrong with him?

With each movement Count George makes, she has a revelation. The Count, unfortunately, mistakes her reaction for passion, and proceeds to tweak and lick and squeeze with far more intensity than is usually required in a two-minute quickie.

I push away people who try to get close to me.

Tweak.

I'm doing this because I'm afraid of how I feel about Manny.

Lick.

I can't get Manny out of my head.

Squeeze.

I see Manny's face in the window.

Not seeing Jodine anywhere in the bar, after leaving the bathroom, Manny wandered over to the window. She'd been in there for ten minutes at least. It was too early to be counting the money, wasn't it? Was everything all right?

Manny now sees Jodine with some man rolling around on top of her and thinks he is going to be sick. Jodine realizes that Manny is not some kind of manifestation brought about by her multiple epiphanies. Count Zeus, of course, can't see any of this; his back is turned to Manny, and he chooses this second to unbuckle and drop his pants.

Manny turns away and leaves the bar.

Shrieking, Jodine's brain is saying to her, *Isn't that what you wanted? Manny to catch you and push you away?*

As the Count pulls his impressive erection out of his jockeys, Jodine thinks, *What did I just do?* She realizes (a bit late) that she wants Manny to be the one leaning against her, the one telling her he wants to come inside her, the one nestling her into his chest.

And that she has just purposefully hijacked any chances of any of those things ever occurring again. She can feel the beads of sweat collecting on her forehead.

"Do you have a condom?" the stranger asks, holding himself in his hand.

"I have to get out of here. I'm sorry, but my boyfriend just saw us."

The look on his face is one of outrage. "Your boyfriend! You didn't tell me you had a boyfriend."

"I didn't tell me my name, either, but that didn't seem to stop you." *Or me.* She hooks on her bra and pulls her dress back over her head. "I'm sorry, Count George. It was nice knowing you."

She opens the door, revealing to the world a confused, almost naked bartender. Sprinting after Manny, Jodine sees him disappear outside and bumps smack into Clint. And Allie and Emma. And Monique. (Monique takes a few steps backward when she realizes that there's about to be a huge commotion, happy in the knowledge that she will not have to attempt to take a piece of anyone.)

Unaware of the drama taking place at the bar, Jodine's eyes fill with tears. "I just did a really stupid thing," she says, squeezing Allie's arm.

Allie shakes her off and Jodine realizes that no one has heard her. This entire side of the bar is staring at Allie.

"I don't understand," Allie says in a tinny voice. "How did she see you two making out? You two couldn't have been making out, right? She must have seen something else, right?"

Emma's and Clint's gazes flick toward each other and then back to Allie. "She saw us," Emma says slowly, and then closes her eyes. "I'm sorry."

Allie looks completely confused. "I don't understand."

Clint shakes his head. "We didn't mean for it to happen."

Still confused, Allie thinks she may have been beamed into another dimension. She looks into the drink she's holding, searching for an answer. Her lips begin to quiver.

Jodine, though in an emotional daze of her own, tries to comfort Allie. "They didn't mean to hurt you," she says, taking her hand. (Nobody means to hurt anyone, now do they, Jodine? You'd think she'd be able to come up with something a little more original.) "When they hooked up at the Halloween party, you hadn't even introduced them yet. They didn't know who they were!"

Allie drops Jodine's hand. "Halloween party? Monique said she saw you on New Year's."

Oops.

"This has been going on for three months? YOU'VE BEEN SEEING EACH OTHER BEHIND MY BACK FOR THREE MONTHS?"

No one comments.

Everything is starting to make sense to Allie. "That's where you've been when you said you were at your dad's?"

Emma can't look up. She stares at her boots. "I'm sorry."

Jodine tries Allie's hand again. "They didn't mean to hurt you," she repeats.

Allie squirms her hand away from Jodine's grasp. "You knew about this."

"I...I did."

"I hate all of you. You," she says, stabbing a finger at Jodine, "are a terrible friend. I've been nothing but nice to you and you let them lie to me. You're a...a bitch." Way to go, Allie! You used the *B* word! "And you," she says, pointing to Clint, "are an asshole." Ooooh, she's really mad!

Clint puffs himself up. "I'm an asshole because I've never been attracted to you? Is it my fault you're not my type?"

Allie feels as if a large pail of ice water has been dumped over her head. "But that kiss..."

Emma pokes him angrily in the stomach. "What kiss?"

Clint flaps his arms all over the place. "I didn't kiss her! She slobbered all over me five minutes ago! I would never kiss her!"

"You don't have to be rude about it," Emma says.

"Now you care about how I feel?" Allie screams at Emma. "You are nothing but a liar and a slut."

"I am not a liar!" Emma protests. She narrows her eyes. "Clint was never attracted to you, Allie. You just wouldn't read the signs. You kept throwing yourself at him. We all thought it was pathetic." She looks around the room, pausing her stare on Jodine and Clint for effect. "All of us."

Tears stream down Allie's cheeks.

Jodine picks up Allie's hand again. "Don't listen to her."

"Who are you to give advice?" Emma yells. "Miss Perfection. Miss Never-Does-Anything-Wrong. Miss-Frigidity-Personified-Who-Makes-Out-with-Bartenders-Even-Though-She-Has-a-Boy-friend. I saw you on New Year's. We all did." Emma looks around the room, pausing her stare for effect, and then closes her eyes for effect. "All of us."

Jodine swallows angrily. "I never claimed to be perfect."

"Yeah, right," Emma pipes in, eyes still closed. "What a joke. It would almost be funny if it weren't so pathetic—and expensive."

"What are you talking about?"

"Oh, you know all right. Why don't you tell us, Jodine? We already know about what really happened the night of the fire. That you were using the stove. Not only did you practically burn down the whole place and nearly kill us all, you lied to us, making us believe it was all our fault. Yeah, you're perfect, all right."

Allie snorts, flabbergasted at Emma's version of the fire. "What are you talking about? It was your damn cigarette! You dumped a lit cigarette in the garbage! You're the one who suggested we keep the truth from Jodine and get her to pay."

"You're the one who broke the smoke detector," Emma says. So there, she thinks.

Allie starts laughing and crying simultaneously. "Yeah, blame me. Blame the stupid naive girl who can't even get a guy to go to bed with her. I sure made it easy for you, didn't I? You know something? It *was* my fault. I should have seen what you two are. You with your constant whining and anorexic phobias," she says to Jodine. "You with your lifelong ambition to operate a combination brothel/drug ring," she says to Emma. "Both of you, with your self-centered neuroses, have managed to lose my apartment, the apartment I've been in for three and a half years. Congratulations. You've managed to make me homeless." Shaking, she puts her drink down onto the bar. "You're both lying whores and I never want to talk to either of you again." Allie sobs, turns around and walks away.

Emma rolls her eyes. "She's so dramatic."

"Oh, shut up," Jodine mumbles.

"Please fuck off."

"I'll say whatever I want."

"Fine, but at least brush your teeth first. Your breath smells like diarrhea."

Jodine wonders when it was she was transported back to kindergarten. "Bitch," she says through clenched teeth.

Running her hands through her hair, Emma realizes Clint is smiling. "Clint, why are you smiling?"

"I can't help it. You girls are so hot when you scream at one another. Can I come to your place tonight? Do you think any of you will end up making up and making out?"

"You're a pig," Emma says, and pushes him away with her hand.

"A horny pig. Rrrr."

His leering grin makes her want to knee him where only a few moments ago she was caressing. "It's over," she says instead, with great restraint.

His leer disintegrates. "What, us? Why?"

She doesn't answer. She crosses the room, climbs the steps toward the VIP bar. How could she have said those things to Allie? How could she have done those things to Allie? What is wrong with her? Why does she need every man to like her best? Half the time, she can't even stand men. They always turn out to be such disgusting pigs.

She takes a seat at the bar. *We're* the pigs, she thinks ruefully. Me, Jodine and Al. Only we *all* built our houses out of straw.

"Excuse me," Leslie (the real Leslie) says. She puts down a cosmopolitan. "This is from that guy on the other end of the bar."

She looks up to see Nick smiling at her.

I'll huff and I'll puff and I'll blow your house down.

What house?

She shakes her head and pats the empty seat next to her.

35
WHEN HARRY MET ALLIE

ALLIE

I am the world's biggest moron. If they gave out cash rewards for morons, I could have paid for the repairs a long time ago, and I would not have had to go through this supreme humiliation.

They've been fooling around since Halloween.

I'm not going back to that apartment. Ever.

Walking down Queen Street, I try not to bump into all the couples who are on their way home for a little Valentine's Day loving. I've been trying not to cry for blocks now, because I'm certain that each tear will turn to ice on my skin. I wipe clean whatever lipstick is still on my mouth with the sleeve of my jacket, and I run my tongue over my lips to moisten them, which I realize is a terrible plan because now my lips and my tongue are going to freeze. I nibble on a fingernail, and it breaks off easily in my mouth. I nibble on a second fingernail. And a third. Soon, my mouth is filled with pieces of nail. The taste of polish in my mouth is almost metallic, and I spit the fragments into the snow. My lips are cracked and dry. There are cracks in the sidewalk—of course there are, this city is falling apart and I hate it and I want to go home—but

I try not to step on the cracks because the only people who love me are my mother and father and I'd hate to break either of their backs.

You are so pathetic. Why did I tell them a hundred times that he was my soul mate? Why did I think he cared at all?

Jodine was right when she said that we wander aimlessly through life, and if we happen to trip over someone who wants to be with us, great; if not, that's show biz.

My steps quicken as I try to come up with a new plan. My family loves me, right? I can go home. I'll just go to the station and wait for the next train to Belleville. I'll send a truck to pick up my stuff next week. I'm sure if I beg, my parents will help me pay for someone to pack for me.

I count the cracks as I step over them, trying to forget the cold.

At fifteen my face feels numb.

At thirty I'm concerned my ears might shrivel and fall off.

At forty my feet have turned into ice rubber blocks and I need to sit down to defrost. I can't breathe anymore it's so cold, so I duck into a Second Cup and let the heat spread over me like a warm bath.

I feel a tap on my shoulder and I turn around.

"Hi," Josh says, his cheeks red, his hair windblown, his blue puffy jacket zipped halfway up his face.

"What are you doing here?"

"Did you think I was going to let you wander around Toronto alone at this hour?" He unzips the top of his jacket and I see that he's smiling. I burst into tears, and a little part of the frozen me melts.

A half hour later, I'm sitting on the couch in his living room. "Do you want to hear about what happened?" I ask. Sob.

He shakes his head. "I already know."

The whole bar probably knows. Maybe the whole city. They'll probably make a movie and call it *Valentine's Valueless Virgin* or something. A comedy, for sure. "I'm a moron, eh?"

"You're not a moron."

"You probably thought I was so dumb, chasing some guy the whole year when he didn't even notice me. The whole time he was chasing someone else. You probably thought I was a complete fool." Sob.

He's watching me, smiling. "Imagine that. Chasing someone for a whole year, someone who spent the whole time chasing someone else."

Sniffle. Right. Sob. I'm moronic and insensitive. Sob.

He wraps his arms around me and pulls me into him. "Don't cry. It's killing me to see you so miserable."

I can't help it, I'm a faucet on perma drip, and I know I must look like someone smeared lipstick all over my face. "I can't stop," I wail. "I have no career and nowhere to live and no roommates and nobody loves me...." Sob.

"*I* love you," he says softly.

"And I love you," I say. Sniffle. "But that doesn't count."

He runs his fingers along the side of my neck. "No, I mean I *love* you."

Oh.

"You—" he runs his fingers through my hair "—are the sweetest, cutest, most warmhearted woman I have ever met. I've felt this way about you since the day we met and you threw up on me."

I giggle. "I did throw up on you, didn't I?"

"You did."

He's awfully cute when he smiles, the way his single dimple seems to wink at me. "That must have been a real turn-on," I say.

"I kind of liked taking care of you."

Josh is smiling and I think about how he laughs at my jokes and the way he takes classes just because and the way he fidgets with his hat and the way he always tries to make things better. Right now he's playing with my hair, and I wonder, would my lips feel less chapped if he helped moisten them?

He pulls away. "And taking care of you is what I'm going to do. You need some food. And then I'll take the couch."

Oh.

* * *

An hour later, my eyes have dried up, my body has defrosted and I am oddly content (considering what I've been through) after devouring two grilled cheese sandwiches that he made himself and insisted I eat.

"Are you sure you don't want my room?" the sweetest man in the world asks, spreading a blanket over the couch.

"Don't be silly. Who knows when the last time you changed your sheets was?"

"Ha ha." He fluffs the pillow. "You sure?"

I crawl into the made-up bed. "Yup."

He sits down beside me and pulls the blanket up to my chin. "You'll feel better in the morning."

"I feel better already."

Is this it? Is he going to kiss me? He leans toward me.

And then...he kisses me.

On the forehead.

On the forehead? "Good night," he repeats.

Did I want him to kiss me on the lips? Why didn't he kiss me on the lips? What's wrong with me? "Good night," I say.

He closes the door to his room, then opens it again. "Wake me if you need anything, okay?"

"Thanks."

That must be Sydney, Australia, I think, staring at the blown-up photograph on the wall facing me. The walls are covered in photos he's taken around the world. One of the windows is slightly open and the sounds of the night rustle through the apartment. Seeping through the blinds, the city lights dance across the ceiling.

What if tonight never happened? I would be spending the next two months chasing after Clint. Would he have ever told me he didn't *like* me, or would I have just given up, not knowing, and gone home to Belleville? Why didn't I tell Clint a year ago how I felt? Then at least I would have known. I wouldn't have wasted so much time pretending he was something he could never be.

I've been running after someone who doesn't exist, someone I thought was caring, sensitive, sweet, understanding…

Someone who doesn't exist?

Here I am lying alone on a couch. What's wrong with this picture?

I creep toward the slightly open door and knock softly. "Josh?"

He sits up, topless, in his bed. "Are you okay? Do you need something?"

All that moving furniture around seems to have done great stuff to his chest. And I've never noticed that before because….? Right. Because I've never seen him topless before.

"I changed my mind," I say, standing by the bed. "I want to sleep in here."

"Is it too light in there? I can take the couch."

I slip under the covers and lay my head on the pillow next to him. "Stay." I whisper the word, sounding relatively calm considering that my insides are shaking.

He turns on his side and gently strokes my cheek. "Are you sure?"

My face begins to tingle and the warmth spreads down my neck and over my skin and down my body.

"A hundred percent," I answer, and he laughs and I laugh and then our laughing stops. The room is silent except for our breathing and I can feel the hairs on his thighs tickle my legs. He smiles—there's that dimple again—and he looks sweet and strong and vulnerable.

"This is all my roommates' plan to get you to overlook the rest of the money we owe you."

He swallows and his Adam's apple moves across his throat. "Emma paid me off at the bar," he says, touching my lips with his fingertips.

"Consider this interest."

"How much interest are we talking about?"

"A hundred percent," I repeat.

36
JODINE LETS GO

JODINE

I pick up the phone. I slam down the phone. I pick up the phone. I slam down the phone. I pick up the phone and dial. I close my eyes and pull the covers over my head, hoping this conversation will be less scary in the dark.

"Hi, this is Manny. I can't come to the phone right now, so please leave your name and number and I'll get back to you as soon as I can. Thanks."

"Hi, Manny. It's me. I know you're home. And I know you probably never want to talk to me again. And you have every right to feel this way. I'm really, really sorry. This is going to sound awful, but I don't think I realized how important you were to me until you walked out of the bar tonight. I'm sorry I made it so hard for you to get close to me. And I'm sorry I had to put you through hell today. Especially today, with your grandmother being sick. I hope she's okay. I feel really awful and—"

Beep. The answering machine cuts me off.

Damn.

I dial again. "Sorry. Where was I? Right. I picked a terrible day

to do this, didn't I? I want you to know that the bartender means
nothing to me—"

Beep. This is so annoying.

I dial again. "And that I'm really, really, sorry. Terribly sorry. I
hope I haven't lost you. And that—"

Beep. Is it my imagination, or is the recording interval getting
shorter and shorter? These things don't normally irk me, but
there's so much I want to say. For example, I probably should tell
him that I love him. That would probably be the right thing to do
at this point. I'll call back, one more time.

I dial again. "Hello?" a voice answers.

It's him. He's there. I don't know what to say.

"I don't want you calling me anymore."

"Manny, please. I am so sorry."

"Me, too."

"He didn't mean anything to me. I was just trying to push you
away."

"Congratulations. Job accomplished."

"I really need you to try and understand."

"You know what I thought about today? At the airport? I was
thinking about my grandfather. About how much he worships
my grandmother. And about how much she worships him. And
I compared it to me chasing after you and you not giving a shit.
I want to be with someone who isn't afraid to try. Someone who
doesn't make out with men she doesn't even care about."

"I'm sorry."

"I know. But right now I don't care. Goodbye, Jodine."

"Okay, I understand. Goodbye."

I wait for the click of the telephone, keeping my head under
the covers. My chest hurts and my head hurts and even my eyes
hurt. I once heard that a person can feel pain only in one spot at
a time. Apparently I heard wrong.

I'm still awake and under the covers two hours later when the front lock rattles.

"Hello?" It's Emma.

I climb out of bed and move into the living room. The lights are off, but in the moonlight streaming in through the window I can make out the red bulb of Emma's cigarette. I sit down beside her.

She blows out a mouthful of smoke into the dimness.

For a few minutes we sit in complete silence. Then she shakes her head. "We fucked up pretty royally, didn't we?" She blows out another mouthful of smoke.

I nod and watch the smoke fade into the walls.

"I don't usually smoke without opening the window," she says, and I raise my eyebrow, this time skeptically, and she starts laughing as she inhales.

I laugh, too, and she hands me her cigarette and lights herself another one, and the two of us sit, smoking and laughing and shaking our heads.

"Where are you going to go?" I ask after the laughing dies down and the cigarette is ashes.

"Shit, I don't know."

"Back to Barbie land?"

"No. I ran into Nick tonight. He offered me a room in his Yonge and Eglinton castle."

"You're going to get back together with Nick-the-Prick? You hate Nick! What about Clint?"

She shrugs. "There is no Clint. That's over. He's useless. And you're right. I do hate Nick. But hey, it's better than living with the stepbitch. What about you? Any plans?"

"I don't know. I'm only here for a few more months, so I don't want to sign a lease. My parents, I guess."

"Where do you think Allie will go?" Emma asks. "Where *is* Allie?"

"I don't know."

"Should we be worried?"

"You think? She left the party over four hours ago. Where could she have gone?"

Emma scrunches her nose. "Maybe we should wait for her here until she comes home."

My eyelids weigh a hundred pounds. "But can we close our eyes?"

"Okay."

I lay my head on the couch pillow and Emma's foot kicks me in the nose.

"Sorry." She giggles.

"No problem." I feel myself falling asleep.

I blink twice and open my eyes. Sunlight spears through the window and I'm lying on Emma's knee.

"Are you awake?" she mumbles.

"Uh-huh. How long have you been up?"

"Awhile. Allie's not home yet."

I glance at my watch. "It's ten o'clock. Do you think she's lost?"

"Lost? Can grown-ups get lost?"

"Is Allie a grown-up?"

Emma sits up. "What should we do?"

"Let's call around," I suggest.

Emma reaches over to the coffee table and picks up the phone. "Maybe she went to Clint's."

I raise my eyebrow. Somehow I doubt that. But on second thought, maybe she's still delusional. Maybe she's still hoping...

"Call him."

Dialing, Emma whispers, "I'm calling an ex and I'm not even going to yell at him. Pretty mature, eh? Hello? Who is this? Monique?…Monique from the bar last night? This is Emma." Her voice raises angrily. "Yeah, Nick's ex. What a fucker. He offers me a room in his place and then takes you home. Un-fucking-believable. I'm sorry, I didn't mean to call Nick's number. Habit, I guess. *Bad* habit. I must have dialed it by accident… Oh… I didn't call Nick's? No, I don't want to speak to Clint. Will you just give him a message for me? Can you tell him he's a hemorrhoid on a horse's ass? And that if he ever comes near this apartment again I promise to set both of his minuscule testicles on fire? Thank you." She hangs up the phone and gawks at me openmouthed. "Monique's at Clint's."

"So I figured. Should we cut down one of his prized possessions, too?"

Emma snorts. "I think it's time to bury *that* particular hatchet. Where do you want to call next?"

"Do you think she would have gone back to Belleville?"

"No. How would she have paid for her ticket? She doesn't have a credit card. Could she be at Josh's?"

"I'll try him." I press down the arrow on our call display, find his name and number, and dial.

He answers on the first ring. "Hello?"

"Hi, is this Josh?"

"It is."

"Hi, it's Jodine. How are you?"

"Fine, thanks. You?"

I feel moronic making small talk, but it doesn't make sense to rush a conversation concerning a runaway roommate, does it? "Okay, listen. We're looking for Allie. She's a bit lost. Any idea where she might be?"

"She's not lost, she's right here."

I breathe a sign of relief. "She is?"

"She is."

"Can I talk to her?"

"She's taking a bath at the moment. I can ask her to call you back."

"Oh. Okay. Do you think she will?" I can't imagine Allie staying angry with anyone for longer than a half a second.

"Eventually. But she might need some time, okay? You guys were pretty horrible."

Sigh. "I know. I'm sorry."

I'm sorry. Seems I'm doing an awful lot of apologizing lately.

I hear a voice shout from another room, "Josh! Come in! The water's getting cold!"

Gasp.

"Um...I g-gotta go," Josh stammers.

"Josh?"

"Yes?"

"Take care of her."

"I always do."

He hangs up the phone and for the second time in the last twenty-four hours I find myself staring dumbfounded at a telephone receiver. "You're not going to believe what's going on over there."

A knowing smile spreads across Emma's face. "I bet I do."

On Wednesday morning, I'm in the living room stacking boxes when the front door opens and Allie walks in.

"Hi," I say.

"Hi."

She undoes her coat, and I see she's wearing men's sweatpants. "Need help packing?" she asks.

"Thanks, but I'm almost done." I take a deep breath. "I should have told you about Clint and Emma. Or I should have forced her to tell you. And about the fire—I don't know what I was thinking. I got scared and I behaved horribly, and completely shirked my responsibility. It was probably me, leaving the stove on like that. Or maybe it was Emma. So I'm sorry I lied and I'm sorry I might have started the fire."

Allie's eyes are composed, and for a second I think she's going to tell me to shove it, but then she smiles and her eyes crinkle. "Okay," she answers slowly, and I burst into tears.

Me. Bursting into tears. I didn't know I was capable of bursting. "You forgive me?"

She nods and hugs me, then wipes the corner of my eyes with her sleeve.

"You're ruining your shirt."

She giggles. "It's Josh's."

I want to ask her about Josh, about how it was, about what she thought, about how she feels. But right now, I'm not sure if I have any right to know. "Are you staying here tonight?" is what I ask instead.

She shakes her head. "No, I'm just here to pack my stuff. My clothes. I don't own much of anything in this apartment."

"You're moving back to Belleville?" How awful. We've driven her out of Toronto.

"I think I'm going to hang around the city a little longer."

Really? "Where are you going to stay?"

"Josh's."

Josh's? She's moving in with Josh? You can't move in with a guy after you've been dating for...four days. "Is this a wise move?"

Allie shrugs. "Who knows?"

"Maybe you should do a little more planning."

"I don't want to plan." She shrugs again and heads toward her room.

Not plan? I follow her. "How can you not plan? It doesn't make sense not to plan."

"I'll be fine. Stop worrying about me. It's fate."

Again with the fate theory. I sigh. "Are you sure?"

"A hundred percent," she says, and giggles. "It was just like *When Harry Met Sally* last night. I was crying and he was making me feel better and suddenly I knew he was the one for me."

Again with the soul mate. "I thought Clint was the one for you."

"I think Clint was my diversion. Maybe every action that took place in my life this year happened so that I could end up at Josh's apartment last night. If we hadn't had the fire, we never would have hired him. If Clint and Emma hadn't started sleeping together behind my back, I never would have realized what an ass Clint is, and what an incredible guy Josh is. See? Fate."

I see why Allie needs to believe this, but I don't think I can swallow it. "So do I exist simply to fulfill my role as the roommate who didn't tell you about your other roommate's deception?"

"No, I'm sure there's some greater reason that you were needed to live with us. Maybe you were put here to learn something. *Have* you learned anything in the past six months?"

How can I analyze what I've learned? I can barely concentrate. I can't eat. I can barely get myself up to go to the gym.

What have you learned, Dorothy? asked the scarecrow.

I learned that Aunt Em was sleeping with the Tin Man?

"I've learned that I didn't think losing someone I cared about was going to hurt so much."

Allie looks shocked. "What happened?"

"Manny broke up with me."

"I'm so sorry...but I didn't think you cared about him."

"I didn't, either. Something else I learned, apparently."

She squeezes my arm. "That's a pretty big one."

A box in red wrapping paper is sitting on Allie's bed. "You got me a present?" she asks.

"No." I didn't know there was a surprise for her on her bed. "It must be from Emma."

"I'm not opening anything from Emma."

"Oh, come on. What's going to happen if you open it?"

"It might blow up."

We sit down on the side of her bed and she opens the box. Inside are a tube of cherry lip gloss, cherry-scented soap, cherry-flavored gum and a bag of cherry blasters. She opens the note and I read over her shoulder.

"Congratulations on finally losing it. Love, Emma."

"How crude," I say.

Allie giggles.

Here's something else I've learned: I miss her giggles. "Why don't you stay here tonight?"

She sighs. "I'm not ready to see her right now. I'm sure I'll get over it eventually, but I'm still angry. I'm afraid to see her, I think."

"So bring Josh, too. We'll all hang out."

"You want me to put Josh and Emma in the same room? And risk her flouncing around here in a towel or something?"

"You're crazy. Josh couldn't be wooed by Emma."

"I may be crazy, but I'm not stupid. Do you think I can take the microwave? Josh's is really old."

"I'm sure it'll be fine." I suddenly have a brilliant idea. "I have a present for you, too."

I scurry into the living room and carry my present back to her room. "Here you go! Think of it as a house-warming present for you and Josh."

"You're giving me Fish?"

"If you'll have him."

She claps her hands. "Fab!"

Finally. I got rid of it.

Allie claps her hands again. "Can I change his name?"

"To what?"

"Jay?"

"No. You can't name Fish after me. It will be too confusing."

"Jo?"

"No."

"Toto?"

"No!"

"Jon?"

"No."

"Juice?"

"No."

"Juicy-Juice?"

"No."

Allie grins. "Fish?"

"Perfect."

Fish swirls in his bowl, apparently in agreement.

Epilogue
THE OMNISCIENT NARRATOR TELLS YOU WHAT HAPPENS TWO AND A HALF MONTHS LATER

Emma storms out of Nick's front door gripping two of her bags. "You need to put a tampon up your ass to stop the shit from coming out of you," she screams, and unlocks her car door.

"Me?" he yells back. "I want you out of my house. And this time don't come crawling back to me when your next boyfriend dumps you."

She rushes back to the front door and pulls her last two bags over her shoulder. "It's over," she says. "Do you understand? Over." She dumps the bags into her car. "I hope you fall into the subway and have each of your limbs ripped off."

"What kind of idiotic expression is that? When have I ever taken the subway?"

She slams the car door. Shit. Her sweater is stuck. Should she open the door and remove her sweater or just drive away and hope he doesn't see it flapping out the car?

She presses on the gas.

They spent the first month in bed, the second month getting on each other's nerves, and the last two weeks threatening to commit mutual homicide.

Jodine had predicted it would end this way, with Emma screaming expletives.

Yes, she and Jodine go out for a drink now and then, to catch up. They make it a point to try various bars around the city. New bars. They decided they've seen enough of 411 to last them a lifetime. Six months, anyway.

One day in early March, Emma showed up at Josh's with flowers, intending to make up with Allie. Allie invited her in and the three of them sat in the living room, drinking hot chocolate. Allie promised to keep in touch, but she hasn't called.

Emma occasionally still feels pangs of guilt. They're like PMS cramps—nothing a Midol won't take care of, but still annoying.

Now here she is, pulling into her father's driveway. At least I had the foresight to send my furniture here and not to Nick-the-Prick's, she thinks.

Here she is again. Home sweet home. She takes her key out of her purse and opens the door. AJ and her dad are in the kitchen, eating breakfast.

"I'm moving back in and I don't want to discuss it, so don't even talk to me," Emma says. She climbs up the stairs to her room and wonders if there are any design job openings in Montreal.

"Stephen," AJ says to Emma's father, "will you please remind your daughter to take off her shoes before trampling all over the carpet like some sort of hoodlum?"

Emma reaches into her purse and takes out a cigarette.

"Stephen," AJ says to Emma's father, "will you please remind your daughter there's no smoking in my house?"

There's no place like home there's no place like home...

Neither Emma nor Allie ever speak to Clint again. Rumor has it that he got another promotion at work and was awarded with a young blond secretary. One Friday afternoon, after a long lunch infused with Long Island ice teas, he squeezed his secretary's behind and before he could say harassment, HR was escorting him out of the building.

Allie and Josh have become one of those nauseating couples who speak to each other in baby voices and never let go of each other's hands. When Jodine hangs out at their place, which is at least a few times a week, she insists that they refrain from referring to each other as either Baby Doll or Muffin while she is in their presence.

Allie is enrolled in Ontario University's cooking college. She's decided she wants to be a chef.

She has the hands of a chef, Jodine tells her.

And her nails look great.

When Jodine told her brother she was planning on moving back home, he insisted she move into his spare bedroom until she finished classes. "Family bonding," he called it.

In mid-March, Jodine invited Manny out for coffee and reapologized. He accepted, but said that she had broken his heart and he would never be able to trust her again. She said she understood, and she does.

After the Valentine's party fiasco, Manny decided to sit in the back row in class. With Monique. Monique, apparently, felt the need to help him deal with his pain.

It is now the beginning of May. Jodine has packed up her meager belongings and said her goodbyes. Allie already bought a ticket to come visit her at the end of the month. Jodine suggested that they rent bicycles and go to Central Park to teach Allie how to ride.

Emma also mentioned coming to visit sometime soon, and Jodine is secretly hoping they end up coming on the same weekend.

When she settles in her seat on the plane to New York, the

headphones to her Discman are firmly in place and her *New York Times* is opened on her lap.

Someone taps her on the shoulder. She sees a man in his late twenties, neatly dressed, with short curly brown hair and hazel eyes. He seems to be saying something, but she can't make it out.

He taps her earphones.

Right, she thinks, and slides them down sheepishly. "Sorry."

He smiles, revealing perfect teeth and a strong jawline. "No problem," he says. "I have the window seat next to you."

She pulls her paper toward her and pushes her legs into her seat so he can get by.

He sits down beside her and puts his hands on his lap. "Anything interesting in there?" he asks, still smiling.

"Not really," she says. She folds up the paper and smiles back at him. "So how are you doing today?"

Eeeeeeeeeeeeeeeep.

Thirty-second pause.

Eeeeeeeeeeeeeeeep.

No one has moved in yet. Carl was a little hasty in throwing the girls out immediately and won't find new tenants until July.

Eeeeeeeeeeeeeeeep.

So what do you think? Is it the smoke alarm or another mouse? If a smoke alarm beeps in an empty apartment, is it really beeping at all?

Too bad Fish is gone. He'd know. He sees everything.

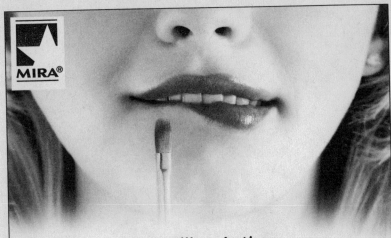